# THE LIGHT OF LOVE

"It's true," Hunter said softly. "You *are* my wife! I don't know where you've been or what happened to you while you were away. I don't even care. We can't pretend things are the same as they were before the war. But I promise I won't speak of that again. Come here."

She approached him shyly. Nothing in life had prepared her for this moment. She stood uncertainly beside the bed, wondering what this stranger expected of her.

Hunter gazed up at her. "Come here, darling. Come to me."

She eased down to sit on the edge of the bed, her fingers toying nervously at the frayed folds of the blue-and-white summer-winter coverlet. All the while, he kept murmuring Larissa's name, coaxing her to lift her gaze to his.

His dark eyes fairly glowed with the light of love, the light of recognition. No stranger could look at her that way. In an instant, she knew for certain they had loved before. Somewhere far back in the mists of time.

"Hunter," she whispered, not sure what she would say next, not knowing if she could say anything as tears were so close again.

He sensed her turmoil of emotions. "You don't have to say a word, darling. Just let me look at you. Let me touch you, Larissa. I've dreamed of holding you in my arms for so long. . . ."

Pinnacle Books by Becky Lee Weyrich

ONCE UPON FOREVER
WHISPERS IN TIME
SWEET FOREVER

Zebra Books

SPELLBOUND KISSES

# ONCE UPON FOREVER

## Becky Lee Weyrich

**PINNACLE BOOKS**
**WINDSOR PUBLISHING CORP.**

PINNACLE BOOKS are published by

Windsor Publishing Corp.
475 Park Avenue South
New York, NY 10016

First Printing: March, 1994

Printed in the United States of America

Author Photo by Gary Gay.

*To Pat Laye, for being my special friend and #1 pen pal.*
*To Bill Laye, for all those great lunches.*
*My thanks and love to both!*

# Chapter One

*Bluefield Farm, Kentucky*
*August 20, 1861*

Everyone in Fayette County knew that eventually Larissa Flemingate Courtney would marry one of the Breckinridge twins of Bluefield. The question was, which one. No one spent more time pondering the matter than Larissa herself. In her own way, she loved them both. So how could she possibly choose between handsome, serious, compassionate Hunter, the elder by seven minutes, and his equally handsome, but unpredictable daredevil of a brother, Jordan? Jordan was the one who got the three of them into scrapes as they were growing up. Hunter always got them out.

Larissa's mother had sent her to the library earlier, demanding that she think through her choices and come to an immediate decision. But the harder she thought about it, the more confused she became. Then the storm had begun and the sound of the rain pounding against the tall windows had lulled her to sleep.

Her dreams were anything but peaceful. She'd been

fighting two men, screaming for help, while one of the horse barns went up in flames. The Thoroughbreds' cries of pain and fear had torn at her heart. Wrenching free of her two attackers, she dashed into the burning building, mindless of the danger, bent on saving Bluefield's prize mares and stallions.

Larissa twisted in her chair, grimacing in her sleep as she felt the heat, the terror. Her sleeve caught fire. She felt the searing pain in her arm as she tried to beat out the flames. Suddenly, at the moment when it seemed that all was lost, she spied a shining bridge of light—all colors like a rainbow—and a voice called to her: "Come across, darling. I'm waiting for you. I need you, and there's so little time."

Larissa rubbed her arm, shivering from the terrible dream that seemed almost real it was so familiar. She'd had this same vision many times before when she was visiting at Bluefield. She always woke up before its end.

Her mother's voice made her jump. "Well, Larissa? Have you made your decision yet?"

Mrs. Courtney had entered the library at Bluefield without a sound. Now she stood by the door, waiting to hear her sixteen-year-old daughter's answer to the perplexing question. She received only silence, however.

"Larissa, you begged me to bring you to Bluefield so that you could make up your mind," her mother reminded her. "We came here to settle this matter once and for all. You've had a week already, and it will soon be time to return to Lexington."

"But the week's gone by so quickly. It isn't long enough," Larissa argued, smoothing her damp palms down the skirt of her lavender-sprigged cotton frock.

Exasperated, Mrs. Courtney replied, "You've had your

whole life to make this decision, Larissa. We've all been patient with you up till now, but you owe it to the Breckinridges to give Jordan and Hunter your answer before we leave."

Larissa stared out the library window at the rain pounding the rose garden, turning the ground below Mrs. Breckinridge's prize bushes into a rainbow of fragile petals. Beyond the garden, the horse farm's rolling fields of bluegrass looked like undulating waves on a restless sea. The storm had raged most of the afternoon. Even its high winds and sheeting rain fell far short of the tempest gripping Larissa's mind and heart.

"Why do I have to marry either of them?" she asked quietly, almost as if she were talking only to herself. "Why can't life simply go on the way it's always been—the three of us. One for all and all for one? We've shared such lovely times growing up. How can I put an end to all that?"

Mrs. Courtney's voice took on an impatient edge. "Because you're not a child any longer, Larissa, and neither are Hunter and Jordan. It's unseemly for the three of you to go romping about the countryside as you did when you were youngsters. Besides, you know very well that neither of the twins will marry until you decide between them. *You*, Larissa, hold their fate in your hands. Colonel Breckinridge has decreed that the son who marries first shall have Bluefield, while the other twin will inherit Broad Acres along with all its problems. So, you're not only deciding your own future, but the fortunes of Hunter and Jordan and the entire Breckinridge line as well."

"It's not fair to put this all on me!" Larissa cried, allowing some glint of childish resentment to slip out. "Why can't I have more time?"

"I wish it were in my power to grant you more, dear," her mother answered with a sigh. "But now that war's been declared, there's simply no time left. Hunter is already drilling his cavalry unit for duty, and I'm sure Jordan will ride with his brother to fight. Need I point out the necessity for haste in this matter? Should they leave with this unsettled, you might find the choice taken out of your hands by a Confederate bullet, my dear."

Larissa shuddered slightly at the vision her mother's harsh words evoked. This all seemed great sport to see Hunter and Jordan, strutting about in their fine new uniforms while they bragged about how they'd whip the Rebs in jig time and be home before Christmas. But the very thought of battle and bullets and blood froze Larissa's heart. She didn't want them to go. Why, without Hunter and Jordan, her whole world would be turned upside down. And she couldn't bring herself to think of one twin without the other—the way the dark hair waved over their foreheads in identical fashion, the way the passionate lights in their black eyes always betrayed their emotions before she could read it in their faces, the way they both sat a horse with a slight list to the right so that from a distance she could identify a rider as one of the brothers. But which one?

She closed her lavender-blue eyes for a moment, trying to think, trying to make herself give up one twin for the other.

"I can't choose," she said finally. "I love them both."

"Larissa, shame on you! Why, that's positively indecent! Besides, you needn't love either of them to make your choice. Good common sense, not your heart, should be your guide in something as important as the proper marriage. I'll leave you now to consider this matter further. But before I go, I must remind you that we leave for Lexington in only two days. I want the name of my future son-in-law before our carriage rolls out of Bluefield's drive."

Larissa sat for a long time after her mother left her, staring out the windows at the retreating storm, and twirling one sausage curl the color of corn silk around her fingers. She had been certain until they arrived here that she'd made her decision. Deep down she had begun thinking of herself as Mrs. Jordan Breckinridge. She had decided upon Jordy because he could always make her laugh and forget the war or anything else more serious than which gown she would wear to which ball. But on closer consideration, she wondered if she could go through life with the same careless abandon of a bright butterfly flitting from flower to flower. She wasn't sure. There were times when she needed calm and peace and thoughtful reverie, when she longed for a companion who shared that simple need.

"Mrs. Hunter Breckinridge." She tested the sound of the name in the silence of the library. It had a pleasingly calm ring. But the calm didn't last. "Jordan and Hunter. Hunter and Jordan," Larissa muttered, desperate for a flash from heaven that would give her the proper answer.

The identical twin brothers had always seemed to her like halves of a single whole. Since earliest childhood, she had roamed the fields with the two of them, ridden Bluefield's fine Thoroughbreds through the woods with them, danced with them, laughed with them, and adored both twins equally. But something had changed in the past week. Maybe, now that Larissa was a more mature sixteen, she was seeing the pair as they really were for the first time in her life. Or maybe the serious business of war was making her look at life from a different perspective.

As hard as Larissa tried not to think of the war, it kept coming back to mind. The longer she waited to marry, the shorter time she'd have to be with her husband before he rode away. Tears came to her eyes just thinking about that parting. In spite of what both Hunter and Jordan said about how grand it would be to ride out against the Southern Rebels, defeat them in a month, and then return home victorious, she couldn't quite believe it would be that simple.

To distract her mind from the unpleasant subject, she rose and went to the bookshelves, searching until she found a naughty French novel she'd been reading the last time she visited Bluefield. She unlaced her tight shoes and slipped them off, then rolled down her stockings and discarded them as well. Finally, she was comfortable, with her bare feet tucked up under her in Colonel Breckinridge's massive, leather reading chair.

She plunged into the story eagerly. But to her dismay, the torrid tale of love and heartbreak only served to make her yearn for something, although she couldn't quite put her finger on exactly what that something was. She wasn't even sure it had a name, but the feeling made her more restless than ever.

After a time, Larissa sighed and closed the book. She was in no mood to spend a quiet afternoon alone with her thoughts. She couldn't imagine where Hunter and Jordan had run off to today, but whatever their plan, it hadn't included entertaining her. By ignoring her and leaving her bored, they could both be faulted with contributing to her nagging indecision.

She put aside the novel and chose another—a slender

tome entitled *Legends of the Moonbow at Cumberland Falls*. The author was Hunter Breckinridge.

"Why, I'd forgotten all about this." She paused in thought. "Hunter must have written it ten years ago, when he was my age. I remember Jordy teasing him unmercifully about his 'great literary accomplishment.' "

Hunter had always been the man of letters in the Breckinridge family. Everyone knew that he kept a secret journal, but no one, not even Larissa, had ever been allowed to read its closely guarded entries.

Larissa settled back in her chair with Hunter's work. Beautifully illustrated, the book told in words that read like poetry of the natural phenomenon that occurred at Cumberland Falls in Kentucky's eastern mountains on nights of the full moon—a shimmering lunar rainbow that appeared in the mist. Along with documented facts about the area, Hunter related tales of ancient Indians worshiping at the sixty-foot falls, of people disappearing over the moonbow, and of magic and mystery present at the site to this very day.

For a long time, Larissa remained entranced by Hunter's words. This was a side of him she seldom saw. He was a mystical, romantic visionary. A man who seemed as fascinated by the past and the future as he was with the present. Reading his words again after so many years touched Larissa deeply. She felt for the first time as if she knew the real Hunter Breckinridge. Not the man who worked tirelessly at managing Bluefield, who could calculate lists of figures in his head and tell the breeding of a Thoroughbred by simply gazing into the animal's eyes. This side of him was not all facts and figures and work. No, not at all. He was a sensitive being with more heart and soul than his finest stallion.

The short book came to an end all too soon. Without the stories of the moonbow to occupy her mind any longer, Larissa's thoughts returned to her present delimma.

"Which one?" she murmured. "Which brother will I wed?"

She got up and walked over to the wide French doors that opened onto a terrace overlooking the west garden. The roses were a riot of pinks, golds, and scarlets. Their mingled perfumes hung heavy, almost cloying, in the hot, humid air. The whole farm looked half asleep. Nothing moved. Only the bees droned on in their never-ending search for sweetness.

Suddenly, a movement in the distance caught her attention. Shading her eyes against the bright sun that had just broken through after the storm, she noticed a rider coming straight for the house at breakneck speed. As he galloped his horse through the arched gate to the garden, Larissa recognized the oncoming figure—Jordan Breckinridge—and her heart beat a bit faster.

"Jordy!" she called, stepping onto the terrace. "Where have you been all day? If you're looking for Hunter, he's not here."

Jordan flung himself down from the saddle. His shirt was open to his belt, showing a sweating expanse of deeply tanned chest. Larissa found it hard not to stare at the dark man-hair that grew like a forest from his neck down. The sight made her feel a funny tingling inside.

"Hell, I know Hunter's not here. But *you* are. Why do you think I came in such a hurry? Ol' Hunter's right busy at the moment, so it's just you and me, little darlin'."

In spite of how many times she'd heard it, Larissa always blushed when Jordan called her that. Hunter would never have taken such liberty. He treated her like

14

a woman while it seemed that Jordan still teased her constantly and looked upon her as the girl she had always been. Their outrageous flirting had gone on for years—more a game between them than anything of a serious nature. But now it seemed different somehow.

"Where is Hunter?" she asked, perching on the damp stone banister of the terrace.

Without even thinking about what she was doing, Larissa allowed her skirt to ride up just enough so Jordan got a tempting glimpse of bare feet and ankles. His gaze went straight to the bait.

Jordan cleared his throat, then looked up at her face. "Can't tell you where he is. It's a secret." He let his hot, lazy gaze travel over Larissa's sweat-dampened frock until it stopped at the tight cotton bodice.

His refusal to answer annoyed Larissa. "Hunter's never kept secrets from me. I want to see him. I've just finished reading his book about the moonbow and I've questions I'm dying to ask him. Besides, Mother's just told me that we'll be here only two more days. I want to make the most of my time. Why won't you tell me where he is?"

"Nobody's keeping secrets from you, Larissa. I'm not sure where he is right this minute, that's all."

Larissa's attitude went instantly from anger to alarm. "You mean to tell me he's off somewhere in this storm? Jordan, we'd better go find him. Anything could have happened. A tree might have fallen on him. Or that crazy, wild stallion of his might have been frightened by the lightning. He could have taken a spill. He could be badly hurt."

Scenes from the romantic novel she'd been reading flashed through her mind—the dashing hero, thrown from his mount, lying in pain until the heroine, weeping and sighing, came to rescue him and nurse him back to health. Larissa could see herself doing that for Hunter. Yes, she definitely could.

"Don't be a goose, darlin'. Hunter's never been thrown in his life. But you're right, he could well be in the saddle this afternoon."

Something about the smirk on Jordan's face and the way he said the words made Larissa suspicious. The two of them were up to something and she meant to find out exactly what.

Setting her chin at a haughty angle, she demanded, "Jordan, you take me to find Hunter right this instant! I mean to get to the bottom of what's going on."

Jordan looked down at the lawn and dug the toe of his scuffed riding boot into a soft patch of clover.

"Aw, hell, Larissa, what do we need Hunter for?"

"Talk louder, Jordy. You know I hate it when you mumble."

In two long strides, he was on the terrace, standing so close to her that Larissa could feel his heat and smell horse and sweat and bourbon and musk on him. The heady scent fairly took her breath away. More amazing, the odor smelled sweeter to her than any roses that ever bloomed. She breathed him in deeply.

"Is this better?" he asked in a husky whisper.

"Well, I can hear you now, but you—" She paused, not sure what she was about to say. "You smell, Jordy."

"You do, too, darlin'," he said with an impish grin. "You smell like sweet, hot woman flesh."

Larissa gasped and took a step back. "You stop saying things like that. It isn't decent."

"It's a lot more decent than what I'm thinking right about now."

16

Larissa felt uncomfortable suddenly. There was something about the hot glitter in Jordan's black eyes and the tenseness of his stance that set her on edge. He'd been drinking, there was no doubt about that. And when he was in his cups, he could be highly unpredictable.

"I think we'd better go find Hunter," she said.

Jordan's dark eyes flared with something akin to anger, then he glanced away, toward his gray gelding. "You'll have to get up astride in front of me if you're set on going."

His words were a challenge. Larissa looked at the horse, then back at Jordan. He was grinning again, daring her to do it.

She knew better, but it seemed the only way to get Jordan to take her to Hunter. "All right," she said. "But we'll have to walk till we're clear of the house. It wouldn't do for your mother to see me astride your horse."

"Damn!" Jordan cursed. "That woman! She still watches you like a hawk eyeing a biddy-chick. You know she's got it all figured out that you're going to marry Hunter. Well, the joke's on her! The way I see it, you're bound to choose me. Any woman would be a fool not to. I never met the woman yet who could resist me."

Larissa felt her cheeks go hot. She stared at Jordan openmouthed, then said, "Well, I never!"

She fell silent for a moment, realizing suddenly that sometime before Jordan rode into the garden she had actually made her decision. Jordan might be wonderfully devilish and carefree and fun-loving. Yes, he was all of those things. But for a husband she wanted a man she knew she could depend on. She loved them both and she always would. But she loved Hunter in a deep, wonderful, secret way that she could never love Jordan.

She looked up into Jordan's handsome, darkly tanned face, her own solemn. "I'm sorry, Jordy, but I can't marry you," she whispered. "It's Hunter . . . I suppose it always has been."

For a moment, she saw anger flare in his eyes. Then he threw back his head and laughed long and hard. "Now, ain't that just like a woman? Of course you won't marry me because I haven't asked you and don't intend to. I'm not ever going to get married. Now, do you want me to take you to Hunter or not?"

Stunned by Jordan's words—he had asked her to marry him many times—and embarrassed to the tips of her bare, pink toes, Larissa murmured, "I need to talk to Hunter as soon as possible, but I think I'll wait for him here."

"Suit yourself, little darlin'. But you may have a long wait. I hear tell he's had his eye on a pretty little high-yeller gal over at Broad Acres. The way you've been stalling around, I figure he must have got tired of waiting and went looking for some prime poontang to soothe his nerves."

Larissa gasped and felt a cold shiver down her spine. Although it was common knowledge that men often spent their lust in the slave cabins, such a topic was never mentioned in a lady's presence, and certainly not to the gentleman's intended or in such crude terms.

"He's been gone quite a while, though," Jordan continued. "I reckon he'll amble on home directly—all tuckered out and grinning like a fool . . ."

Suddenly, before Larissa could react, Jordan grasped her about the waist, drew her close, and kissed her firmly.

"You're going to make me a mighty fine little sister, darlin'."

18

She tried to fight out of his grip, but he held her fast. "Yes, mighty fine, indeed!"

The second horse trotted in through the arch at exactly the moment Larissa fought her way free, but not before Hunter had a chance to see that something intimate had been going on between his brother and the woman they both wanted. Larissa felt her face go scarlet the moment she glanced up and saw Hunter dismounting. He was not smiling.

Jordan threw up his hand in greeting and shouted, "Just leaving, brother. She's all yours!" Then he jumped in the saddle and churned mud in the garden in his haste to depart.

Hunter walked slowly up the stairs to the terrace, a frown on his face. "Larissa, what's happened? You look so pale."

"It's nothing," she murmured, wanting to rush into Hunter's arms, but knowing that first she must officially accept his proposal. She was still trying to form the proper words when Hunter spoke.

"What was Jordan doing here at the house? He's supposed to be over at Broad Acre, supervising work on the new barn."

She didn't answer his question. Instead, she asked, suspicious in spite of her best intentions, "Is that where you were—over at Broad Acres?"

He shrugged out of his wet coat and tossed it over an iron chair. "No. I had to ride over to Fairview to see a mare I'm thinking of buying. That damn storm caught up with me halfway home and one of the bridges washed out so I had to take the long way back."

"A mare," Larissa murmured under her breath, wanting to believe him, but still hearing Jordan's lurid tale ringing in her ears.

Silence stretched between them—an uneasiness that Larissa had never before experienced when she was with Hunter. Finally, he managed to get out what was on his mind.

"Larissa," he said in a tone dull with disappointment, "I'm sorry, but I couldn't help seeing Jordy kiss you. I suppose I should wish you all the best, but I'm not sure I'm man enough for that." He paused and looked directly into her eyes. "I do wish you all the happiness life has to offer. You above all people, Larissa. You and Jordan are the two people who mean the most to me in the whole world. He'll make you happy. He'd better, or, by God, I'll . . ."

Suddenly, Larissa realized what he must think. "Oh, Hunter!" she cried. "No! That's not the way it is. Jordan kissed me, yes." She paused, formulating a tiny lie. "But he was only congratulating me, welcoming me to the family. You see, I'd just told him that I'm going to marry *you.*"

Hunter's face had been as dark as the receding storm clouds. Now, a bright light straight from his heart beamed through his eyes. A smile wavered at the corner of his lips, then spread across his whole handsome face.

"I want to marry you, Hunter," Larissa said softly. "I think I always have. I should have accepted immediately when you proposed last April. But when a girl's only fifteen, marriage seems so far away."

Too emotional to speak, Hunter swooped down on his betrothed and wrapped her in a full, strong embrace. When his mouth came down over hers, it was their first real kiss. A kiss that left Larissa dizzy with pleasure and

20

desire. She clung to him, fearing she might fall if she let go too quickly.

"I can't believe this," he murmured. "It's too good to be true."

"But it is true," Larissa whispered. "I realized while I was reading your book about the moonbow how much I love you, Hunter."

He smiled into her sparkling, lavender-blue eyes, then threw back his head and laughed. "You read my poor little attempt at great literature? I thought I'd hidden that copy so no one would find it."

"But it is great literature. You put your heart and soul into that work. It's beautiful, Hunter. Beautiful and moving and mystical."

"If it made you love me, I'll have a copy bound in gold for you, darling."

He hugged her again, cradling her in his strong arms and rocking back and forth. "Oh, Larissa, Larissa! I've loved you for so long. I've waited all my life for this moment. How soon can we be married?"

Suddenly, a bit of the joy drained from Larissa's brimming heart. "How long do we have before you go away?"

"Jordy and I plan to leave in three weeks."

Larissa gave a cry of dismay. *"Three weeks?"*

"I'm sorry, but we're stretching it to stay here that long. We'll have a hard ride before we join up with the other troops."

"Oh, Hunter!" Larissa clung to him, tears stinging her eyes. "Why did I waste so much time?"


The time Larissa had wasted making up her mind, Mrs. Courtney made up for by hurrying along with plans for the wedding. She and Larissa made a hasty trip to Lexington to make necessary arrangements, then sped back to Bluefield. There would be no time for a honeymoon, so it was decided that the wedding would be held at the groom's home. That would give the newlyweds as much time as possible to be together before Hunter rode off at the head of his Cave Hill Cavalry.

Jordan, meanwhile, packed everything he owned and moved to Broad Acres. He remained in seclusion there while the wedding plans rushed forward.

A week before the wedding, a combination engagement celebration and birthday party for Mrs. Breckinridge was held at Bluefield. Friends and relatives came from miles around. The mansion was bursting at the seams with guests, and hansom carriages cluttered the wide, curving drive. Larissa had never been more excited in her life.

The grand gold-and-red ballroom at Bluefield was decked out with giant vases of roses that perfumed the air, while waxy green magnolia leaves reflected the candlelight from chandeliers and sconces. Wine and bourbon flowed freely, and there was enough food to have fed Mr. Lincoln's Grand Army of the Republic for a week.

At the appointed hour, once all the guests had arrived, Larissa waited nervously on the landing of the wide staircase until a tall servant in immaculate livery intoned, "Mistress Larissa Flemingate Courtney, Lexington Manor."

All heads turned toward her. A buzz went through the crowd. Young men smiled. Young ladies tried to pretend they hadn't the slightest interest in the beauty's shimmering gown of lavender shot through with silver or her halo of gleaming blond curls or the moonstone resting at her breasts—a gift from her intended. Older men readjusted their spectacles for a better look while their wives whispered news of the hasty engagement and forthcoming wedding, wondering if they might not be well-advised to count months on their fingers when Larissa gave Hunter his first child.

Hunter stood below, oblivious to all else but his bride-to-be. He beamed. He glowed. He showered her with the light of love.

Larissa noticed only one person below who neither smiled nor looked away. Jordan lounged against a far wall, surrounded by twittering lady-birds. He stared directly into Larissa's lavender-blue eyes, his own hard and scheming. Even from a distance, he threw a clear challenge her way. He might as well have shouted his rage for all to hear. Larissa certainly heard it. It frightened her and turned her cold inside. His very look mocked her and warned her that, even though she might be engaged to Hunter, Jordan was not done with her yet.

Larissa stood frozen on the stair, trembling, unable to tear her gaze from the taunting glare of Jordan's eyes.

Then a warm hand closed on her gloved fingers. The next moment, Hunter kissed her hand and she warmed to the feel of his breath through the dainty lace. Their eyes met. They smiled.

"Darling, are you real?"

Larissa laughed lightly. Hunter's question was so unexpected.

"If you don't believe it, my love, you should feel how my heart is fluttering."

His eyes went to her lovely, silver-clad bosom. "If only I dared," he murmured.

Larissa spread her fan to hide a blush. She let Hunter

23

lead her down the stairs. Dozens of guests clustered there to greet her. They congratulated Hunter on winning such a lovely creature's heart. They complimented Larissa on her gown. They asked a hundred questions about the upcoming wedding. But all the while, Larissa was aware of Jordan still raking her with his steady, calculated gaze.

"Hunter, might we dance now?" she whispered, sounding more urgent than she meant to, but knowing she could not endure Jordy's eyes on her a moment longer.

"Why, darling, I was just about to ask you the same thing."

Hunter ushered her out of the adoring throng of guests and into the perfumed ballroom. The other dancers parted, mesmerized by the glitter of Larissa's shining gown that almost, but not quite, matched the love-light in Hunter's dark eyes. Oblivious to all else, Hunter whirled Larissa in sweeping turns about the polished floor.

As the sad-sweet sound of the violins swelled, Larissa felt her heart swell with ever more love for Hunter. The gentle but commanding way he touched her to guide her through the steps of the dance, the caressing look in his wonderful eyes, the husky tremor in his voice when he spoke—all these things told her that she was adored by this man, cherished beyond all others.

They danced once and then again. It was during that second turn on the floor that Jordan tapped Hunter's shoulder to break in.

"Share and share alike," Jordy quipped to Hunter as he stole Larissa away.

Larissa heard Hunter's light laugh, but there was little humor in it. He was obviously pained by having to entrust his sweetheart into his brother's care, if only for the space of a waltz.

24

Although Larissa had always felt perfectly at ease with Jordan, such was not the case tonight. He held her a bit too close and pressed his hand into the small of her back in such a way that her body was forced to curve against his. And, too, he'd been drinking tonight. He was dangerous.

"Smile for ol' Jordy, little darlin'," he coaxed. "Why, you look like you're headed for your execution instead of your wedding. Could it be that ol' Hunter caught you off guard and pressured you into this?"

"Don't be ridiculous!" Larissa snapped. "I told you my decision before I told Hunter."

"Ah, yes, you told me all right. But could it be, now that you've had more time to think things through, that you're not pleased by the choice you made? Could there be someone else you'd rather have?"

"Like *you?*" Larissa answered sarcastically.

He chuckled. "I'd guess that if you marry Hunter, you'll always wonder just a bit how it would have been with me."

"You're insufferable!"

He laughed again. "I won't argue that point. I'm also mean-tempered, a sot, and the biggest carouser in the county." He leaned closer to her ear and whispered, "But I'm damn charming and you know it, Larissa. And besides that, I'm quite generous with my women. I would give you anything your little heart desires—in the bedroom or out of it."

Larissa tried to pull away, but he held her fast. She felt that his comments deserved no reply. Furious and more than a bit frightened, she longed for the music to end. Fully aware of her discomfort, Jordan only gripped her closer and grinned.

When she realized that she was his prisoner, at least for the next few moments, Larissa determined to be firm with him.

"You have your nerve, talking to me this way when I'm already engaged to your brother. I told you, I'm going to marry Hunter. I could never have married you, Jordan."

He threw back his head and laughed. "There you go again with those crazy ideas of yours. I'm not proposing marriage, little darlin'. I told you weeks ago that I don't plan to marry. I'm only thinking that you're going to get mighty lonely once your husband rides off to do his gallant duty to his country. If you feel the need of company . . ."

Only the circumstances of their surroundings stayed Larissa's hand. Mentally, she slapped Jordan's grinning face as he so richly deserved.

"Of course, since I know how fond all you girls are of men in uniform, darlin', I'll be joining up, too. But I plan to join the winning side. John Hunt Morgan is putting together his own troop to operate right here in Kentucky. I'll be riding with him, so I'll still be close—in case you need some male company."

Larissa stumbled over her own satin dancing slippers. Hunter's twin brother, joining the Confederacy? She couldn't believe it.

"Does Hunter know your plans?" She had meant to guard her icy silence for the rest of their dance, but she had to ask him.

"Not yet. Since you chose to tell me first about your marriage, I decided it was only proper that you be the first person to hear my news."

"You can't do this, Jordan. How could you be so disloyal to your own family—your own brother? Not to mention your disloyalty to your country. You know Hunter means to make you second in command of his troop. He's counting on you. You can't let him down."

"I don't see it that way at all. Home comes before everything else. And Kentucky is my home. Besides, without slaves this rich man would be a pauper. I plan to guard my fortunes well. It's what any real man would do."

Larissa felt tears gather in her eyes. What if Hunter and Jordan met on the field of battle—on opposite sides? It was too terrible to contemplate.

"Please, Jordy," she whispered. "Won't you reconsider this decision? It's wrong. You'll be sorry. We all will."

He looked into her eyes, his face solemn. "Do you really think so, darlin'?"

Larissa nodded vigorously. "Yes, with all my heart."

"I'll think it over, then. But I make no promises. We can't talk here. Come to Broad Acres tomorrow afternoon. Come alone. I'll listen to what you have to say and consider it."

He sounded like his old self again. Larissa felt reassured.

"I'm so glad you'll think it over. But, Jordy, you know I can't visit you at Broad Acres alone. I'd be ruined if word got out."

"Who would find out? Besides, you're almost my sister."

"Oh, Jordan," she stalled, trying to think of something.

"Have it your way, Larissa. But you're the only one who can change my mind. And I won't even consider any options unless you come, as I've asked. If I don a Confederate uniform, it's your doing. You can remember all through the war that you might have changed my mind."

"That's not fair, Jordy!"

"Life's not fair, darlin'. Didn't anyone ever explain that to you?"

Before she could reply, the music stopped. Hunter was there to claim her.

"I can't dance any longer. I need a breath of air," she told him.

"My thoughts, exactly. Let's slip out to the garden so we can be alone for a time."

They left the ballroom, by one of the side doors that opened onto the terrace. Hunter took Larissa's hand and led her into the garden, down the moon-silvered paths to the clipped maze of boxwoods. They strolled through the night, Larissa clinging to Hunter's arm, hanging on his every quiet word.

They were far from the house when the rain started—not a storm, but a gentle, soaking downpour.

"The old gardener's cottage is just over there," Hunter said. "Let's make a dash for it."

Moments later, they burst through the door of the snug little house.

"This place hasn't been used for years," Hunter said. "But Mother has it kept tidy. She keeps saying that someday she'll turn it into her own private studio where she can come to rest and paint her roses."

Larissa glanced about the two tiny rooms of the octagonal cottage. They stood in a sitting room with windows across one side and a cushioned seat beneath them. A game table, two chairs, and a tea cart took up most of the space. Beyond, a door led into a second chamber. Through the opening, she spied a daybed.

"You're soaked, darling," Hunter said. "Here, let me help you."

Hunter took her to the long window seat. Once they

28

were settled, he drew the gloves from her hands, easing the lace over each finger until the tingling flesh of her palms was naked to his touch.

He kissed her hands with warm, soft brushes of his lips. When she sighed with pleasure, he grew bolder still. In one slow, sensual slide, he drew off her damp, cobweb-thin shawl. A moment later, his hands touched her bare shoulders, tensing and relaxing on her flesh. And then his mouth and tongue took up the lazy, wonderful work.

Larissa might have felt faint on the dance floor, but now she was near swooning. If ever a man was made to give her pleasure and bring joy to her heart, Hunter Breckinridge was that man.

When he drew her into his arms, kissing her with slow deliberation, Larissa shivered against him.

"You're cold, aren't you?"

She wasn't cold. Far from it!

"Hunter, I wish we were married already. And I wish you never had to go away."

"Hush, love," he cautioned. "Let's don't talk about my leaving. We'll have time before I go to create some wonderful memories. I'll take them with me when I ride out. I'll take *you* with me, in my heart."

Larissa knew what she longed to say. But dared she be so bold?

"Hunter?" She paused, the words difficult to form.

"What is it, darling? What's bothering you?"

"Would it be so wrong if we began creating those lovely memories tonight?"

In answer to her question, Hunter let out a pent-up breath. He drew her back into his arms and held her. A long, intimate silence passed between them. Then his mouth came down on hers and his hand found her breast. No words were necessary after that.

Her complex question had a simple answer: Love.

Larissa felt her whole body come alive as Hunter touched her breast and kissed her open mouth. For a long time, there in the dark, silent cottage, he held her and caressed her. He kissed her so many times that she lost count of the number. She lost track of time and of the world outside their own sweet, intimate space.

At some point, she heard him whisper, "We're on stolen time, my love." At that point, they began shedding their clothes. Hunter helped Larissa out of her gown and hung it gently over one of the chairs. His own coat rested already on the other.

A moment later, he lifted her in his arms and strode the short distance across the small room to the door . . . to the daybed. The coverlet smelled of lavender and summer sun, and she knew that she would always remember those scents when she thought of their first making love.

When he lay down beside her moments later, she felt his bare flesh. There was no way she could disrobe completely in the dark, removing stays, petticoats, and other underthings too intimate to mention. But with Hunter's help, she removed what she could manage.

Larissa trembled at the thought of what they were about to do. She knew something of lovemaking from the French novel she'd read. She knew she would probably weep, but for joy, not for pain. She knew, too, that like the French hero, Hunter could not be kept waiting. She reached for him, murmuring his name.

He pressed hard against her, letting his hands knead her aching breasts. When she moaned softly, he dipped his head to kiss the proud peaks. Larissa caught her breath as fire raged through her body. She arched her back toward him.

"You want this as much as I do, don't you, Larissa?" Hunter's voice betrayed his surprise and his delight.

Any other woman might have blushed at such an accusation. Not Larissa. She defended herself boldly. "I want *you* more than I've ever wanted anything in my life. And why shouldn't I? I'm going to be your wife."

"You're wrong about that, my darling." His voice was dark with urgent desire as he positioned his body over hers. "You *are* my wife—my own—as of this moment."

His thrust was quick and sure. Larissa felt heat like lightning striking through her. A moment later, they were moving together as Hunter ventured ever deeper. Larissa's eyes were wide open, staring at the wonder of him through the darkness. She could see the sharp planes of his face, enhanced and highlighted in the play of shadows. But more than that, she could feel him moving inside her, lighting fires that had never known flame.

And then the room began to swirl and the whole world turned upside down. She felt nerves twitch in her toes and fingertips and somewhere deep down inside her that she couldn't name. That nameless place throbbed and pulsed, then turned her whole body into something too wondrous to describe. All feelings, all sounds, all pleasures, all colors.

She was flying high above, playing with the stars, dancing across the moonbow, and Hunter had taken her there. Hunter on a silver stallion with wings on its heels.

Larissa heard Hunter moan her name. She opened her eyes at last. The rain was over. The full moon was shining in the window, glowing softly with all colors of a rainbow.

"Look, darling!" she whispered. "The moon has watched you love me. The moon knows our secret."

31

He kissed her deeply, then sighed and rested his head on her bare breasts, teasing her nipple with his lips. "But the moon won't tell what it knows."

"Hunter, when you leave me . . ."

"Sh-h-h! Don't talk about that."

"I must. Only this once," she promised. "While you're away, let the moon be our messenger. I'll stare up every night and send you a kiss by our moon."

He smiled and Larissa thought she saw the glint of a tear in his eye. "Yes, we'll have the moon to share. And I don't mind at all that it shares our secret. I feel like shouting it to the whole world. I only wish we could stay here all night."

Larissa gave a sharp cry. "What if they come looking for us? We'd better get back to the party."

"One more kiss?" Hunter begged.

She turned back into his arms and he held her for a long time, kissing her, touching her, wondering at what miracle had made her his for all time. But her total happiness was marred by two things—the thought of Hunter and Jordan going into battle on opposite sides and her terrible dream. Even as they made love, for a fleeting instant, Larissa had felt the hot pain in her arm and seen the dreaded flames.

# Chapter Two

Although Larissa and Hunter thought their long absence from the party the night before had gone unnoticed, they were mistaken. One person, other than the man in the moon, had kept a close watch on them all night. And by the next morning, Jordan Breckinridge was nursing a hangover and a grudge, while making plans to cause his brother and soon-to-be sister-in-law an equal amount of suffering. The note he sent to Larissa bright and early the next morning set his plan—and her fate—into motion.

Larissa hadn't slept particularly well. She'd thought all her problems would be solved by her marriage. But life wasn't that simple, she realized. All night she'd tossed and turned, dreading Hunter's leaving only two days after their wedding, and wondering what she could do to change Jordan's stubborn mind. When a servant brought Jordy's note that morning, she knew what she must do. She dressed quickly in her new riding costume of heather-colored gabardine, told her mother that she needed a gallop through the fields to clear her head, then struck out for Broad Acres.

Thunder rumbled off in the distance as she rode away

from Bluefield. Another storm was approaching. The very air had a sickly yellow cast that brought with it a sense of foreboding. Larissa was tempted to turn back. She knew it was foolish to meet Jordan alone, especially so soon before her marriage to his brother. But if she could change Jordy's mind about joining the Confederacy, then Hunter would never have to know that they had met privately.

She drew courage from reminding herself that she was doing this for Hunter. Jordan had said last night and again in his message this morning that only she could make him rethink his decision. She owed it to the entire Breckinridge family to do what she could to keep peace between the brothers.

"And if I can make Jordy see the light, then the risk I'm taking will be well worth it," she told herself, taking a measure of comfort from the sound of her own voice.

Larissa reached a grove of cedar trees a good distance from the house. She tied her horse there, not daring to ride on in broad daylight. She couldn't risk being seen. On foot, she could follow the high yew hedge along the drive or duck behind a tree if anyone approached.

After a long, hot hike, the old mansion loomed ahead—a ramshackled pile of columns and verandas that had been magnificent in its prime, back in the early part of the century when the first Breckinridge settled in Kentucky. Larissa eyed the place closely, imagining how it could be, if only Jordan would invest the time and money needed to restore it to its former glory.

What the place needed was a mistress. And what Jordan needed was a wife. Of course, he continued with this nonsense about never marrying. But Larissa had a feeling that was just an act to make her feel guilty for choosing Hunter.

Suddenly, she remembered their dance the night before—how closely he'd held her and how suggestive his gaze had been. She remembered, too, the kisses he'd stolen on the garden terrace the day she told him she meant to marry Hunter.

*"That,"* she assured herself, "will *never* happen again! I'm wise to you now, Jordan Breckinridge."

In order to move more quickly across the patchy expanse of lawn, Larissa lifted her long riding skirt and hurried toward the back entrance of the house. She knew that Jordan had only two house servants, and the rest of the slaves would be in the fields at this time of day. She could slip in quietly and no one would ever know she was there. They would talk. She would leave. And afterward everything would be fine between Hunter and Jordan. Then she could stop worrying and get on with the business of enjoying her wedding and brief honeymoon at Bluefield.

Exactly what she would say to Jordan to persuade him to join the Union army and ride with his brother, escaped her for the moment. But she felt sure the right words would come to her. She would do whatever she had to in order to make Jordan come down off his high horse and confess that he was only doing this to spite Hunter.

"Well, I simply won't let him spoil things for all of us," she declared determinedly.

With one final dash, Larissa made it across the backyard and to the steps that led to the hallway door. Crouching behind a huge gardenia bush, she held her breath and listened. Suddenly, she heard Jordan's voice from an open window on the second floor.

"That'll be all, Pompey. Shut the door on your way out. I don't want to be disturbed the rest of the morning."

Larissa tingled with nervousness at his words. She hadn't bargained on this turn of events. But she might have guessed that he'd stay in his room, nursing his hangover till noon or after. It was so like him to force her to confront him there instead of meeting her downstairs like any civilized host.

She crouched lower still as she heard Pompey head for the back door. Jordan's old valet came out and crept down the stairs, then turned toward the kitchen a distance away across the yard. Larissa waited until he entered the cook house, then made her move. She couldn't let that old gossip see her here.

Her heart thundering, she raced up the stairs and into the cool, shadowed hallway. Once inside, she flattened herself against the wall until she could catch her breath. She listened. Not a sound came from above.

"Jordan?" she called.

No answer.

After two more times with the same lack of response, she shrugged, then started up the stairs to the second floor—to Jordan's bedroom.

She froze halfway up when a board groaned under her slipper. She wasn't concerned that Jordan might have heard, but somewhere in the house was the maid, the second servant who always hovered about. After a moment's thought, Larissa decided that she must be out in the kitchen now, preparing the master's noon meal.

Larissa moved on confidently, certain that she and Jordan were alone in the house. All the way up, she kept hearing her mother's voice, reminding her that no lady ever enters a gentleman's chamber. The admonishment was

36

almost enough to make her run away, but not quite. She was perspiring, trembling. But too much depended upon this meeting, and she'd come too far to turn back now.

Finally, she stood outside Jordan's room. She paused and listened. She heard a rustling sound and then a low laugh. He must be reading a humorous book, she concluded.

She knocked briskly and called his name. When she heard his muffled voice from the other side of the door, she took that as permission to enter.

In the next heartbeat, Larissa turned the knob, then froze. Her face turned quickly to pale horror. She longed desperately to flee, but her body refused her urgent command. She stood in the doorway—eyes wide, mouth agape.

"What the almighty hell?" Jordan roared. "Jesus Christ, Larissa!"

Larissa felt her lips move as she tried to form words, but not a sound came from her. She heard only her heart thundering and a warning buzz in her ears. She was going to faint and that would be dreadful—she knew it, but there was no help for it.

Had she swooned a moment sooner, she might have been spared the second shock—the sight of Jordan, completely naked, rushing his dark-skinned and equally unclothed bed partner into the next room. For a moment before the beautiful young slave disappeared, she turned and looked Larissa right in the eye, her dark gaze bewildered and pleading.

And then the floor rushed up to meet Larissa.

A short time later, she came around, the acrid odor of smelling salts stinging her nostrils. She was stretched out on Jordan's rumpled bed. He was leaning over her, clothed only in a tobacco-brown silk robe, his handsome face smiling down into hers.

"Had I known you'd really come, I would have waited for you, little darlin'."

He leaned closer, as if he meant to kiss her, but she shoved him away.

"You bastard!" she cried. "You set this whole thing up. That note you sent—'Such a dilemma . . . how can I ever decide without talking to someone who understands . . .' Well, I hope you're satisfied, Jordan Breckinridge. You certainly pulled the wool over my eyes. I feel like the world's greatest fool. How dare you?"

He rose up and glared down at her. "How dare *you?* This is my bedroom, therefore, I dare whatever I please. As for your coming here at my invitation, I assumed you would arrive like any other guest, in a carriage and *announced.*"

"You know I couldn't do that. Why, if anyone found out I was here, my reputation would be ruined. Hunter would be forced to cancel our wedding. It would be the scandal of the century!"

A slow smile, lacking all warmth, curved Jordan's lips. "Yes. Wouldn't it!"

Larissa felt suddenly like a small trapped animal, a wounded bird, a stupid child. Jordan had planned this, all right, and she'd walked right into his trap.

She lurched off the bed and past him.

"Wait a minute! Where do you think you're going?"

"Back to Bluefield! Back to Hunter!" she called over her shoulder.

"I thought we were going to talk."

"I've changed my mind. Do whatever you please."

She was almost at the door before he rushed ahead of

her and barred the way. "Is that an invitation?" he said with a smirk. "If so . . ."

Slowly, he bent and kissed her cheek. Larissa gasped and tried to pull away, but it was too late. He had a grip on her arms, holding her so that he could steal a longer, deeper kiss. Larissa felt tears pooling in her eyes.

*You will not cry!* she ordered silently.

"Come on, little darlin'. You know you've always wondered what it would be like with me. Now's your chance. You can compare, before it's too late, and see if you've made the right choice."

Larissa gasped softly.

"Don't try to act like a startled virgin, for God's sake. I know what you and Hunter were up to last night in the cottage."

"You spied on us?" She could hardly get the words out. The thought of Jordan doing such a thing turned last night's time with Hunter into something tainted and shameful.

"Like you always used to say, darlin', 'All for one and one for all.' Now, it's our turn. Hunter never has to know."

Larissa felt as if she were choking. Her cheeks flamed. She wanted to scream at him, scratch out his eyes, beat him to a bloody pulp. But when she opened her mouth to shout the obscenities she felt boiling up in her throat, all that came out was a trembling whisper. "You're a terrible person, Jordan Breckinridge!"

He nodded. "Yes, I am. And ornery and good for nothing and a cad, and I think you'd better get out of here before I decide not to let you go. As for my joining Hunter's cavalry unit, I'll think about it, little darlin', since you've asked me to."

"Don't bother!" she flung at him. "U.S. Cavalry officers have certain standards to uphold. I'm not sure Hunter would want you in his troop."

Before Larissa could get past him and escape, Jordan offered one final insult. Turning toward the door to the adjoining room, he yelled, "Arabella! Get back in here. I'm not finished with you yet."

Then looking back at Larissa, a cunning smile on his face, he said, "I now intend to resume where you interrupted me. If you'd like to stay and observe, feel free. A lesson might be helpful on your wedding night."

Mortified and humiliated, more embarrassed than she'd ever been in her life, Larissa raced out the door and down the stairs.

Riding back to Bluefield, she kept telling herself that at least one thing good came out of this terrible morning. No one, other than Jordan and his slave lover, had seen her at Broad Acres. For the rest of her life, she would live with the shame of her foolish action, but at least Hunter never had to know.

It was a long ride back, but once she returned—safe and sound and nearly untouched by her future brother-in-law—the last-minute wedding preparations took her mind off what had happened. Then came her final sitting for her wedding portrait, gowned in shimmering white and a long, mistlike veil, with Hunter's gift, the moonstone necklace, as her only adornment. But, as she tried to sit still for the artist, her thoughts strayed back to Jordan. She soothed away her unbidden guilt by reminding herself that only hours remained until she would be Mrs. Hunter Breckinridge and all would be well. This morning's unpleasantness would be forgotten forever.

* * *

The bride might not have felt quite so confident had she known of the brothers' plans for the evening before the wedding.

It was all Jordan's idea, of course. He was a great one for bachelor parties. He gathered the "boys" from the neighboring farms at Broad Acres to give Hunter a prime send-off into the "stormy waves of matrimony," as he styled his twin's coming wedding.

Much bourbon was consumed, many songs were sung, and not a few wenches were bedded before the raucous evening came to an end. By midnight, only the brothers remained, downing one last glass before calling it a night.

The parlor at Broad Acres was a shambles. Empty jugs littered the Oriental rug. Cigar butts still smoldered in ashtrays. A few articles of hastily discarded clothing were strewn about since Jordan had brought Arabella in to share her pleasures with his friends.

"You shoulda given her a shot," Jordan drunkenly told Hunter. "She's a mighty fine piece and I should know."

"I've given up that sort of sport," Hunter answered with a smile. "I'm getting married tomorrow, remember?"

"Hell, how could I forget?" Jordan's tone turned suddenly belligerent. "But you've got every right to partake of what's offered, brother. Tonight of all nights."

"I think not," Hunter answered, rising and stretching as if he meant to leave.

"You aren't going yet?"

"It's time. I don't want to show up for my wedding all worn out and haggard."

Jordan caught his brother's coat sleeve and tugged him

back toward his chair. "Hey, did you ever think it would come to this?"

"I don't know what you mean, Jordy." He yanked his coat free of his twin's grasp. "Let go now. I really have to leave. It's a long ride back to Bluefield."

"You know what I mean. Did you ever think that Larissa would marry you instead of me? I always thought I was the one she had a hankering for."

Hunter laughed. "I don't know that she ever showed either of us any special favors."

Jordan gave a deep, low chuckle. "Oh, you think not? Well, I'm here to tell you I know better."

"You're drunk, brother. That's the whiskey talking."

"Yeah? Well, whiskey always speaks the truth. And I think you're rushing into something you'll be sorry for later."

"Shut up! I don't want to hear it!"

"You're going to hear it. I don't care if you knock me on my ass for saying it, but Larissa's nothing but a damn tease. Why, when she came over here the other morning . . ." Jordan let his words trail off, as if he'd let something slip unintentionally.

Hunter leaned closer, squinting at his brother. He was not smiling. "Larissa came here? When?"

"She stopped by a couple of days ago—said she was out riding and decided she wanted to see me. Seems she wasn't quite sure she'd made the right decision. It wasn't anything. You know how girls are, especially when they're about to tie the knot. The grass always looks greener, and all that shit."

Hunter grabbed his brother by the shirtfront and shook him. "What the hell are you saying, Jordan? Spit it out or, by God, I'll knock you from here to next Sunday."

42

Jordan shrugged away from Hunter, looking embarrassed, ashamed. "It's like you said, brother, I'm drunk. I should never have opened my big mouth."

"Dammit all, you did open it, so let's have it. *All of it!* What the hell happened? And you'd better tell it straight!"

Jordan avoided his brother's angry gaze. He slumped down in his chair as if he were trapped in some terrible situation, not of his making.

*"Nothing* happened, Hunter! I swear it." But the fact that he still refused to meet his brother's eyes made the words seem pure lies.

"You'd better be telling me the truth," Hunter warned. "Goddammit, you'd better be!"

Jordan took a long pull at a whiskey jug from the table, then let out a weary sigh. "Hey, it's all in the family, brother. I mean, even if we had done anything . . . even if it took and she got pregnant, who'd know? We're twins—*identical* twins. Any son of mine would look like yours. So what's the big damn deal?"

Hunter roared out of his chair and grabbed Jordan. "You stinking, lying bastard! You dirty sonuvabitch!"

Hunter's right cross to Jordan's jaw sent him flying across the room, where he crashed into the wall, then slid to the floor in a pool of whiskey. The last thing Hunter noticed before he stormed out was that his twin brother, although unconscious, was still smiling.

"Damn you to hell, Jordan Breckinridge!"

It was on the tip of his tongue to damn Larissa as well. But he loved her too much to curse her name. She was still young, still impressionable, still vulnerable. There was no doubt in his mind that Jordan had forced her to do whatever she had done. Yet he couldn't deny that the thought of his bride with his brother twisted his gut with jealousy.

"I'll put it out of my mind," Hunter told himself as he galloped headlong through the night. "That's all I *can* do."

Before he reached Bluefield, he swore to himself a thousand times that he would forget everything that Jordan had said . . . *if he could.*

The morning of the wedding dawned bright with promise. Droplets of dew shimmered on the fields of bluegrass and sparkled like newly cut gems in the brilliant sunshine.

Larissa was more than happy to see an end to the night. She'd slept off and on, but the dream had come again to trouble her each time she closed her eyes. Last night, however, the nightmare had changed. At the end, when her gown was afire, no shining bridge had appeared out of nowhere to save her. And sounds of battle had mingled with the crackle of the fire and the screams of the horses. The dream had always been unsettling, but last night it had brought sheer, unrelieved terror.

As hard as Larissa tried to forget the night and think only of her happiness to come as Hunter's bride, the fear continued to lurk at the edge of her consciousness. She moved about, preparing for the grand occasion as if she were in a daze.

Not until she was gowned and veiled and waiting on her father's arm to descend the broad stairway did the full impact of her happiness strike her. A tremor of anticipation shivered through her whole body.

"Are you all right, my dear?" her aristocratic, white-haired father whispered.

"Perfect!" she answered, staring up at him through dewy eyes.

"Then smile, won't you?"

She smiled. Then the music began and they started down.

Not until they reached the foot of the stairs and Larissa spied Hunter did she almost lose her grip. In fact, she nearly stumbled. He had never looked more dashing, more handsome. But she hadn't expected to see him in uniform. The crisp blue of his coat, the brass buttons, the red sash and gleaming saber. The whole picture of him only served to remind Larissa how little time they would have together.

Somehow, Larissa made it into the flower-decked parlor to stand beside her groom. She glanced up to see their two wedding portraits, newly hung above the fireplace. Her vision blurred as she stared at them. She seemed to see a double image—two brides, two grooms. Then the moment passed.

Hunter took her trembling hand into his, but his touch seemed different. He didn't cling to her, caressing her fingers with his as he had the night they made love. His touch was light, almost formal. She guessed he must be nervous, too.

When time came for Hunter to speak his vows, Larissa looked up into his face. Something in his eyes made her catch her breath. She had expected to see the warm light of love shining down on her. Instead, the look she saw in Hunter's eyes seemed almost haunted, faintly accusing. Once again, she attributed his expression—and what she imagined she saw in it—to wedding-day jitters. His and hers. Once all this formality was over and they could be alone, everything would be perfect between them. Surely, their time together in the gardener's cottage had proved that.

"I now pronounce you man and wife. You may kiss your bride," the robed parson intoned.

Larissa braced herself for a crushing embrace, a long, hard kiss—both of which she would welcome. Instead, her new husband pressed her sleeves lightly and brushed his lips past her cheek, barely touching her flesh.

She leaned close and whispered, "I love you, my darling."

"Do you?" he murmured back.

All through the celebration that followed, Hunter acted his usual cordial self, chatting with the many wedding guests, toasting his bride with champagne when he was called upon to do so, smiling when he realized it was expected of him. But Larissa knew him well enough to see through the pleasant facade. Something was *very* wrong!

Jordan arrived late—after the ceremony was over. He looked the color of swamp slime—hideously hungover, Larissa surmised—and sported an ugly purple bruise on the side of his jaw. It almost seemed to her that he sneaked in, then hung back in the crowd, not wanting to be noticed. He never bothered to give his brother a congratulatory handshake or his new sister-in-law a kiss for good luck. Not that she would have welcomed it. Still, his behavior did seem extremely odd.

Late in the evening, Larissa noticed Jordan motion to Hunter. For several moments the brothers stood together, away from everyone else. They exchanged a few words. Hunter looked angry for an instant, then paled. Jordan turned and strode out of the house. The thought of what might have passed between them made Larissa go faint with fear.

Not long after that brief episode, Hunter came to Larissa's side and touched her arm. "Time for you to toss your bouquet. We're expected to go to my room now."

Larissa stared at him uncertainly. No word of endearment, no eagerness to have her all to himself. Only, "We're *expected* to go . . ."

She tested a bright smile on him. "Of course, darling. I've been waiting. I thought we'd never get to be alone."

For a moment, she glimpsed the old light of love in his eyes, but it flickered out quickly. "Time's come," he said stiffly.

Hunter hated himself for acting so cold. But he was in pain. Over the years he had broken both arms in accidents, he had been bitten by a snake, stung by bees, and stabbed in the side in a barroom brawl. But no physical agony he had ever known could equal what he was feeling now, on his wedding night. The two people he cared most for in all the world—Larissa and Jordan—were suddenly like strangers to him. They had betrayed him. And he had betrayed Larissa in turn by going ahead with their marriage when he had such grave doubts.

What did he mean to prove? he wondered. That he was man enough to win her from his brother? Man enough to raise his nephew as his son, if she were pregnant with Jordan's child? But how would he know? They had both been with her—identical twins with the same woman. There would be no way this side of hell to determine which one was the father. So, if Larissa presented him with a child—his own child—he would never know for certain that it was his.

He knew he should confront his bride with his suspicions, but what was the use? Jordan had sworn his tale

47

was the truth. He had lied to cover up their sin, but he was a poor liar under the best of conditions. Drunk, Jordan was even worse at the game.

And now this . . . this final blow. A few hurried words from his brother had shattered any dreams that remained. Jordan in the Confederate army! It was unthinkable. How long would it be before they met in battle on opposite sides? And who would shoot first?

Hunter felt his heart breaking as he climbed the stairs beside his bride. With her silver-blond hair and her lavender-blue eyes, his Larissa was as lovely as an angel. If only she were all his and truly an angel. He wanted her right now more than he'd ever wanted anything in his life. He needed her to hold him and soothe away this final insult—this betrayal by the brother who was his other half. He longed to take his bride in his arms and kiss her until she swooned, love her until all the pain was driven away and only sweetness and happiness remained in the universe.

At the door of his room she paused and turned. Were those tears swimming in her eyes? he wondered. Why was she crying? Could it be that she knew she'd made the wrong choice?

"You shouldn't cry on your wedding night," he said softly. "You should be happy."

"And so should you, my love. But you aren't, are you?"

Ignoring her question, he pushed open the door. "Come inside, won't you?"

She hesitated. "I don't know. Should I?"

"What do you mean? Of course, you should. We're married now."

"But do you love me, Hunter, or has this all been a dreadful mistake?"

His heart twisted into a tighter knot. She was about to

48

tell him that it was over before it ever had a chance to begin. "Of course I love you, Larissa. I always have and I always will. I think I loved you long before we met in this life. And I'm sure I'll love you if we live again."

His strange declaration was not what Larissa wanted to hear. She longed for *real* words of love—words that would make her feel warm and comforted and sure that he needed her as much as she needed him *right now*.

He took her hand and drew her inside. A moment later, his arms were around her, crushing her against him. His lips moved over her face, kissing her mouth, her eyelids, her cheeks.

"Oh, Larissa," he moaned. "No more talk. I don't want to try to sort things out with words. I want to hold you and touch you and fill my eyes with the sight of you so that when I'm gone I have only to will it so and you'll be there in my mind—in my heart."

His words seemed so strange. What was it he didn't want to talk about? Then Larissa realized what it must be. The brief conversation between the two brothers came back to mind. That had to be it.

"Jordy told you tonight, didn't he." It was not a question; she was that sure.

"Yes, but it doesn't matter," Hunter said, still kissing her neck, holding her close.

"How can you say that? We both know it's wrong!"

He was tugging at her gown, fumbling at the tiny pearl buttons. "We can make it right, Larissa. Just you and I. We'll forget about him."

"How can you say you'll forget about your own brother and what he's done? We have to face this and figure out what we're going to do about it."

49

"I'm going to do something about it. I'm going to leave you with *my* son."

Larissa failed to note the emphasis Hunter put on that one word. Nor could she think how leaving her pregnant would do anything to change Jordan's mind about joining the Confederate army.

Soon they were in Hunter's bed, but he was so different tonight. His lovemaking was neither slow nor tender. He went about it like a man in a frenzy, taking her over and over until Larissa begged him to let her rest for a time. Even as she drifted off to sleep, he continued stroking her breasts, touching her in tender places, nibbling at her shoulder.

Larissa had no idea how long she slept before the nightmare began. She only knew that it was horrible and that she woke up crying and screaming, "No! No! Please, no more!"

She realized something else, too, when she came fully awake. Her husband had entered her while she slept. He took her frantic cries personally and rolled away from her.

"Oh, Hunter, I didn't mean to deny you," she begged.

"But you couldn't help yourself, could you?"

He rose from the bed and pulled on his clothes. "I think I'll get some air."

"Please, darling, You don't understand. It's just a bad dream."

He looked at her, his expression dark with anger. "Well, at least now you admit it."

And then he was gone. Larissa sat up all night waiting, but he never returned to their bed.

* * *

By suppertime the next evening, Hunter was still missing. He'd left a note downstairs saying that he had to spend his last day readying his troops for their departure. Larissa was disappointed by his absence, but she tried to take it in stride. He would be home before bedtime, she assured herself. After all, this would be their final night together.

Larissa was gowned and robed for bed by the time she heard Hunter enter downstairs. She perched at the vanity, hoping to make a pretty picture for her husband when he opened the door. But the velvet-covered stool grew hard and uncomfortable long before he came upstairs.

When he finally stumbled through the door, Larissa had given up and gone to bed alone. She sat up and smiled at him.

"Darling, I was worried," she said. "But everything's fine now that you're home, safe and sound."

She purposely failed to mention that, although safe and sound, he was obviously quite drunk.

He stared at her as if he were surprised to see her there in his bed. For a moment, she saw the old light of love kindle in his dark eyes. But the next instant he quickly masked all his emotions.

"I figured you'd be asleep by now."

"Of course not, Hunter. Not with you leaving tomorrow morning. I stayed up to wish you a proper goodbye."

He stumbled over and flopped down on the bed. "You mean last night wasn't an end to it? I thought you'd run to Jordan today, telling him what a brute I was last night and begging him to take you in."

Larissa's heart lurched in fear when he mentioned Jordan. She prayed Hunter's twin hadn't told him about the other morning. She didn't want Hunter to find out that she'd visited Broad Acres alone—not ever!

"Why did you marry me, Larissa?"

His question struck her speechless. When she had gathered her wits, she said, "Hunter, I don't know how you could ask me that. I love you. That's why I married you. Do we have to waste these last precious hours fighting? I had more pleasant things in mind."

He laughed—a cold, hard sound. "You're quite the little actress, aren't you? Well, save your act for a more appreciative audience. I know you hated every minute of last night. You made that plain enough. And you have every right to despise me for demanding my husband's rights. It won't happen again, ma'am. You have my word on that. I do have enough pride left to know when I'm not welcome."

"You're wrong, Hunter!" she cried. "So wrong! I *do* love you!"

As if he never even heard the words, he said, "Chin up, darling. Maybe you'll get lucky and some Reb bullet with my name on it will find its mark. Then I'll be out of your way and you and Jordan can be together. That's what you want, isn't it? What you've *always* wanted."

Larissa couldn't hold back her tears. Hunter knew! He knew she'd gone to Broad Acres. She'd ruined everything.

"Darling, please!" she begged. "I want you. You're my husband. We have so little time left."

Suddenly, the old Hunter returned. He reached up and wiped the tears gently from her cheek. "I'm not worth crying over. And, if you *truly* love me, darling, I can forget everything else. We can pretend last night never happened."

"Oh, Hunter, yes! Let's do start over. I wish we could

turn the clock back to the night in the gardener's cottage. That was wonderful, beautiful. I'd give anything if we could live it all again. And you're here now, and we're married, and there's nothing to stop us from . . ."

She glanced down, only to realize that her words were falling on deaf ears. Her husband, still fully clothed, lay stretched out on the bed, fast asleep. Most of that night, Larissa sat beside him, staring down at his face through her tears. What a mess she had made of things. What a ghastly, sickening, miserable mess!

The dawn brought no easing of her pain. She awoke to find Hunter already dressed in his spanking new uniform—brass buttons gleaming and his shining saber swinging from its scarlet sash.

"You needn't stir," he told her when she started to get out of bed.

"Well, of course, I'm getting up," she replied. "I want to see you off."

Her words were ill-chosen and brought a grim smile to Hunter's face. "I should have suspected," he said.

Within the hour, he left. Long after he had ridden away, Larissa stood on the lawn where they had said their final farewell, where he had kissed her for what she suspected might be the last time. The morning breeze rustled her pink ruffled skirt and a misting rain began to fall. But she could not make herself move. She could not bear the thought of going back into the house, empty now without her love.

"Come back to me, my darling," she whispered through her tears. "Come back soon so that we can start all over again. I do love you so."

# Chapter Three

Within a few weeks of Hunter's departure, everything changed at Bluefield. And everything changed for Larissa. Jordan left the same day as his brother, only his uniform was gray and he rode under a different flag.

Mr. and Mrs. Breckinridge removed themselves from Bluefield to Broad Acres, leaving Larissa to care for her new home alone. Although it was a huge responsibility, she welcomed the task. She needed to work long and hard to make the time go more quickly until Hunter came home. Reports of the war made it seem unlikely that the Union forces would put down the rebellion in a few short weeks or even months.

On their wedding day, Hunter had freed all the slaves at Bluefield. His parents had followed suit at Broad Acres once they heard of their other son's defection. Many of the Negroes left immediately, making even more work for those who remained. But it relieved Larissa's mind to know that those servants who stayed were loyal to Hunter and to Bluefield. Things seemed to be going along smoothly.

Not until two months after Hunter's departure did

disaster strike. Larissa told herself long after that she should have seen it coming. She'd had her terrible dream every night for a month before nightmare became reality.

She'd ridden into Lexington for a brief visit with her parents—the first trip she'd made since her marriage. On the ride home she became more uneasy with each mile.

Leaning out of the carriage window, she called up to her driver, "Cassius, can't you make the horses go any faster? We need to get home before dark."

He'd mumbled back something about bad roads and rough going, but he had urged a bit more speed out of the team. Still, it was long past dark before they came within sight of Bluefield.

Far down the road, Larissa had seen an eerie glow in the sky. A forest fire, she'd imagined. Not until they were almost home did she realize that some of Bluefield's outbuildings were ablaze. She leaped from the carriage and raced to the huge bell in the yard, clanging an alarm for all to hear. But no one came.

"Cassius!" she yelled. "Go find the others. We have to form a bucket brigade from the well to the horse barn."

"But that's the corn barn burning, ma'am."

"Never mind the corn. We have to save the horses. Their stable is going up any minute now. Hurry! Get help!"

Larissa knew this scene. She had lived with it in her dream for years. But would there be a shining bridge at the end of it to save her? She doubted it.

Even as she raced toward the horse barn, she saw sparks from the other burning building land on the roof. Wrenching open the heavy doors, she hurried inside, opening stalls as she ran. The high-strung Thoroughbreds, panicked by the smell of smoke, danced frantically.

She knew if she didn't get them out of the stalls quickly they'd injure themselves. She led Hunter's best pair of stallions to the open door and gave each a sharp slap on the rump, then hurried back inside.

The wind was coming up, making the sparks swirl and fly through the air. Larissa glanced up and spied the first orange flames eating through the roof. The smoke grew thicker by the minute, while the horses still trapped in their stalls grew more frantic.

Back and forth, back and forth Larissa ran, freeing the horses. She could hardly see the door any longer. The smoke choked her and filled her eyes with tears. She heard a crash. One of the mares screamed. A back corner of the roof had crashed to the barn floor, trapping the unfortunate animal. Larissa raced back to try to help, but her problems had only begun. The skirt of her gown caught fire. While she tried to beat that out, her sleeve began to smolder.

Stumbling, gasping, crying, she headed for the door. She had done all she could. All the stall doors were open. She would have to leave it to the horses to seek safety for themselves. Just as she staggered into the open and drew the first breath of clear air into her smoke-clogged lungs, someone grabbed her burned arm.

"Well, lookee here!" the man said. "If we ain't flushed us out a right fine filly. You must be Larissa, wife of ol' Jordy's Yankee brother. Course Jordy don't know nothing about it, but after hearing all his tales about this fine place and his right handsome sister-in-law, me and my buddy, we lit out from the army and figured we'd pay you a call. So, how 'bout some of that fine Kentucky hospitality we've heard tell of?"

*Deserters!* A warning alarm went off inside Larissa's brain. She'd heard tales of soldiers—disgruntled that the war was not all glory—leaving, then using the conflict as an excuse to burn and loot. Hunter had warned her in a letter that she might be in danger at Bluefield since he and Jordan were fighting on different sides.

Larissa went limp, but by design, although it took very little acting on her part. "I'm badly burned," she moaned. "You're hurting me. Please."

Sure enough, the scruffy fellow eased his tight grip on her arm. And when he did, she jerked away from him and leaped to the back of one of the Thoroughbreds. She dug her heels in and the horse shot away across the yard.

Behind her, she heard the man shout, "Goddammit, let's get her! We can chase her down. There's the two of us. You head her off and I'll catch her."

Larissa had to cling to the horse for dear life. She was without a saddle, astride with her skirts bunched up under her. And once she got away from the glow of the fire, the night was pitch-black. Had she had time to study the stars, she would have known that she was headed southeast. But there was little opportunity to do anything but hold on tight and pray.

All night the men chased her. She could hear their horses pounding on determinedly and the men shouting curses after her, calling out what they meant to do to her when they finally caught up.

Suddenly, they were no longer on the open road, but in deep woods. Larissa's whole body ached and her burned arm throbbed painfully. She put her head down on the horse's neck and cried into his mane.

"Hunter," she whispered. "Oh, Hunter, where are you? I can't get away. I can't save myself. I need you! I love you!"

Then a total, black void swallowed her up.

* * *

*Who am I?* She couldn't think—didn't know.

*Where am I? How long have I been running?*

As hard as she tried to remember, it was no use. She knew she was cold, wet, weary, lost, and that someone was chasing her, closing in fast. Beyond those obvious facts, her mind seemed incapable of functioning properly to give her the answers she sought.

Exactly who her pursuers were or what their intent, she wasn't sure. She only knew that she had to keep moving in order to escape.

The woods loomed thick and black around her. She couldn't see them, but she knew they were still out there somewhere. She glanced about, frantic, then realized that they couldn't see her either. In that moment, the sinister darkness was her only comfort.

Relieved, she slumped down and huddled close to the dark trunk of a massive ironwood tree. She had to rest, to think, to plan some strategy. She'd come too far to let them capture her now. If she weren't so exhausted, she'd keep going. But she had never been this weary in her life. Her body ached with fatigue. Her arms and legs burned and itched from insect bites and bramble cuts. And she was weak with hunger. The few berries she'd picked in the woods earlier in the day had hardly served to stave off starvation. How long had it been since she'd had a decent meal? She couldn't remember. Days? Weeks?

Somewhere off in the distance she heard the rush of water, perhaps a swollen river or a waterfall—perhaps a way of escape.

*If only my horse hadn't gone lame.*

Her blue eyes widened in the darkness. Yes! She remembered something; she had been on horseback when she set out. That thought spawned another. She recalled horses—many horses—screaming, dying, while flames leaped all around. She touched the tender burn on her arm. She had tried to put out the fire. But then the men had spotted her and swooped down like so many vultures, ready to capture her and kill her . . . or worse.

The tender throb of her injured arm seemed nothing compared to the pain she felt deep inside. It was a pain of need and loss and bewilderment. There was something else, too. *Guilt!* Why? What had she done that was so terrible? If only she could remember.

Somehow she knew that whatever had happened to her, her life would never be the same again. Everything she knew was gone. Everything from now on would be as strange and unfamiliar as this black, forbidding forest.

"Gone . . . all gone . . ." she murmured, brushing at tears with the back of her hand.

She closed her eyes and leaned her head back against the tree trunk. As she forced herself to relax, bits of scenes—like unfocused dreams—floated just at the edge of her memory. She saw a great white-columned house set in rolling blue-green fields as a backdrop for a tall, dashing U. S. Cavalry officer. His brass buttons gleamed against his blue uniform as he mounted his horse. The coal-black stallion stamped the earth, anxious to be off. She heard music playing at a ball and cannons firing on some distant field of battle. She heard men screaming and dying. She shivered and gripped the tattered sleeves of her ruined gown. What did all this have to do with her? She was simply too tired to think.

"If only I dared sleep for a time."

But sleep would be suicide. Somehow she had

managed to elude capture, even though the men had pursued her for days. She could take no chances now, not even in the sheltering darkness of the thick forest.

She gave her sore body a good shake, forcing herself to remain awake and alert. The moon would be up soon. Then she could see to move on. But they would be able to see, too. The thought sent a shiver through her.

"How long?" she murmured. "How long do I have before they find me?"

She hadn't realized that the forest was alive with night sounds until everything suddenly went deathly silent. Gone now were the soft whispers of creatures scurrying through the underbrush, owls hooting, and the wind sighing through branches overhead. She held her breath, waiting. Waiting for what? she wondered.

Then in a terrible moment, she knew.

"Jesus-H-Christ!" she heard one of the men curse. "I can't see my dad-blamed nose on my face. Where the hell did she go to?"

A harsh laugh erupted in the night. "Take it easy, Jeb. She ain't gone far. And she sure as hell ain't crossed the river in the dark. We got her penned up good as a shoat ready for slaughtering. Come moonrise, that silver hair of hers'll glow like torchlight. I reckon we ain't tracked her all this way for nothing. We're about to have that little gal. All we gotta do now is sit tight and bide our time. Pass me that jug while we wait."

So, they were still there—rough and mean and drunk. She began to tremble—tremble so violently that her teeth chattered. They were right, of course. Her long, silver-blond hair would shine in the moonlight, a dead give-away. She clawed at the earth, scooping up handfuls of rich, dark dirt, rubbing it into her hair. It was no use. If only she had her hooded riding cape, but she'd lost that somewhere along the way. The river was her only chance. She might drown trying to cross it, but better that sort of death than what those men had in mind for her.

She took a deep breath and clutched at the cool moonstone dangling from the silver chain around her neck. Someone had given her this token, someone she loved. Perhaps the handsome cavalry officer? At the moment, the smooth crystal felt like a talisman, a good-luck charm that had brought her this far and might save her yet.

Moving carefully—blindly—through the dark woods, she edged ever closer to the sound of the rushing water. Her heart pounded. It was so loud she feared the men might hear it even over the roar of the falls.

Just as she crept out of the thick forest and onto the uneven rock ledge that verged the river gorge, the full moon broke from the clouds. Her heart sank. She found herself on a high cliff over the river. There was no way across, no way of escape.

Behind her she heard one of the men give a whoop. "Well, lookee there! She done come out of hiding, just a-standing there waiting for us, Jeb. Come on! Let's get her."

Seized with panic, she turned back to the deep river gorge and the falls dashing on the rocks below. A single step and she would be free of her pursuers forever. But could she take that step? Could she leave this world? Could she desert the man she loved even to save herself from the unspeakable horrors her tormentors promised?

Even now, she heard them crashing through the woods, coming closer and closer. She held her breath and closed her eyes.

"Only one step," she urged. "One tiny step and this nightmare will end."

Suddenly, just as the men broke out of the forest near her, she was blinded by a brilliant glow. The throbbing, silver light seemed to radiate from the falls, forming a pulsing, glowing bridge across the gorge. The soft colors of a rainbow shimmered in the rising mist.

"Grab ahold of her 'fore she jumps, Jeb!" came the cry from behind her.

Holding her breath, she stepped off solid ground and onto the shimmering bridge. At that moment, the men's cries faded in the distance. She felt the warm silver light enfold her. Her fear vanished. She was safe at last.

Then the light of the moonbow faded and total blackness closed in around her.

Somewhere off in the distance, the woman from the other side of the moonbow heard the crackling sound of a man's voice. "Dateline: Chicago, October 1, 1982. Cyanide placed in Tylenol capsules has now caused seven deaths in the Chicago area. The makers of Tylenol have recalled two hundred sixty-four thousand bottles of the pain reliever. As yet no one has been arrested for the crime."

She glanced toward the sound. It seemed to be coming out of an odd-looking brown box that sat on a nearby table. She was in a strange bed, in a strange room. As she slowly regained consciousness, the unfamiliar words added to her confusion.

Then she heard other, clearer voices—a man and a woman. They seemed to come from far, far away, but somehow she knew they were very near her, watching her.

"Switch that blame radio off, Lonnie. It's all static," the woman said.

There was a soft click, then the more distant voice died.

"Who is she, you reckon?" the man whispered in awe. "She's a right pretty little thing, ain't she? But it looks like she's been through some bad times of late."

"Her name's Clair de Lune," the woman declared. "Clair de Lune Summerland, I vow."

The shaggy-haired coal miner turned and squinted at his wife. "Go on with you, Rachel! There ain't no such person."

"There is now!" she stated emphatically. "We always wanted a daughter, Lonnie. This girl ain't from around here. My guess is she's a moon child come to us to answer our prayers. So I'm claiming her for my own."

"Look! She's coming around, Rachel. I reckon now we'll find out who she really is and how come she walked up to our cabin steps and collapsed."

"Where am I?" the silver-haired girl asked in a groggy voice. "What happened?"

She stared up at the pair hovering over her. The woman looked thin and frail, aged by hard work and a hard life. The man, tall and muscular, had permanent dark lines etched in his face so that his worried expression was accentuated by the embedded coal dust from years spent in the mines.

"Don't you remember your own name, child?" Rachel Summerland asked, hoping against hope she'd receive a negative answer.

"It's gone. Everything's gone. I have no name."

"Why, of course you have a name," Rachel answered,

beaming. "You're Clair de Lune Summerland. I'm your ma and this here's your pa. You remember us, don't you, child?"

Relief flowed through the weary young woman. She stared into the faces of two strangers, but they were kind faces. The woman's eyes were watery-blue, her smile sweet and motherly. The man wasn't smiling, but his warm brown eyes were filled with concern. She wanted them to be her parents.

"What happened to me?" she asked.

A flicker of something wiped the smile from the woman's face for an instant, but then it returned, broader than ever. "Why, you just took a fall, darlin'. You hit your head and knocked yourself senseless. I reckon that's why you can't remember nothing. But you'll be all right. You just lie easy and rest a spell."

"My arm hurts."

The woman took her hand and frowned at the ugly burn.

"Don't you worry, honey. I'll put some salve on that and bind it up real good." The woman fabricated a tale as she tended the girl. "I reckon you must have been carrying the lantern when you fell. But it'll be all right in a day or so. There now, all done! Me and Lonnie will leave you be for a time so you can rest."

When the two people who claimed to be her parents left the room, Clair de Lune Summerland closed her eyes. For a long time she heard the murmur of their voices coming from the next room of the cabin. Her parents seemed to be arguing about something, but she couldn't hear their words distinctly. Finally, the drone of muffled sounds lulled her to sleep.

She was home at last. The nightmare was over.

Clair de Lune Summerland never recalled that her name had been anything else, that she had ever lived in any other time, or that she had crossed the moonbow on that cold and terrible night, leaving behind the dark and handsome man she loved.

Some nights, though, as she gazed up at the full moon, a powerful lonely longing ached deep in her heart.


The next ten years passed swiftly for the "moon child," as folks in the mountains of Eastern Kentucky called the Summerlands' foundling daughter. However, they never called Clair de Lune Summerland that to her face. As far as Cluney knew, she'd had a lick on her head at age sixteen and simply forgotten her past—a past that remained as mysterious as the day she showed up at the coal miner's cabin on Baldy Rock Mountain.

Once she was well enough, her parents sent her to school down in the valley. "Smart as a whip!" her teachers said she was, although it did seem peculiar to them that she was so amazed and fascinated by such everyday inventions as radios, television sets, computers, and even telephones. But she soon adjusted to her new world and took these things for granted.

Rachel and Lonnie Summerland lived to see their daughter graduate from high school at the top of her class. They saw her accept a full scholarship to Whitley College down there in the valley. They knew some day she'd make a fine teacher.

After a few years, the Summerlands stopped worrying that someone might come to claim their "daughter." She was a Summerland through and through and no doubt about it. They even had witnesses. Old Miss Redbird from up on the mountain and Wooter Crenshaw, the coffin-maker, both swore before a judge that they'd been there the day that Rachel gave birth to Clair de Lune. Redbird and Wooter were friends, *good* friends; it was the least they could do for the grieving couple, who'd lost their only son in a mine accident. And so the "moon child" became a legal Summerland, with a twentieth-century birthdate, a birth certificate, and a Social Security number.

As for her old life, all that remained were the occasional nightmares, a few vague memories, and that lovely moonstone necklace.

But on nights of the full moon when a moonbow spanned Cumberland Falls, Cluney Summerland got a strong yearning to leave the mountain and travel somewhere far away.

However, it wasn't until March 1, 1992 that her longing became an obsession. That was the day she found Major Hunter Breckinridge's Civil War diary—the very same day she received word that Jeff Layton was dead.

# Chapter Four

"Major Breckinridge, don't you reckon we better head back to the lodge now, sir? Don't look like there'll be no moonbow tonight—not with them clouds all boiling like stew in a witch's pot."

The persuasive voice, as deep and powerful as the water pulsing below them in the Cumberland River gorge, came from a man as black as the Kentucky night—Private George Washington Abraham Lincoln Freeman.

That was his new name, the one the former slave "Jimbo" had chosen for himself when his Tennessee master had reluctantly read the Emancipation Proclamation to his people a few months back. As soon as Jimbo—or "Free," as he now called himself—was able, he'd hot-footed it over into Kentucky and joined up with the first Federal regiment he bumped into, the Cave Hill Cavalry, commanded by Major Hunter Breckinridge.

Private Freeman had been in uniform only two weeks before the Cave Hillers ran smack-dab into Morgan's

Raiders at the Campbellsville bridge. Although Morgan had been forced to retreat, leaving behind seventy-one bodies, the Rebel troops had done their fair share of damage before giving a final war whoop and hightailing it out of there.

Major Breckinridge wasn't dead from the skirmish, but with five Reb bullet holes in him, Free reckoned he was as close to expired as a human could get without actually passing over.

The private had managed to get his commander to the lodge at the edge of the Cumberland River where he'd heard tell a preacher and his wife took in soldiers and nursed them back to health. But Free wasn't sure Parson Renfro's missus would be able to do anything for Major Breckinridge.

Free couldn't rightly figure just what was keeping the major alive, except, maybe, that he had his heart set on glimpsing the moonbow over Cumberland Falls one last time. Then, too, he pined away night and day to see his pretty bride who'd somehow got lost in the war. There was one more thing, too, that seemed to give Major Breckinridge an almost superhuman strength. He had a bitterness in his heart and a craving for revenge.

"Major?" Free tried again to draw the man's attention away from the dark, roaring falls.

"You go on back, Free, if you want. I'll stay a spell longer. Looks to me like the clouds are thinning. Could be the full moon'll break through yet."

Free neither left nor said another word. He wasn't about to remind this man he admired so much that his injuries would keep him from returning unless a strong arm was lent to help him back up the hill. The private

70

stood steadfastly beside his commanding officer tonight just as he had all during that fateful battle.

"You hear me, Free? Go on now. I'll be fine." The major turned and glanced up, saw Private Freeman still there, and shook his head. "Do what you want, then."

Hunter Breckinridge was a big man—hard as the coal that came out of these Eastern Kentucky mountains—but his thready voice bespoke the war's toll on his strength. Had Free not known better, hearing that old voice, he might have taken the major for a man nearing eighty rather than someone fifty years younger. It was a crying shame, he reckoned, what this war was doing to Kentucky's finest.

"I ain't in no hurry, Major. I'll just bide here with you awhile longer. I'd like to see me one of them moonbows. I hear tell they got magic in 'em." He reached out to make sure the blanket was still around his commander's shoulders. "You warm enough, sir? There's a mite of a nip to the air tonight. Winter'll be coming on soon."

"Winter," Breckinridge echoed dully. Winter was already here for him—a black coldness that chilled his body, his heart, his very soul. As for the season itself, he doubted he'd live to see it. A man knew when he didn't have much longer; he could feel his blood slowing, his heart straining, and old memories seemed far back in the past like you were gazing at them through the wrong end of a telescope.

By next full moon, next chance to see the moonbow, there'd be an end to it, he figured. Things would be decided one way or the other for Hunter Breckinridge. But maybe that wasn't so terrible. If Larissa was truly gone—gone for good—what did he care about going on? No, he'd rather not stick around. Maybe on the other side it would be warm and sunlit. And for certain there'd be no more war, no more pain.

"No more Larissa," he muttered to himself.

"What's that you say, sir?"

Hunter hadn't realized he'd spoken his wife's name aloud until Free questioned him. He cleared his throat, trying to get past the lump, before he could speak again.

"Nothing, Free. I was just thinking about my wife. Wondering where she could be. It's hard not knowing what happened to her. I ache with wondering, nights like this."

"I reckon I can sympathize with that, Major." Free nodded his dark head solemnly. "My woman got sold off, sent here to Kentucky, so I heard. I ain't seen her in over two years."

Free could feel the major's eyes on him even though he couldn't see the man's face in the dark.

"I didn't know you were married."

"I ain't exactly, sir," Free said, pain edging the words. "We jumped the broomstick, slave-fashion. We planned to make it legal with a parson and all once we was free. But before we could do it, Belle got sold off like I said. That's why I come to Kentucky—to look for her. Hell, once this war's over, I'll search this whole damn state, if I have to, but I mean to have her back."

A long silence stretched between the two men. They were both thinking of the women they loved and had lost.

"I hope you find her, Free," the major said at length. "There's no pain in the world like losing the woman you love—the only one you'll ever love. There's a loneliness, like a wound that won't heal. But there's a worse pain, too. The pain of not knowing."

"  'Scuse my asking, sir, but what you reckon happened to your wife?"

Another long silence followed Free's question. Major Breckinridge wished he'd never brought up the subject. It was like digging at a fresh wound, just thinking about Larissa.

Finally, he said, "I wish I knew. We were wed right before I left to join my troop. One of those whirlwind courtships, you might call it. We'd known each other all our lives, but I never thought she'd consent to marry me. I always figured she had her sights set on my twin brother. But then the war broke out. I proposed and—Glory be!— she said yes. Seemed like it couldn't have been more perfect—big, fancy wedding, then afterward the two of us together at Bluefield. Only two days later I had to leave her."

He paused and let out a long sigh. When he spoke again, his voice dropped to a husky whisper. "But it wasn't perfect and now it never will be. I hadn't figured on this damn war lasting so long. When I left, I thought I'd go help whup the Rebs and be home in a few weeks. It was six long months before I got back to Bluefield on leave. When I finally did get there, my wife was gone— not a trace as to where."

"Didn't no one know what happened, sir?"

"Oh, there were tales—lots of them. One of my neighbors said Larissa got real restless once I was gone and started riding out alone. I figured when I got to Bluefield and she wasn't there that maybe she just took off to Lexington to stay with her folks for a while. But she wasn't with them.."

Major Breckinridge paused. He couldn't bring himself to tell Free the tale that seemed most likely the truth—that

Larissa had grown weary of waiting and left to find Jordan. Hunter had tried a million times to tell himself that his wife and his brother wouldn't do that to him. But the longer he waited and searched, the more he believed that Larissa simply had no intentions of being found. It was like she'd dropped off the face of the earth.

Ever since they were boys, Hunter and Jordan had vied for Larissa's favors, performing breakneck stunts on horseback to dazzle her and doing any other tom-fool thing they could think of to win her praise. She had teased and flirted and played one against the other until she nearly drove them wild. While still in their teens, they had even fought a duel over her. Thank God, they'd both had sense enough to aim high, so the fight turned out bloodless. Larissa had been delighted that they both survived, and afterward she'd continued to give them equal attention. For a time, it looked as if her heart would never find a home. Hunter wondered even now if that wasn't the case. She'd made her choice at last. But it looked like Hunter had finally won her only to lose out in the end to Jordan. Hunter couldn't stop thinking about Larissa's rendezvous with his brother shortly before their wedding.

"What you reckon become of her, sir?" Free's question interrupted Hunter's grim thoughts.

"Lord knows," the major answered, shaking his bandaged head. "It scares me to think. One tale I know to be true. A Confederate raiding party came through one night and stole a dozen or so horses. Thoroughbreds, the best in my stable. The servants were all scared out of their wits and hid till after the Rebs torched the barns and left. They told me, though, that they didn't think my wife was there that night—that she'd ridden off somewhere to go visiting. But she could have come back while those sca-

74

vangers were there. If she did, she would have tried to keep them from stealing the stock, and . . ."

"Oh, Lord God! Don't even think about that, sir," Free moaned.

"Hard not to, I'm afraid."

Hunter was lying and he knew it. If any Confederate soldier had come for Larissa, he figured the bastard's name was Breckinridge. It would be just like Jordan to lead a raid against Bluefield out of pure spite. And he wouldn't put it past his brother to kidnap Larissa in the bargain. But deep in his heart, Hunter truly believed that it was much more likely Larissa had left with Jordan of her own free will. And considering the way he had treated her on their wedding night, he figured it served him right.

He kept waiting and hoping for some sign, something that would let him know that Larissa—wherever she was—was still well and still his. But he figured death would catch up with him before he caught up with his wandering wife. And why shouldn't she wander? He had all but sent her away before he left for the war.

The two men fell silent. Only the roar and hiss of the falls and the crisp rattle of dry leaves overhead disturbed the quiet.

Hunter felt the cold creeping into his bones, making his head ache and his eyes smart. He stared up at the purple-black clouds. They seemed to have changed slightly, taking on a tinge of silver. As he watched, a thin sliver of the full moon slid into the open, casting a glow down on the falls and turning the dark clouds gilt-edged. Behind him, he heard Free catch his breath.

"It's coming, Free," he whispered. "The moon's found a crack to slide through."

Even as he spoke, the big luminous moon—its face

seeming to smile down on them—shouldered the clouds aside, chasing away the darkness. All around them an eerie light stole through the gloomy woods. The skirt of the falls glowed as frothy white as a bride's petticoat. The mist rising into the air looked like silver smoke.

"Magic!" Free breathed. "It pure-tee is!"

But Hunter didn't hear the private's exclamations. He sat entranced, the ache of his bullet-riddled body forgotten as he watched a shining halo spread itself over the falls. The moonbow gleamed like a new silver dollar. Then colors glowed faintly, giving the rushing water an aura all its own. A heartbeat later, as the moonbow pulsed and gleamed its brightest, Hunter saw something—something he had never expected to see in this place, in the dead of night.

"Free! Free, look there!" he yelled. "Do you see?"

"Yessir, I see it! And ain't it a lovely sight, that moonbow?"

"I don't mean the moonbow, man. Can't you see, there atop the falls?"

Just then, a fat, greedy cloud gobbled up the moon. The magic faded, but not Hunter's excitement.

"Help me up the hill, Free."

The major was trying to struggle to his feet. He was so eager to get back to the lodge and record in his journal what he'd witnessed that he failed to realize he needed Free's help.

Long into the wee hours of the morning, the lamp in the major's room glowed as he tried and tried again to write in his diary a description of what he had seen. Finally, bone-deep weary and aching with something far different from pain, he gave up the impossible task and penned the final entry in the journal he had kept for so

76

many years. It was short and simple, but it would suffice, he decided.

"I went to the falls tonight. I saw the moonbow and now I know, Larissa, that love is the greatest power on earth or in heaven. I know, too, what is to come; I have seen the future. And I saw an end to all manner of suffering. I am ready to surrender to Fate."

One hundred and twenty-nine years off in the future, Cluney Summerland rubbed her tired eyes and closed the old journal. How many times had she read that final entry? Would she ever discover what Major Hunter Breckinridge had seen in the moonbow that night? The Civil War soldier's flourished handwriting was easy to decipher now, but the last paragraph in the diary still baffled her.

Sitting in a sunny corner of the living room of her apartment in faculty housing on the campus of Whitley College, she rubbed her fingers over the brittle leather that bound the mysterious journal. Hunter Breckinridge and his wife Larissa now seemed as much a part of Cluney's life as her best friend and co-teacher, B.J. Jackson. She'd been helping B.J. clean out the basement of the school library two months ago when she'd unearthed the major's chronicle of the Civil War.

Had it been *only* two months since her fiancé's death? The pain made it seem so much longer. She and B.J. had worked late that afternoon at the library. When she'd arrived home, the telegram informing her that Lieutenant Jeff Layton's plane had crashed during carrier exercises in the Mediterranean Sea had been waiting. Numb with shock—too numb even to cry—Cluney had buried herself that night in Hunter Breckinridge's diary, sharing his pain because she could not yet face her own.

War, however, had not been the major's main topic. He'd given an occasional line or two to some battle or skirmish, but his obsession had been Larissa—his beloved wife, missing in the midst of the conflict.

Over the weeks, Cluney had become more and more obsessed with the major's writings, and especially with his final, mysterious entry. She had even launched a campaign to save his former home, Bluefield, which was up for sale and likely to face the wrecker's ball soon, unless a buyer could be found who was more concerned with preserving history than with building a new shopping mall.

Putting the diary aside, she opened her window to let in a breath of spring breeze. The very air smelled green and new. Commencement season was here again. The Class of 1992 would graduate in just two weeks.

"And then what?" she wondered aloud. "Shall I stay or go?"

For weeks now, she'd been toying with the idea of simply throwing all her belongings in her van and taking off. Her longing to leave this place had grown ever stronger since Jeff's death. His hitch in the Navy had been almost at its end when the accident happened. After their marriage, they had planned to move to his home state, California. Cluney knew only the mountains and the college. Lately, though, something out there somewhere had been calling to her, urging her to hit the road. And she knew where the highway would lead her. Jeff's mother lived in San Francisco. She longed to go there and share her own loss with the other woman who had loved him.

Now that the end of the college year was approaching and her history students were about to graduate and go out into the world, the only things holding her here were the mystery of Hunter Breckinridge and her seemingly futile battle to save Bluefield.

"But none of that's really my problem," she told herself. "And besides, it's ancient history. I *need* to get away. I want to see . . ." She thought for a moment, then her violet-blue eyes misted. "I want to see Jeff's home."

The phone rang, interrupting her thoughts. She reached for it, feeling her usual annoyance at the bothersome instrument.

"Yes? Who is it?"

"Hey, take it easy! No need to bite my head off, girl."

"Oh, B.J., I'm sorry. I was in the middle of something . . ."

"You don't have to tell me. The major's diary."

"Well, yes, that, too, but I was mostly making plans for my trip."

B.J. laughed. "Yeah, sure! Where are you going this time? You know you won't leave this place."

"No, I mean it. I'm really going—right after graduation."

B.J. brushed her friend's declaration aside. "Well, before you take off, how about helping me straighten the library for next year's crop of students?"

"Oh, sure. No problem. But then I'm off."

B.J. chuckled. "Whatever you say, girl. I'll see you around later."

Cluney hung up the phone, but kept staring at it. Why did she feel so odd everytime she had to talk into a telephone? She got the same queer feeling when she worked at her computer. She didn't understand where

79

her typed words went or how they got from the keyboard to the printer. It made her head swim just to think about it. She didn't like watching television either. The faces on the screen gave her the eerie feeling that she was being spied upon, her every move being carefully watched. She'd never turn on the small black-and-white set she owned if she was alone in her apartment. Jeff used to laugh at her, but then Jeff had laughed at life in general. She didn't think he had ever taken anything seriously except his flying and their love for each other.

Cluney rose quickly from her chair and strode across the small room. She tried not to, but she couldn't help thinking about Jeff and how their life would have been. His sudden death had done something to her; she would never be herself again. Thinking about him made her feel restless—out of sorts and out of place. A misfit. A lost soul.

"All the more reason to get away from here," she told herself.

She stood for a moment at her window, looking out over the greening mountains. Here and there, she spied bright dots of pink and white—the redbuds and dogwoods just bursting into bloom. She could see Baldy Rock in the distance.

The old cabin was still there on the mountain, but empty now. She'd removed a few mementos after her parents' deaths two years ago. Since then, she hadn't been back. Without her ma and pa the place no longer felt like home. It almost seemed as if she had no home.

"Maybe that's why I have to leave," she mused. "Maybe I think that somewhere out there I'll find a place where I really belong."

Nervous suddenly, she rubbed the old burn scar on her arm. After all these years, it still itched when she got upset.

Her ma had explained that she'd been holding a lantern when she fell and her arm had been burned in the accident that took her memory. But in her nightmares, she saw a burning building. What building? Where? She didn't know.

Pure impulse moved her suddenly. She hurried into her small, neat bedroom and pulled open the desk drawer. On a piece of old motel stationery, with a leaky ballpoint pen, she quickly scrawled her letter of resignation. With her intentions down on paper, she leaned back and sighed. Later she could type it up on her computer. But the deed was done.

"No turning back now," she said. "I'm going to California. I need to be with Jeff's mother."

When Jeff's plane had crashed, Cluney had felt that her fiancé's death signaled the end of her world. Now, for the first time in months, she felt the clouds part to let the moon shine through.

## Chapter Five

The Whitley College Library was quiet—too quiet—on that hot Monday morning, May 18, following the graduation ceremonies of the Class of '92. The whole campus was like a ghost town, but the library was more like a morgue. The two women, working side by side, broke the stillness only occasionally, most often when Cluney Summerland sneezed explosively from a combination of book dust, spring allergies, and a cold she'd picked up in the past week.

B.J. Jackson shoved a box of tissues toward her. "Here—help yourself." Then as Cluney blew loudly, her friend asked, "Hey, how'd you ever get a name like Clair de Lune anyway?"

"Didn't I ever tell you that, B.J.? It was my mama's favorite piece of music. She used to sit on the front porch on summer evenings and play it on her dulcimer. Seemed like it would flow out over the mountaintop until the birds all hushed to listen."

With a cackle and a smart-aleck crack, B.J. quickly erased the pretty picture Cluney had painted. "I'll bet you're real glad your ma wasn't partial to 'Jimmy Crack Corn' or 'Froggy Went A-Courtin'.''

Both young women laughed, but their humor was forced since they both knew they were spending their final few hours together. They understood how difficult it was going to be to say goodbye when the time came. And that time would come very shortly—as soon as they finished rearranging and dusting the books on the shelves and sorting through the last box of long-stored textbooks from the library basement.

Eight years they had been best friends—Cluney Summerland and B.J. Jackson—through their undergraduate years at Whitley College, through graduate school, and, finally, as staff members at their alma mater, Cluney in the history department and B.J. as assistant librarian.

They made an odd pair. Cluney was tall and slender, delicate-looking with her long, silver-blond hair and pale-blue eyes tinged with lavender, the exact shade of a type of Chinese porcelain called "moonglow." B.J., on the other hand, was smaller and more compact, and as dark as one of the polished stones beneath nearby Cumberland Falls—her ebony hair and eyes only a shade darker than her smooth skin. Their friends kidded them, calling Cluney "Ms. Sunlight" and B.J. "Ms. Shadow."

Now the inseparables were about to part. B.J.—a transplant from Tennessee—would stay on as Whitley's head librarian next year, while Cluney—born and bred in these mountains of Eastern Kentucky—was bound and determined to strike out for the first time in her life to see California. Her van was all packed and her apartment key turned in. The moment they finished straightening the library, she meant to hit the road and hang a sharp left, headed west.

"Are you really going to leave?" At the quivery sound in B.J.'s voice, Cluney glanced up from the stack of dusty books she was sorting. Sure enough, she saw tears in her friend's black eyes, making them look larger and brighter than usual.

"You know I am," Cluney answered, a catch in her voice at B.J.'s sudden loss of control. They had both vowed to avoid any messy farewell scenes. "I figure on being out of Kentucky by nightfall, headed west as far as the road will take me."

"But it's full moon tonight, Cluney," B.J. said in a pleading tone. "I thought you'd hang around at least long enough to see if the moonbow appears. We could drive up to the falls like we used to. Don't you want one last chance to see what Major Breckinridge wrote about in his diary?" B.J.'s voice rose on a hopeful note. If anything could make Cluney stay one more night, it was the moonbow. "Come on, girl, let's do it."

Cluney thought for a minute. The idea was tempting. But wasn't the diary one of the reasons she'd made up her mind to leave? It had become an obsession with her. She'd been using it and her futile fight to save Bluefield to block out facing her grief over Jeff's death. That wasn't healthy. She had to face her loss and learn to live with it.

Still, she had hoped to get an early start and that obviously wasn't going to happen. She was tired after the hectic graduation weekend, and feeling dragged out from the antibiotics she'd been taking for her cold. Maybe it would be better to begin her long trip tomorrow, rested and in better spirits.

"You want to," B.J. said, "I can see it in your face. Do! Let's have one last blast together. We can go to Mac's

Pizza Castle for supper, then head on up to the falls. Who knows? Tonight could be *the* night."

Cluney laughed at her friend's arm-twisting. B.J. was good at it, always had been. "Okay! Okay! You talked me into pizza, but I'm not going to the falls again. I'm all done with that—end of chapter, clean page. No good-byes, no looking back. I've given that diary too much of my time and attention, but no more. Whatever happened to Hunter Breckinridge and his wife, it's clear to me now that it's none of my business. Obviously, I was never meant to find out the answer to that mystery. And it's clear I've lost my battle for Bluefield."

B.J. glanced at Cluney, but said nothing. She didn't believe for a minute that her friend meant to walk away from those characters out of Kentucky's past. She might be trying to run away from them, though.

Cluney interrupted the silence once more, talking as much to herself as to B.J. "There is one person I need to say goodbye to. I'll just have time to drive up there before supper."

Both B.J.'s frown and her question held a world of disapproval. "You don't mean you're going up the mountain to see that crazy old witch-woman?"

"Don't call Miss Redbird that. She's not a witch and she's a lot saner than most of the people up on Baldy Rock."

"How can you say that, girl, when your own folks lived up there? When you were born and raised there, too?"

"I never claimed to be anything *but* crazy," Cluney joked, with a wink. "As for my folks, I've always had a strange feeling about them. All that business they told me about how I fell down the cellar stairs when I was a teenager and got a lick on my head and couldn't remember anything afterward. Amnesia? I mean *really!* B.J., would you believe a story like that? It's like I never even existed until I was sixteen years old."

"If my folks said it was so, I'd believe it."

"But they never even took me to a doctor as far as I know. Mama said they sent for that old healing woman that lived across the mountain. In her *learned* opinion, I was sound, if dented."

"Well, you must have been okay. You're here now, aren't you?"

"The part of me that's lived since right before my seventeenth birthday is here. As for the rest—the earlier years of my life—I might as well not have lived at all. Why, it's like I was never really born—just popped up out of the mountain, nearly grown."

"That *is* crazy talk, Cluney! If you don't believe you were born, take a look at your birth certificate."

"I don't have one."

"Say what?" B.J. squinted hard at her friend.

"The courthouse burned the same year as my accident. All the local records went up in flames. Mama got me one of those substitute certificates by getting Pa, Miss Redbird, and Wooter Crenshaw to swear they knew I was born. But what if they all swore to it just because my mama asked them to, B.J.?"

B.J. rolled her eyes, then climbed to her feet and carried a stack of books to a nearby shelf. "Lord, girl, what an imagination you have! But maybe you're right, maybe you never were born. Maybe you're that moon child I hear tell of that came down off the mountain one dark and stormy night."

B.J. made the eerie *do-do-do-do* sound from "The Twilight Zone," then giggled.

"Go on, B.J.! You and your mountain tales! I thought librarians were suppposed to be levelheaded."

"I am, if *anyone* in this room is. You certainly aren't—fixing to run off to California and traipsing all the way up to the top of Baldy Rock before you leave to see that old witch-woman. I'd be scared to go up there alone. They say she eats bats." B.J. gave an exaggerated shiver. "Thank goodness you're meeting me for pizza. At least you won't be staying at her cabin for supper."

Cluney had to giggle at B.J.'s antics. When she crossed her eyes and shook her hair into a tangled mess, she did resemble Miss Redbird, except that the old woman's hair was snow-white and her mouth puckered inward since she'd lost the false teeth Social Services bought her awhile back. Miss Redbird claimed they fell down the well.

"I have a very good reason for going," Cluney explained. "Miss Redbird's been claiming for years that she had a secret to tell me 'when the time's right.' Well, it's now or never. Once I leave this place, I doubt I'll ever be back. That and the fact that Miss Redbird claims to be over a hundred years old would seem to mean that there's no time like the present."

B.J. stopped shelving books and leaned closer, her dark eyes wide with interest. "What kind of secret?"

Cluney shrugged. "I have no idea. When I was younger and scared of old Redbird, I figured she used to tell me that just to get me to come up and visit her. But the last couple of times I've gone to her cabin, she's mentioned this secret and promised that I'd know soon. Or as she put it, 'The time's right nigh for the tellin', child.' "

B.J. rubbed her bare arms briskly. "Cut it out! You're giving me the creeps, girl."

"Well, anyway, I am going up to see her."

Finally, at three o'clock B.J. locked the library door. It had been a job and a half, but now the shelves were all neat and dusted, ready for the new wave of students in the fall. Students, they both realized with a touch of sadness, that Cluney would never meet.

"Want to come on over to my house?" B.J. asked hopefully.

"No, I'd better go on and finish what I have to do." Cluney tried to keep excitement from creeping into her voice. B.J.'s mention earlier of the diary had brought it to mind for the first time in days. In spite of her declaration to B.J. that she meant to forget about the Breckinridge mystery, Cluney was eager to go off somewhere quiet and go over the entries in the diary one last time before she left Kentucky. Maybe there was something she had missed—some clue hidden in its pages that would unlock the meaning of that final entry made by Major Hunter Breckinridge on that long ago September night back in 1863— the night he saw the moonbow.

"You're sure?" B.J. asked.

Cluney waved and headed for her purple van. "I'll meet you at eight at the Pizza Castle."

"Don't eat any bats! They'll spoil your appetite."

Cluney laughed and started down the steep hill to the parking lot. The mountains in the distance looked a cool blue-green, but a mirage of heat shimmered up from the pavement. She climbed into the ovenlike van and turned on the motor, switching the AC to full blast. Before she pulled out of her parking place, she leaned over the seat and pawed through the clutter in her huge leather purse until she found what she was looking for. She rubbed her hand gently, lovingly over the water- and blood-stained leather cover of the old diary. Then she placed it on the seat beside her and wheeled out of the lot, headed for Baldy Rock.

As Cluney turned off the main highway onto a narrow country road, her mind flipped back like pages in the diary itself.

She remembered so well that feeling of excitement the afternoon she discovered it in a box of old books at the library.

"Hey, come look at this," she'd called to B.J. "It's an old diary written during the Civil War. Wonder how it got here."

At first glance, neither of them could read it. The handwriting was all fancy flourishes and curlicues and some of the pages were badly water-stained.

"You take it home and see if you can decipher it," B.J. had told her, obviously less than interested in the old, illegible work. "Somebody probably donated it years ago and it's been locked away in our basement ever since. I doubt there's much of interest in it, even if you can figure it out. Looks like a foreign language to me."

Cluney did take the journal home that day. She poured over the script, straining to make out each letter, each word. She made her own handwritten duplicate of the book and finally typed the entire contents, donating one copy to the Whitley College Library and sending another to the Filson Club in Louisville. She had hoped the historical club's members might be able to tell her something about Major Breckinridge, but nothing had come of it, other than finding out—disappointingly—that Bluefield, the old plantation house at the site of the Breckinridge horse farm, would soon be leveled to make way for a suburban Lexington shopping mall.

The journal was all she had of the man—all except a lot of fantasies. She no longer needed her neatly typed pages; she could now read Major Breckinridge's handwriting at a glance. Better than that, she knew every word he had written by heart. Still, she felt closer to him when she could hold his diary in her hands and watch the ebb and flow of his fanciful script. In the margins, the romantic U. S. Cavalry officer had drawn hearts with lilies and roses springing from their centers and the moon in all its phases.

*The moon!* It had been their secret talisman. On many nights while they were apart during the war, Hunter had noted in his journal that the moon was especially lovely or that he had sent his wife a kiss by way of the moon. Cluney felt she knew this couple as if they were part of her own family.

Hunter's feelings had changed markedly after his wife's disappearance. A bitter tone had crept into his words. He seemed to doubt his wife's loyalty, and often confided his fears to his diary that she had gone away with another man. He still loved Larissa, clearly, even though his entries were edged with pain and jealousy. In spite of his suspicions, he obviously blamed himself more than he blamed his wife.

Cluney had no idea what had happened to either Larissa or Hunter Breckinridge, or what he had seen that night of the moonbow—the same night he had written the final entry in his journal. He had said he "surrendered."

"Surrendered to what?" She sighed. "I guess I'll never know. But at least I won't lie awake nights any longer, staring at their moon and wondering."

Cluney frowned suddenly. She hoped once she was away from here she could sort out and separate her feelings for Jeff and those strange yearnings she felt for Hunter Breckinridge. It was almost as if her mind were playing tricks on her, blending the two men into one image, making her heart ache equally for both of them. She was sure this had happened because Hunter's diary had come into her hands the same day she received news of Jeff's death. Still, her mingled emotions for the two men grew more puzzling as time passed. It was almost as if she had convinced herself that if she could solve the mystery of Hunter Breckinridge and his lost wife that she could get Jeff back.

"And that borders on insanity," she warned.

An enormous pothole jounced Cluney's thoughts back to the business at hand. The road to Miss Redbird's was a narrow, tortured mountain trail. Folks said that in the old days horse-drawn wagons had made this same treacherous climb. But Cluney doubted if a horse could stay on his feet to pull a load clear to the top. She leaned forward in her seat, physically trying to urge her van upward.

Easing around a hairpin curve, Cluney hit the brakes suddenly. A familiar sign—one that she hadn't seen on the road for the past month or so—sat propped against a rotting fence post. COFFINS, the weathered board announced in uneven black letters. And below that, WOOTER CRENSHAW.

"I wonder where he goes when he takes his sign in," Cluney mused aloud.

The whole county knew that this strange little man made coffins and moonshine, and that if his sign was not out, you might as well drive on by because Wooter Crenshaw was no longer in residence—his residence being a rough, one-room log cabin that perched crazily on the side of Baldy Rock.

On impulse, Cluney turned into the lane. Wooter had known her ma and pa all their lives. Saying goodbye to him seemed the proper thing to do, since her folks were both gone now, buried in twin coffins hewn by Wooter himself. Her parents would expect it of her, Cluney told herself. Besides, she liked the old geezer. He'd been as much a part of her life as the mountain itself.

She drove slowly down the rutted lane between fence posts that leaned this way and that or just lay on the ground resting for a spell. Her arrival was announced by Wooter's pack of "critters." Most were dogs, all were strays. Besides assorted hounds, Wooter had a cat that barked like a dog and an old pair of raccoons that he claimed were really his own ma and pa who just refused to stay in the grave they missed their boy so. Like everyone else in the county, Cluney was always careful to pay her proper respects to Ma and Pa Crenshaw. As she pulled into the coffin-cluttered yard, she fished in her purse, coming up with a bag of peanuts for the 'coons.

Rolling down her window, she called, "How are you, Wooter?"

He yelled a stream of disparaging remarks at the hounds who were leaping at the van windows. They immediately shushed their racket and slunk under the cabin. The raccoons then scuttled forward and sat on their haunches near her door, awaiting the payment of respects. As Cluney handed them the peanuts, it suddenly struck her how much old Wooter resembled the pair—squat, bowlegged, with dark smudges around both his eyes from squinting in the sun while he worked.

"Good to see you again, Mr. and Mrs. Crenshaw,"

Cluney said dutifully, and loud enough for their "son" to hear. She watched the pair carry her offering to an old enamel dishpan, where they washed each nut industriously before consuming their feast.

The bearded mountaineer had been stooped over one of his pine boxes, coaxing the splinters into smooth edges. When Cluney approached, he straightened up to his full four-foot, eleven-inch height. He whipped a red bandanna out of his overalls pocket and wiped his dripping face, then nodded.

"Howdy, little girl."

Cluney smiled. No matter that she was twenty-seven years old, taller than him by several inches, and a college teacher to boot, to this man she would always be "the little girl from up near top of Baldy."

"We've missed you around here, Wooter." She hoped he'd let slip and mention where he'd been for the past couple of months. But it was not to be.

He answered simply, "Well now, won't be no need for that no more. I'm back, ain't I?"

"What are you making?" Cluney knew it was a dumb question, but she always asked.

"Coffin." He was back at smoothing edges.

She glanced at the stacks of pine boxes all about. "Looks like you're ahead on your work. Who's that one for?"

"Redbird."

Cluney gasped.

"Warn't meaning to scare you, little girl. Ol' Redbird, she ain't dead yet, just fixin' to be."

"I didn't know she was sick."

He squinted up at her as if to see is she was serious or

94

just joshing. "Ain't," he replied. "She was always one to plan ahead, you know."

"But you said she was fixing to die, Wooter."

"You get Redbird's years on you and you'll be fixin' to, too. Come hot weather, it don't pay to wait around for something to happen."

Cluney covered a smile by brushing at the perspiration beading her upper lip. "I'm on my way up to visit her now, to say goodbye."

Wooter's head shot up and his little, beady eyes flared wide. "She going ahead with the wake 'fore I even finish her box?"

"No, no," Cluney answered. *"I'm* the one going."

He reached in another deep pocket and pulled out a measuring tape. "Well, why didn't you say so in the first place, little girl? Somehow I hadn't reckoned on you coming to put in a order just yet."

When he approached her with his tape, Cluney backed away, horrified. "No, you don't understand, Wooter. I'm going away to California."

"Oh." He stuffed the tape measure back in his pocket.

"I saw your sign on the road and thought I'd stop to say goodbye on my way up to Miss Redbird's."

"That'll be a end to it, then," he said with a sigh.

"An end to what?"

"Your people in these parts. They come here from Virginny a long time back, through the Cumberland Gap. They's a good lot of them back then, the Summerlands. Five brothers and two sisters and their spouses and young'uns all pulled up stakes to come to Baldy Rock. Summerlands used to be so thick in these parts you couldn't stir 'em with a stick. Yessiree! Then, slow but sure, they went to drifting off." He raised up and gave her a long, hard look. "And now you, little girl, the last of your line." He shook his head sadly and went back to his work.

Wooter made her feel like she had to explain her decision to leave the mountain. "I don't feel like I belong here. I never really have."

He stopped scraping and squinted at her. "Don't belong? Who you been a-talking to, little girl? What they done told you?"

"Nobody! Nothing!" she answered quickly, defensively.

"You belong here as much as anyone in these parts. All our people come through the Gap together back in the olden times—the Crenshaws, the Summerlands, the Renfros, the Breckinridges . . ."

"*Breckinridge?*" Cluney interrupted. "There's no one by that name on the mountain or even in this county."

"You sure?" he asked almost sarcastically. "You just ain't been the right place at the right time, little girl."

"You know these people, Wooter? The Breckinridges, I mean."

"Course! I know ever'body. They all come to me sooner or later—for a box for the burying and a bottle for the wake."

"Do you know a Hunter Breckinridge?" Cluney had no idea why she asked such a question. How on earth could Wooter know a man who had died, probably from his war wounds, over a century ago?

He answered her question with another. "Who's been telling you about him?"

"Nobody. I just read his name somewhere and wondered. Do you know anything about him, Wooter?"

"I know where he's buried—up by the falls."

Wooter had said the very thing that Cluney did not want to hear. She couldn't make herself think of Hunter

96

as dead and buried. To her he seemed as alive today as he had been back on that September night in 1863 when he'd gazed at the moonbow over Cumberland Falls.

Cluney didn't ask any more questions. "I guess I'd better be getting on up to Miss Redbird's now," she said. "So long, Wooter. Take care of yourself."

He just stared at her, so Cluney turned and started for the van, feeling curiously unsettled by her visit.

His deep voice boomed, stopping her in her tracks. "Moonbow tonight!"

She whirled back around. "How can you be sure? No one ever knows for certain when it will appear."

*"I know.* All the signs is right. You oughten to go, though. Best stay away from the falls tonight."

"I'd just changed my mind about going. How did you know?" Cluney asked.

"Never you mind," he said. "You best listen to ole Wooter, little girl. Stay clean away from there tonight."

She turned to leave without another word, but he stopped her again.

"Take this on up to Redbird," he said, handing Cluney a Mason jar of moonshine. "Tell her I'll haul her box up for her to try it on the next day or two."

With that, Cluney was obviously dismissed. The old man's warning left her so befuddled that she almost climbed into her van without saying goodbye to Mr. and Mrs. Crenshaw, but at the last minute she stooped down to scratch their furry heads. For one wild moment, she considered unscrewing the lid on the jar and giving them each a swig of white lightning. It would serve Wooter right, she figured, if she got his folks drunk on 'shine. He'd gotten her that upset with his warning about the moonbow.

97

\* \* \*

Two long, mournful whistles stirred the cool air and then a third. This was the call of the redbird. Cardinals, hearing the sound, came darting through the trees and swooped down to the dirt yard at the edge of the cabin's porch. The old woman in the rocking chair scattered handfuls of sunflower seeds for the birds. Soon her yard was as bright as a garden of poppies in full bloom.

"There you go, pretties," she crooned to her visitors. "Eat your fill, now."

Miss Redbird watched as the less vibrantly colored females of the species hung back, waiting for the males to finish before they stepped forward to eat. The animal kingdom wasn't so different from the human females' lot, she mused.

All of a sudden, Redbird forgot all about her feathered friends. She sat up straighter in her rocker and keened an ear.

"Somebody's a-coming."

At that moment, Cluney Summerland was still far down the mountain, but Redbird had lived enough years to sense a change in the very air when company was on the way. With surprising agility for one of her advanced years, she rose and went inside to put on a fresh apron. Moments later, she was settled again in her rocker, waiting.

"Reckon it's Clair de Lune Summerland headin' up here," she told the birds. "And, sure as shootin', she's fixing to light out. I seen it coming these past weeks. Restless, that girl's been, seeking answers there ain't even any questions for. She'll be wantin' to know the secret today. Don't 'spose I can keep it from her no longer.

98

Still . . ." Redbird paused and sighed, rubbing one arthritic hand over her rheumy eyes. "It'd be a whole lot better could she just find it out for her own self. She won't believe the tellin' of it no how."

Redbird leaned her head back with another sigh and rocked gently. She gazed out over the mountains, watching the misty smoke hover over the tall peaks. Some said that blue-gray haze that gave the Smokies their name was the restless spirit of Indians, wanting their sacred burying grounds back from the thieving white man. Others claimed the smoke marked mystical places hidden away in the mountains and valleys—places where time stood still or doubled back on itself.

"They's mystery here, all right," the old woman said. "More than a body could ever understand. Me and ole Wooter know, but is the secret ours to tell?"

Redbird was still pondering the question when Cluney's van crested the top of the mountain and came to rest by the cabin steps.

Cluney climbed out, smiled, and waved. "How are you, Miss Redbird?"

"It shore took you long enough. You must of stopped to yammer awhile with Wooter. 'Bout time you got here, girl. Come on up and rest a spell."

Cluney stared at her old friend curiously. If she lived to be as old as Redbird, she would never understand how the woman always knew when she was coming. But there were a lot of things the mountain woman knew that went beyond normal comprehension. B.J. wasn't the only one in these parts to call Miss Redbird a witch.

"You're looking fine, ma'am," Cluney noted with pleasure. All Wooter's talk of coffins and wakes had left her unsettled.

The bright-eyed woman laughed. "You sound surprised, girl. You shouldn't be. I'll be fine till the day I die. And I reckon that's a ways off yet. How come you're leaving us?"

The question took Cluney by total surprise. Before she could answer, Redbird fluttered a thin hand in the air. "Never mind," she said. "I reckon I know your reasons. There's lots of other things I know as well. Come on up here on the porch. We got to talk, girl. Time I was telling you a thing or two. High time!"

*The secret!* Cluney knew she was about to hear it at last.

She frowned slightly and a shiver ran through her. All of a sudden, she wasn't so sure she wanted to hear the secret this ancient soul had kept to herself for so many years. Cluney had a feeling that she was about to hear something that would change her life forever.

# Chapter Six

As Cluney settled herself in the creaking, willow rocker next to Miss Redbird's, a hush fell over the forest surrounding the cabin. Birds stopped singing and the breeze stilled. The whole mountaintop seemed isolated suddenly in its own silent, rarefied air. It was as if Baldy Rock itself were waiting expectantly to hear what the old woman had to say.

Redbird gave Cluney a long, quizzical look. "Well? Didn't Wooter send me something for samplin'? He said he was gonna make up a new batch special for my wake."

At the moment, moonshine was the farthest thing from Cluney's mind. She fumbled in her deep leather purse, then drew out the forgotten Mason jar. When she produced Wooter's sample, Redbird smiled and smacked her lips, then reached eagerly for the container of colorless, fiery corn likker.

"Well, now! That's more like it. It wouldn't do to strain myself telling tales without some fortifying spirits. When you get to be my age, child . . ." She broke off, cackled, then patted Cluney's hand. "You wouldn't understand, I reckon. 'Tain't many likely to get to be my age."

Redbird unscrewed the lid and breathed deeply of the 'shine's potent bouquet. "Reach me that gourd dipper yonder, will you, honey? And one for your own self, too, if you care for a nip."

"No, thank you, ma'am," Cluney answered. She was more than happy that she had a legitimate reason to decline Miss Redbird's offer. "I have to drive back down the mountain."

She smiled and handed the old woman the carved-out gourd.

"Suit yourself, but it'd do almighty wonders for that head cold of yours."

"I'd better not mix that with my medicine, ma'am."

Cluney watched as her hostess poured a generous portion of white lightning into the dipper, then took a deep, long sip.

"Ah-h-h!" Redbird sighed, eyes closed, head tilted back in satisfaction. "Wooter outdone hisself on this here batch."

Shadows had begun to cloak one side of the mountain. It was growing late. Cluney could feel herself getting more fidgety by the minute. But she knew there was no rushing Miss Redbird. The woman would say what she had to say, all in her own good time.

Suddenly, Redbird set down her gourd and turned her full attention back to her guest. Without preamble, she said, "You don't remember nothing back from your early years growing up, do you, child?"

Startled by the woman's abrupt question, Cluney shook her head and leaned closer. "Not a thing, ma'am."

"Well, that ain't surprising. You see, the secret I been waiting to tell you all this while is that you wasn't reared

102

here like Rachel always claimed." Redbird paused dramatically, allowing her statement time to soak in.

Cluney realized she was trembling. She fought to find words, but could barely get them out. "Then where?"

Redbird scratched her thatch of white hair with one long nail and shook her head. "Can't say as I can answer that question, 'cause you never said yourself. The night you showed up on the mountain, you was scared out of your wits. Then you collapsed right there on the doorstep and was out of your head for nigh onto a fortnight. When you finally did come around, you couldn't tell us your name or where you come from or who your folks was or nothing. It was like you dropped out of nowhere—maybe fell right down out of the sky."

"There was nothing to give anyone a clue as to who I might be?"

Redbird's eyes focused on the dainty necklace Cluney always wore. "You had that there polished bit of moonstone 'round your neck, but nothing else out of the ordinary."

Cluney's hand went to the thin, silver chain at her throat. She touched the small, round, pearly blue stone and it warmed against her fingertips.

"I brought this with me?" she whispered. "I never knew."

"There was a lot you never knew and maybe never will know. You knew you were scared, though. You was just a-babblin' on and on about someone after you—gonna get you."

"Who?" All Cluney remembered was waking up with a man and a woman staring down at her—two total strangers with kindly faces. The next she recalled, they were explaining to her gently that she'd had a bad fall and burned her arm when she dropped a lantern.

"Who was after me, Miss Redbird?"

The woman shook her head. "You never could tell us that. As I said, you never told us nothing 'cause that was exactly what you knew. Whoever or whatever frighted you, scared the wits clean out of your head. Oh, you was a smart girl, no doubting that. You learned real fast, then got that scholarship to college and all. But as for recalling what happened before you came here, it was like you just locked it up somewhere in your mind 'cause it was too fearsome to be allowed to wander about in your thoughts. After a time, you claimed that whatever fragments you did recall was no more than pieces of a nightmare from falling and banging your head."

"Hysterical amnesia," Cluney said under her breath. The very thought chilled her through. People who had committed terrible crimes or been victims of heinous acts often reacted in this manner. What in her past was so horrible that all these years later she still couldn't face it?

"But you didn't fall down no stairs," Redbird went on to explain. "Least not after you come up to the Summerland cabin that night of the full moon. Rachel and Lonnie just figured that was as good a way as any to explain things to you, and they wanted you to stay with them real bad. They'd lost their only son in a mine cave-in, you see."

"Yes. They told me all about my older brother," she said wistfully. "It always made me feel sad that I couldn't remember him."

"You never knowed Horace Summerland, is why you can't remember him. He died three years 'fore you showed up here."

"There was a full moon that night I came?" Cluney asked, her head spinning.

"Yep, and the brightest moonbow you ever seen. It was a beaut!"

"Wooter says there'll be a moonbow tonight," Cluney said, her thoughts drifting.

"That Wooter!" Redbird gave a snort—half amusement, half disgust. "He claims he knows ever'thing. So how come he don't know when I should plan my wake for? Tell me that!"

"Will there be a moonbow tonight, Miss Redbird?" Cluney ventured.

"Of course! But Wooter don't know that for sure. Only I do. Him, he's just guessing."

"Do you think the bride of the falls will show herself?"

Many people over the years had claimed to have seen a young woman dressed all in white at the top of Cumberland Falls in the mysterious glow of the moonbow. Cluney herself had never witnessed this phenomenon, but she knew plenty of folks who said they'd seen the bride.

Instead of answering her young friend's question outright, Redbird asked another. "Are you fixing to go to the falls tonight, child?"

"I thought I might," Cluney answered. "One last time before I leave."

"Then mayhap you'll see her."

"Have you ever seen her, ma'am?"

Redbird nodded and took another sip of Wooter's 'shine. "Many's the time back in the olden days," she answered. "She's a right sad woman. Lovely as a angel, but with grieving in her eyes and tears on her pale cheeks. I've heard her wail, too, calling out to him that she's lost.

It'd just break your poor heart to hear her. Loved that man, she did. Loved him something powerful!"

"Wooter claims that wailing isn't the bride's, that it's just an owl hooting," Cluney said.

"Wooter Crenshaw don't know diddley squat!"

Cluney looked down at her lap to hide her smile. Wooter and Redbird were best friends and worst adversaries. Both claimed to know *everything* about the mountains and the people who'd inhabited these parts—past and present—and each claimed that the other knew less than nothing. They had practiced this mountain-style one-upsmanship for decades. Everyone else tried never to side with either of these ancient souls for fear of incurring the wrath of the other. Cluney carefully sidestepped Redbird's comment.

"Wooter warned me not to go to the falls tonight." She gave Redbird a sidelong glance. "Why would he do that?"

Miss Redbird sniffed indignantly. " 'Cause he's a old fool!" she snapped. Then her craggy face settled into gentler lines and her voice softened. "He just don't understand, is all, honey. 'Twere it up to Wooter, he'd never let the sun go down nor the moon come up. He don't like to see time slipping away. He mourns them that's gone and wants to hold his dear ones close forevermore. Just look how he treats them two 'coons." She leaned close as if she meant to impart another secret to her guest and whispered. "Take it from one who knows, they *ain't* his ma and pa!"

"Really?" Cluney gasped to keep herself from laughing.

"Don't tell Wooter I told you. He'd be mighty upset. He knows, of course, but he's got hisself convinced other-

106

wise. That's just my point, though. Wooter don't want nothing to change—not ever. But there comes a time when all things *must* change, and we ain't got no right to try and stop them from it."

A male cardinal flitted through the woods, perched on the porch railing, and cocked his head at Cluney. For a moment, she was distracted by the bright bird's intent gaze. Then she realized that Miss Redbird had yet to answer her question about Wooter's warning.

"I don't understand what all this has to do with my going to the falls tonight."

The mountain woman scattered a handful of sunflower seeds, then sighed wearily. "I was working up to that, honey. Me and Wooter don't see eye to eye on a lot of things, but we both know that if you go to the falls tonight something's gonna happen. Something that'll change things around here from now on. I've had this abiding feeling all day that there's a end coming, and a new starting-over about to happen."

Cluney stared at the woman whose eyes now glistened with unshed tears. She never thought to question this premonition. Everyone on the mountain knew that Miss Redbird had been born with a caul and had second sight.

"Well, of course, Miss Redbird. I'm leaving for California tomorrow. That would explain your feeling of an ending and a new beginning."

Redbird shook her head. "Nope!" she said firmly. "You won't never see Californy, child."

Cluney felt a tremor run through her. What was Miss Redbird saying—that she'd be killed in a wreck on her way?

As if sensing the younger woman's distress, Redbird added, "You won't never get no farther west than the next mountain over. Still, you'll be taking a trip, mark my words. A right long trip, at that."

"But how can I go anywhere if I never leave here?"

"There's ways," Redbird answered cryptically. "As you come here, so you'll depart."

Cluney half rose from her chair, so startled was she by what the woman implied. "Do you mean I'm going back where I came from? But how can that be when I don't know where I was before I came here? And what if I do go back and *they* are still looking for me?"

Suddenly, Cluney was shaking with fright. She had no idea who *they* were, but even though she remembered nothing of her past, she sensed how dreadful that time had been. She had no desire to return to that netherworld from which she had escaped ten years ago.

Miss Redbird rose abruptly. She reached down and took Cluney's trembling hands in hers. "It's time you was going now, child. There's a need for you."

"A need?" Cluney mumbled, so unnerved suddenly that she could barely think straight.

"Yes, honey. *He* needs you, and there's not much time."

"*Who*?" Cluney begged. "Who needs me?"

"That's for me to know and you to find out, child. I've told you all that's fit to tell. The rest is up to you. I reckon you better be on your way now."

For some strange reason beyond Cluney's comprehension, Miss Redbird's words almost made sense to her. She knew she had to go, although her destination remained a mystery. And she knew that *he* would be waiting there for her, although she had no idea who he was or why he needed her.

"How do I find him?" Cluney asked as she was getting into her van.

"Just go back the way you came," Redbird called from her rocker. "He'll be waiting for you there."

Cluney's mind was spinning, her heart racing. For years she had yearned to find out Redbird's secret. Now that she knew it, she was more confused than ever. Thoroughly shaken and totally distracted, she choked down the van three times before she managed to get it started. When it finally coughed to life, she leaned out of the window and called, "I'll see you soon, then, Miss Redbird."

" 'Tain't likely," the old woman said under her breath. " 'Tain't likely a-tall, Larissa."

Bouncing over rocks and in and out of potholes, Cluney charged down the mountain at a much faster speed than was safe, but her mind was not on her driving. Her big purse flew off the seat, scattering its contents all over, but she never slowed down. She was bursting to talk to someone about the things Miss Redbird had told her.

"Thank God for B.J.," she mumbled as she turned onto the highway.

Once she reached the restaurant's parking lot, she realized the things from her purse had all spilled out.

"What a mess!" she grumbled.

Digging under the seat, she tried to retrieve all the junk that had rolled in all directions—lipsticks, tissues, wallet, plastic pill bottles, a package of condoms, fingernail files, shoelaces, a can of Mace, earrings, chewing gum, and an assortment of toiletries from a motel bathroom—anything she might possibly need during the course of a day at school. Finally, she was satisfied that she had recovered everything. She stuffed it all back into the scarred leather shoulder bag and climbed out of the van.

A short time later, she was waiting at one of the tables in the pizza place when B.J. came through the door, right on time.

"Over here!" Cluney called.

"Hey, girl, the thought of traveling must make you hungry. I figured I'd be waiting a half hour as usual before you showed up."

Cluney waved her friend into the booth impatiently. She was in no mood for idle chitchat.

"What's happened?" B.J. asked.

It didn't take second sight to know that something extraordinary had transformed Claire de Lune Summerland since the two women had parted outside the college library several hours before. She looked pale, weary, older, in fact.

"Don't tell me the van broke down on you."

Cluney shook her head. "No, no! Nothing that commonplace. I went to see Miss Redbird."

"And she made you eat bats!" B.J. couldn't help cracking jokes when she got nervous. And she was certainly picking up jittery vibes from across the table.

"I wish she had," Cluney said. "They'd have been easier to swallow."

Quickly, Cluney filled B.J. in on Miss Redbird's tale of her uncertain origins.

"So, nobody around here knows where you were born, where you came from, or who you really are?" B.J. rubbed her bare arms. "Gad, I'm all goosebumps, girl! Are you sure she was telling you the truth?"

A pimply faced college student in a greasy paper hat

110

came by and interrupted to take their order. Once he ambled off, Cluney said, "Miss Redbird would have no reason to make up such a tale. And it all fits, B.J. The fact that I can't remember anything before my supposed fall and those nightmares I've had all these years about trying to run away from something or someone."

"Well, did she tell you who's after you?"

Cluney took a deep breath, then shook her head. "No, that's the worst part. Miss Redbird claims she doesn't know. I think she knows more than she was willing to tell me." She reached across the table and gripped B.J.'s smooth, dark arm, drawing her closer for more privacy in the crowded room. "But, get this! Redbird says I'm about to go back where I came from."

"You mean California?" B.J. whispered back. "You started out there as a kid?"

"No. Miss Redbird said I'll never see California."

"That old woman's crazy as a tick!" B.J. snapped. "Not that I wouldn't like to see you stay here, but what right's she got scaring you so, trying to make you call off your trip?"

Cluney swallowed hard, struggling with a lump that had suddenly formed in her throat. For some unfathomable reason, whenever she thought about Miss Redbird's statement that *he* needed her, she had to fight hysterics. She'd been in love not so long ago. She'd been engaged to be married, in fact, until the accident at sea one dark night when Lieutenant Jeff Layton's jet flew into the Mediterranean instead of onto the flight deck of the carrier. Oh, yes, Cluney knew what love and the loss of love felt like. And this man who was waiting for her—whoever he was—surely, was someone she had loved long ago. Perhaps someone she still loved.

She felt B.J. shaking her arm. "Hey, snap out of it, Cluney! What's come over you? You were a million miles away just now."

"Not a million." Cluney tried to smile, but failed. "Only a few thousand. I was thinking about Jeff and the crash."

"Don't tell me that old witch-woman brought that up, too!"

Cluney shook her head and dabbed at her damp eyes with her napkin. "No." She sighed. "Only by association. You see, Miss Redbird said that I have to go back because there's someone waiting for me. A man who needs me. She also said that time is running out."

"What the hell'd she mean by that?"

With a shrug, Cluney admitted, "Beats me! All I know is, I have to go."

"Where exactly are you going, if not to California?"

A sheepish look stole over Cluney's face. "I'm not sure. To be perfectly honest, I haven't a notion. I do know, though, that I have to go to the falls tonight. Miss Redbird says there'll definitely be a moonbow."

"So?" B.J. said, uncomprehending.

Again Cluney shrugged. "I don't know, B.J.," she admitted. "Maybe I'll see some sign or something in the moonbow that will give me a clue to where I'm supposed to go. Miss Redbird didn't explain."

"Lord a-mercy!" B.J. swore. "I think you two were up there this afternoon sipping on Wooter's 'shine." She leaned across the table. "Here, let me sniff your breath, girl."

"Cut it out, B.J. You know I don't drink that rotgut. I'm completely serious about every word I've said. And I'm worried, too. Real worried!"

Their waiter set their large, deluxe pizza between them and for a time the pair fell silent as they dug into the steaming hot mass of cheese, tomato sauce, olives, sausage, and pepperoni.

The metal platter was half empty before B.J. broke the munchy silence. "I think we need to figure out where you came from and what happened to you before you go running off half-cocked. Can't you remember anything from back then?"

Cluney continued chewing, but now with a thoughtful expression on her face. Finally, she said, "I have a few jumbled-up memories, but I'm pretty sure they come from that nightmare I keep having, not from anything that actually happened to me."

"Well, tell me," B.J. insisted.

Cluney stared into the pizza plate as if it were a crystal ball and she were seeing the scenes there. "I remember a fire and someone screaming for help."

"Someone? Who?" B.J. prompted.

Cluney frowned and shook her head. "It's not a who? It's animals—horses maybe. Can horses scream?"

"Beats me! What else?"

"People running. Men! Running after me!" She looked up suddenly, her face stricken. "They're trying to kill me, B.J."

B.J. glanced about the pizza parlor, hoping no one had overheard. "Take it easy, girl. Nobody's after you—not really. Can you remember anything else?"

"A man, and he's calling my name."

"What name, Cluney?" B.J. asked excitedly. "What's he calling you?"

Cluney shook her head and sighed. "I don't know. I only know that he's calling for me."

"Anything else?"

"I've had a dream about being lost in the woods. It's cold and wet and I'm *so* scared. And I keep crying for somebody—somebody who can save me from them. But I know it's no use. He's far away."

*"There!"* B.J. all but overturned their table in her excitement. "You said it! That's the very man old Redbird was talking about, I'll bet." At Cluney's puzzled stare, B.J. added, "You just said it, girl. You said, '*He's* far away.' That has to be the man who's waiting for you."

"This is all just crazy," Cluney said. "Why, it makes no more sense than that psychic who came to our Halloween party last year. You know, the one who could see auras. She told me that she saw a figure in my aura and that was real strange because usually she saw only colors. When I asked her about this figure, she got real cagey about it. All she'd tell me was that it was someone who was dead already and that he was watching out for me. Now, wouldn't you think that if she had the power to see auras and figures in them that she'd at least be able to identify the character floating around my head? It's a lot a nonsense, if you ask me."

"Sh-h-h!" B.J. hissed in warning. "Don't you go making fun of spiritual things. There's more we don't know about than you or I will ever understand. My ancestors were slaves, remember? I know a lot of tales that have been passed down, and let me tell you, girl, they'd curl your hair. When that psychic said you had a figure in your aura, I believed her. And now I think I know who he is."

"Well, would you mind telling me?" Cluney asked almost flippantly.

"The same guy that Miss Redbird said needed you,

114

that's who. And I'll tell you another thing. I'm going to the falls with you tonight."

Cluney reached nonchalantly for the last slice of pizza. "I never said I was going for sure."

"But you know you are. And there's no way I'm letting you go alone. If there's any magic to be seen up on that mountain tonight, I mean to see it, too."


A short time later, Cluney and B.J. were in the old van as it chugged up the winding, tortuous road toward Cumberland Falls. All the signs looked good. The full moon was on the rise without a cloud in sight. The woods that formed a canopy over the narrow road looked haunted by silver ghosts. A strange mist rose from the ground, and silence hung over everything.

They passed the old Dupont Lodge on the left and a few minutes later arrived at the entrance to the park, open late tonight for moonbow watchers. No cars were in the parking lot, however. Only the ranger's truck. The mountain air had turned chilly and now a strange, blustery wind was whipping around the falls.

"Looks like we'll have the place all to ourselves," Cluney remarked as she climbed out of the van, leaving her keys in the ignition, but bringing along her purse. Then she added in a deep, dramatic voice, "All the better for weird happenings!"

"Now don't you keep on poking fun, girl," B.J. warned. "Let's go down the stairs to that little overhang near the bottom of the falls. That's the best view, if there is a moonbow."

Flashlights in hand, the two women carefully maneuvered the narrow rock stairs that were slippery with damp mist. The roar of the sixty-foot falls was all but deafening. The sound seemed to Cluney to block out all else. With each step she took, she became more and more aware of an odd feeling creeping over her. She felt light-headed, almost dizzy, and it seemed as if she could feel that powerful roar deep inside her chest.

"B.J.?" she called back over her shoulder. "Are you coming?"

"Fast as I can," her friend answered. "You better slow down or you'll slip and take a real fall."

Cluney heard B.J.'s warning, but there was no holding her back. It seemed as if the falls were calling to her, urging her to hurry. Suddenly, she realized that the voice she kept hearing was real—a man's voice, deep and urgent.

"There's little time left. Come to me. Oh, please, my darling, come quickly."

Without realizing she'd uttered a sound, Cluney answered, "I'm coming. Wait for me."

A short distance behind Cluney, B.J., breathing heavily, had stopped dead in her tracks. She was shaking all over, but not from the night's chill or the effort of the downward climb. Staring at Cluney through the darkness, she couldn't believe her own eyes. At first, she thought she was imagining things. But after a moment, she knew that the vision was all too real.

"Cluney!" she screamed, but it was obvious her friend was beyond hearing.

# Chapter Seven

"Cluney?" B.J. yelled. "Can you hear me? Answer me!"

Only moments before, B.J. had been forced to move slowly in the darkness. Now, suddenly, she had to shield her eyes against the bright light up ahead. When the moon sailed over the dark treetops, it appeared to burst in a shower of silver-white fire, lighting up the whole landscape before coming to rest on Cluney, where she stood on the small ledge that overhung the falls.

B.J. remained paralyzed. Her mouth was wide open, but no further sound came out. All she could do was stare. Yet, could she believe her own eyes?

As the brilliant light dimmed slightly, she could once more make out Cluney's form. It was Clair de Lune Summerland, all right, but she had been totally transformed, as if she were enveloped in a veil of shining mist. She'd been wearing jeans and a heavy blue sweater, hiking boots on her feet. Now she was dressed all in glowing white. Her long skirt billowed about, sweeping the ground in a shimmering train. Sparkles of silver, like stars twinkling in the night, circled the high neck of her gown and came to glittering points over her wrists. And over it all—adding a soft glimmer—flowed the long, frosty-white veil.

B.J. caught her breath, then gasped, "The bride of the falls!" Swallowing hard, she called out. "Cluney! Cluney, can you hear me?"

The bride turned, and when she did, B.J. saw her face. She was smiling and her eyes glowed silvery lavender-blue through the mist that enveloped her.

B.J. tried to rush down the stairs to her friend, but it seemed as if some invisible barrier barred her way. She could no more descend the stone stairs than she could fly. All she could do was stand and stare and try to convince herself that what she was watching was real.

Suddenly, the sound of the falls increased to a deafening roar. B.J. covered her ears, but still the sound grew louder by the minute. Then through that noise came the mournful baying of a hound—the loneliest, most heart-wrenching sound she had ever heard in her life. Goose bumps rose on her arms and tears sprang to her eyes.

She continued to watch. She saw the moonbow span the falls, forming a silver bridge from one side of the gorge to the other. As she stared, the bride mounted the eerie beam of light and rose higher and higher into the air. Over the falls she soared, into the brightest moonlight. At the very top of the arch, high above the roaring water, she paused and turned back to look directly at B.J. She raised her hand in an unmistakable sign of farewell. A moment later, she vanished along with the moonbow.

Suddenly, the woods grew still, as silent as death. A shiver ran through B.J. It took her a moment to recover her senses. As soon as she did, she hurried down the stone steps, slipping and sliding on the damp surface.

"Cluney!" she screamed. "Answer me, dammit! Where are you?"

But B.J. knew that her friend would not answer. Before she ever set foot on the overhang, she knew she would find it deserted. She stood clutching the handrail, staring down into the swirling dark water far below.

"Oh, God, Cluney," she moaned.

B.J. wasn't sure what she had witnessed, but she'd heard tales from her old aunties about seeing the spirit of a dead person rise from the body. If Cluney had slipped and fallen into the gorge below, there could be no hope that she had survived. If that was the case, and it certainly seemed likely, B.J. was sure she had seen her friend's ghost.

"Get a grip!" she snapped at herself. "I've got to get help."

As fast as B.J. had come down those stone steps, she made it back up in half the time. Luckily, there was still a light on in the office next to the tiny gift shop. The ranger wouldn't leave his post until all the cars had left the parking lot.

B.J. ran to the door and banged on it, screaming, "Help! Help me! My friend's fallen over the railing!"

A big, rugged-looking ranger opened the door at once. He fired a few quick questions at B.J., then put in a call for help. A short while later, the overhang and surrounding areas were flooded with spotlights as men searched high and low. When they finally switched off their lights at dawn, they had yet to find a clue to Cluney's whereabouts.

"It's been a long night. You'd better head on back to town, Miss Jackson," the ranger said with sympathy in his tired voice. "I'll let you know the minute we find her."

"I'd rather stay," B.J. insisted.

"I know," the man said, "but you're beat, and there's nothing you can do here. Go home and get some rest. I have your number. I'll call, I promise."

B.J. had never felt more helpless or hopeless in her life than when she started down the mountain, alone, in Cluney's van.


"Lord have mercy, Free! Have you lost your senses?" The tall, gaunt woman in a faded gray frock the same color as her hair and eyes stared down at Major Breckinridge as he tossed and turned feverishly on the bed.

"There wasn't nothing I could do to stop him, Miz Renfro. He was bound and determined to go to the falls last night. If I hadn't of gone with him, he'd of dragged himself down there and probably died on the spot with no help to get back up here. He was pining away to see that moonbow."

Mary Renfro, her eyes dark with concern, sponged the major's brow, then tucked the blanket up closer under his chin. There was little more she could do for him. That wound through his shoulder wasn't looking good. No, not good at all.

"Well, I suppose a dying man's got a right to be pampered. Still, it sure didn't do him no good to be out in the night damp. Then his lamp was burning near all the night through. I glanced in twice and he was propped up in bed, writing away. What do you reckon he sets down in that book of his?"

Free shrugged. "Even if I was the nosy type, which I ain't, ma'am, I wouldn't know. I can't read a word."

She glanced at the big, gentle private—a recently freed

120

slave. His eyes were downcast. He was obviously embarrassed by his admission of ignorance.

"First chance I get, Free, I mean to teach you. A man's gotta know how to read and write to get by in this world."

He beamed a smile at her, grateful for her offer and also for her calling him a man. Most folks still just called him "boy." But deep down Free knew that Mrs. Renfro would never find time to teach him his letters. Upstairs, she had seven wounded soldiers to tend all by herself, the preacher being off most of the time procuring supplies when he wasn't saving poor sinners' souls. And she had given up her own bedroom on the main floor to Major Breckinridge on account of his being so poorly. From the looks of it this morning, though, she wouldn't be out of her bed much longer. The major was in a bad way.

As if reading Free's thoughts, Mary said, "If I only had some help here with the nursing, it'd be better for us all. The major's mighty lucky to have you to tend him, Free. Now, soon as he wakes, you see he gets this squirrel broth. It ain't much, but it should strengthen him some."

"Yes, ma'am. I'll sure do that." Free took the ironstone crock she handed him and placed it on the hearth to keep warm by the fire.

Mary Renfro glanced once more at Hunter Breckinridge and shook her head sadly. "He ain't got long and maybe that's a blessing."

Then she turned and left Free to watch over their restless patient.


The odd sensation Cluney had experienced as she was going down the stone stairs to the overhang intensified with every step she took. She felt a strange dizziness, yet she kept going. It almost seemed as if she were being drawn along by some will stronger than her own.

She must have blacked out for a moment. When she came to, she was standing on the little stone ledge out over the falls, her face damp with mist. She looked around. Everything familiar had disappeared. She seemed to be trapped within a glowing ball of white light that distorted her vision.

She heard B.J. calling her name. But her friend was somewhere out there in the darkness, beyond the blinding circle of brilliance.

Sometime during this odd phenomenon, Cluney felt as if the earth were moving beneath her. She lost her balance, and for one terrifying instant she thought she was falling over the railing into the dark, dangerous water far below. Then the next moment, she glanced up to see the moonbow before her. Soon she found herself walking over the shimmering bridge that spanned the falls. The light surrounded her, casting its glow over the forest and down into the gorge. Glancing back, she caught a final glimpse of B.J. She looked so worried, so frightened. Cluney raised her hand and waved, trying to let her friend know that everything was all right.

Cluney felt warm and safe, sure of her actions as she continued across the high, glowing bridge. Far below, she could hear the water dashing on the rocks. Far above, she could see the full moon shining its brightest. Off in the night, a lonesome hound bayed his mournful moon-serenade. The sound brought tears to her eyes.

Then it happened! The wind shifted, the forest sighed, and, in the distance, Cluney spied someone waiting for her, beckoning to her across time and space. She quickened her step, eager to be by his side.

Suddenly, everything went black. No more moonbow. No more falls. *No more Clair de Lune Summerland!*

The next thing Cluney felt was the morning sun warming her. Then she became conscious of something wet and rough scrubbing at her face—lapping her cheeks, tickling her eyelids, kissing her lips. She fought her way up out of the shadows, trying to fend off her enthusiastic attacker.

"Hey, cut it out!" she cried, covering her well-licked face with her arms. "What's going on?"

When she came fully awake, she found herself lying on the damp ground, her head pillowed by her purse. She was staring into the baleful eyes of a bone-thin, long-eared hound.

"Well, hey there, fellow." She fended off another tongue attack, and scratched his wrinkled forehead. "Where'd you come from?"

The old black-and-tan hound whimpered and nuzzled her neck. Cluney looked for a collar and tag, but found only a frayed length of rope around the dog's neck.

"Come on to the van with me, pal. I'll find you something to eat."

Only vaguely wondering why she had slept on the ground beside Cumberland Falls, Cluney headed up the slope toward the parking lot.

"I guess we missed the moonbow last night," she told the friendly pooch. "The last I recall we were headed down toward the falls. B.J. must have given up and gone back to curl up in the van for the night. I should be so smart!"

Not until she came out of the deep woods at the verge of the gorge did Cluney realize that all was not well. The paved path she had taken from the parking lot to the edge of the falls was nowhere in sight. She glanced around, trying to get her bearings. Suddenly, her heart did a jackknife. Not a thing in sight looked familiar. Oh, the falls were there, all right, but in their natural state, with no ropes or warning signs to keep sightseers safe.

But the rangers' office, the gift shop, the concession stand, the parking lot, her van, even B.J.—all were gone.

"What the . . . ?"

The dog whimpered, sensing her confusion and anxiety. She reached down and patted his head, extremely happy for his company at that moment.

"Now this is just crazy," she muttered, still glancing about, searching for anything, *anything* that looked the least bit familiar. "I know this park like the back of my hand. The road should be right over there."

She walked a few yards, the hound at her heels, then stopped dead. "No road! *No road?*"

Feeling weak with panic, Cluney sank down into a bright pile of crisp, autumn leaves. Her head was spinning. Suddenly, she spotted smoke rising beyond a copse of trees. In that instant, her lopsided world seemed to right itself. Whoever lived there could tell her where she was. Maybe they'd let her use the telephone to call . . .

"Call who?" she wondered aloud. "This isn't the place I knew last night."

Dismissing those thoughts for the moment, she hurried toward the rising smoke. "I know what happened," she said with a laugh of relief. "I just wandered farther down the trail than I thought. Come on, boy. I'll get you some breakfast yet."

Even though she was relieved to see signs of life, Cluney still had the lingering feeling that something was wrong.

Surely, B.J. wouldn't have left her to sleep all night on the ground, not with the cold she'd been nursing.

Cluney stopped, wrinkled her nose, and sniffed. Her head was perfectly clear, her cold gone. But how could that be? She'd been sneezing and sniffling like crazy just hours ago.

When she cleared the trees, she was sure something was very wrong. The park buildings she had expected to see were nowhere in sight.

Instead, before her in the clearing stood a rough, two-story log cabin that she had never set eyes on before. Suddenly, she saw a bearded face peering at her from the woods beyond the house.

Cluney waved frantically. "Hey! You there!" she called. "Mister?" But he disappeared the moment she spoke to him. Rubbing her eyes, she wondered if she had only imagined the gaunt face, sunken eyes, and scruffy black whiskers.

She turned her attention back to the house. Smoke rose from the chimney, a few chickens scratched about in the edge of the woods, and several scrawny horses ambled lazily about inside a split-rail enclosure attached to a lean-to that adjoined the house. A clothesline strung between two saplings sported several sets of red long johns, flying as proudly as flags in the breeze. Nearby, a big black tub simmered over a wood fire, giving off the distinctive, eye-smarting odor of lye soap.

None of this should have struck Cluney as particularly odd. Deep in these mountains of Eastern Kentucky, some men still wore long johns, some women still did their wash outside in boilers, nor were chickens in the yard anything of particular note. But something about the entire scene was all wrong. To begin with, by her calculations the date was Tuesday, May 19, 1992. Yet the few leaves left on the trees were the bright scarlet and gold of late fall rather than the lush green of spring. Surely, she hadn't slept right through the summer!

"Well, we'll just find out about this," Cluney told her hound.

Smiling to let these mountain folk know she was friendly, but squaring her shoulders to let them see she was tough, Cluney marched up to the rough plank door and knocked. She waited long moments before anyone opened, then found herself staring into the weathered face of a woman who was probably in her fifties, but who wore the work-hardened look of someone much older.

Cluney was about to introduce herself and beg for help when the woman gripped her arm and pulled her inside.

"Well, Lord save us!" the stranger cried. "If I ain't happy to see you! Get yourself right on in here, girl. There's more work for the both of us than you could shake a stick at. I thought you'd never show up. I sent word to Tilda over a month ago that you was needed."

"Excuse me?" Cluney said, trying to pull away from this stranger, who had obviously mistaken her for someone else.

The woman's smile faded and she gave Cluney a closer look, then a severe frown. "Don't tell me you're not my Cousin Tilda's youngest, come to help out with the soldier boys?"

"Soldier boys?" Now it was Cluney's turn to frown. "I don't understand, ma'am."

The woman leaned closer to Cluney and whispered, "Me and my husband figured we'd best not tell it around that we're taking in Yanks and Rebs to tend. Kentucky being a border state and split on its opinion of the struggle, things could get a mite touchy was it general knowledge. But I say, a wounded boy is a wounded boy. Besides, you strip 'em down to their union suits and you can't tell one from another. I thought sure, though, that your ma would explain to you that I needed your help with the nursing."

When Cluney made no reply, the woman asked, "Did your brother Lem bring you in the wagon? Tilda said she'd try to send me some supplies."

Cluney kept blinking rapidly, sure that this whole scene would soon dissolve before her eyes. But it didn't. It seemed as if she was caught up in a dream in which she was expected to play a major role, but had been given no script. She'd have to wing it, she decided.

"I came last night," Cluney answered at length, "in my van with B.J."

The older woman clapped her hands to her cheeks and her gray eyes danced with happy lights. "Land sakes! That *is* good news! I didn't know your brother Bobby Joe had come home from the war. Last I heard from Tilda, he was missing after that battle down to Virginny. Holler at him to come on in here and have some coffee and fried squirrel. I'm afraid that's about all we got right now. And even at that, the coffee ain't real, just parched corn boiled up. But it passes well enough for what we're lacking."

"Please, ma'am," Cluney begged. "I'm not your Cousin Tilda's daughter. And I don't know any Bobby Joe. I came up here with my girlfriend, B.J. Jackson. We drove to the falls last night to see the moonbow. I don't know what happened, but I seem to be lost. I can't find B.J. or my van or anything familiar."

Mary Renfro looked disappointed, then impatient, then suspicious. "Two women got no business coming up

127

this mountain alone at night. Don't you know there's bushwhackers hereabouts?" She eyed Cluney's tight jeans curiously. "Course, I guess that's why you're dressed up like a boy—to fool 'em, should you run into any. But it still ain't fittin'."

"I only wanted to see the moonbow," Cluney explained lamely.

The woman made a sound of disgust. "That blamed moonbow last night sure enough stirred up more than its share of trouble. The poor major! But never mind that foolishness, just tell me this. Did you or didn't you bring supplies? We're getting desperate, I can tell you."

Cluney shook her head. "I had some things in my van, but now it's gone, like I said."

Suddenly, the woman's thin face brightened. "Oh, never you mind. We won't fret a minute about that now that you're here to help out. I don't know where you come from and I can't say as I'm carin'. All I know is the good Lord sent me another pair of hands, and it's high time we put His gift to use. You can watch over the major and I'll send Free out to hunt us up some game." She turned and headed toward the back of the sparsely furnished house. "Step lively now. We best be getting to work. We've wasted enough time jawing like two old broody hens."

"Ma'am?" Cluney said, not at all sure she wanted to follow this stranger anywhere. "Could you tell me who you are and exactly where I am?"

The woman turned so suddenly that the hem of her long, ragged skirt flared, showing a bit of worn leather boot. "I swan! I just don't know where my wits are today. Forgive my lack of manners." Extending her hand like a man, she said, "I'm Mary Refro and this here's the house my good man built me with his own two hands and the

128

help of the Lord. You've heard of my husband, I reckon," she added with more than a touch of pride. "The Reverend Lewis Renfro? Baptist, of course. Why, we've been on this land for thirteen years, since way back in 1850. Everybody hereabouts knows us."

Cluney's mouth dropped open, but she couldn't utter a word. Her head was spinning. Maybe everyone in the midnineteenth century knew the Renfros, but, to Cluney's knowledge, this was the first time she'd slipped out of the twentieth century to go visiting this far away. From what the woman had just said, the year must be 1863.

*1863?* Her history teacher's keen mind kicked in. The Civil War. The Emancipation Proclamation. If this was the autumn of '63, that meant Lee's army and the Union forces of General Meade were now at a stalemate in Northern Virginia, while the Federal forces under General Rosecrans in Tennessee and General Ambrose Burnside in Kentucky were marching south on Chattanooga and Knoxville. Knoxville was only about seventy miles away. Cluney tried to imagine the long-dead generals, whom she had read about so often, alive now and waging war at this very moment.

That war explained the "soldier boys" Mary Renfro had mentioned earlier. But *nothing* explained what Cluney herself was doing here or how she'd gotten here or, more importantly, how she would get back.

Her first impulse was to say to the woman, "You're joking, right? You're a friend of B.J.'s and the two of you set me up." But somehow Cluney knew that this was *no joke!*

Panic seemed the normal course of action. Still and all, Cluney's natural curiosity and her enthusiasm for history made her want to stay here, at least for a time. If she was hallucinating, let the hallucination continue, she thought. She'd often wished she could send herself back into some earlier period to see and feel the living history that she read in dry books and tried to make come alive for her students. If she was only dreaming, that was fine, too. At least her dream seemed to be historically accurate.

Shaking the woman's hand firmly, Cluney said, "I'm happy to meet you, Mrs. Renfro. I'm Cluney Summerland from Baldy Rock."

Mary looked at her visitor more closely and gave her a warm smile. "Well, I declare! We got some relations over to Baldy—third cousins, twice removed on my husband's ma's side. You reckon we're kin?"

"Most folks in these mountains are, by blood or marriage," Cluney replied evasively.

"Then, too, we got a real good friend lives on Baldy Rock. Ever' time I think we ain't gonna have a morsel of food to put on the table, here he comes up the mountain with a wagonload of victuals in the nick of time. Mayhap you know him . . ."

A loud call for help from the back of the house interrupted her. "Miz Mary, come quick! It's the major!"

With Cluney right at her heels, Mary Renfro whirled about and raced for the door at the far end of the main room.

The moment they reached the bedroom, Cluney noted the tall, kind-faced, young black man and guessed he must be the one her hostess had referred to earlier as "Free." She nodded to him as she hurried in, but he seemed not to notice. Indeed, the man had good cause for calling for help. On the bed was one of Mrs. Renfro's patients, swathed in bandages and thrashing about as if he was having some sort of fit.

"What happened here?" Mary demanded as she rushed over and tried to restrain the man.

"I don't rightly know, ma'am," Free admitted, his eyes wide with alarm. "One minute he was sitting up in bed and I was feeding him broth, and the next he hollered that he couldn't see nothing. Then he claimed he heard his dog howling—that old hound the raiders kilt—and he about went wild."

"Hand me that bottle of laudanum, Free," Mary ordered calmly. "We got to get him quiet or he'll hurt hisself worse."

Cluney stood by helplessly, wishing there was something she could do. Free got the medicine, then held the major down while Mary spooned it into his mouth. With all the thrashing about, most of it ran down his chin.

"Is there anything I can do to help?" Cluney asked. "Maybe if I lifted his head a bit."

The moment Hunter Breckinridge heard Cluney's voice, he stopped fighting. Mary quickly slipped him another dose and all of it went in this time.

"Where is she?" the major asked, sitting up in bed and reaching his arms out in front of him like a blind man feeling his way.

"Where's who, Major Breckinridge?" Mary asked, gently trying to press him back down to the pillows.

"Larissa!"

"Now, Major, don't you start fretting about your wife. You'll just get yourself all worked up again. You need to rest."

Still staring blindly about the room, he called, "Larissa? Are you there? You are! I know you are!"

"There, there, Major," Mary soothed. "You lie down now and try to sleep awhile. I brought a nice lady to sit with you. She's right pretty, too. You just tell her if you need anything. I'm going to send Free out to shoot us some supper."

Major Breckinridge was slipping away as the laudanum took effect. But even as he drifted off to sleep, he kept murmuring his wife's name over and over again. When Cluney took the chair beside his bed, he reached out and grasped her hand.

"You just call now, Cluney, if you need me," Mary whispered before she left the room.

Cluney never heard her. Transfixed, she stared down at Major Hunter Breckinridge. All she could think of was that the dry, hot hand holding hers in a grip like steel was the same hand that had penned the beautiful and loving words to his wife Larissa in the old journal.

Still, holding his hand, she dug into her purse to find his precious diary, but it was gone. It must have slid far under the seat of the van at the same time her pocketbook got dumped. Now that treasure was lost to her somewhere off in the far-distant future.

Even as the sad thought crossed her mind, she glanced across the room to spy that very leather-bound book lying closed on the desk. Next to it lay several turkey quills, a pot of ink, and a stained blotter. Her heart raced. She glanced down at the face of the sleeping man.

"You *really* are Hunter Breckinridge," she whispered in awe. So many thoughts were spinning through her head that she felt quite dizzy.

Still staring at him, she realized that he looked exactly as she had imagined, heart-stoppingly handsome even though his fine features were pale now and sharply chiseled. His hair was dark and thick. A stubble of bluish beard shadowed his square jaw. His darkly furred chest was bare except for the linen strips binding his left shoulder. His hands were large, with long fingers and neat, square nails. She could tell he had once been a man as strong as the mountains. But the war had taken its toll. Her heart went out to him.

Suddenly, she heard Miss Redbird's voice in her head. "He needs you and there's not much time."

She knew in that moment that Hunter Breckinridge was, indeed, the man who needed her, and it seemed that there certainly wasn't much time. He was gravely wounded; she could tell that just by looking at the pallor of his flesh. How terribly, terribly sad that he had lost so much—that only imagining he heard the baying of a favorite hound could send him into such an emotional state.

Just then Cluney heard the door to the room creak. She saw a damp, black nose nudge through. The next moment, the old hound who had befriended her slunk in and across the room, eyeing her as if asking permission to enter. He licked their joined hands, then climbed onto the bed, settling himself close against the major's side.

Hunter stirred in his sleep. A slight smile softened the pain-hard lines of his face. Still clinging to Cluney's hand, he reached out his other to stroke the hound's head. The dog let out a long, satisfied sigh and inched even closer to its master.

"Good boy, Trooper." Hunter's words were only the barest whisper. Breathing heavily, he finally managed to get out one more word. It was a name, his wife's name.

"Larissa."

Cluney thought she had never heard a man speak a

133

woman's name with such tenderness, such passion, such love, such pain. She bit her lip to hold back tears, and all the while she clung desperately to his dry, fever-hot hand.

"I'm here," she whispered. Then, shocked by her own words, she lapsed into watchful silence.

She had to figure out what had happened to her and what she was going to do. She thought back over the events of only yesterday. No, not yesterday! If the Civil War was truly still in progress, her *yesterday* was far, far off—over a century in the future. Was she really here or did she only *think* she was back in the nineteenth century? She was supposed to have left for California today. She'd said her goodbyes, met B.J. for supper, then the two of them had come to the falls to see the moonbow.

But that wasn't all she'd done yesterday. Her eyes went wide suddenly when she recalled Wooter Crenshaw's warning about the moonbow: "You oughten to go. Best stay away from the falls tonight."

What had Wooter been trying to tell her—that if she went to the falls she wouldn't be herself after seeing the moonbow? Or that she would be herself, but no longer in the right place and time?

She *had* seen the moonbow! She remembered now. She had seen it as never before, as if she were inside its glow, viewing the world through a shimmer of silver.

"But things like this don't happen," she murmured. "Not to a sane, ordinary schoolteacher, anyway."

The major's hand had slipped from hers as his body relaxed in sleep. She rose for a moment and went to the journal. Glancing first toward Hunter to make sure he was still sleeping, she opened his diary and read at random.

"The same," she whispered, a shiver going through

her. "It's the very same book. He's the very same man."

"Larissa . . . my darling . . . where are you?"

Without Cluney's reassuring touch, Hunter had grown restless again. She hurried back to her chair beside his bed and took his hand in hers.

"Here! I'm here," she told him.

But *where* exactly is here? she wondered. And *who* exactly am I?

# Chapter Eight

B.J. went home as the ranger told her to, but she got little rest, no sleep. She flopped down on the made-up bed, her nerves tense. For a couple of hours, she tossed and turned, trying to remember exactly what she'd seen at the falls. She recalled the light almost blinding her, but nothing much after that. It was almost as if the brilliant glare had erased part of her memory. If she could just think what it was she had forgotten, she felt sure she'd know where to find Cluney.

Still dressed in her jeans, sweater, and red cowboy boots—the same clothes she'd had on at the falls—she lay sprawled on her bed, staring at the silent telephone. It was almost noon, but still there was no word on Cluney's whereabouts.

"Damn!" she muttered, shoving herself up from the rumpled spread. "I can't lie around here and do nothing. I'll go crazy!"

She grabbed her car keys and headed for the door, but the ringing phone stopped her—all but stopped her heart, in fact. She dived across the bed to answer it.

"Hello!" she shouted.

"Miss Jackson?"

"Yes, this is B.J. Jackson."

"This is Sonny Taylor, the ranger from up at the falls?"

His tone asked for recognition. "Yes, yes! I remember you. Any news?"

"I'm afraid not, ma'am. It's right puzzling. Sheriff Elrod asked me to call and see if you'd mind coming down to the station house to answer some questions about last night."

B.J. gulped and swallowed several times before she spoke, but her voice still betrayed her panic. "You don't mean I'm a *suspect*?"

"Of course not, ma'am. We got no body nor any proof of foul play—*yet*," he added ominously. "The sheriff just wants to clear up a few details, is all."

"I was just heading out," B.J. told him. "I can be at the sheriff's office in ten minutes."

"Good," Ranger Taylor answered. "I'll see you shortly then."

The town that had sprung up after Whitley College was founded as a place to educate coal miners' children was little more than a whistle stop. The students liked to joke that if you were passing through and blinked your eyes at the wrong time you'd miss the whole damn place. So, even though she caught the town's single red light, B.J. still made it, in only eight minutes, to the sheriff's tiny station house—one office, one empty cell, and a less than sanitary unisex john.

When she opened the door, two men rose to greet her—the tall, muscular ranger, Sonny Taylor, and the short, barrel-chested sheriff, Clewis Elrod.

"Sheriff, this is Miss Jackson," Taylor said. "She's the one from up at the falls last night."

"Howdy, ma'am." Sheriff Elrod touched the brim of his hat without removing it. "Thanks for coming down here so quick. It appears we're going to need your help."

He motioned toward a beat-up folding chair. B.J. sat down, gripping her purse in her lap, nervous and feeling oddly guilty simply because she was at the jail.

"I don't know what help I can be," she said. "I just don't understand why you can't find my friend. I mean, she was right there with me, then she was gone in the blink of an eye. She must have slipped over the railing. There was nowhere else for her to go. She got to the overlook before I did. I was still on the stairs, and those stone steps are the only way off the overlook except straight down."

"If she'd fallen over the railing," Sonny Taylor said, "we'd have found her right off. You see, ma'am, the water's real shallow down below there. She'd of hit the rocks right beneath the water's surface and been hurt real bad, if she wasn't killed outright."

"Oh, no!" B.J. cried, visualizing Cluney lying sprawled and still on the boulders.

"You said you saw a light last night, Miss Jackson?" the sheriff asked.

B.J. nodded. "Yes. It was real bright, almost blinding."

The two men exchanged glances. "Sounds like a hunter's searchlight to me," the sheriff said. "Did you hear any shots fired, ma'am?"

B.J. shook her head. They were definitely on the wrong track. "What I saw wasn't any searchlight, Sheriff Elrod. This was like no light I've ever seen before. Eerie—silvery—with colors sort of shimmering through it."

The ranger gave a nervous laugh. "Sounds like the moonbow."

"Yes! I think it was," B.J. agreed excitedly. "In fact, I'm sure of it."

Sheriff Elrod shoved his hat back on his head and let out the type of sigh he reserved for liars, fools, and crazy people. "Well, little lady, if you're telling me the moonbow swooped down and carried your friend off, I'm afraid there's not a damn thing I can do about it. No, ma'am, that dog just don't hunt!"

B.J. bristled. Who did this character think he was, calling her "little lady?" And she never claimed nor believed that Cluney had been kidnapped by the moonbow.

"All I know is that my friend was there before I saw the light, then gone after it appeared."

"Didn't you say she meant to leave for California today?" the ranger asked in a cautious voice, fully aware of B.J.'s rising anger.

"Well, there you are!" the sheriff said, as if dismissing the entire matter. "That gal just decided to take off last night instead of waiting till daylight. And we done wasted all this time, manpower, and taxpayers' money searching for her."

B.J. jumped to her feet, furious. "Do you think she's going to walk all the way to California, Sheriff? She left her van in the parking lot at the falls. She left all her clothes, all her belongings. Does that sound like someone who took off across country in the middle of the night?"

The sheriff shrugged, unperturbed by B.J.'s outburst. "Shoot, I know how you young people nowadays live. She's probably off in the woods somewhere, shacked up with her boyfriend. I figure you've wasted enough of my time on this gall-durned foolishness. If we find a body up around the falls, I'll get in touch with you. Otherwise, I

140

don't see as there's much more I can do. Why, it's too early yet even to file a missing person's report."

"Well, a good day to you, too, Sheriff!" B.J. snapped, jumping up from the chair. She was so mad she could hardly get the words out. If they didn't want to help, she'd find Cluney herself. She headed out the door and slammed it behind her.

"Miss Jackson, hold on a minute," Sonny Taylor called after her. "I need to talk to you."

B.J. was already in her car. She put the key in the ignition and cranked it, but left it in park. "I think we've about said all there is to say."

"No, ma'am, we haven't. It's about the falls and some strange things I've seen up there from time to time."

His words piqued B.J.'s interest. "What sort of things?"

He seemed embarrassed suddenly. "Well, you know . . . We get all sorts of lunatics up to the falls on nights of the full moon. I never know what's coming next. We've had so many jumpers lately that when I see some guy climbing over the rope I just tell him I'd appreciate if he'd commit suicide on somebody else's shift."

B.J. bristled. "If you're suggesting that my friend killed herself, you can forget it."

"No, I didn't mean that. I'm sorry." He blushed under his tan, before continuing in a hesitant voice. "I'm just trying to explain about the moonbow and all the weird stuff that goes along with it. There's the 'moonies,' as we call them, the religious cult folks that come out in their long robes, beating drums and chanting all night. It'd make your skin crawl to hear their racket."

"What's all this got to do with Cluney?"

The tall ranger glanced about to make sure no one was listening before he resumed in a whisper, "Nights when there's nobody but me up there to see the moonbow, that's when the oddest things happen."

"Such as?"

"I've seen the bride," he answered. "And I've seen faces staring back at me from the falls—faces that were there one minute, then gone the next. And there's an old man who comes and goes."

"Comes and goes?" B.J. repeated. "What do you mean? Is he real or only a vision like the bride?"

Ranger Taylor shook his head. "You got me, there," he answered. "I'm not from around these parts. I've been here only since early last year, so I don't know everybody hereabouts. Seems like I've seen this little old guy in town a time or two, but then again, I can't be sure he's the one from the falls."

"How often do you see him at the falls?"

"If there's even a hint of a moonbow, he's there. There and then gone. I'll catch sight of him moving around at the edge of the cliff and the next thing I know, he's vanished."

"Vanished?" B.J. repeated. "Like into thin air?"

Taylor nodded solemnly. "You got it, ma'am. Like smoke blown away in the wind. Like your friend vanished."

A shiver went through B.J. even though she was sweating inside her heavy sweater.

"So are you saying that you think wherever this man goes is where we'll find Cluney?"

"I'm not saying that, ma'am. I just wanted you to know that your friend's not the only one to disappear out there, and that she could come back next moonbow just like he does."

"Have you told Sheriff Elrod about this?"

"Hell, no!" Taylor said, his horror at the thought evident in his voice. "He'd most likely slap me in jail for drinking on the job if I told him such a tale. He'd never believe a word of it. I'd be a laughingstock or worse."

B.J. chewed at her bottom lip, deep in thought. "Yes. I can see why you'd be reluctant to talk about these visions." She looked back up at the lanky ranger. "But what if this disappearing man is real? You said you thought you'd seen him in town. I know everybody around here. What does this guy look like?"

Taylor rubbed a hand over his eyes, trying to envision the fellow. "Well, he's short—under five feet, I'd say. And I know he's got a beard, and he walks kind of funny—side to side like he's real bowlegged. And he's always dressed in baggy overalls. That's about all I can tell you."

B.J. grinned. "Thanks! That's enough. I think your man is flesh and blood. I think I even know where he lives. I'll be in touch."

Before the ranger could say another word, B.J. shoved the gearshift into drive and stepped on the gas. Her tires sprayed loose gravel in all directions as she wheeled out of the parking lot.

It was high time she paid Wooter Crenshaw a visit. If he was, indeed, the little man who disappeared then reappeared at the falls with the moonbow, she had quite a few questions he might be able to answer.

B.J. had never met Wooter personally, but she'd heard Cluney talk about him so much that she felt like she knew him. It seemed he'd been around Baldy Rock forever and knew everyone who'd ever lived in these parts. He also knew everybody's business and their coffin size. B.J. gave a shudder at the thought. That was one reason she'd

143

never gone with Cluney to visit the old geezer. She was afraid he'd try to measure her.

"No thanks!" she muttered. "When my time comes, I'll take cremation and sprinkling. Give me wide, open spaces!"

As she turned onto the rough mountain road that led up toward Wooter's cabin, she remembered something Cluney had told her about his sign. "If it's not propped up against the fence post, Wooter's not home. He goes off sometimes; nobody knows where."

B.J. almost hoped his sign was gone. How was she supposed to explain to him what she wanted without sounding perfectly insane?

"Hey, ole Wooter, I know you don't know me from Adam's house cat, but I hear you disappear occasionally and I'd like to know how you do it and where you go."

B.J. laughed humorously and shook her head. "Sure! *Wonderful* approach, girl!"

She stopped trying to figure it out so she could concentrate on the rutted road. Maybe something would come to her when she saw him.

Wooter's sign came into view. There was no turning back now. B.J. wheeled into the lane and slowed as a pack of dogs and one yapping cat charged toward her car. Sitting beside the drive were two raccoons who seemed to consider themselves above all the noise and excitement. B.J. grinned. "That'll be Ma and Pa Crenshaw, of course."

Just then, B.J. saw the gnomelike coffin-maker come around the side of the cabin. He stopped dead in his tracks and stared hard at the unfamiliar yellow compact car in his drive. Since he was holding a shotgun in his hands, B.J. decided her best course of action was to cut the motor, then get out slowly—*very* slowly.

She did just that, but Wooter never moved. He wasn't aiming his gun at her but, to B.J.'s way of thinking, it posed a threat nonetheless.

"Hello!" she called.

No answer. Not a muscle moved.

"Are you Wooter Crenshaw?"

At length, he called back, "May be. Who wants to know?"

"I'm B.J. Jackson—a friend of Cluney Summerland's."

B.J. was aware of the pair of raccoons sniffing around her boots, but she tried to ignore them.

"She ain't here!" Wooter yelled back.

"I didn't think she was, but I thought you might have some idea where I can find her. I know she came to visit you yesterday."

A sharp claw reached up and pawed at B.J.'s hand—the one holding her purse. "Get away!" she snapped.

"Here now! You got no cause to speak harsh to her. That ain't no way to treat my ma," Wooter growled. "She's just hankerin' for a treat. You got anything to eat in that there bag? Best give her something—my pa, too."

B.J. fished into her purse and found some sticky, lint-covered peppermints. She scattered several on the ground and watched as the two raccoons gathered up the candies, then ambled over to wash their feast.

Wooter propped his gun against the cabin steps. "That's better," he said. "Now, what's this about that little Summerland girl?"

B.J. quickly filled him in on what she knew of the night before. He stroked his long beard as he listened, nodding his head from time to time.

145

"Well, that's about all we know," she finished. "Cluney told me that you said she shouldn't go up to the falls last night, so I figured you might have some idea what happened to her."

"Tarnation and gall-durn!" he sputtered. "She ought to know to listen to me instead of letting old Redbird fill her head full of crazy notions."

"Do you think Miss Redbird knows where she is?" B.J. asked hopefully.

"I reckon me and Redbird both know, but that don't mean we're gonna tell no strangers."

"But I'm not a stranger," B.J. pleaded. "I'm Cluney's best friend. I have to find her. Please, won't you help me?"

Wooter's shaggy brows drew together over his beak of a nose. He kept pulling at his beard and making a grumbling noise deep in his throat. When he finally looked at B.J., his eyes were dark and glittering.

"Just 'cause I know where she's at don't mean I can do nothing about it. I 'spose I could go there myself, though, and make sure she's all right."

"But where is she?" B.J. demanded.

"You wouldn't understand was I to try and explain it to you."

"Is it far way?"

He squinted hard at her. "Farther than you might figure."

"Then how'd she get there without her van?" B.J. persisted.

"Wheels ain't the only way to travel, you know. Time I was going now."

"Can I go with you?" B.J. asked excitedly.

He snorted and gave her a look of disgust. "Hell, no,

146

you can't go with me! You don't go to this here place 'less you been called for a reason." He gave her a cool look, up and down. "And you can take my word for it, you wouldn't like it there no way, you being of the darker persuasion."

B.J. bristled, but she could tell the old man meant no offense. Still, she wondered at his words. None of what he said made much sense. She realized, totally frustrated, that she still had no idea where Cluney was.

"How soon can you get to her and bring her back?" B.J. asked.

Wooter shaded his eyes with one hand and squinted up at the sky. "Depends," he answered.

"On what?" By now, B.J. was truly exasperated.

He pointed off to the west. "See them clouds? If the mountains keep them at bay, could be the moonbow'll show itself again tonight. But if things get overcast, won't be no use trying till next full of the moon."

"Oh, no!" B.J. cried. "That'll be nearly a month from now. Why, anything could happen to her. You just tell me how to find her and *I'll* go right now."

Wooter shook his head and made his growling noise again. "I done told you, girl. You can't go and that's that! Now, you just run along home and leave this to me."

Refusing to be put off so easily, B.J. suggested, "Maybe Miss Redbird could help."

"You best leave her out of this," Wooter raged. "Ain't she done stirred up enough trouble already? I'm so mad at her right now that I'm thinking of trimming her coffin a inch all around, so it'll squeeze her too tight all through eternity. I tell you, she's nothing but a meddling old busybody. She had no cause to tell that little Summerland

147

girl the secret. Now, you get on outta here and leave me be. I got some tall thinking to do."

When Wooter reached for his shotgun, B.J. needed no further inspiration to get her moving. She was in her car and peeling rubber in seconds, without even a "by-your-leave" to Ma and Pa Crenshaw.

But she didn't go home. Instead, she headed up to Cumberland Falls again. Maybe Sheriff Elrod and his men had given up the search, but B.J. still felt sure that she could find some clue to Cluney's whereabouts if she went back to the very spot where the two of them had been the night before.

An hour later, B.J. pulled into the parking area beside the falls and got out of her bright yellow car. The sun felt warm on her face and the spring air was like subtle perfume. Taking a deep breath, she closed her eyes.

"Oh, Cluney, I wish you were here," she murmured. "It's one of those soft, perfect afternoons—the kind you love."

Of course, B.J. had no way of knowing it, but Cluney Summerland *was* there—only a short distance away, maybe fifty or sixty yards. Even if B.J. had gone to the very spot where her friend was, however, she wouldn't have seen her. Cluney hadn't traveled the distance in miles, but in time. As Wooter had said, it was "farther than you might figure." One hundred and twenty-nine years farther, to be exact.

B.J. headed toward the stone stairway that she and Cluney had taken the night before. She heard the birds singing, the wind sighing in the trees, and the roar of the falls, but there was no way that any human ear in the year 1992 could hear what was going on only a short distance

148

away, up the hill and beyond the copse of trees. Nor could B.J. have seen her friend. But Cluney was there all right!

"Has he settled down any?" Mary Renfro asked quietly as she passed the open bedroom door.

"Yes," Cluney answered. "The major's sleeping peacefully."

Mary nodded, but Cluney noticed the grim look on her thin face.

"That's the way of it," the woman whispered. "Dying takes a lot of energy—as much as being born. So a body needs to sleep a good bit right before—restin' up to pass over."

"No!" Cluney gasped. "It's the medicine you gave him that's making him sleep."

Mary merely nodded, then went on about her work.

Sitting beside Hunter Breckinridge, still holding his hand, Cluney tried not to think about what Mary had said. Hunter couldn't die; it wasn't fair. But then Jeff Layton had died, hadn't he? Jeff, who had been so young and full of life, who had seemed invincible. Jeff, who had meant everything to Cluney, who had been her whole world.

Her emotions in turmoil, Cluney couldn't hold back her tears. She couldn't imagine how she had come to this place, but surely she was here because Hunter Breckinridge needed her. Or, perhaps, she thought suddenly, she was here because she needed him.

Her thoughts drifting, her senses dulled by the stillness of the late afternoon, Cluney nodded off sitting up in her chair.

She had the oddest dream. She wasn't herself any longer. She was instead Larissa Courtney Breckinridge, and she was seeing her husband off to the war. But her husband wasn't Hunter in his spanking-new U.S. Cavalry uniform. He was Jeff Layton in crisp khakis, his Navy wings of gold gleaming in the bright sunlight on the airstrip as he stood beside his sleek jet, saying a final farewell to his fiancée before he went into the hangar to don his flight suit and leave her . . . *forever*.

The big, brown-haired, brown-eyed lieutenant draped his arm across the bare shoulders of the delicate, silver-haired beauty at his side. Her long gown, hoop skirt, and dainty lace gloves looked startlingly out of place with jets screaming overhead, but her beau seemed not to notice.

He leaned down and nuzzled her cheek. "Darling, do you still respect me after last night?"

A tremor ran through Cluney, or was she truly Larissa? She felt a blush warm her face. "Please don't joke about last night, Jeff. It was wonderful. It was precious. Something I can hold onto until you come home."

"Wait for me?" he said, his husky voice, serious now.

"You know I will." She was trying so hard not to cry, but it was no use.

"Hey, you better cut off the waterworks or you'll have me getting all misty, too. Come here, sweetheart."

He drew her into his arms, pulling her so close that her hoops tilted dangerously. Then he kissed her—a long, deep, soul-rending kiss. It was the kind of kiss that tasted of parting—the kind that was meant to last for months so that they could both dream about it at night or just lie in bed savoring its memory when they couldn't sleep because they were apart and, oh, so lonely.

"I love you," he whispered when they finally parted. "Have I ever told you that before?"

"About a million times," she answered, forcing her bravest smile, "but it sounds better every time I hear it."

"Do you love me?"

She clung to him and suddenly her tears flowed freely; there was no way she could stop them now. "You know I do, Jeff. Oh, yes, I love you, darling."

"Write to me?"

"Every single day!"

She hated the pause that came next. She knew what he was working up to. They'd been separated before—not for months, but only weeks was bad enough. Right now, holding him and having his arms around her, knowing that she wouldn't feel his embrace again for at least six months, was almost more than she could bear. And his next words to her, she knew, would be, "Well, so long, darling. I'll be home before you know it. Meantime, take good care of yourself for me."

She bit her lip until it almost bled when he began that goodbye speech. Tomorrow would be easier than today. Jeff would be gone, but he would also be one day closer to returning to her. Right now, this minute, he was as close to her as he could be in public, yet as far away from coming home as he could get.

He said the very words she'd dreaded, kissed her one last, quick time, then turned to leave. In that moment, her loneliness was so deep that her soul ached with it.

Just when she thought she couldn't bear to be without him, he reached out and squeezed her hand.

Cluney jolted awake, but still seemed in a fog. She thought she heard the scream of a jet taking off just before her eyes opened. But that couldn't be. There were no planes in 1863. There was only the Civil War and the wounded man lying beside her in the bed—the man who had squeezed her hand.

"Who were you dreaming about, Larissa?"

"My one and only love," she whispered, not in answer to Hunter's question or even for his ears, but as a final, hopeless plea for her doomed lover to come back.

"I suspected as much," he said in a raspy voice. "You seemed a million miles away. I sensed you were not with me."

"I'm right here," Cluney answered softly. Then she added silently, *I was only a hundred and twenty-nine years away.*

Hunter's next words gave Cluney a jolt, as if she were hearing an eerie echo. "I suppose it's useless to say this to you now, but I love you. Have I ever told you that before?"

Likewise, her answer echoed from her dream. "About a million times."

His hand slid from hers. His face suddenly etched with pain, his voice almost surly, he replied, "Then I won't impose upon you by ever saying it again, Larissa."

She could only stare at him, wondering what she had done to anger him so.

"I'm sorry," she whispered, without a notion why she felt compelled to apologize. She knew only that she must.

# Chapter Nine

When Hunter Breckinridge had first heard Larissa's voice hours before, he'd figured for sure he was dead. By rights he certainly should be. How else could he find old Trooper and Larissa at the same moment? He'd told himself that he'd simply passed through the Pearly Gates sometime while he slept, and there they both were waiting for him.

Although preachers claimed that animals had no souls and, therefore, couldn't get into heaven, Hunter knew for certain that his old hound, Trooper—reportedly shot by a mean-spirited Reb—was lying right beside him. He knew the feel of his dog, the sound of his voice, the very smell of his beloved companion. Wherever they were, there was no doubting that he and old Troop had been reunited.

Then, for a time, there had been the other heavenly evidence—the woman beside him. He was pretty sure she was his Larissa—the only woman he had ever loved. It was sobering to admit that he knew his dog better than he knew his wife, but it was true all the same. He and Larissa, although they'd known each other all their lives, had shared a bed only twice before he went away to war, whereas he and old Troop had slept on the same feather mattress every night for as long as Hunter could recall. Except, of course, on his wedding night and the night before he left for the war.

Still thinking he was dead, Hunter had decided that it wasn't so bad. If passing over meant he and Larissa could be together the way he'd always hoped it would be, then heaven really was paradise. That line of thinking had ended abruptly the minute Larissa mentioned another man—her one and only love. He shouldn't have been surprised. But how did she expect that to make him feel?

Rigid on the bed, Hunter seethed silently, but tried to cover the pain in his heart. He supposed it was brave of Larissa to admit to her husband that she was still thinking of his brother. But, damn! It hurt so bad to hear her admit that Jordan was still on her mind after all that had happened.

Didn't she know he was dying? Couldn't she have pretended for just a short while? Why hadn't she simply taken salt and rubbed it into his open wounds? But then Larissa had ever been honest, sometimes too honest for her own good.

"Hunter, are you all right?"

He knew Larissa's voice so well. She sounded genuinely concerned and loving. How could she do this to him? Didn't she know she was tearing him apart?

If he were able, he would rise up from the bed this minute and grab her and shake her. Then he'd take her in his arms and make fierce love to her, punish her for ever thinking about anyone else.

*No, I wouldn't!* he told himself. He knew that, if he were able, he would make love to her—yes, *fierce* love. But it would be with all the tenderness and passion that he had withheld from her on their wedding night.

He had thought once that all would be perfect harmony when they married. How wrong he had been! And it was all his fault. He could blame his brother if he liked, but Hunter knew he had been unfair to the woman he loved.

Yes, this was Larissa, there was no doubt in his mind. But having her here was more hell than heaven, he decided. He wanted her! And he wanted everything to be right between them again.

All night she had stayed right beside him. He was so aware of her presence that he ached. His dreams had been happy ones for a change. He had drifted back to their happiness before their wedding night instead of wandering dark paths, searching for her. He had relived her sweet shyness the night they first made love. He had heard her once more swearing her everlasting devotion to him. He had kissed her so tenderly that night, holding her in his arms until he ached to possess her forevermore. She had returned his gentle affection, letting her hands trail over his hard body, exploring and glorying in his strength. Jordan had not come between them that night, and what a wonder their love had been!

Everything had been wonderful until the night before their wedding, until he found out his bride's secret.

Now, as he lay in the darkness, feeling her near, he could only wonder if he would still have to do battle for his wife's affections. Was Jordan even now a part of her life?

At times during the night, he'd heard her crying softly. The sound broke his heart. He knew the source of her sadness. Her tears were not for him. She was crying for his brother. The two of them were together again—Hunter and his wife. So why else should she sound so sad?

For the longest time now, he'd been drifting in and out. He opened his eyes every now and again, but saw only darkness. Earlier, he might have cursed aloud at not being able to see Larissa's face. But not now. Now his blindness seemed a blessing. How could he look on her beauty, knowing that she was thinking of another?

He ached, remembering the sweetness of her face. Her countenance was imprinted forever in his mind's eye— her lovely blushrose skin, her searching eyes of Clair de Lune-blue, her delicate mouth, and all that long, wonderfully silky hair the color of moonlight that wrapped around him when they made love.

No, he needed no eyes to see Larissa. Nor could he exorcise her image from his dreams.

Both Hunter and Cluney slept fitfully till dawn. She woke first and watched him for a time, wondering at his sudden flash of anger last night. She still couldn't think what she might have done to upset him so.

His lips moved silently and she guessed that he was finally waking up. She hoped he was. She'd been sitting up in a hard chair all night and she ached to move about, to stretch her arms and legs and back. But she dared not leave him until Mary or Free came to relieve her.

As she watched, his eyes flickered open.

"Hello there," she said softly. "You're awake at last."

"You're still here, Larissa?" He sounded pleased, yet surprised.

"You still can't see, can you?"

He raised one hand to his eyes, then waved it impatiently. "That doesn't matter. What would I want to see, anyway? A little while ago, I was sure I'd died and gone to heaven. But that's not so, is it?"

Cluney glanced around the shabby room. "No. This certainly isn't heaven."

"I should have figured," he answered. Then he gave a sharp laugh, followed by a ragged cough. "If it were heaven, there'd be no pain any longer, and I'd be able to see the whole universe at a glance."

"Do you really believe that's the way heaven will be?" Cluney asked. She'd never given it much thought.

"I certainly hope so," he answered. "I suppose I'll be finding out soon enough."

"Don't talk that way. You're going to get well."

"Why should I want to get well?" he asked. "So I can go back to the war and let the Rebs finish me off?"

"What about your home, your family?"

"My home has probably been burned to the ground by now. As for my *family*—you tell me, Larissa."

Cluney didn't know what she expected her to say. And she didn't know what to do. He obviously was convinced that she was his lost wife, but something seemed wrong between them. Maybe the medicine Mary Renfro had given him had confused him.

Hunter clearly wanted and needed to believe that Cluney was his wife. But how could she, in good conscience, participate in such a strange masquerade? It was dishonest and, in the end, it could prove far more painful to him than the truth. She sighed, unwilling to deal with the problem at present. If he was truly dying, as Mrs. Renfro said, what harm could it do to give him a few days' happiness by pretending? Maybe that was the true reason she was here.

157

"You really shouldn't waste all your strength talking," she warned gently. "You need to rest."

The old hound shifted positions on the bed and Hunter reached down to pat him.

"The servants at Bluefield told me my dog was dead, shot right through the heart. I never believed it, though. Did you have old Troop with you all the time, Larissa?"

Cluney thought for a moment, then answered honestly, "No. He just wandered out of the woods when I was coming up to the Renfro place. You know how faithful hounds are. He probably followed your scent all the way here from Bluefield."

Hunter tugged his dog's ear affectionately. "Good old Trooper! You're my family, aren't you, pal?" Then he turned back to Cluney. "What about you, Larissa? Where have you been all this time? How did you find me here?"

Cluney squirmed in her cane-bottom chair. She had no answers for his questions. Should she try to make things up as she went along or simply tell him the truth? Evasion, she decided, was probably the best course.

"I'll tell you everything later. Right now, you need something to eat. I'm sure Mrs. Renfro has breakfast ready for you."

She rose and stretched.

"Don't go just yet."

"I'll be back before you know it," she assured him.

"Larissa?" He spoke the name sharply.

Cluney hesitated, then finally said, "Yes?"

"Before you go, kiss me, won't you? It's been a long time. After so long, a man aches to touch his wife."

Cluney stared down at Hunter. The pain in his face tore at her heart. He needed to be kissed and he deserved to be. Any man who adored his wife the way Hunter

158

Breckinridge obviously adored his Larissa should be kissed. Cluney reminded herself that she'd kissed a lot of other guys with a lot less reason for doing so. Besides, what could it hurt?

She moved to the bed. "Of course, I'll give you a kiss."

Trying to be careful not to hurt him, Cluney leaned down over Hunter, closing her eyes as her lips pressed his gently.

Her shock was total when he captured her with his good arm and pulled her close. Cluney hadn't meant to kiss him this way. She'd thought to give him only a swift, soft press of lips. But Hunter had other plans for his long-lost bride. His mouth claimed hers with a fierce hunger. She sprawled—half on the bed, half off—as his fingers tangled in her hair, holding her for a long, deep, thorough kiss.

Cluney was very aware of her breasts crushed to his bandaged chest. She knew this must be hurting him since his strong grip was hurting her. But, obviously, any pain Hunter felt was far overshadowed by the pleasure of embracing the woman he assumed to be his wife.

By the time he released her, Cluney felt perfectly dizzy and thoroughly confused. No one had kissed her that way since Jeff. Dear Jeff—their last night together. They had made love for the first time the night before he left for that ill-fated deployment to the Mediterranean. Before that evening, she had managed to stall his sweet advances with promises of a more exciting honeymoon if they waited. But when Jeff had told her jokingly that everyone did it the night before a deployment because you never knew who might not come back, his words had twisted Cluney's heart. She had finally given in to her own need as well as

Jeff's. Little did she suspect at the time that it would be their only chance, ever, to share love.

She stared down at Hunter. How could this total stranger from another century stir the same emotions, light the same fires that had been hers and Jeff's alone?

"You taste good, Larissa," Hunter whispered. "Now I know for sure that I didn't die during the night. I may even last through one more night if I can look forward to more of your kisses."

His mention of dying brought a flood of tears to Cluney's eyes. "Don't say things like that, Hunter Breckinridge! You're not going to die. I won't let you!"

With a sob that came straight from her breaking heart, a sob that Cluney could neither understand nor control, she fled the room. Just outside, she ran right into Mary Renfro.

"Land sakes, child! What's come over you?" Mary caught Cluney by the shoulders and stared into her tear-streaked face. Then she glanced toward the bedroom door and frowned. "It's not the major, is it? He ain't up and died on us?"

"No!" Cluney cried. "He's not dead and he's not going to die. I won't let him!"

"Here now, girl. That's not for you to decide. When the Lord figures it's time to take the major home, he'll go right enough."

"The Lord can't have him!" Cluney cried.

"You hush that blastphemy this minute! And you under the reverend's very roof! You ain't got no right to say what happens to that poor man in there. If you ask me, he'd be a whole lot better off with the Lord, what with all his pain and his sorrow over losing his wife."

Cluney managed to calm herself. Mary was right, of

course. But somehow, she couldn't make herself believe that Hunter Breckinridge would be better off dead.

"I don't know what I'm going to do," Cluney muttered to herself.

"About what?" Mary said. "All you can do is keep him comfortable till his time comes."

"You don't understand, Mrs. Renfro. The major thinks *I'm* his wife. He's convinced of it. Do I tell him the truth or go along with him? I don't want to hurt him. He's taken all he can stand already."

Mary gave Cluney a sharp look. "I don't hold with lying, girl."

"It wouldn't be lying—not exactly. I'd just be avoiding the truth, and it would only be for a time. But you and Free would have to go along with it. You'd have to call me Larissa."

"Well . . ." Mary was still frowning, deep in thought over whether she'd be sinning outright if she joined this outlandish conspiracy. Finally, she made up her mind. "Well, if it eases the major, then I don't reckon I see the harm in it." She glanced heavenward. "Forgive me, Lord!"

Cluney hugged the woman. "Oh, thank you, Mary!"

"Here, now!" Mary said, putting Cluney at arm's length. "We got work to do. But before you take the major's breakfast in to him, I reckon I better find you something suitable for his wife to be wearing."

"But he can't see me."

"All the same, them trousers ain't fittin'. Besides, a body that's got no sight's got a keener sense of hearing. If he don't hear petticoats rustling, he'll think it a mite odd. The Breckinridges are high-toned folks with a big, fancy

161

horse farm up Lexington way. I can't rightly picture his Larissa in a pair of work britches, can you?"

Cluney did her best to envision a nineteenth-century plantation mistress in jeans, a black turtleneck, and hiking boots. No! Her dream of Larissa in her hoopskirts and filmy ruffles returned to mind. She smiled. "You're right, Mary. I should dress properly for him."

"Well, come along with me, then. I got a trunk full of my daughter Lorettie's old frocks—rest her dear soul. You needn't worry about catching nothing from wearing her things. She wasn't took by disease, but choked on a fish bone right yonder at the supper table."

Stunned by the woman's matter-of-factness concerning her own daughter's death, Cluney said, "I'm so sorry, Mary."

The woman shook her head. "No need. The Lord giveth. The Lord taketh away. Her time come while she happened to be eating crappie for supper. That was all."

Poor Lorettie had hardly been a fashion plate as Cluney discovered a short time later. Her trunk contained a limited assortment of plain, high-collared, drab frocks befitting a parson's teenaged daughter.

Dressed in the best of the lot—a guinea-blue gingham with a bit of a ruffle at the neck and wrists—Cluney approached Hunter's room a short time later. She felt perfectly odd, wearing the old gown with its accompanying petticoats and pantalets. She'd drawn the line at lacing herself into Lorettie's narrow corset. No way was she donning that torture device! As for shoes, her own hiking boots had to suffice. Luckily, her long skirt hid them. Lorettie's foot must have been all of a size four. Cinderella might have worn those slippers, but not Cluney Summerland with her size eight clodhoppers.

Carefully, Cluney balanced a wooden trencher filled with fragrantly steaming squirrel stew on her forearm while she opened the door to Hunter's room. To her utter shock, she found him sitting up in bed.

"Well, look at you!" she cried, delighted. "How did you manage that?"

"I told Free my pretty wife was coming and I might get another chance to grab her if I was propped up, so he helped me."

Cluney laughed. "I'm glad you feel up to grabbing this morning. You were pretty restless during the night."

She glanced across the room to see the black man leaning against the window frame. He gave her a nod to let her know he'd said nothing to shatter the illusion that she was Larissa Breckinridge.

"I reckon I'll be going to help Miz Renfro now," Free said, "if you don't need me for nothing else, ma'am."

"Oh, there is one thing," Cluney said. "Is there a basin and a razor about? I thought the maj . . ." she paused, stumbling over the words, then forced herself to say, "my husband might like a shave."

Hunter ran a hand over his bristly chin and grimaced. "I suppose that's a good idea. I scraped you pretty badly before, did I? But don't you think Free should do that? It's hardly a task for a lady."

"I believe I can handle a razor well enough not to slit your throat. Besides, I want to do it." Cluney meant that. She wanted to do whatever she could to bring comfort and pleasure into Hunter's life.

"Yes, ma'am," Free answered with a twinkle in his dark eyes. It truly warmed his heart to see the major

163

getting such fine treatment. "I'll go heat some water right now."

"Thank you, Free," Cluney answered, smiling.

She perched on the edge of the bed to feed her charge. The stew smelled wonderful. What Hunter didn't eat, Cluney finished for him.

But soon, Hunter was all questions again. "You still haven't told me how you found this place, Larissa. Who brought you here?"

Cluney thought quickly. She did have an advantage in this situation. She had memorized Hunter's journal and knew things about him and his wife that would lend credence to her performance.

"It was the moon—our moon," she said. "I had no idea you were here, but I came up to the falls to see the moonbow."

"Incredible!" Hunter exclaimed. "You couldn't have possibly come all this way by yourself. Besides, I would have seen you out there. Free took me to the falls. I saw the moonbow, and I saw something else, too."

"Yes?" Cluney prompted.

"I saw the bride of the falls."

"Tell me about her," Cluney begged.

"The bride was you, Larissa. First, there was the soft glow of the moonbow. Then it grew brighter and brighter until I was almost blinded by the light. Then you stepped out of that glowing silver ball, dressed exactly as you were the day we married. I knew then that you were coming, that I'd see you soon. I stayed up all night writing in my journal, trying to explain all my feelings for you." He paused, seeming weary suddenly. "But it was no use. I suppose I shouldn't have even tried. What difference does it make now?"

His words confused Cluney. He sounded so hopeless suddenly. But why should the moonbow make him sad?

"Now you don't have to write anything down," she said softly. "I'm here and you can tell me what you feel."

He muttered something under his breath that sounded like, "I'm not sure you want to know."

Cluney rose to put the empty stew dish on a nearby table, and Hunter shifted himself higher on the pillows. With nourishment he had obviously gained strength.

"Come sit beside me, won't you, Larissa?"

Uncertainly, Cluney perched on the side of the bed.

"Closer," he demanded.

"Hunter, I don't want to hurt you."

He laughed—a short, sharp sound that made Cluney cringe.

"You don't want to hurt me, eh? Don't worry about it."

The rest of his thought went unspoken. His wife couldn't hurt him more if she tried. He knew the truth about her and Jordan. *That hurt,* really hurt, but the pain seemed to be fading now that Larissa was back. Maybe there was still time to put things back to rights between them.

Suddenly, he clamped his good arm around Cluney's shoulders and kissed her deeply. She felt heat suffuse her body and tried to pull away. She couldn't let this stranger make love to her. She'd thought he posed no threat in his weakened condition, but apparently she'd misjudged his prowess.

"No, please!" she gasped, drawing away.

"I've missed you, Larissa," he whispered. "Haven't you wanted to lie with me? I've thought of little else all this time. And now I'm dying," he stated bluntly. "Would you deny your own husband his last wish?"

This was absolute insanity! Cluney had lost one man she loved and she knew how that hurt. And yet she felt herself longing to give in to Hunter Breckinridge—not only because he wanted her, but because she wanted him. As crazy as it sounded, it was almost as if she had found Jeff again. She had suffered so over Jeff's death. Now, suddenly, this stranger was kissing her as Jeff had kissed her, making her feel the same things Jeff had made her feel, forcing the love she had buried with Jeff to come out of the grave and burst into full flame once more.

How could Hunter Breckinridge do this to her? How could she let him?

Cluney knew she was only setting herself up for another fall if she gave him her heart. As Mary had warned her, he had little time left, but there seemed nothing she could do to resist. It was almost as if her sole purpose in coming back here to Hunter's time was to love him—to give him all the affection and passion that still smoldered deep inside her for Jeff.

Still unconvinced that she should allow this to happen, Cluney said, "No, Hunter. You're not well enough."

"I feel well enough," he said. "Maybe I'm not as strong as other men, but take my word for it, darling, I can please you."

Cluney swallowed hard, sure that his bold words were true. Casting about for some other excuse, she said, "You haven't had your shave yet."

He gave a low chuckle. "So, that's the only problem. I forgot about my whiskers. I apologize, my dear. You must look as if you've been grazing in a briar patch. I promise

166

to behave until after I've had my shave. Shall we do that right now?"

"Hunter," Cluney said in a somber tone, "you're badly wounded. Mary said . . ."

"Mary's a prude!" he exclaimed. "How could she know that the ache in my heart is far worse than the pain in my shoulder, my leg, or my head? You know, if it weren't for Free, I'd be dead now, and I've cursed him many's the day for saving me and causing me all this agony. But it's worth it, Larissa. I wouldn't have missed being with you again for anything. Maybe we still have time to make things right. Unless you and your love . . ."

The blood drained from Cluney's face. She couldn't stand this any longer. How could he know about Jeff? And why did he keep bringing up their relationship?

"Please don't," she whispered. "He's gone."

Her words shocked him into silence for a time. Did she mean it was all over between her and Jordan? Finally, Hunter said, "I'm sorry. But, Larissa, I'm still here and I want you back. I can't promise things will be as they were before, but we'll have each other no matter what. You will stay this time, won't you?"

Cluney's thoughts were spinning. "I don't know," she cried. "I mean, I hadn't thought past today or tomorrow. But then, I don't know where else I could go, at least for the time being."

There was a world of hurt in Hunter's silence.

"Oh, Hunter! You know I didn't mean it that way."

"Never mind how you meant it," he said with deadly calm. "Whatever has happened between us in the past, you're here with me now and I don't intend to let you go as long as I have a single breath left in my body. I want you to be a wife to me again. Now, come here!"

167

Cluney hesitated. Jeff had never ordered her about. Even when he had finally made love to her, he had convinced her with gentle teasing and persuasion. So why did she even consider complying with Hunter's command? She didn't know. All she understood was that she could not refuse him. He might not have long, but what time he had left she wanted to share with him. She felt like his wife. It almost seemed to her that they had shared years and years together. Years that she couldn't remember, but had read about in his diary.

Careful of his wounds, Cluney slipped her arms around him and held him close, tears spilling down her cheeks.

"What do you want me to do?" she whispered.

"I want you to love me, Larissa. Love me as you have never loved any other man. A kiss, perhaps?"

Aroused by the sudden tenderness in his voice, Cluney brought her open mouth to his. His tongue was as smooth as his beard was scratchy. The opposing sensations sent tingles of fire through Cluney's blood. Still kissing her deeply, Hunter brought his hand to her breast. He squeezed gently, then harder. Cluney caught her breath.

"You were always so tender there," he murmured, "so pleasing to touch."

Just then, a footstep in the hallway caused Cluney to pull away.

"We can't," she said breathlessly. "Not in the daytime. Mary might come in—or Free."

"I don't care. Do you?"

Cluney thought about it for a moment. No, she decided, she really didn't care. What they had started needed finishing. With that thought, a new terror suddenly gripped her. What if he found out she was not Larissa? Would he send her away in one of his lightning-flash rages? She knew she wanted him, this minute, as she had never wanted any other man but Jeff. And it wasn't simply a physical need, although there was that, too. No, she wanted Hunter Breckinridge as a part of her life from this day forward. She wanted him to promise her as he had promised his Larissa that their love would last even beyond the grave.

Hunter's next words only added to her fears. "Larissa, I think my eyesight's returning. I can see some light and vague shapes. I'm sure that bright glow at the falls coupled with my writing all night did the damage. But it seems to be only a temporary disability." He cupped her face between his palms and gazed at her. "I can hardly wait to see your face. When we make love tonight, I want to be able to see you again. All of you!"

"Please, Hunter, you're embarrassing me," Cluney whispered.

Actually, he was doing far more than embarrassing her. He was both frightening her and arousing her. She knew with a dreadful certainty suddenly that she would let him make love to her once darkness fell, that she wanted him with all her heart and soul. But she had a feeling that would never happen. Once he realized she had tricked him, she was sure he would hate her for deceiving him.

Before Free arrived with the basin and razor, Hunter had drifted off to sleep again. Cluney, feeling as if she'd been granted a reprieve, slipped out of the room for a time. She went in search of Mary Renfro and found her out by the washtub in the yard.

"Mary, can I talk to you a minute?"

Still stirring the laundry with her long stick, the woman motioned to Cluney to come on out.

"How's the major?" Mary asked.

"Sleeping again. He ate most of his stew, and he thinks his eyesight is coming back."

"Well, glory be!" She glanced up. "Thank You, Lord, for all small favors." A look back at Cluney told her that the young woman did not share her relief. "What's got into you, girl?"

"Once his sight comes back, he'll know I've tricked him, Mary. What will I do then?"

Mrs. Renfro looked hard at this strange girl who'd wandered up from nowhere. She couldn't quite figure her. "You can't be blamed. You didn't trick the major, child. He done it his own self. He wanted you to be his Larissa so bad that he just made it all up in his mind. Could be he won't see no difference once the truth is right before his eyes."

Cluney spelled Mary at stirring the wash while they talked. "I'm afraid I don't understand what you mean."

"Well, I've had a lot of sick men and boys through here the past year or more. Some heal up and go on back to the war. Others are buried yonder in the woods. But they all got one thing in common; they're all missing someone—wife, sweetheart, mother. And more than a few times, I've been taken for that loved one. I reckon it helps them a mite just to pretend."

Cluney frowned. "I don't think Hunter is pretending. I'm sure he really believes I'm Larissa."

Mary nodded and smoothed a work-roughened hand over her brow. "Right now, he does because he needs to. Don't you see? He's got nothing left to live for without his wife. If he gets worse, likely he'll keep on believing. If a miracle happens and he starts recovering, he'll be well enough to deal with the truth, I reckon."

170

"So, you think I should just go along with him and hope for the best?"

"Can't see as you have much choice, now that you got yourself into this. Not 'less you want to kill him outright by telling him the truth right out."

Any mention of Hunter's dying went straight through Cluney's heart like a sharp knife. Mary's words brought immediate tears to her eyes. She sniffed loudly, trying to hold them back.

Mary gave her a sharp look. "Here, now! What's come over you, girl? You got to keep up a bright face—let the major see you smiling all the time, not blubbering like it was the end of the world."

"Oh, Mary . . ." Cluney paused, choking on her emotions. "Something's all wrong!"

"This whole war's wrong, honey, but we can't go to sobbing over it all the time."

"I know! I know! But that's not what I mean."

"What then?" Mary waited for an answer that didn't come. "What ail's you, girl?"

Gathering her breath for a rush of words, Cluney blurted out, "I think I'm in love with him!"

"Lord, help us!" Mary muttered, shaking her head. She put her hands on Cluney's quaking shoulders and looked into her eyes. "You *knowed* he was dying. I told you, if you couldn't see it for yourself. A sane woman don't go giving her heart to baby lambs that's raised for slaughtering or dying men who love somebody else. It just ain't done!"

"I know," Cluney whispered "But he's so much like a man I loved and lost."

"Well, that's sure a weight off my soul!" Mary exclaimed. "I reckon it all makes sense now."

"It does?"

"I believe so, child. You're doing about the same as the major is—taking love that's got no home no longer and finding it one. Just mind you don't get too wrapped up in this poor soldier boy. He ain't got long!"

Mary said the last words in such a stern tone of voice that Cluney felt as if she'd just had a good scolding. How could the woman be so hard-hearted?

Just then the front door to the cabin banged open and Free yelled, "Miz Larissa, come quick! He's awake and he can see clear as day. Wants his wife there, right now, he does!"

Cluney and Mary exchanged quick, uncertain glances before "Larissa" turned and ran for the house. She was eager to be with her "husband," but troubled and fearful at the same time.

Who would Hunter see before him—Larissa Courtney Breckinridge or Clair de Lune Summerland?

# Chapter Ten

Hunter immediately regretted telling Free that he had his eyesight back. He realized that he had missed the perfect opportunity to observe his wife closely without her knowing that he was watching her. He was sure she was Larissa; she was the same as he remembered in almost every way. But there was something about her that was different, too.

During the many months that they had been separated, Larissa seemed to have lost some of her fine polish, her "prissiness," as his mother used to call it. He'd always objected to that characterization, even though he knew it was accurate. Larissa, like all the young blue-blooded ladies of her class, had been expected to be a bit vain, flighty, and self-centered. They were pampered from birth, so they expected to be for life.

But that capricious part of her was gone now. Vanished! In its place, he sensed a more genuine tenderness of heart, a deep compassion that Larissa had been lacking before. He had no idea what had wrought this change in his wife.

Suddenly, he scowled when he thought again of Larissa

with Jordan. Could it be that his twin brother had taught his wife the true meaning of love?

"No," he murmured. "I won't allow myself to believe such a thing."

Then another troubling thought struck him.

"Or is it not compassion at all, but *pity*?" he wondered aloud. He would know the minute he saw her face. "Please, God, don't let it be pity!"

Hearing the front door squeak on its hinges, Hunter sat up straighter in the bed, his heart pounding so hard that it made his chest ache. Larissa would come into his room any moment now. He almost dreaded seeing her for the first time. Could she possibly be as beautiful as he remembered?

He reached over and patted his sleeping hound, feeling a nervous need for companionship. "You and me, old boy," he said, "we're a team for life no matter what. Tell me, Troop, will she look the same? You've seen her. I haven't."

The hound opened one eye and thumped his skinny tail against the bedspread. Then he gave a sigh and drifted off to sleep again.

Hunter continued thinking, talking to himself, but addressing the dog. "Of course, it could be a trick. Mary Renfro's a sweet woman, but she's not above trying to pull the wool over a fellow's eyes in order to make him want to live. It does seem mighty odd that my wife didn't show up here till I'd lost my sight. Then, too, Mary had me all doped up with that foul-tasting medicine."

Hunter didn't believe a word he was saying, however. He knew! He knew for certain that Larissa had returned to him, for whatever reason.

A moment later, the bedroom door eased open. Hunter

174

held his breath. He wanted to see and he didn't. He wasn't sure he could bear to look into her eyes. What would he read there? She had never been able to hide any secrets from him. Not even the one that had changed both their lives.

He closed his eyes, not ready to look at her just yet.

"Hunter?" she called to him quietly.

With what seemed a great effort, he raised his head and looked directly at her.

For a moment, he couldn't find his voice, too many battling emotions were raging through him—his love for the beautiful young bride he had left, his fear for her, his anger and hurt when he found out she'd gone to his brother.

Finally, in a hoarse whisper, he said, "Larissa. This war has aged you, aged us both."


Cluney caught her breath. She wasn't sure what she had expected, but certainly not this. Was Hunter Breckinridge seeing his wife in her only because he wanted to? Or was he merely pretending, playing some sort of twisted joke on her for deceiving him?

She glanced toward Mary and Free, who were standing behind her in the doorway. They were both staring at her as if they'd never seen her before in their lives. Mary's eyes held only accusation, while Free looked pleased and surprised.

"Mary . . ." Cluney began, seeking an explanation rather than hoping to offer any.

Mrs. Renfro quickly cut her off. "You'll be wanting some time alone with your husband. So, we'll leave you now."

Without another word, the woman shut the door, leaving Cluney to face this man who claimed to be her husband. She stood in awkward silence a few feet from the bed.

"Larissa, I didn't mean that as an insult—about your aging. It's just that you were a girl when I left you. Looking at you now, no man could take you for less than a woman. You've filled out fine and handsome, my darling."

Cluney had never known such a mingling of embarrassment and bewilderment. Now that Hunter could see, he was giving her the once over, head to toe. She noted with a deep blush that his gaze lingered at the bodice of poor Lorettie's too-tight dress, where the faded fabric strained over her full, bra-less breasts.

"Come here to me, Larissa." He stretched his good arm toward her and beckoned. "Let me have a closer look."

"Why are you doing this?" Cluney's voice was shaking so she could hardly get the words out. She stood her ground, waiting for an answer.

"Doing what? I only want my wife here beside me."

"*Your wife!*" Cluney echoed in a flat tone.

He nodded. "Yes, you, Larissa. Is there something wrong with that?"

Cluney spread her arms, palms up in an imploring gesture. "Look at me, won't you, Major Breckinridge? I'm *not* your wife!"

He frowned. "Major Breckinridge? What kind of games are you playing, Larissa? Of course, you're my wife! Or do you figure now that you've been with another, that makes you his instead of mine?"

Tears brimmed in Cluney's eyes. "Look, I don't know

what's going on here. I have no idea how you even know these things about me, but that's over now."

Her head was spinning. She fell silent when a thought struck her: *No, it isn't over with Jeff; it won't even begin for over a century.* Then as if to remind herself of what was real, Cluney whispered, "He's gone. He died in a plane crash."

The moment the words were out of her mouth, Cluney realized the mistake she'd made, but it was too late. Hunter leaned closer, his face dark with something that verged on anger.

"Make sense, woman! What do you mean 'plane crash'? And if you insist upon claiming you're not my wife, then tell me who in hell you think you are."

*Who, indeed, was she?* Cluney wondered.

This was not going to be easy and Cluney knew it. She sighed and sank down into the chair beside the bed, trying to think how to begin.

Looking at him, staring directly into his dark eyes, she only hoped that he would believe her. But how could she blame him if he didn't? She hardly knew what to believe any longer.

"Please don't think I'm crazy when you hear what I have to say. I'll tell you everything, but it may take some time." She glanced about and shrugged. "How to begin? I'm not from this place." Already she realized she had screwed it up. Backtracking, she corrected that statement. "Well, yes, I am from this place, but I'm not from this time. I'm from over on Baldy Rock Mountain, and I teach history at a college that will be built in the valley shortly after the war is over."

He interrupted, as she guessed he would. "There's nothing down in that valley but a few coal miners' shacks."

Cluney nodded. "Not now, but there will be a college and a town there in a few years. A place for the miners' children to be educated. Please, won't you just listen? This is very difficult to explain. Maybe it will make some sense when you've heard *all* I have to say."

She glanced at him. He nodded, but looked thoroughly confused and chagrined.

Trying to figure out how to continue, Cluney gazed up toward the ceiling as if she might find some clue there. When she looked back down, her eyes lit on his diary.

"That journal over there, I've read it, so I know a lot about you."

"You read my diary while I was sleeping? That's my private property and you know it. That's the only thing I ever asked you not to do, Larissa."

Cluney tried to remain at least outwardly calm in the face of his justified anger. "You don't have to worry. As far as I know Larissa has never read your diary. But I have. My name is Claire de Lune Summerland, by the way. My friends call me Cluney."

"*Your husband* calls you Larissa!"

Ignoring that, Cluney continued. "You know the college in the valley I mentioned? Well, I found your diary there, in the basement of the library. It had been stored away for years. I know things about your early life at Bluefield because you recorded them in your daily entries. I know, for instance, that your dog, Trooper, was the only one in that litter to survive, and that your father wanted to destroy him because he was sick, too. But you nursed the pup back to health. I know that you were in love with Larissa for a long, long time, and that she was several years younger than you are. I know that you asked her to marry you in her parents' garden in Lexington . . . that

178

you got down on one knee . . . that there was a full moon overhead. I know about your wedding. I even know the intimate details of your wedding night." Cluney rubbed her cheeks with her hands to cover a sudden blush.

*"My* wedding night? Somehow I've always thought of it as *our* wedding night. But I guess your lover changed all that for you."

"Will you please shut up about him!" Cluney shouted. Then she looked down, embarrassed, and murmured, "I'm sorry. But it's just that I loved him so much and you make it sound like it was something dirty, something I should be ashamed of."

Hunter's face went ashen. His words came out sounding cold. "If you loved him so damn much, why didn't you stay with him? Or have you only come back to me because Jordan's gone and you have no one else to turn to?"

*"Jordan?"* Cluney cried. "You think I loved your brother?"

When Hunter stared at her, confused, Cluney explained, "I know about him from your diary. But I've certainly never been in love with him. To tell you the truth, Hunter, I could never understand why the two of you remained close. He was always such a schemer."

"What game is this, Larissa? You said you loved—"

"The man I loved was named Jeff Layton."

Hunter growled, "No matter his name, you loved him all the same."

Cluney had had about enough of his temper. Sick or dying or whatever, he didn't have to act like such a bastard.

"Damn your hide, Hunter Breckinridge, turn over and

listen to me! I will not be ignored! You asked me to tell you about myself and that's what I'm trying to do."

Slowly, inch by inch, he turned back toward her. But the meanness was still in his eyes. "Who's this Jeff Layton?"

"He *was* the man that I, *Cluney Summerland*, loved and planned to marry. As I said, he was killed a short time ago, on March 1, 1992."

For the first time, Hunter Breckinridge was at a loss for words. He stared hard at Cluney, his eyes narrowing, then going wide. "The hell you say! *1992*?"

She nodded slowly. "I know you find that impossible to believe, but it's true. Night before last, which was May 18, 1992, I came up to Cumberland Falls with a girlfriend to watch the moonbow. I saw it, then something happened—something I can't explain. I don't remember anything after that until I woke up the next morning and it was 1863. Or, come to think of it, maybe I'm still asleep and dreaming all this."

"Take my word for it, you're not dreaming," Hunter said sternly. "And regardless of when or where you came from, you *are* Larissa Courtney Breckinridge!"

"How can you be so sure?"

"For one thing, you know about old Trooper. That's not in my diary. But you would know about it anyway, Larissa. You were there the day the pups were born in the stable. You helped me save Trooper's life. Why, if you hadn't cried and begged so, Father would have done away with him."

Cluney knew her mouth was hanging open, but she was too numb to close it.

"Then there's the necklace," Hunter continued. "I gave you that moonstone you're wearing around your

180

neck. I gave it to you on your thirteenth birthday as a promise that I meant to marry you someday."

Cluney's hand went to the slender chain around her neck. She rubbed the smooth stone with one fingertip. "*You* gave me this?"

Suddenly, Cluney believed what he said. She knew she was Larissa and that Hunter Breckinridge was her husband. Tears flooded her eyes, then streamed down her cheeks. Miss Redbird had told her that she was wearing the moonstone when she turned up at the Summerland cabin, that she had brought it with her.

Covering her mouth with her hand to keep from sobbing aloud, Cluney could only shake her head.

"It's true," Hunter said softly. "You *are* my wife! I don't know where you've been or what happened to you while you were away. I don't even care. All I know is that I love you, Larissa. I may not have much time left, but I want to spend all of it with you."

"Oh, don't!" Cluney sobbed. "Please, don't say that!"

"We can't pretend things are the same as they were before the war. But I promise I won't speak of that again. Come here."

Cluney hesitated, fighting back her tears. "Hunter, there's something you have to know. I don't remember. I know the things I read in your diary, and somehow I remembered about Trooper. But I can't remember ever being your wife. The only things I recall happened off in distant time, over a century from now. From your diary, I know far more about Hunter Breckinridge than I do about his wife, it seems. Larissa is a total stranger to me."

"Don't worry about that," he whispered. "Come. I'll help you remember, darling."

She approached him shyly. Nothing in life had prepared her for this moment. She stood uncertainly beside the bed, wondering what he expected of her.

Hunter gazed up at her. "Come here, darling," he repeated. "Come to me."

She eased down to sit on the edge of the bed, her fingers toying nervously at the frayed folds of the blue-and-white summer-winter coverlet. All the while, he kept murmuring Larissa's name, making Cluney tremble at the tender, passionate sound of his voice. Finally, he coaxed her to lift her gaze to his.

His dark eyes fairly glowed with the light of love, the light of recognition. No stranger could look at her that way. In an instant, she knew for certain that they had loved before. Somewhere far back in the mists of time.

"Hunter," she whispered, not sure what she would say next, not knowing if she could say anything as tears were so close again.

He sensed her turmoil of emotions. "You don't have to say a word, darling. Just let me look at you. Let me touch you, Larissa. I've dreamed of holding you in my arms for so long."

He brushed a tear from her cheek with his fingertips. Their eyes met and held. In that electric moment, she saw a blinding flash of light and felt a tremor shake her soul. It was the same sort of sensation she had experienced when the moonbow appeared.

"My beautiful, wonderful wife," he whispered, letting his fingers trail down her cheeks to caress her quivering lips. "How I do love you."

He slid his hand around her slender waist. He drew her nearer. They were close now, so close that she could feel his warm breath on her face. Then he leaned toward her, pressing his lips to hers. His hand cupped her breast.

Fireworks seemed to go off inside Cluney's head, sending shock waves all through her body. What was this stranger doing to her? But suddenly he was a stranger no longer. His every move, his every touch, his every word stirred warm memories that had been hidden away in the deepest part of her heart. Yet the feelings confused her. Was she remembering Larissa's husband, Hunter, or was it Jeff's touch she recalled with such emotion?

Hunter obviously wanted to make love, but Cluney was afraid. She didn't remember him as a wife should remember her husband. But she had to admit to herself that wasn't really the problem. She wanted to know him—to have him touch her, caress her, and take her to that blissful place that lay somewhere over the moonbow.

But Hunter was wounded, ill, and weak. She couldn't bear the thought of hurting him or making him worse. As much as they wanted each other at this very moment, she wanted more for him to live and be with her always.

Reluctantly, she eased away from him. "You'll have to give me a little more time, Hunter. I have to get used to . . . things."

"Please, Larissa, I've waited so long already." He reached out and caressed her breast once more. "Just let me hold you."

Sitting beside him on the bed, Cluney closed her eyes and let her head fall back. He was teasing her nipple through the threadbare fabric of Lorettie's shabby gown. It felt *wonderful!* When she sighed, his touch became bolder.

"You'll rip the dress," she gasped.

"Then take it off," he begged.

Cluney glanced toward the door.

"They won't come in," he assured her. "They'll know

183

we need privacy right now. Besides, darling, you want to remember, don't you? A woman's mind may forget, but never her body. Her body remembers everything—always and forever."

Without giving her time to answer, Hunter began fumbling at the tiny bone buttons of her bodice with his one good hand. "Damn!" he cursed. "I can't manage these stubborn things."

Cluney gripped his fingers and kissed them. "Let me," she whispered.

His gaze never wavered as she slowly undid the little buttons. She wore nothing underneath, so inch by inch her bare flesh offered itself to his hungry gaze. When she finished her task, Hunter smiled and sighed.

"That's better, darling. Ah, so much better!"

Cluney was still sitting beside him, facing him. He reached out to her and slipped his hand inside her open bodice. She stiffened when his cool fingertips brushed her nipple. He played with her ever so gently for a time. When he felt her relax, he cupped her breast with his hand—fondling her, stroking her, making her ache with longing.

Soon only warmth flowed between them. Ever so carefully, Hunter eased the gown off her shoulders. A shaft of sunlight came through a rip in the curtain at the window to fall across her bare breasts.

"See how you glow," Hunter whispered. "All soft and golden."

Larissa wanted to hear these words and to feel her husband's touch. But the part of her that was still Cluney Summerland felt painfully shy with him suddenly. She moved to cover her sun-brushed breasts with her arms, but Hunter caught her wrists, forcing them down.

184

"No!" he said. "I want to look at you. I want to fill my gaze with your beauty."

Hunter slowly stroked her breasts—one and then the other. Then he left them, letting his fingers trail down her ribs. She moved against his hand. He let it slide up through the valley between her breasts, then on to her shoulders and her slender throat. All the while, the sunlight played over her, gilding her burning flesh.

Finally—her body relaxed—but tingling, Cluney closed her eyes and sighed. And then she cried out softly with surprise as Hunter leaned down and touched one nipple with his tongue. The hot, moist contact was electric.

Cluney's first impulse was to pull away, but his arm was clamped around her waist. She could only sit where she was and let him do as he pleased. She needn't try to fight him since there was no hiding how much he was pleasing her. Her breath came in ragged bursts as he continued stroking her with his tongue. Then his mouth closed over her, sucking at her nipple, torturing it tenderly with little nips of his teeth. Cluney felt as if she were melting. Soon she would be nothing but a pool of golden sunshine on the blue-and-white coverlet.

Satisfied that he had given sufficient attention to her right breast, Hunter moved to her left. A new shock wave raged through Cluney. She trembled all over and tried *so* hard not to moan aloud. But it was no use. As he lazily tongued her nipple, he worked at her gown, easing it down over her hips. A moment later, he pressed his palm against her smooth belly, making her sit up straighter, making her breasts jut forward with even more pride and thrust.

"Hunter, what are you doing to me?" Cluney moaned.

185

"You're making me want things no decent woman should even think about."

He chuckled softly. "You needn't be decent with me. I'm your husband, remember? And I'm starved for you, and I want you to be starved for me. I don't want my wife to be one of those prissy women who only *allows* her husband his due—the kind with a dry mouth and tight thighs. No, Larissa, it would please me no end to have you beg for what I so long to give you as a gift. Lie down here beside me, darling. Let me make you beg."

Silence fell in the room. Hunter's ragged breathing and Cluney's pounding heart were the only sounds. In some other part of the house—what seemed another world—Cluney could hear men talking, pans clanging in the kitchen, footsteps, a slamming door. But it seemed as if she and Hunter existed in a charged realm all their own. She couldn't believe this was happening to her, yet she didn't want it to stop. Hunter Breckinridge was, indeed, an extraordinary man. And, as he kept reminding her, he was her husband.

His hand, playing at her breast again, brought her out of her reverie. She pulled away and closed her bodice.

"Darling?" he said softly. "Won't you lie with me?"

"I can't," Cluney admitted with regret. "I want to, but I can't right now. Not with everyone moving about just on the other side of the door. I'd be too nervous. I'd spoil everything."

He laughed softly. "If you plan to keep putting me off to give me something to live for . . ."

"No!" Cluney cried. "It's the truth, Hunter. We just can't do this now."

"Tonight, then? Will you come to me and share my bed? Lie with me as my wife should?"

His words stunned Cluney. Of course, if she was really his wife, she should sleep with him. But what would Mary Renfro say?

"I'll have to give Mary some sort of explanation. She thinks I was only pretending to be your wife. She has no idea . . ."

Hunter reached out and turned Cluney to look at him. He smiled. "You'll find a way to explain to her, won't you?"

The pleading in his dark eyes mesmerized her. "Yes," she answered. "I'll find a way. I must!"

For several charged moments, Cluney and Hunter could only stare at each other—she, realizing that she had committed herself unconditionally, while he could think only of the woman before him and what pleasures she promised him once the sun had set.

But sounds in the hallway soon broke the spell. Cluney quickly slipped Lorettie's gown back into place and fastened the buttons. She knew her face was flushed. She probably looked as guilty as hell, but there was no help for that. She had herself back in order by the time Mary knocked at the door.

"It's way past noon, Major. Aren't you wanting something?"

He gave Cluney a leering grin and said softly, "How did she guess?"

"Oh, hush that!" Cluney warned playfully. "You let me handle Mary, now, you hear?"

"What are you going to tell her?"

Cluney rolled her eyes. "Something so crazy that no one in his right mind would believe it. But I think it just might be the truth."

When Cluney turned to head for the door, Hunter said, "You're leaving me?"

Cluney couldn't help but laugh at the pitiful tone in his voice. "I have to go talk to Mary now. I'll send Free in. He'll sit with you this afternoon."

"You'll be gone that long?"

"Hunter, I have things to do."

"What, besides talk to Mary?"

She held out the skirt of her sorry dress. "For one thing, I need to find some more clothes. For another, if you want me to sleep in your bed tonight, I'm going to have to clean up a bit. I'm sure I must smell worse than your old hound."

Hunter grinned boyishly. "Well, I suppose I can do without you for a few hours, if you'll be getting ready for tonight." He rubbed a hand over his bristly face. "I'll get that shave before you return."

Cluney was halfway out of the door when he called her again.

"Larissa?"

"Yes, Hunter?"

"I love you."

She smiled and felt her heart dance in her breast.

"Until tonight," she said softly.

"And after tonight," Hunter answered, "we have the rest of eternity to share."

For some unaccountable reason, his mention of eternity made Cluney tremble with a sense of dread. But she managed a smile for her "husband" nevertheless.

# Chapter Eleven

Cluney came out of Hunter's room just in time to catch Mary between errands. She had to tell Mary something before tonight, and there was no time like the present. She did dread it, though.

"How's the major doing?" Mary asked.

"He's resting right now," Cluney answered. "But I think he's feeling better."

"That's good," the woman said distractedly.

She was about to hurry on to her next task when Cluney caught her arm. "Mary, I need to talk to you about something important."

"What's on your mind? Is the major feeling so much better that he's starting to give you problems? I know how men are—when they're *awful* sick, they're like babies, but when they're just *kindly* sick, they can be a peck of trouble."

"No, Hunter's being a perfect patient."

Mary cocked an eyebrow when Cluney called the major by his first name.

"Why don't we sit down?" Cluney said, motioning toward the rough chairs by the fireplace in the main

189

room. "You look like you could use the rest while we talk."

"Whatever," Mary said, glancing about before she took a seat as if something far more important than Cluney's problem occupied her mind.

When they were settled across from each other, Cluney jumped right in. "Mary, I have a confession to make. When I came here, you thought I was your Cousin Tilda's daughter. For all I knew then, I could have been. You see, I had no idea who I really was. I'd lost my memory temporarily."

"My, land!" Mary exclaimed. "You poor child! Took a fall and bumped your head, did you?"

Cluney smiled brightly so Mary wouldn't worry needlessly about her condition. "Well, I'm not sure exactly what happened, but I'm sure I'm going to be all right now. You see, Major Breckinridge—that is, *Hunter*—remembers me. He says I really am his wife, Larissa."

Mary eyed Cluney skeptically. "Go on with you!"

"No, it's true, Mary. See this necklace? Hunter gave it to me years ago."

Mary was still unconvinced. "You remember that, do you? Or did he just say it was so? Now, Cluney, that poor man has been through a lot. And he's been pining away for his wife ever since Free brought him here. Betwixt the pain and the laudanum, he's likely to believe anything and try to make you believe the same. Do you remember him?"

Cluney had to confess that she didn't. "But I'm sure it's the truth, Mary. Awhile ago, I said something to Hunter about when his dog, Trooper, was born. I remember that, Mary, truly I do! I can recall it as plain as something that

190

happened yesterday. How could I know that, if I'm not Larissa?"

"Well, *iffen* it's the truth, then I'm mighty pleased for both of you. But . . ."

"No buts, Mary!" Cluney answered emphatically. "It *is* true! I may not remember the man, but I certainly recall my love for my husband. And once we've been together, I'm sure everything will come back to me."

"*Once you've been together?*" Mary repeated suspiciously.

Cluney bit her bottom lip, embarrassed. She nodded silently.

"You can't mean that man—sick as he is—figures on doing his husbandly duties. Why, the very idea!"

"You're right, Mary, my husband is very ill," Cluney answered quietly. "But all the more reason I should share his bed, if that's what he wants."

"And what do you want?"

Cluney blushed and cast her gaze down. "I want whatever is best for my husband."

"Well, that's more like it," Mary answered. "Share his bed, indeed! It's bad enough he's let that mangy old hound climb up on the quivvers alongside of him."

"Mary, I promised him," Cluney admitted quietly. "I'm not asking your permission; the minister who married us gave that. All I need is a nightgown and a place to bathe."

Mary sat up rigidly and gave a sniff of indignation. "Well, I 'spose that's an end to this discussion. As for bathing, the best place is down to the falls. There's a mineral spring alongside of the big tulip tree. The rest of Lorettie's clothes are in the cedar chest in the major's room. You might as well help yourself, I reckon. She won't be needin' 'em. Now, I've got to get to work and

191

scrape together something for these men to eat for supper. The good Lord always provides, but He's been offering mighty slim pickings of late."

"I'll just get my bag and head on down to the mineral spring, if there's nothing I can do here."

Mary gave Cluney one last, exasperated glance, then waved her along. "You go have your wash. I'll look in on the major in a while."

"Thank you, Mary, for everything."

"You got nothing to thank me for . . . Larissa."

Cluney could tell that the name was like bitter gall in Mary's mouth. The woman didn't believe her story for a minute. The preacher's wife now looked on her as a fallen woman, Cluney suspected. But before long, everyone would know the truth; Cluney was sure of it. If she'd remembered the puppies' birth, she would remember everything in time.

When she tiptoed back into Hunter's room to get her purse, he was sleeping soundly, a smile on his lips. The thought of what he must be dreaming embarrassed Cluney. She hurried out and closed the door soundlessly.

As she went out the front door, she saw the same strange man she had glimpsed upon her arrival. Once more she spoke to him. Once more he disappeared around the side of the house without a word to her.

Dismissing him from her mind, she glanced toward the falls and spied the tulip tree at once, so tall it towered over the others around it. Slinging her bag over her shoulder, she headed for the spring only a short distance from the lodge.

The afternoon was still warm enough so that she wouldn't catch a chill bathing out in the open. The mineral spring, which bubbled up into a Jacuzzi-sized bowl of

# MORE PASSION AND ADVENTURE AWAIT... YOUR TRIP TO A BIG ADVENTUROUS WORLD BEGINS WHEN YOU ACCEPT YOUR FIRST 4 NOVELS ABSOLUTELY *FREE* (AN $18.00 VALUE)

Accept your Free gift and start to experience more of the passion and adventure you like in a historical romance novel. Each Zebra novel is filled with proud men, spirited women and tempestuous love that you'll remember long after you turn the last page.

Zebra Historical Romances are the finest novels of their kind. They are written by authors who really know how to weave tales of romance and adventure in the historical settings you love. You'll feel like you've actually gone back in time with the thrilling stories that each Zebra novel offers.

## GET YOUR FREE GIFT WITH THE START OF YOUR HOME SUBSCRIPTION

Our readers tell us that these books sell out very fast in book stores and often they miss the newest titles. So Zebra has made arrangements for you to receive the four newest novels published each month.

You'll be guaranteed that you'll never miss a title, and home delivery is so convenient. And to show you just how easy it is to get Zebra Historical Romances, we'll send you your first 4 books absolutely FREE! Our gift to you just for trying our home subscription service.

## BIG SAVINGS AND FREE HOME DELIVERY

Each month, you'll receive the four newest titles as soon as they are published. You'll probably receive them even before the bookstores do. What's more, you may preview these exciting novels free for 10 days. If you like them as much as we think you will, just pay the low preferred subscriber's price of just $3.75 each. *You'll save $3.00 each month off the publisher's price.* AND, your savings are even greater because there are never any shipping, handling or other hidden charges—FREE Home Delivery. Of course you can return any shipment within 10 days for full credit, no questions asked. There is no minimum number of books you must buy.

smooth limestone, she found to her delight was warm. She had the urge to dive right in, clothes and all. But she'd have to wear Lorettie's gown back to the house.

Glancing about to make perfectly sure she was alone, Cluney quickly removed her boots and socks, then slipped out of her dress, careful not to snag the thin chain of her moonstone necklace on the buttons. The air felt too cool against her naked flesh. Goose bumps rose on her arms and breasts. She hugged herself and shivered, then stepped into the warm, effervescent water.

She sighed with pleasure as the bubbles foamed up around her, tickling her flesh. Reaching for her bag, she pulled it closer and rummaged through its contents until she found a tiny bar of motel soap. Soon, she was lathered all over. Another search through her purse produced a small bottle of almond-scented shampoo from the same motel. In no time at all, she wore a tiara of iridescent bubbles.

"God, it feels good to be clean!" she said.

She dipped her head underwater to rinse her hair thoroughly, then swam about to get all the soap off her body. When shadows stretched longer, she reluctantly decided that it was time to end her frolic. Since she had no towel, she'd have to stretch out on a rock in the sunshine until she was dry enough to get dressed again. She'd spotted the perfect place—a smooth, flat rock that had been baking in bright sunlight all day.

Before Cluney climbed out, she glanced around again to make sure she was still alone. Satisfied that no one was watching, she scurried over to her rock and stretched out on her stomach.

"Hm-m-m," she sighed. "I'll bet this is as good as any of those nudist beaches on the Riviera."

The warmth of her rock and the sun beating down on her back soon lulled her almost to sleep. Then, suddenly, she felt the damp hair rise at the nape of her neck. Her eyes shot open. She had the unmistakable feeling that someone was watching her. When she heard the sound, she knew she was right. Something moved in the bushes a short distance away. With one hand Cluney grabbed for Lorettie's gown to cover herself, with the other she snatched up her purse.

"Who's there?" she cried, struggling to get into her clothes. "Don't come any closer."

He didn't have to; he stepped out of the bushes right behind her. He grabbed her around the waist with one arm and tangled his other hand through her hair.

Cluney fought for all she was worth, but the guy had caught her by surprise. He had her before she could use any of the defensive moves she had learned in her self-protection classes.

Cluney saw her attacker for the first time when he wrestled her around to face him. It was the silent, bearded man who had watched her leave the lodge.

"I got you now, gal," he said, his foul breath making her gag. "You ain't getting away again. You can't leap no falls once I hog-tie you. I ain't been with a woman for a mighty long time, and I got me a powerful hankerin'."

Cluney had managed to get into her dress before he caught her, but the buttons were undone, leaving her exposed to his leering gaze. When he let go of her hair to grab at her bodice, Cluney jerked away and landed a staggering blow to his chest with her well-loaded purse. Then she ran like the devil himself was chasing her.

But she knew she'd never outrun him. The man was tall and lanky, with long legs that could quickly outdistance

194

her. Fumbling in her purse, her hand closed on the cool, metal cylinder she always carried. She'd never used it before, but there was a first time for everything.

She glanced over her shoulder. He was gaining on her. She could hear him right behind her. She imagined she could feel his hot breath on the back of her neck.

Cluney was ready to whirl and attack, when suddenly a searing pain shot through her neck. He had reached out and grabbed the chain of her necklace. He was twisting it tight, choking her. Cluney felt a trickle of blood as the thin strand of silver bit into her flesh. With a scream and a jerk of her body, she broke his hold on her and whirled to face him.

The next scream was his. Cluney aimed a stream from her canister of Mace right into his face. Dancing about like one possessed, the man coughed and gagged, cursed her and wailed for mercy.

Free from him at last, Larissa headed at top speed for the house. When she finally reached the door, she all but fainted from relief and exertion. Off in the distance, she could still hear her attacker screaming in pain.

Not until Cluney was safely inside the house did she realize that her necklace was gone. She'd dropped her can of Mace, too. She wanted both back and her boots as well, but there was no way in hell she was going back out there right now to search for them. She'd get them later, after she stopped shaking.

"And I'll take Free along with me for protection from that crazy bastard," she assured herself.


B.J. decided to stay at Cumberland Falls until the moon rose on the outside chance that there'd be another moonbow. It didn't happen often, but it was not unheard of for the phenomenon to occur three nights in a row.

Besides, she wanted to see what Wooter Crenshaw was up to. If the moonbow did appear, and if the old man did manage to disappear, B.J. planned to be right on his coattails.

The afternoon was warm for spring. One of those lazy days when even the bees' buzzing seemed to drone softly and slowly. B.J. sprawled on a rock high above the falls and let the sound of the dashing water lull her. Removing her sunglasses, she stared at the gorge far below, watching the play of light and shadow, her eyes peeled for anything that looked the least bit unusual.

Sonny Taylor, arriving at the ranger station for his shift, saw her and sauntered over.

"Spot anything?" he asked.

B.J. shaded her eyes and glanced up. "Nothing," she answered. "How about you?"

He shook his head. "Sheriff Elrod called off the official search—said there wasn't any evidence that anything had happened to your friend. He's convinced she just wandered off, 'to do whatever young folks nowadays do,' as he put it. But some of the fellows from around here are still out in the woods trying to find her. If she's out there, they will."

B.J. stood up and brushed the grass and leaves from her jeans. "I had a talk with your vanishing man, Wooter Crenshaw."

Sonny grinned his gratitude. "Man, that's a relief! I sure figured I was seeing a ghost or something. But this guy is real, huh?"

"He's real all right, but he didn't tell me much. He seems to think he knows where Cluney is, but he wouldn't

196

give me a clue. Wherever she is, he said I couldn't go there. But if there's another moonbow tonight, he plans to try to find her. Go figure, eh?"

"Does this guy's elevator stop at all the floors?"

B.J. shook her head and laughed. "I'm not sure he even has an elevator. He's one weird old dude. Seems harmless, though."

"And you're figuring on staying here till after dark to see what happens, aren't you?"

B.J. gave a brisk nod. "You bet I am! I don't have any idea what's going on around here, but I mean to find out. Cluney's the best friend I've ever had and I won't rest easy till she's back, safe and sound. She's not the type to just take off on some crazy whim."

"Well, I hope she does turn up—and soon." Ranger Taylor seemed distracted suddenly. He glanced all around, then turned back to B.J., frowning. "Hey, you haven't seen an old sorry-looking hound around here, have you?"

"No. You missing your dog?"

Sonny laughed. "He's not mine, he just thinks he is. He took up with me a few days back. Every afternoon when I come to work, he lopes over, begging for a handout. I brought him a steak bone today—figured he'd go crazy over it. Now he's nowhere around."

B.J. thought for a minute, then said, "You know, I'm sure I heard a hound baying at the moon last night. Maybe he figured the pickings were better on the other side of the moonbow or maybe he followed Cluney, wherever she disappeared to."

"He'll turn up," Sonny assured himself. "Always does. Come to think of it, I know where he sleeps. Want to walk over there with me and have a look? It's not far."

"Sure," B.J. said. "Why not?"

Sonny led the way past the gift shop and the ranger station, then into the woods and over a rise. Beyond a copse of trees lay a clearing in the forest with a mound of earth in the center and charred bricks scattered around.

"I never saw this place before," B.J. said.

"Then you never walked over this far from the gorge, 'cause it's been here right along."

"What was it?" B.J. asked. "Somebody's house?"

"That's what they say," he answered. "I've heard tell that back during the Civil War a preacher and his wife lived here and took in wounded soldiers. There were some mineral springs nearby and the water was supposed to be real healthy." He pointed across the clearing to an old iron fence. "That's the burying ground, where Preacher Renfro and his wife laid the ones to rest that were beyond their help."

"Wow!" B.J. exclaimed. "I'm a nut for old graveyards. Can we take a look?"

"Sure. Follow me. It's quite a sight—Union and Confederate soldiers lying side by side. I guess their taking in Yanks and Rebs is what caused the Renfros to leave the area finally. There were some harsh feelings toward them from both sides before the war was over. When the house burned, no one could ever say for sure whether it was by accident or what."

Rhododendrons flamed pink and scarlet in the deep shadows between the graves. Rough slabs of rock had been carved crudely to give names, dates, and where the soldiers were from. Maine, Georgia, New York, South Carolina, and all points, north and south. Perhaps twenty graves dotted the overgrown enclosure.

"Hey?" Sonny called out suddenly.

"What's wrong?" B.J. asked, sure that something was by the sound of his voice and the dark look on his face.

"We must have had some vandals up here. There's a marker missing. I remember it just as plain as can be because he was the only one from Kentucky buried up here."

"But why would anyone steal a grave marker?" B.J. shuddered at the thought.

"Beats me, but it's gone. And it was right here just yesterday. 'Major Hunter Breckinridge, Lexington, Kentucky.' "

"Say *what*?" B.J. gasped. "Hunter Breckinridge?"

"Yep, that was his name all right."

"I know him!" B.J. cried.

When Sonny looked at her real hard, she stammered, "Well . . . I mean, I know *about* him. My friend, Cluney, found his diary hidden away in the college library. She got a real fixation about the guy. He lost his wife during the war. She didn't die, she just disappeared. Cluney's spent all her free time lately trying to find out what happened to both of them, but she didn't have much luck."

"Then she's probably the one who swiped his tombstone."

"Cluney?" B.J. scowled at the big ranger. "She'd never do such a thing!"

"Wait . . . a . . . minute!" Sonny edged between the graves, trying not to step on any sleeping soldiers. "Something's not right about this. Damned if I can figure it."

"What is it?" B.J. hurried over to stand beside Sonny.

"Man, this is so weird!" he whispered. "It's not just the stone that's gone, the whole damn grave is missing."

"What do you mean?" B.J. cocked her head and looked

up at him. His suntanned face had gone pale—the color of ashes.

"You see there," he said, pointing. "That's Captain Van Dyke from New York and right beside him now is Private McClenny from Florida. Well, Major Breckinridge used to lie right between the two of them. But you see, now there's no space. Van Dyke and McClenny are slap side by side, like there never was another grave between them."

B.J. rubbed the goose bumps that had just risen on her arms. "Are you *sure*?"

"Of course, I am! Why, I've been here a hundred times or more. I even recorded all the names and dates and where they were from, hoping I might be able to contact some of these fellows' descendants. I'll show you my chart back at the office, if you want."

"I believe you," B.J. said. "But how do you explain this?"

Sonny Taylor took off his hat and scratched his head. He gave a deep sigh, then said, "I can't! *No way!*"

"Let's get out of here, okay?" B.J. was already heading for the broken-down fence. "This place is giving me the creeps."

Ranger Taylor wasn't far behind her. He'd heard of some mighty strange things happening around Cumberland Falls, but this beat everything.

When they reached the clearing and the mound that had once been the Renfro lodge, B.J. stopped suddenly. The place felt cold to her, as if she'd just stepped into a freezer locker. She tried to move, but found she couldn't.

"Hey, Sonny, I think this place is haunted. It's grave-cold," she called out with false bravado. "You better come over here. Quick!"

He laughed. "You must be standing over the crack."

"The *what*?"

"There's kind of a seam in the earth somewhere around here. Cold air comes up from the caves down below, or that's what I've been told. Even on the hottest day, you can be sweating up a storm, then you hit that crack and all of a sudden you got air-conditioning up your pant leg."

"Man, is that a relief! I thought the buggers had me for sure."

Once her fear dissolved, B.J. found she could move again. She glanced at the ground to see if she could see any sign of a crack, but only the mound of century-old debris lay around her. Something gleamed in the sun. She reached down.

"Hey, look, it's an old medicine bottle." Scattering more of the earth with the toe of her boot, she spied something else and picked it up. "A piece of crockery with a fancy transfer design," she said.

"There's bound to be all kinds of old junk in that pile," Sonny pointed out. "The Renfros were still living here when the place burned down. Everything they owned went up in the blaze. They were lucky to get out alive, I've heard tell."

"Did they have cans of Mace back then?" B.J. asked, eyeing a shining canister a few feet away. "Hey, that's just like the ones Cluney and I carry. Our instructor in a class we took for self-protection sold them to us." She picked the can up and frowned, feeling an uneasy tingle along her spine. "Yes, it's exactly like the one I have in my purse right now."

"Hey, in that case, remind me to keep my distance," Sonny joked.

B.J. continued turning over bricks and kicking away weathered fragments of charred wood until the glint of silver caught her eye.

"Hey, Sonny! Wasn't there supposed to have been a silver mine under the falls?"

He laughed. "Some guy spread that tale around in the eighteen-fifties, trying to sell land up here, but nobody ever found any silver that I know of."

"Well, I just found some!"

B.J. dropped to her hands and knees, digging at the gleam in the dirt. When she pulled the thing free, she gave a sharp cry.

"What is it?" Sonny called.

"Oh, my God! Oh, no! And there's blood on it!"

He was beside her instantly. "Let me see. What did you find?"

B.J.'s hand trembled as she held up the necklace, then her whole body began shaking uncontrollably.

"This belongs to Cluney," she whispered. "Her moonstone necklace. She always wore it. And, look! The stone is all smeared with blood." She pointed to the canister, lying where she'd dropped it. "And that's her Mace. Somebody attacked her on this very spot. She tried to protect herself, but it looks like she failed. Oh, dear God . . . *Cluney!*"

"Heaven help her!" Ranger Taylor groaned. "Looks like she might've been kidnapped. I'd better call Sheriff Elrod."


After finding Cluney's necklace, B.J. was more determined than ever to remain at Cumberland Falls until the moon rose.

"Why don't you go on home?" Sonny begged. "I'll keep an eye on our old guy."

"No!" B.J. was adamant. "If Wooter does take off for parts unknown, I need to be here to follow him. It wouldn't do any good for you to follow him. I know Cluney; you don't. Besides, now that Sheriff Elrod's men are searching again, I can't leave the park anyway. They're bound to find something. I'd go crazy if I was way down the mountain, waiting all alone."

So B.J. set up watch in the ranger's office, fortified with hot coffee and pleasant company. There was one thing about Ranger Sonny Taylor—he sure was a talker.

"Were you raised around here, B.J.?" Dire circumstances had put them on a first-name basis.

"Nope. Born and raised on the French Broad River in Tennessee."

"That's pretty country. How come you left there to come to the coal-mining section of Kentucky?" he wanted to know.

They were both in his office, keeping a sharp eye on the falls even as they chatted. It was dark. The moon was on the rise. But so far Wooter Crenshaw had yet to put in an appearance.

"I don't know exactly why I came; I just know I had to come. It's funny, but I never did feel like Tennessee was the right place for me. And there was something about Kentucky . . . well, I just couldn't stay away. I've had this feeling all my life that I'd find myself in these mountains. It's like there's some secret here that I could never discover anywhere else on earth."

"Like Kentucky, do you?" He gave her a big grin and handed her a donut.

She smiled back and accepted his chocolate-glazed offering. "I guess you could say that."

"You married?"

"Nope," she answered. "Never even close." She laughed. "Maybe that's the secret I'm supposed to discover in Kentucky—how to find and hold a fellow."

"You know the kind you want?"

"Oh, sure! I could practically draw you a picture of him." She tapped her temple with one finger. "I've got him right up here, even though I've never seen him. Seems like I was born knowing what he'll look like and how it'll be between us."

Sonny stretched and gave a big yawn. "Well, you're one up on me. I been married and divorced twice already. Looks like I never know what I want. I just know what I *don't* want, after it's too late and I'm stuck with it."

Suddenly, B.J. sprang to her feet and peered out the window. "Hey, looka there! It's Wooter pulling into the parking lot."

"You sure?"

"He's the only one around here I know of that has COFFINS painted in three-foot letters on the side of his wagon. I'm going to sneak out there and keep an eye on him."

Sonny rose, too, and looked out. "Okay, but you be real careful, now. If anything happens, you holler."

She turned and gave him a wink. "You can bet on it!"

B.J. eased out and went around the side of the building so Wooter wouldn't spot her in the lights. Lurking in the shadows, she watched him urge his mules closer toward the edge of the gorge, near the spot where she and Cluney had been the night before. She followed, but at a safe distance to avoid detection.

204

Wooter sang a toneless song to himself as he climbed off his wagon and headed down the stone steps. He had no flashlight, nor did B.J. She wondered how he could maneuver so well in the dark. She was having her share of problems—stumbling over loose rocks and tripping on roots. The moon was out, but not high enough yet to be of much help.

Then it happened! Just as B.J. reached the head of the stone staircase that led down to the overlook, a bright glow shimmered over the falls. She looked down and saw that Wooter was now standing in the middle of the brilliant light. He turned and glanced up at her.

"Go back!" he warned.

"No! I'm coming with you!" she cried.

Taking advantage of the light that now blazed around Wooter's form, B.J. hurried down the stairs, slipping and sliding on the damp, mossy stone. Suddenly, a brilliant flash blinded her. She cried out and threw a hand over her eyes. The next thing she knew, her foot slipped and she was bounding down the stairs, tumbling head over heels.

She screamed, flinging her arms out, trying to grab hold of something to stop her fall. But it was no use.

Wooter's face flashed before her, then Cluney's face, then everything went black.

The next B.J. knew, she was back inside the ranger station. Sonny Taylor was bending over her, holding a damp cloth to her forehead.

"Don't try to move," he cautioned. "Something may be broken. I've called an ambulance. You just lie easy till they get here."

"Sonny," she whispered through bruised lips, "I saw

her. I saw Cluney. She's out there, just like Wooter said. He found her and he's brought her back. I saw her!"

"Take it easy now," Sonny soothed. "I don't know what you saw, but old Wooter's left us again, wagon and all. I followed you out there, scared of what might happen. I saw him down on the ledge a second before you took your tumble. But when I got down to you, he was gone—vanished!"

B.J. closed her eyes and moaned.

It was nearly dark that evening and Cluney had almost recovered from her episode earlier that afternoon when the unexpected visitor arrived. She was still shaken, but was trying to hide it. So far, her bearded attacker hadn't returned to the lodge. She'd asked Mary a few guarded questions about the man and found out he was a Reb from Alabama named Jeb Smith, who'd wandered up one day dazed and belligerent, but with a wound in his leg that needed tending. So Mary had taken him in and nursed him along with the others.

"He's all mended now," Mary had told Cluney, "except in the head. Crazy as a bedbug, he is, all the time talking about some woman that leaped over the falls. I don't know why he keeps hanging around here. Looks like he'd go on his way. I reckon he's just hiding out from the war. Most of these boys don't look forward to going back. To tell you the truth, I figure he deserted and he can't go back."

Cluney confided in Mary that she thought he might have changed his mind quite suddenly about leaving. She only hoped she was right.

The two women were folding bandages by the fire in

the main room when Mary cocked her head and asked, "Did you hear that?"

"Hear what?" Cluney asked. "All I hear is Free outside splitting wood."

"I'm going out and have a look-see."

Mary walked over to the front door and peered out, then gave a glad cry as she ran into the yard.

"Well, bless my soul! Look who's coming up the mountain. And bringing a wagonload of supplies. If he ain't a welcome sight. I declare, if I had to eat one more squirrel, I'd go to burying nuts and jumping through the treetops. Free, run over yonder and unhitch them mules for him."

"Yes, ma'am, Miz Mary."

Her mind on other matters, Cluney listened only distractedly to Mary's voice as she welcomed their gift-bearing visitor. Cluney had to agree, though, that something other than squirrel would be most welcome on the menu. Hunter would be pleased, too. Maybe she'd fix the two of them a little candlelight supper. Yes, that would be nice, she decided. If only she had a bottle of wine . . .

Just then the door banged open. Mary ushered her visitor into the room.

"Cluney, look who's come. It's my friend from Baldy Rock. Wooter Crenshaw! And he's as welcome a sight as I ever saw." She gave the old man a squeeze. "Bless my soul, if you don't show up ever' time when I'm just about at my wit's end and the larder's down to rat droppings."

Cluney spun around—eyes wide, mouth open. There before her stood the little old coffin-maker, a jug of moonshine in his hand, which he gave to Mary Renfro.

"Thank the Lord, you brought more medicine!" she cried. "We been needin' it bad."

"Wooter?" Cluney could hardly believe her eyes.

He touched the brim of his battered straw hat, smiled real wide, and said, "How do, little girl?" just as if this were any normal day when his sign was out and Cluney had stopped by his place for a chat.

# Chapter Twelve

Cluney couldn't quite believe her eyes. She had almost convinced herself that she was, by some hook or crook, back in the nineteenth century. Then up pops Wooter, making her doubt her own senses. Once again, she felt as if she had blundered into the rehearsal for one of the college plays and she was the only one on stage without a script.

As Mary and Wooter talked a mile a minute and Free stood by silently, Cluney sat back to listen and observe, trying to figure out if she was dreaming or what.

Her gaze roamed the room. If this was a play, the costumes and props were certainly genuine. There stood Mary in her homespun frock and long, muslin apron. Behind her, Free looked the part of a slave in his baggy trousers, much-patched shirt, and ill-fitting boots. But then, Wooter appeared much the same as the other two. He wore washed-out overalls and a red flannel shirt that could have come from either century. Even his gun was as ancient as the hills.

As for the lodge, Cluney knew from experience that it had no electricity, no indoor plumbing, no heat except that provided by the big fireplaces. Even the poorest home in the mountains had some sort of fuel oil heater in the 1990s.

"Little girl?" Wooter's voice interrupted Cluney's thoughts. "You and me need to talk a spell. I got a message for you from a friend of yours."

Cluney sat up, all attention. "Miss Redbird?"

"Nope, a young gal name of B.J."

Mary Renfro laughed delightedly. "Well, I swan! I figured you two must be acquainted, both of you coming from Baldy Rock. I reckon I was right." She motioned to Free. "Come on. I need to get some supper going now that I got victuals to cook. And you better go set a spell with the major, give the girl time to catch up on things with Wooter."

Once Mary and Free had left, Cluney said, "Wooter, how in the world did you get here?"

He snatched a straw out of the broom by the fireplace and chewed at it thoughtfully for a minute, then perching it in the side of his mouth, he said, "Same way as you did. I come over the moonbow."

"Is *that* what happened to me? I wasn't sure how I got here. I wasn't even sure I really was here."

"Well, now you know." He inspected her face closely. "How's it been for you?"

"Strange and scary at times, but sometimes it's wonderful."

He nodded and scratched at his beard. "I reckon Redbird was right, then."

"Right about what?"

"She vowed and declared you needed to come back here—to have another chance where you started out."

"Where I started out?" Cluney parroted.

210

"Yep. I figured you'd of guessed that by now. You was from here all along. But something happened to you awhile back, something dreadful, me and Redbird figure. The only way you could escape was by way of the moonbow, so you took it. That's when you wandered up to the Summerland cabin, out of your head."

"Then I really am Larissa Breckinridge?" Wooter's words seemed to confirm her suspicions.

"According to Redbird you are. She told me she didn't want to say nothing while your ma and pa were still living. She was mighty fond of your folks and claimed it would have broke their hearts had you come back sooner."

"So, this is really the secret she's been promising to tell me for years." Cluney thought that over for a few moments, then looked back to Wooter. "But why didn't she explain everything to me? It would have been so much easier if I'd known my true identity before I came back here."

He cocked his head and squinted at Cluney. "Would you have believed her?"

"Not a word of it," Cluney admitted.

"That's what Redbird figured. You had to come here to believe it was so."

Cluney sat for several moments, shaking her head in silence.

"That friend of yours is sure stirring things up back yonder," Wooter said. "I don't know what's going to happen next."

Cluney tried to think how she'd feel if B.J. had disappeared without a trace. "I imagine she is. I wish there were some way I could let her know I'm all right."

"Well, she almost come right along with me. Had she

made it down those steps in time to grab my britches leg, she'd of been standing here right now."

"She tried to follow you?"

"Damn right! Near about did, too. Come next full moon, I figure she'll try coming over by herself. She's stubborn, that one!"

Cluney laughed, but she was aching inside. She truly missed B.J. She wished she were here. Everything would be easier if she could share her feelings with her best friend.

"Is there any way for her to come here?"

Wooter switched his straw to the other side of his mouth, then said, "Nope! Not a way in the world unless she's needed. Major Breckinridge needed you. Mary Renfro needed me to bring supplies. But who'd need one more poor slave wench over here?"

Cluney bristled. "B.J. Jackson is no slave and never has been! She's a fine, educated woman—a librarian."

"You can't hardly be a librarian 'less you can read," Wooter countered. "And this day and time—right here, right now—there's laws against teaching her people their letters. Ole Free can't read a word. Ask him, if you don't believe me."

Cluney's mind was clicking away, trying to figure out all of this. "So, if B.J. did manage to get over the moonbow, she'd lose everything she's worked for all her life. She'd be just like Free—homeless, penniless, just emancipated, but with nothing to gain from that freedom."

"That's about the size of it," Wooter answered. "I done warned her, but I don't think it took. She's bullheaded that one. Come right up to my cabin, looking for you. And fed Ma and Pa peppermint candies, mind you. They 'bout went crazy. You know what happens when a 'coon

212

washes a peppermint? My ma and pa's real neat. They won't eat nothing till it's washed down real good. Well, them striped candies melted clean away. My folks didn't have nothing left but a pan of syrupy pink water. Mad as hell, Pa was!"

Cluney put her hand to her lips to hide a smile, but tears flooded her eyes. What she wouldn't give to see B.J. and Ma and Pa Crenshaw again! She missed them. She missed everything in the twentieth century.

As if reading her thoughts, Wooter asked quietly, "You gonna make it all right here, little girl?"

Cluney wiped at her tears and shook her head. "I don't know, Wooter. I just don't know."

He leaned down close and looked real hard at her. "What happened to your neck? You got blood on it."

She put her hand to the place where her necklace had cut her. It felt sticky and tender; her necklace was gone. Quickly, she explained to Wooter about her bearded attacker and how she'd fended him off.

Wooter first frowned, then cackled. "You don't have to worry no more about that sorry sonuvabitch. I passed him on the road—me coming up and him going down. He was hightailin' it, I can tell you. Staggering around like a mad dog and whooping fit to kill. I reckon your Mace done a job on him. He won't be back."

"Thank God!" Cluney breathed. "I've never been so scared in my life." Suddenly, she stopped and thought. "Yes, I have! I've been exactly that frightened before and for the same reason. That's not the first time that man's come after me. It was a long time ago, but I remember now."

"How'd you get away from him the other time?"

She looked Wooter straight in the eye and answered, "I

escaped over the moonbow, that's how. My memory's coming back, Wooter. It really is!"

"Talk to the major," Wooter said solemnly. "He'll help you remember everything."

"I'm almost afraid to remember," she admitted.

"There's no fear like the unknown, little girl. You take my advice, you find out everything you can as quick as you can. Before it's too late."

Cluney never got a chance to ask Wooter what he meant by his final comment. With a quick nod, he turned and headed out the door.

The lodge that evening took on almost a party atmosphere. Delicious smells wafted through the house all afternoon as Mary cooked up ham and corn and squash. She even found the makings for a sweet potato pie. The men who were ambulatory came down to the big kitchen for their meal. But Cluney had other plans in mind.

"Mary, I'd like to take my supper into Hunter's room and eat with him, if that's all right with you."

The last ounce of disapproval had vanished from Mary's eyes. She smiled at Cluney and patted her arm. "According to what Wooter told me after you two talked, that's exactly where you belong, Larissa Breckinridge, with your husband." Then she leaned close and whispered, "When it comes time to dress for bed, you put on the pretty batiste gown that's in the bottom drawer wrapped in brown paper. I made that myself for my Lorettie's wedding night. But she never got to use it, poor child. I think she'd like you wearing it for her tonight."

Cluney leaned over and gave the motherly woman a

quick kiss on the cheek. "Thank you, Mary, for everything."

Mary whacked Cluney's behind with her big wooden spoon. "Go on with you, now. Don't you keep that man of yours waiting a minute longer."

Turning quickly, Cluney snatched her big purse off the wall peg where she'd hung it while she was helping Mary with supper. The strap slipped from her hand and the contents scattered over the board floor. Cluney scrambled to retrieve everything before Mary or any of the others saw the odd assortment of articles she carried around with her and guarded so carefully. She wasn't sure she could explain about her ballpoint pen or tampons or the package of condoms, and her charge cards would certainly baffle them.

But she wasn't quick enough. Free, standing nearby, spied a photograph that slipped out of her wallet. He only meant to help her pick up her things, but when he caught sight of B.J.'s photo, he grabbed for it.

"What's this?" he demanded in a deep, gravelly voice.

"It's only a picture of a friend of mine. Let me have it, please."

Free was on his knees, holding the snapshot with his big hands. He was trembling all over and tears ran down his cheeks.

"My Belle," he murmured. "It's my Belle."

"Excuse me?" Cluney said.

He glared at Cluney, accusation in his eyes. "Where'd you get this likeness of my Belle."

"Free, I'm sorry, but you're mistaken. That's a friend of mine named B.J. Jackson."

"She live around here?" he demanded.

215

Cluney shook her head. "No. She lives a long way away. Now, please, give it to me."

Free reluctantly surrendered the photo, but it was clear he was unconvinced by Cluney's explanation.

"I been missing my Belle for two long years. I mean to find her. I need her something powerful. I do love that woman, Miz Larissa!" He pointed one big finger at B.J.'s face. "And that be her, no doubt about it."

Cluney didn't stay to argue any longer. Slinging her bag over her shoulder, she lifted the tray she'd prepared for herself and Hunter and left the kitchen.

When she entered the bedroom, Cluney found Hunter shaved, his hair trimmed, and his face beaming. His color was better than when she had seen him earlier. All in all, he looked like a new man. If only the bandages weren't there to remind her of his true condition.

"High time you got here!" he scolded good-naturedly. "I was beginning to think you'd forgotten you have a husband."

Cluney placed the tray on a table near the bed and smiled at him. "You look fine, Hunter. Are you feeling better?"

For the briefest instant, a shadow seemed to pass over his face. Then he chuckled and said, "How could I not be feeling better with you here beside me, Larissa?"

Cluney's emotions were in true turmoil. More than anything, she longed to keep everything at a surface level and provide Hunter with a pleasant evening. But she had so many questions, so many doubts, and this man who claimed to be her husband seemed to be the only one she could turn to for answers and comfort.

"Hunter, can we talk for a minute before we have supper?"

He nodded, his smile fading at the solemn tone in her voice. "I'd like that," he answered quietly. "Is something bothering you, darling?"

Cluney sat down on the side of the bed. She shrugged and spread her palms before her in a helpless gesture. Hunter took her hand and held it.

"I don't even know where to start," she admitted. "I've always felt that I was a very logical person, but what's happening to me at the moment defies all logic. At times, I doubt my own sanity."

"You've been through a rough time, sweetheart," Hunter soothed. "It may take you awhile to regain your equilibrium and your memory. But we're together again now. We can work things out, you and I."

She gave him a brave smile and gripped his hand in both of hers. "Yes, I believe we can," she whispered. "And I think my memory is beginning to return, Hunter. I was talking to Wooter Crenshaw, a friend of Mary's, this afternoon. Something he said sparked a memory—not a very pleasant one, I'm afraid. I remember being chased by a man or men through these woods. I was all alone and I've never been so frightened in my life."

Hunter drew her close and kissed her cheek. "Those aren't the sort of memories I want you to recall, my love. There are so many beautiful things we shared that I want to tell you about."

Cluney looked into his dark eyes and felt the impact of his gaze. "I want you to help me remember, Hunter. I want to recall everything we ever did, everything we ever said to each other. I want to love you the same way I used to."

Hunter's whisper almost escaped Cluney. He said, "I want you to love me even more than you used to."

217

While the new Larissa spread the bedside table for her husband, Hunter watched her closely. He couldn't guess what had transformed her, but his wife was not the same flighty young woman he had married. Granted, he had won Larissa's hand, but he had never believed that he had won her heart completely. His brother's shadow had always loomed between them, larger than ever after Jordan told him of Larissa's clandestine visit to Broad Acres shortly before their wedding.

Hunter had hoped that in time he could make Larissa love him completely, with all her heart. But there had been no time after their marriage to induce that miracle, if indeed such a feat was even possible. And Hunter realized now that he had behaved badly and handled his wife all wrong from the moment they were married. All she had ever needed was to be truly loved. Certainly, he loved her, but had he ever bothered to show her just how much? Had he allowed his jealousy to disrupt their love even after their marriage?

Now, miracle of miracles, Larissa seemed to have forgotten Jordan entirely. Could Hunter find it in his heart to forgive and forget his brother's transgressions as well? Could he possibly hope to claim Larissa's love for his own at long last?

She was talking to him, saying that she hoped he liked ham and squash and sweet potato pie. Didn't she realize that none of that mattered—that supper was only an unavoidable interruption on this night of nights?

"A feast," she called it. A feast was what he wanted, all right. He longed to feast his eyes on her beautiful, pale body. And once he had her beside him, he would let his

218

mouth feast at her lips and her breasts. His hands ached with his need to touch her warm, soft flesh. He wanted to hear her voice in the darkness, begging for him as she sighed and moaned at his tender caresses. Such was his hunger, and such would be his feast.

"Aren't you hungry, Hunter?"

"Oh, yes!" he said in a voice, raspy with emotion. "I am truly starved!"

How tenderly she ministered to his every need. She fed him slowly, carefully, dabbing at his mouth with a napkin. She talked, she laughed, she smiled into his eyes. He would have eaten his supper with greater haste, but she seemed to be drawing it out, urging his hunger for her to grow ever stronger.

Finally, he cleaned his plate. He watched, fascinated, as Larissa tidied up—something she would never have dreamed of doing in the old days. "What are servants for?" she would have said.

She rose from the bed, tray in hand. "I'll just take this to the kitchen now."

"But you'll be back, won't you?"

She smiled at his urgent tone. "Oh, yes, Hunter. I'll be back."

Before she left the room, she pulled out the bottom drawer of the chest and removed something wrapped in brown paper. Placing it on the chair beside the bed, she turned and smiled at him. "I'll *definitely* be back!"

Once she was gone, Hunter reached over and opened the brown paper. Inside, he found a dainty nightie—all white and soft and pure.

"Ah, Larissa!" he said with a sigh. "If it weren't for the pain in my shoulder and the deeper pain in my groin, I'd swear I'd died and gone to heaven."

True to her word, Larissa slipped back into the room only minutes later. She seemed nervous and uncertain suddenly.

"Do you still want me to stay with you tonight?"

"Need you ask?" he answered with invitation heavy in his voice. "You know I do, darling."

She nodded, unsmiling, looking as jittery as a bride. "Then I'll just slip behind the curtain and change. I won't be long."

It was dark outside and only a single candle guttered on the bedside table. The room was cloaked in shadows. But still Cluney felt the need to change somewhere beyond Hunter's gaze. Quickly, she eased behind the tattered drape that cordoned off one corner of the room for privacy. As she slipped on Lorettie's gown, she could almost feel Hunter's eyes on the burlap curtain.

Even though she had bathed that afternoon, she took time to pour water from the ironstone pitcher into the bowl and wipe herself all over once again. Then she splashed on some lilac water Mary had given her. She was stalling for time and she knew it. But suddenly she felt so afraid. Hunter might claim to be her husband, but to Cluney he was still a virtual stranger.

"Darling?" Hunter called softly. "The night is slipping away."

"Don't be impatient. I'll be only a minute longer."

He laughed. "Those are the very same words you used on our wedding night. Remember?"

No! She didn't remember. That's exactly what made her so nervous at the moment. He knew what they had been to each other and how they had been when they were together, while Cluney remembered nothing of that time. She felt certain things for him that made her realize she must be his wife. But a wife with no memory is not a wife at all. She is little more than a virgin bride about to face the unknown.

She was tempted to call out to him and ask him if he was sure he wanted this. He called to her instead.

"Larissa darling, do you know how long I've dreamed of this night? Do you know how I've ached to hold you again? We never really had a chance to come to know each other as husband and wife. I want that chance! I've lived for it."

Cluney realized in that moment that there was no backing out. Hunter Breckinridge had, indeed, lived for tonight—for the night when he could be a husband to his long-lost wife once again.

Steeling herself, Cluney stepped from behind the curtain. The gown was thin—just how thin she realized the moment she saw Hunter's gaze travel over her. Blushing, casting her eyes down to avoid his, she glimpsed the dark rosettes of her nipples through the sheer white batiste.

"Come here!" he ordered in a husky voice, throwing the covers back for her as he spoke.

Cluney hesitated only a moment. Then she sped across the room and climbed into the bed. Hunter flipped the covers over her.

"Come closer, darling," he commanded.

The bed felt warm—a good, human kind of warmth, all cozy and private and filled with secret promise.

"That's better," he whispered when they were touching, thigh to thigh. "Now, I want you to close your eyes, Larissa. I'm going to tell you a story."

"But—"

221

"Sh-h-h!" He silenced her with a light kiss. "Just listen and remember, my love."

In his deep voice, with its husky Southern drawl, Hunter lulled her with his tale of times gone by.

"Remember, darling, that afternoon shortly after your fifteenth birthday when we went out riding, I on Black Jack and you sitting sidesaddle on your pretty white mare, Dancer? As I recall, you were dressed in a fetching new outfit—a riding costume of sky-blue. I didn't dare tell you at the time, but I could hardly keep my eyes from that finely cut coat with the shiny brass buttons. The way it cupped your proud breasts—well, it gave me ideas I shouldn't have had toward one of your tender years.

The tone of his voice and his quaint confession gave Cluney a certain tingle. She smiled, but kept silent, waiting for him to continue.

"I remember how your skirt blew up slightly when we were at full gallop, even though it was weighted with shot to protect your modesty. What a surge I felt when I got an unexpected glimpse of your snowy, lace-edged petticoats. At that moment, I had the greatest urge to call a halt in order to tumble you right there in the woods."

Cluney almost gasped aloud. Not at Hunter's admission of guilt, but at something his words recalled to her mind. He was telling her his feelings on that sunny afternoon. But suddenly she knew Larissa's feelings as well.

Hunter *should* have tumbled her in the woods, then and there. It would have served the little witch right! Besides, that was exactly what Larissa had wanted, what she had planned, in fact.

The too-tight cut of her jacket was no mere slip of the seamstress's hand. Larissa herself had moved the brass buttons to make the jacket tight in order to accentuate her

222

breasts. As for her shot-weighted riding skirt blowing up, Larissa had removed the bits of lead from the hem only an hour before she set out with Hunter, hoping that a glimpse of lace might give him certain ideas.

And what would she have done had Hunter fallen for the bait? Cluney wondered. With only a moment's thought, she knew. Larissa Courtney, the belle of Fayette County, would have allowed Hunter to have his way with her. Then promptly afterward she would have branded him a cad, only to go running to his brother Jordan for comfort and hopes of a proposal. Damned if the fine Miss Courtney wasn't a nineteenth-century prick-teaser!

Cluney opened her eyes and stared up into the darkness, hardly daring to breathe. *Hunter must* never *know*! she told herself.

With that thought still in Cluney's mind, his next words came as a total shock. "I knew what you were up to that afternoon, my darling little flirt. You gave me every invitation, every opportunity to have at you. And, oh, I was sorely tempted! You put me through hell and then some that afternoon. But I guessed what you were up to. You were trying to get to Jordan through me. You'd wanted him all those years because he always said he'd never marry. He was a challenge. Well, you see, Larissa, there was one thing you never bargained for. I truly loved you! I still do, in spite of everything. I refused that afternoon to be led astray, no matter how hard you tried, no matter how many tricks you had up your pretty sleeve."

"The grove!" Cluney whispered suddenly, not even sure why she had said it.

Hunter chuckled. "Ah, yes, the grove! What a lovely oak glen that was! So private. 'Our own piece of paradise,' you called it. *My* own piece of *hell*, it turned out to be. You claimed the horses needed a drink at the spring. True enough. It was a hot day. Just how hot I didn't realize until you let me kiss you. Ah, that swift little tongue of yours flicking into my mouth. Do you know what that does to a man?"

He paused and laughed softly, waiting for his wife to answer. But Cluney lay, silent and blushing, beside him, so he continued.

"Yes, I'm sure you knew what you were doing to me. Then you removed your tight jacket, pleading the heat. And what harm between friends, your unfastening a few buttons? Before I knew it, my hands were on your cool breasts. A moment more and my mouth would have followed the lead of my fingers. Had that happened, all would have been lost, including your precious virginity, my darling. That was a real struggle for me—mind over manhood. But had I let you win that humid afternoon, you would not be here now. And I would have no right to do this."

Cluney gasped softly as Hunter's hand stroked her breast. She lay rigid as he fondled her almost roughly. Then his touch gentled and she sighed with pleasure, feeling a liquid warmth flow through her.

"Do you remember that afternoon, Larissa?"

"I do," she answered honestly. "I remember everything about it. And you're right," she admitted. "I planned the seduction. But you were too smart for me. You knew all along?"

"I did."

"Then why did you let me . . . ?"

"Because I loved you. And I wanted you—not just for that one moment, but forever. And because I believed that, in time, I could make you love me, too."

224

"But that's crazy, Hunter!" Cluney said. "You should have turned Laris . . . me over your knee and given me a good spanking."

He laughed. "Don't think I didn't consider that—more than once."

"And now?"

"You've changed. You've grown up, darling. Either that, or you've refined your ability as an actress. I'm not sure I care which as long as you're with me again and seem happy that we're together."

"Oh, I am!" Cluney assured him.

"What happened when you went away that changed you? You never seemed sure of your affections before. Can't you tell me what's made the difference, Larissa?"

All the while they talked, Hunter continued his fondling caresses. Now one finger was circling her nipple. He would squeeze it gently from time to time, mounding pleasure upon pleasure for the object of his tender torment.

Cluney caught her breath between words as she spoke. "I can't tell you yet, because I really don't know. I went away. Far away. For a long time. I didn't know who I was . . . where I'd come from. I didn't remember you, Hunter, or anything from my other life. I still don't remember much."

"You remember this, don't you, darling?"

Hunter's hand slipped down over Cluney's belly. Easing her gown up, he slid his fingers between her thighs. The moment he touched her, Cluney began to tremble. His stroke was light, but sure. Obviously, he knew Larissa's body better than Cluney herself knew it. In moments, he brought her to the very brink of orgasm.

"Oh, please, Hunter!" she begged. "Stop! Wait!"

225

He drew away in the nick of time. Cluney lay beside him, breathing deeply, trying to gain control once more.

"Why did you stop me?" he asked.

Oh, this was so difficult, so scary, so embarrassing! How could Cluney ever put her feelings into words?

Finally, she made an attempt. "Becuase it isn't fair," she said. "Sharing is what love is about. The pleasure should be divided equally between the two of us, just like the love we share."

"Are you saying you truly want me?" He sounded surprised.

"Yes! We're husband and wife, aren't we? Of course, I want you. If you . . . I mean, if *we* can."

He laughed—a joyous sound. "The Rebs missed their aim, my darling. Of course, I *can!*"

He pulled her closer then and kissed her deeply, teasing her tongue with his. Cluney's head was reeling. Suddenly, sights and sounds from Larissa's life were flashing through her mind like pictures from a VCR set on fast forward. She watched Larissa as a little girl, pitting one brother against the other. She heard Larissa as a young teenager, making promises to Hunter, then to another young man who was equally handsome, but who had a strange, cold gleam in his eyes. She cringed when another vision flashed, the two boys bloodying each other's noses over the pretty girl as Larissa stood by smiling and cheering them on.

As Hunter held his wife and kissed her and touched her, something happened—something extraordinary. It seemed that Cluney Summerland ceased to exist. She became his Larissa—his bride, his lover, his woman. For the first time in so long, she felt whole again, as if a part of her heart that had been torn away was now back in

226

place. As he held her in his arms, Cluney began to remember more of the past—not her own past, but Larissa's. Not things from Hunter's journal, but things Cluney Summerland had never before known.

Between kisses, she whispered to him, "Darling, remember that spring afternoon we took a picnic to the meadow and it was all golden with forsythia and you cut a whole armful for me?"

"I do," he murmured. "That was the first time I ever kissed you."

She felt a blush. "Why do you think I remember that day? Not for the forsythia."

"That was such an innocent kiss," he said, half laughing. "I'm surprised you remember it at all. I barely touched your lips with mine and it lasted the merest instant."

She snuggled close. "You touched my soul with that kiss."

"You hid your feelings well."

"I did love you," Cluney insisted. "I still do."

"More than you love anyone else?"

"More than I love life itself," Cluney heard herself say.

"Do you remember your first ball at Bluefield, sweetheart?"

She sighed deeply and closed her eyes. "I wore the petal-pink gown of lace that Mother ordered all the way from Paris. The bodice was stitched with tiny pearls. And you, my darling, looked so handsome, so dashing in your evening clothes. Why, you simply took my breath away!"

Hunter uttered a low, evil chuckle. "When I held you on the dance floor, I sorely longed to take far more than your breath away. Lord, how I ached for you that night!" He touched her breast with his open palm. "I still do,

227

Larissa, more than ever. It's a pain only you can soothe."

His mention of pain snapped Cluney out of her haze. She was lying against him, certainly hurting him. Quickly, she moved away.

"Don't!" he urged. "I want you close beside me."

She leaned against him again.

"This is no good," he fumed. "Too much gown. I can't get to you with only one good hand to maneuver. Take it off!"

When Cluney rose from the bed, she realized her knees were weak. She turned toward the curtain, but Hunter stopped her.

"No! Take it off over here in the light. I want to see you, darling. All of you."

Cluney stood staring at Hunter for a moment, her gaze locked to his. There was no hiding from him any longer. He was her husband, demanding his rights.

Slowly, she drew the gown up over her legs, her hips, her breasts. She slipped it over her head, then tossed it aside. Hunter's eyes gleamed in the candlelight as he stared at her.

"Magnificent!" he breathed. "Wonderfully, perfectly fantastic! Come closer."

Cluney did as he ordered. He reached out and passed his open palm over her flat belly and down to her thighs. She bit her lip to keep from moaning out loud. Her eyes closed and her head lolled to one side. Hunter slipped his arm around her waist and drew her closer. Then she felt his lips press against the soft flesh of her hip. He stroked her gently with his tongue.

What was he doing to her? Did he mean to make her stand all night while he tormented her with pleasure?

"Come back to bed," he ordered, a new urgency in his tone.

The moment they were side by side once more, Hunter sought her breasts—suckling her gently, making her sigh and moan.

And then she felt him, hot and throbbing, against her thigh. An instant later, he entered her. This was not the deep, swift thrust she expected. But his slow, gradual entry was far better, making her grope and beg for every inch of him until she was filled. With easy rhythm, they rocked together, locked in a total embrace from mouths to toes.

Cluney experienced a sensation like flying without wings, like gliding through space on a cloud. She knew this man; she loved him. And no matter what she had put him through in the past, she vowed from this moment on never to give him anything but pleasure, the same kind of pleasure he was showering on her this instant.

When their beautiful moment came, Cluney shuddered against Hunter. His groan of release at the same moment was so deep that it frightened her. But her fear passed into a perfect instant of bliss.

She never realized she was crying until he wiped the tears from her cheeks.

"It's over now, darling," Hunter whispered. "Whatever our problems before, they've been solved miraculously. Now we are truly one."

Cluney felt her heart take wing when she heard his words. They were, indeed, like one person—one happy, delirious, miraculous being. Life was beautiful—as beautiful as the moonbow!

But Hunter's next words chilled her soul.

"I know I don't have many days left, my darling, but

they will be the happiest days of my life because you are with me and I know you love me."

Long after he fell asleep, Cluney lay wide awake, listening to an owl sound his lonesome call through the night and trying to think what she would do if Hunter didn't survive.

"I don't know where I belong anymore," she whispered. "I'm like a drifter in time. I felt lost before, and without Hunter I'd be lost again."

She forced herself to stop trying to figure things out. Instead, she thought of B.J., and wondered what her closest friend was doing at this very moment on the other side of the moonbow.

# Chapter Thirteen

B.J. Jackson was hospitalized for two nights after her tumble down the stairs at Cumberland Falls. She was there long enough for the doctors to x-ray every bone in her body and scan her brain from all angles. Of course, she joked afterward that they found "nothing." Other than cuts, bumps, and bruises, she was okay, and having a fit to get out. Not only did she hate hospitals, she couldn't do a thing about finding Cluney as long as she was being held against her will.

Sonny Taylor sent her a big bouquet of blue-tinted carnations and came by to visit her twice. On his second call, he found B.J. out of bed and dressed, waiting for the office downstairs to get her paperwork so she could pay her bill and check out.

"Hey, B.J.! You look real fine," Sonny said, fidgeting with his hat in his hands. "I heard they were letting you go today and I thought you might need a ride home."

"How 'bout a ride up to the falls instead?"

"Aw, B.J.," he groaned. "There's not a blame thing you can do out there. The sheriff's got men searching around the clock."

"All the same, I want to have a look for myself. I might spot something that they'd miss. Has anyone seen Wooter Crenshaw since the other night?"

Reluctantly, Sonny shook his head. He didn't want B.J. getting mixed up in this again, but there seemed no way to stop her. She was one bullheaded lady!

"Wooter's sign's not on the road. Nobody's seen nor heard from him since the night of your accident."

B.J. was busily stuffing odds and ends into her purse. That chore finished, she picked up the vase of carnations, then surveyed the room for anything she might have missed.

"Thanks again for the flowers, Sonny. I don't think I ever saw this exact color before."

He grinned and blushed. "I'm real glad you like them. I had them done up special for you. I noticed you wear blue a lot and figured that must be your favorite color. I would have sent red roses, but I reckon that wouldn't have been fitting. I mean, we just met and all. I didn't want you to think I was being forward."

"The blue carnations are beautiful and perfectly appropriate for a woman who's bruised from head to toe."

Sonny looked stricken. "I didn't mean it that way."

"Just joshing, Sonny. What do you say we get the hell out of this place?"

He offered B.J. his arm, then they headed for the elevator. After a brief wait in the office, she was at last a free woman again.

The sunshine felt wonderful. The morning was almost balmy. She climbed into Sonny's pickup truck with hardly a twinge. Moments later, they were headed up the mountain toward Cumberland Falls.

"Any word from the sheriff on that can of Mace and Cluney's necklace?"

"Yep." Sonny kept a keen eye on the winding road as he spoke. "The lab report just came in this morning. The blood's a match, all right. They checked it against her records at the college infirmary."

When he heard a sharp intake of breath from B.J., he quickly added, "But, look, that doesn't mean something's happened to her. She'll turn up, you wait and see."

"I wish you'd put that another way, Sonny. That's exactly what I'm afraid of—that she'll 'turn up.'"

"Aw, heck, B.J.! You know I didn't mean it *that* way."

"I know, Sonny, but I can't help thinking about it. In fact, I've been doing a lot of thinking while I was lying up there in the hospital."

She paused and Sonny glanced her way. B.J. didn't continue, though. She just sat there, looking out the window at the soft, smoky-green of the mountains and listening to the country music on the truck's radio. Randy Travis was wailing away about "old bones."

"Well?" Sonny said. "Are you going to tell me what you've been thinking or not?"

"You'll figure I'm crazy."

He chuckled. "I reckon I already suspected that. You're not *plumb crazy*, though, just a little tetched."

"Well, thanks, ol' buddy!"

"Go on, B.J. Tell me what's on your mind."

"Okay. I guess I have to bounce my ideas off somebody. Sonny, do you know anything about time slips?"

"Sure," he said, frowning, not making the connection. "I punch a time slip every day when I come to work or leave."

"No, no," B.J. said. "I'm talking paranormal phenom-

233

ena here. A time slip is when someone travels back into the past and sees things that happened years ago as if they were happening right now, this very minute. From what I've read and heard, it usually lasts only minutes. But suppose Cluney has slipped back in time and can't figure out a way to return?"

Even though they were approaching a treacherous bend in the steep road, Sonny turned and looked B.J. full in the face. "Go on with you! Where'd you ever hear such a thing?"

"Look out!" B.J. reached for the wheel as Sonny missed the curve and the truck's right tires slipped off the pavement, bumping the vehicle crazily along the shoulder.

"I never heard of such," Sonny mumbled once he had control of the truck again.

"Well, I've not only heard of it, I know someone it happened to. A friend of mine back home lived in this real old house. One day I was visiting her and we were just fooling around in the rec room—playing records, dancing, giggling like teenagers do. Jeanne decided to go to the kitchen to get us some soft drinks. She was gone a long time. When she finally came back, she was shaking all over and she'd forgotten all about our sodas. Once she could settle down enough to talk, she said that she'd heard a piano playing in the living room as soon as she left me. And they didn't own a piano. So, Jeanne walked on through the house toward the sound. All the other rooms looked normal, but the minute she stepped into the living room everything was changed. The wallpaper was different, the furniture, the drapes, and there was a strange woman sitting at an old-fashioned piano, playing it. Jeanne said she could see out the window, and everything was different outside, too. A horse and buggy drove by in the dirt street. There was no house next door, just a wooded lot. When a man came into the room and started arguing with the woman, Jeanne got out of there fast. And she was plenty scared, I can tell you. She said she thought the man meant to kill the woman."

"You're puttin' me on," Sonny said.

"No! It's true, cross my heart. They even found out later who the woman was. Her name was Martha Everett Olmstead. After what Jeanne saw that afternoon, her daddy checked some old records at the courthouse. He found out that Jeanne was right—if she hadn't gotten out of there fast, she would have seen that man, Curtiss Olmstead, murder his wife. Eighty-year-old court records showed that they had a fight and he knocked her down and she hit her head on that piano. While she was out cold, he strangled her."

Sonny gave a low whistle and glanced at B.J. "So, let me get this straight. You're saying that you think Cluney Summerland slipped back into the past and is still there?" The serious-minded ranger was shaking his head with every word he spoke.

At Sonny's incredulous tone, B.J. became defensive. "I'm just saying I think it's possible. That's all."

He chuckled softly. "About as possible as those two 'coons you told me about being Wooter Crenshaw's ma and pa."

"All right," B.J. said stiffly. "Then you explain to me how Hunter Breckinridge's grave could be missing from that old burying ground."

"I can't," Sonny admitted. "But I suppose you can?"

"I have an idea."

"Well, for God's sake, tell me! That's been driving me batty."

"Suppose I'm right about Cluney going through a time slip. And suppose she's done something back then to keep Hunter alive. If he didn't die at Cumberland Falls, then he wouldn't be buried there, would he? And if she's managed to change history in some way, then it would change some things in the present, too."

"Now I've heard everything!" Sonny wheeled into the parking lot at the falls, switched off the ignition, and turned to stare at B.J. "You think your friend has gone and changed history? Give me a break, lady!"

B.J. arched an eyebrow at him. "You have a better explanation?"

"No, but . . . *how* do you figure she could change things?"

B.J. looked thoughtful for a minute, then said, "She's had a bad cold and she's been taking some pills for it. We haven't found her purse, so she must have it and her medicine with her. Maybe she'll give Hunter some of her antibiotics and save his life. Shoot, they didn't even know enough back then to keep things clean around sick people. Cluney could save him just by making sure everything's sterile. Or maybe just her being there will keep him from dying. I don't know. But I do know that if that's where Cluney is, she'll do something—anything she can—to keep him alive. She's in love with him, you know. She has been ever since she found his diary and read it."

"In love with a guy who's been dead for over a hundred years?" Sonny gave a short laugh and pounded the steering wheel with his fist. "Now, that beats all! What'd they do to you while you were in that hospital, girl? Scramble your brains?"

"I'm serious, Sonny. I told you about Cluney finding that journal he kept during the war. She fell for this guy

236

just from reading what he'd written. Hunter Breckinridge was real to her—as alive as you and I are right this minute. Believe what you will," B.J. said. "But I'm going to find out. If both Cluney and Wooter can find that time slip, then so can I. Next full moon, I'm going wherever they are."

"Like hell!" Sonny boomed.

"You just wait and see," B.J. assured him. "Besides, I think I'm needed back there. I've had this odd feeling ever since the other night. It's almost like someone's calling out to me from way off somewhere."

"Who?" Sonny obviously figured B.J. had just gone around the bend.

B.J. shook her head. "I'm not sure. Could be Cluney, could be someone else. I'll let you know when I find out."

"Yeah, you do that!" Sonny answered. "You do that very thing!"


Free had been trying for days to catch Larissa by herself so he could ask her some questions. But it seemed like she and Major Breckinridge were spending every hour of the day and night together.

Finally, late one afternoon while the major was napping, Free saw her slip out of the bedroom. She headed through the house and into the yard. He followed.

When he went outside, she was standing at the edge of the gorge, just staring out at the falls. She made a pretty sight there, with the mist all around her and the late afternoon sun turning it gold like an angel's halo.

"Miz Larissa?" Free called from a distance away, not wanting to startle her.

For a moment, she seemed not to have heard him. Then, slowly, she turned and smiled.

"Free, aren't the falls beautiful this afternoon? They look all golden in the sun."

"Yes, ma'am," he answered dutifully. "Miz Larissa, there's something I got a hankering to ask you."

"What is it, Free?"

"It's about my woman, Belle." He tensed when he said the words, afraid she would tell him to be on his way.

Instead, she said, "You love her a lot, don't you?"

"Oh, yessum, I do!" When he realized he'd looked Larissa straight in the eye as he answered, he quickly dropped his gaze, ashamed of his own forwardness.

"It's all right, Free," she said gently. "I understand what it means to love someone you can't be with. I understand all too well. Now, what did you want to ask me?"

"That likeness of Belle you got. I know you said it wasn't her and I'm not meaning to dispute your word, ma'am, but if I could just have another look at it."

As always, Cluney had her bag and all its valuable contents slung across her shoulder. She fished into it and brought out the photo of B.J. With obvious uncertainty, she handed it to him.

He cradled the picture lovingly in his big hands. "Oh, my!" he breathed. "Oh, this *got* to be my Belle, ma'am. I couldn't mistake the woman I love so much."

"Where is Belle?" Cluney asked gently.

He shook his head. "I ain't knowing at the moment, ma'am. Our master sold her off to someplace here in Kentucky. I ain't seen nor heard of her since. Soon as I got my freedom, I come straight here, hoping I'd find her so we could marry. But looks like this war has just throwed ever'body every whichaway. Nobody's where they belongs no more."

Cluney mused silently on the truth of his words.

"Do you know the name of the person who bought Belle?"

He gave her a baleful look. "No, ma'am. I heard tell she'd gone to a place called Brodaker."

"I don't believe I've ever heard of a place by that name in Kentucky."

"But, ma'am, if you have her likeness, how come you can't tell me where she is?" Free knew he sounded uppity, but he couldn't help himself. He had to find Belle and Larissa was the only one who might help him.

"I explained to you, Free, that this can't possibly be your Belle. The likeness is of a friend of mine. Her name is B.J. Jackson. She lives down in the valley." She turned and pointed off toward the town that would not be there until long after the war.

His eyes lit up. "Then I'll go down there and find her."

Cluney shook her head. "It's not that easy, Free. You won't be able to find her there now. I can't explain this to you. I wish I could, but I'm not sure I understand myself."

"Then you won't help me?" he said in a dejected tone.

"I *can't* help you. Believe me, I would, if I could."

After one last longing gaze, Free surrendered the photo to Larissa. She held it thoughtfully for a moment, then pressed it back into his hand.

"You keep this. If it looks so much like your Belle, you should have it."

Free's heart warmed at her generosity. He'd longed to beg her for the likeness, but knew he had no right. The major's lady was indeed a fine person. With tears in his

239

eyes, and B.J.'s picture clutched to his chest, he nodded and bowed.

"I thank you most kindly, ma'am. I do!"

"I hope you find your Belle," Cluney whispered.

From that moment on, Free was never without the photo of B.J. He looked at it every chance he got. He thought of her during the day and dreamed of her at night. If she was out there somewhere, he meant to send her a message, from his heart to hers. Somehow, she would know that he was calling to her, begging her to come to him.

Cluney watched the big private amble back toward the lodge. He never took his eyes off B.J.'s picture all the way. She found his insistence that the photo was actually a likeness of his Belle unsettling. She wished she could explain to Free how she'd come from another time, but she had yet to find a logical way to explain that even to her own husband, so there was no way she could tell him.

Deep in thought, her gaze still focused on the falls, Cluney heard Mary Renfro call to her.

"Larissa? You out there? You best come quick. The major's took a turn."

Cluney hurried toward the house. Mary stood in the open door, beckoning to her. She wasn't sure she understood what the woman meant, but one look at Mary's grim face told her that the news was not good.

"Mary? What's wrong?"

"It ain't like this comes as a shock, but he's seemed so much better these past days."

"Mary!" Cluney felt like shaking the woman. "Tell me! What's happened?"

"Your husband's took with a fever, Larissa. He's out of his head."

"Oh, no!" Cluney cried, rushing past Mary and into the house. "But he was fine before he fell asleep."

"Well, he ain't fine now, I'm sorry to say. Looks like that wound in his shoulder's gone septic. There ain't a thing we can do for him now, but try to make him easy and pray."

Cluney turned and stared at Mary. "Septic? You mean it's an infection."

"I reckon. Don't matter what you call it, the end'll come soon all the same. I'm sorry, Larissa. Mighty sorry!"

Cluney hurried into the bedroom. Her heart sank when she spied Hunter. His face was flushed. Although his eyes were still closed, his lips moved constantly, muttering wild, incoherent phrases. He tossed restlessly, tearing with his good hand at the bandage across his shoulder.

Quickly, Cluney dampened a cloth in the ironstone bowl beside the bed and began sponging him off.

"It ain't time yet to bathe him," Mary said in an amazed tone, obviously assuming that the dying man's wife was preparing him for his burial.

"I have to cool him off, get his fever down."

Cluney's mind was groping for something she could do that would help. Her medical knowledge was sorely lacking. She tried to remember how her mother had tended her when she was ill. Of course! *Ice!* She needed ice. But the only ice on this mountain was in the cold fingers clutching her heart.

"Mary, is there any of Wooter's medicine left?"

"A bit. I'll run fetch it," the woman said, hurrying off.

A short while later, after dribbling some of Wooter's white lightning between Hunter's parched lips, Cluney used more of it to try to disinfect the fiery-red wound. Then she carefully rewrapped his shoulder with clean linen that she herself had boiled earlier.

For hours, far into the night, Cluney sat with Hunter, trying to bring his fever down, praying that it would break. His skin felt so hot. She guessed his temperature must be well over a hundred degrees, maybe as high as a hundred and five. If only she hadn't broken the thermometer she usually carried in her purse, she could find out for sure.

"My purse!" she gasped suddenly, joyously.

She always carried aspirin. And aspirin would bring his fever down. But that was only a temporary measure. She had bigger, better things on her mind. The college doctor had prescribed a form of penicillin for her cold. Surely, Hunter's infection would respond to the twentieth-century miracle drug.

Hurriedly, Cluney dumped the entire contents of her purse on the bed, then scrambled her fingers through the mess, searching for the clear plastic pill bottle.

"It's not here!" she cried, totally dismayed. "But I know I had it."

With a sinking heart, she recalled the spill in her van. The round container of pills must have rolled under the seat. Wherever her van was at the moment, so, too, was her one chance to save Hunter's life. She sank down on the bed and put her face in her hands. All was lost!

Her surrender lasted only moments. "No, dammit! I will not let him die!"

Quickly, she found the aspirin and melted them in a little water in a tin cup. Drop by drop, she forced the precious liquid between Hunter's lips. He grimaced at the bitter taste even though he was still out of his head with the fever.

"You'll thank me later, darling," she whispered.

By dawn Cluney could tell that Hunter's fever was down a bit, but they still had a long way to go. She dissolved more aspirin and gave it to him.

Again, she went through everything in her purse, hoping against all hope that somehow she had overlooked the pill bottle before. She was sitting on the bed, staring miserably at the useless collection of junk she'd brought with her when she heard an odd sound outside. It was barely light yet, but someone was digging.

Cluney rose from the bed and went to the window. Holding aside the burlap curtain she stared out. What she saw sent a chill right through her. Free was out in the burying lot, digging a new grave. One of the other men must have died during the night.

While she was still at the window, the door opened softly and Mary looked in.

"How is he?" she asked.

Still mesmerized by Free's grim labor, Cluney didn't turn as she answered, "His fever is down a little."

She thought Mary had left until she heard the woman's voice again. "I was hoping you wouldn't look out the window," she said in an apologetic tone. "I know it's right early for me to set Free to such a task, but I reckon we're in for a hard freeze tonight. It's feeling like snow, too, Larissa. I told Free to dig right next to that nice young Captain Van Dyke from New York since he and the major was friendly with one another. Larissa, you understand . . ."

Suddenly, Cluney did understand and she was mortified. She whirled on Mary. "How could you?"

243

"A body's got to think ahead, child," Mary answered gently.

"Well, fine! You just think ahead all you like. But think to when my husband is up and around again because I will *not*, by God, let him die!"

"Larissa Breckinridge, I done told you about that!" Mary scolded. "When the major's time comes, it comes and that's all there is to it."

Cluney gestured angrily toward the window and the sound of Free's shovel beyond. "I won't have you digging my husband's grave while he's still alive! I can't stand it, Mary." She ended with a sob.

"Try to calm yourself," Mary cautioned with sympathy in her voice. "It won't do nobody any good for you to go making your own self sick with grief. I'll tell Free to hold off a spell."

"Thank you," Cluney murmured.

After a final glance toward the major and a slight shake of her head, Mary turned to leave. But Cluney stopped her.

"Mary, is Wooter still here?"

"He's around someplace."

"Would you find him for me and send him in here?"

"Of course, honey. Now you take it easy."

Moments after Mary left, Cluney realized the sound from outside had ceased. She gave a shudder of relief, then closed her eyes for a moment. She knew, no matter what, she had to remain calm and strong. With Wooter's help, maybe—*just maybe*—she could save her husband's life.

She sank down beside the bed and took Hunter's hand in hers. It wasn't much, but it was all she could do for the moment. The old hound, Trooper, seemed to share

Cluney's thoughts. He sidled over to Hunter, pressing as close to his master as he could get.

"Oh, Hunter," she whispered, "if only I had those pills. If only I could make you well by willing it so. This is damn unfair! You have to pull through or we'll never have a chance at all the happiness we could have shared."

Moments later, she heard Wooter's knock at the door and hurried to answer it.

"Mary said you needed me, little girl." His gaze wandered past Cluney to the restless man on the bed. "He ain't so good, is he?"

Biting her lip to hold back the tears, Cluney glanced at Hunter, then back to Wooter. "No, he's not. Mary says he's going to die. I don't want him to die, Wooter. I mean to save him. That's why I needed to talk to you."

He stroked his beard nervously. "I'd do anything I could. You know that. But I don't see as I can help none."

"Oh, but you can!" Cluney said with pleading in her voice. "You'll be going back soon, won't you?"

"Most likely."

"How soon?"

"Come full moon tonight, I reckon."

"If there's a moonbow, you mean," Cluney corrected.

"Hell, little girl, I don't need no moonbow to shine the way. I been traveling this route so many years now, I know it by heart."

Cluney's spirits soared. "Suppose you do go back tonight, Wooter, how long before you could come back here? Not until the next full moon?"

He waggled his head. "Nope. You see, there's three nights when the way is clear for traveling—full moon, the night before, and the night after. So I could go one night and come back the next. I done it that way before."

245

Cluney had the greatest urge to hug the old man. "Oh, Wooter, this is perfect! Will you do that for me, then?"

He scratched his head thoughtfully for a moment. "I reckon, if there's a need for it."

"There's a need. Oh, what a need! Go tonight. Once you're there—on the other side—get hold of my friend, B.J. It's important that she get medicine for the major. Otherwise, he won't make it."

Wooter squinted at her. "I don't know nothing about no medicines, 'cept herbs and roots and such."

"You don't have to worry about that. I'll write down everything Hunter needs and B.J. will get it for you. All you have to do is bring it back to me as soon as you can. There's not much time, Wooter, and this is desperately important to me."

He waved a hand toward Hunter's still form. "You mean, *he's* important to you, don't you, little girl?"

"Yes, Wooter. I guess he is—about the most important part of my life."

Suddenly, Wooter's face lit up. "Back to my cabin, I got some right powerful snake oil that a peddler-fellow sold me when he came to town. That'll fix him right up. Why, it'll do anything!" he said excitedly. "Cure lameness, make a blind man see, even grow curls on a bald head. I'll bring that along, too. It'll do the trick. You just wait and see."

Cluney started to refuse Wooter's offer of the patent medicine, but changed her mind. It would do the old man's heart good to help make Hunter well.

She touched Wooter's arm and smiled at him. "Do bring that, please. But get the other medicine, too. We don't have much time, and I want to make sure we have everything we need."

246

"I best be getting ready now, little girl. You watch over him till I get back tomorrow night."

"Oh, I will, Wooter. And thank you." Quickly she wrote down her list of medicines, then pressed the paper into his calloused palm.

He glanced at the list, then back to Cluney, shaking his head. "I hope your friend, B.J., ain't hard to find, 'cause these things you wrote down is Greek to me."

"Tell her I'm all right, Wooter. Tell her I send my love."

He nodded, then left the room.

By sunset that evening, Hunter was worse. His fever was raging again. Cluney did everything she could to make him more comfortable, but it was precious little.

As dark seeped into the woods, Cluney stood at the bedroom window, watching the falls. Sure enough, she spied Wooter's dark silhouette against the moon-silvered glow of the mist. One moment he was there. The next moment he was gone.

"Have a safe journey, Wooter," she whispered softly. "And, *please*, hurry back!"

She returned to her husband and kissed his fevered brow.

# Chapter Fourteen

B.J. hated telephone calls in the middle of the night. She'd had one already—some woman who claimed to be calling from California, looking for Cluney. Probably one of the college students with a warped sense of humor, who'd read in the local newspaper about the history teacher's disappearance. B.J. had hung up on the sadistic little creep.

But even more frightening than a late-night phone call was a knock at the front door long after midnight. She'd been sleeping lightly, so the sound woke her immediately. While she pulled on her robe and made a dash for the door, a dozen different scenarios—each one worse than the one before it—flashed through her mind. But all her fears had a common denominator—Cluney Summerland.

She fully expected to find either Sonny Taylor or Sheriff Clewis Elrod on her doorstep, hat in hand. Either of them, at this time of night, had to be bringing back news—the worst possible news about her friend.

She was struck speechless when she opened the door to

find Wooter Crenshaw—grim and dusty—staring back at her.

"Howdy," he said, tipping his beat-up old hat as he would if they passed on the street at any ordinary time of the day.

"Wooter, what in the world?"

"I come about your friend."

"My friend?" Again, thoughts and possibilities crowded B.J.'s mind. "You mean *Cluney*?"

"Yep. She's got big trouble on her hands."

B.J. narrowed her eyes suspiciously. A brand-new scenario had just popped into her mind: Old Wooter had kidnapped Cluney and this was his moment to demand ransom. When he pulled a slip of paper from the pocket of his red flannel shirt, she was sure she was right.

"Here! We'll be needing this from you. Cluney said, 'Fast!'"

B.J. didn't bother to glance at the paper before she reacted. "Now, look, if this is some sort of extortion you're attempting, it's not going to work."

"I don't know what you're a-talking about, but we ain't got time to stand here palavering. I got to get this stuff back to her by this evening. She told me you'd take care of it."

B.J. squinted down at the piece of paper, trying to read it by the dim porch light. The notepaper was definitely Cluney's; she recognized the tiny yellow flowers that formed a border. The handwriting was Cluney's as well.

She stepped back and held the door wide. "Come on in, Wooter. I'll fix you a cup of coffee while you tell me what's going on? Where is Cluney? Why didn't she come herself? And why does she need all this medicine? Is she sick?"

A short while later, they were both seated at B.J.'s scarred pine kitchen table. Wooter was real cagey about where Cluney was. He refused to say exactly. He'd only admit that she was "a right fur piece from here" and that he had to get back to her before it was too late.

"Too late for what?" B.J. demanded, exasperated with her midnight caller's vague approach. "If you want me to help, Wooter Crenshaw, you better tell me what's going on. Everything on this list is some sort of drug. I'm not just going to empty my medicine chest and hand it all over to you until I know where it's going and toward what purpose."

Wooter shifted in his chair and sort of growled low in his throat. "Hellfire! Cluney claimed you wouldn't give me no trouble. She said you'd be keen on helping her."

"I am!" B.J. stated. "But if she's so sick that she needs all this stuff, then she should be in a hospital."

"Ain't no hospital where she's at!" Wooter snapped.

"Then tell me where she is—*exactly*!"

"Up to the falls," Wooter muttered in an undertone.

"The falls? That can't be. The sheriff and his men have searched every inch of that park."

"Not this part, they ain't. They couldn't get there if they tried."

"Is she in one of the caves? In that old mine shaft under the falls?"

Wooter gave a negative shake of his head each time B.J. suggested a new possibility until she felt as if they were playing a game of twenty questions.

Finally, with a sigh and a shrug, B.J. said, "I give up! Where else could she be?"

He looked her square in the eye and said, "Could be she's over the moonbow."

251

B.J. had a sudden flash of memory—a scene as vivid as if she were right there watching it again. She saw the shining silver light and Cluney, dressed like a bride, rising higher and higher up over the falls. She broke out in a nervous sweat.

"You better tell me what's going on, old man, and you better be quick about it."

He leaned closer and squinted hard at B.J. Could she be trusted with the secret? He couldn't be sure. But then, she was a friend of the little Summerland girl. And if he was going to help her, it looked like he'd have to rely on this woman.

"She's gone back," he said at length. "Back to the past to save her husband."

B.J. jumped up from the table with a sharp cry. She rounded on him, "What kind of sick joke is this? Cluney never got married. Her fiancé was killed in a plane crash. Maybe you can explain to me how she can save someone who's already dead."

Wooter remained calm. "Oh, she was married all right, but in another time and place. Somewhere that's long gone now, except to those few of us who know how to find it. But her happiness depends on her saving that man she married. And his time is fast running out. Now, are you going to get me this medicine so I can take it to her, or are you just going to stand around balking like a mule till he's dead and buried?"

B.J. still wasn't convinced. "Tell me where she is?"

"I done told you. She's up to the falls. It don't matter no how *where* she is. It's *when* that makes all the difference."

"I don't understand what you mean."

He was squinting at her again, sizing her up. "No, I

don't reckon you do. So, I'm gonna tell you. But then, you better get me this stuff, and you better get it fast."

He paused for breath and B.J. prompted, "Well? Tell me!"

"She's gone back in time. Back to during the Civil War. She's abiding in the year 1863, along with her husband. And he got hisself shot up real bad by a bunch of Rebs. If he don't get help, he's done for. Then your friend'll be left a-grieving back then over her man just like she's been doing in the here and now."

B.J. couldn't find her voice for a few seconds. Finally, she said, "And you expect me to believe all this?"

"If you want to help your friend, you have to."

B.J. realized in a flash that she did believe every word of it. Cluney had gone back through a time slip just as she'd told Sonny she suspected. Without another moment's hesitation, she hurried to the bathroom, where she kept all her medicine. Wooter was right behind her.

"How will you get this to Cluney?" She was already filling a paper bag with the various prescription drugs on Cluney's list.

"I'm going on back up to the falls and cross back over the moonbow."

B.J. stopped what she was doing and turned to stare at the old mountain man. "Just like that?"

He gave one solemn nod. "Yep! Just like that! It's easy as pie when you know how."

"Could I go with you?"

He frowned in thought, then shook his head. "I don't see no use in that."

B.J. almost blew up at him, but decided that calm reasoning would be her best approach with Wooter. "Listen, if Cluney's having problems, it'll help her just to have a friend close at hand."

"I'm her friend," Wooter snapped.

B.J. touched Wooter's sleeve in a gesture of gratitude. "Of course you are, and Cluney's lucky to have a friend like you. But don't you see? The two of us have been so close for so long. It would give her comfort to have a woman friend with her at a time like this."

"Well . . . ?" Wooter was obviously mulling over the thought, not sure what to do.

"I won't be any trouble, Wooter. I promise."

He made up his mind in a snap. "Go get some duds on then. If we hurry, we can get back across this very night before the moon sets. But we ain't got no time to waste."

B.J. dashed for her bedroom and began pulling on her clothes.

An hour later, Wooter and B.J. arrived at Cumberland Falls. The moon was low in the sky, and there was not the slightest sign of a moonbow in the rising mist.

"Oh, Wooter, we're too late."

"Naw, we ain't," he answered. "You just come on with me. And mind you hang onto my arm. I ain't never took nobody across before, but I figure you got to be holding on fast to make the journey. Was you to let go, no telling where you'd drop off."

The idea of possibly losing her guide and falling into some long-ago year all alone sent a shiver through B.J. She wasn't all that happy about traveling back into the past with Wooter. But alone, she'd be terrified.

They got out of B.J.'s car and started toward the edge of the gorge. When they were standing so close that B.J.

could feel the mist rising from sixty feet below, she balked and gulped in terror.

"Are you sure this will work, Wooter?"

"I ain't sure of nothing," he responded. "But we won't know till we give her a try. You grip me real good, now."

B.J. put a death hold on his right arm. She glanced down again, her fear of heights making her stomach roll. "We don't have to jump, do we?"

"Where'd you get such a crazy notion, girl? Course we don't jump! You want to wind up splattered all over them rocks down there?"

B.J. shook her head because her voice had suddenly deserted her.

"You ready?" Wooter asked.

In answer, B.J. squeezed his arm tighter.

"All right, then. Close your eyes."

Trembling all over, B.J. did as he instructed. Moments passed. Everything remained the same. She was about to decide that she had nothing to fear, when suddenly the wind rose—cold and brisk. She felt like it might blow her off the edge, down into the gorge.

"Hold steady!" Wooter warned, his voice seeming to come from far away.

B.J. braced her knees and clung to Wooter.

"Oh, Lord!" Wooter moaned. "This ain't good."

"What do you mean?"

Terrified by his ominous tone, B.J. opened her eyes. Immediately, she knew what he meant. Directly before them, hovering so large and black that it closed off their view of the falls, towered a vaporous shape. At times, it looked like a whirlwind. Then it would change, taking on an almost human form, cloaked in a hooded shroud. And from the depths of the thing came a low moan that chilled the soul, a stench of rot and decay, and a promise of hopelessness.

B.J. let out a shrill cry.

"Hush up!" Wooter hissed. "Pay it no mind."

"What is it?" she whispered, half choking with fear.

"It ain't really got a name. But I reckon you know as good as I do what it is. We can't leave here till it passes us by. Hold right still and don't let it know you're scared, girl."

That was more easily said than done. B.J. closed her eyes again and tried to think happy thoughts about being reunited with Cluney. She had a feeling the thing would be repelled by any pleasantness.

After a time—what seemed an eternity—she sensed that it was gone. The air about them smelled fresh and felt warmer. Once again, she could hear the roar of the falls and the night creatures stirring. But she dared not open her eyes for fear that it might still be there.

"It's all right now," Wooter whispered hoarsely. "We can get on about our business. Death passed us by."

*Death!* B.J. had not dared put a name to the horrible apparition. But the little coffin-maker knew this phantom intimately. She shivered, wondering just how close a call they'd had.

She was still pondering this question when she felt the warmth of a bright light on her face. She caught her breath as a lovely, weightless sensation flowed through her body.

"Hold tight." Wooter's words were the last she heard.

An instant later, they were rising, flying, leaving the Earth of 1992. B.J. felt herself floating back through time. The years flipped past in her mind like the pages in a picture book turning rapidly. She caught brief glimpses of passing years—astronauts landing on the moon, a flash of pink as the presidential limousine sped through the streets of Dallas, a happy mob scene in Times Square when World War II ended, President Lincoln in his box at Ford's Theater, Generals Lee and Grant at Appomattox. Then all went black.

Cluney couldn't close her eyes to sleep that night. Even in the darkness, she could sense Hunter's pain. Every change in his breathing, every shift of his body brought her instantly to his side. She held his hand and talked softly to him, trying to make him fight for life.

"As soon as you're well, darling, we'll go back to Bluefield. They burned the barns and other outbuildings, but the house is still there. We'll put it to rights again—just the way it was before the war. And then we'll raise our family there. Our sons will learn to ride and hunt just like their father, and our daughters will be the belles of the whole county. The war's over for you, Hunter. It will be over for all of us soon. Then life for us will be the way we've always dreamed it should be. Hang in there, darling. We have a beautiful future ahead of us. Listen to me! Believe me!"

Even as Cluney spoke with firm assurance, tears streamed down her cheeks. She had to keep hoping, but, oh, it was hard! Hunter had gone too long without proper medicines—medicines that didn't even exist in this time and place. What if something happened and Wooter couldn't get back here? Or what if he arrived too late for the penicillin to work its miracle?

She stared out the window at the waning moon. Its glow through her tears seemed to form a new sort of moonbow.

"Oh, hurry, Wooter! Please hurry!"

A moan of pain brought her full attention back to Hunter. She gripped his hot hand and brought his fingers to her lips.

"I'm here, my darling," she whispered. "I won't leave you. Not ever again."

"Larissa," he whispered. "Look to the moon . . ."

His words trailed off. Cluney leaned closer, trying to hear, but he said nothing else for a time.

"Yes, Hunter. What about the moon?"

"When I'm gone . . . look to the moon. I'll be smiling down at you, loving you always."

Swallowing a sob, Cluney answered him sternly, "Don't talk that way! You aren't going anywhere. You're going to stay right here with me. You're going to love me, but here and now, my darling."

Cluney slipped into bed and snuggled close—holding him, feeling the erratic beat of his heart against her breasts. She refused to let him go. She would will his heart to keep beating.

She sensed a change before she actually knew what it was. At first, she thought Hunter's breathing had altered. Then she realized that it was something else—something from out in the night. She heard the wind stir and saw black clouds cover the moon. Then the hair at the nape of her neck rose as she felt a presence enter the room. Even through the darkness, she could see a blacker shape at the foot of the bed. An awful stench filled her nostrils. Her heart thundered with a new kind of fear.

Did she imagine the words or did someone actually speak? "It is time."

She clung more fiercely to Hunter. "No!" she whispered hoarsely, her heart pounding. "Go away! You can't have him!"

*"Tim-m-me . . ."* The ominous word hung in the thick air like some poisonous vapor.

The black shape remained—shifting, swirling, inching ever closer to Hunter's motionless form. His old dog whimpered and slunk down off the bed, then under it.

Cluney, shivering as she clutched at Hunter's still body, heard the beating of wings and the howl of the wind. She closed her eyes and prayed with all her might. She forced herself to concentrate only on willing Hunter to live. She knew she had to block out the awful black vision and the terrible sound of its grim voice. She felt as if she were in the midst of some heated battle—some challenge of wills beyond anything she had ever experienced or even imagined possible.

Hunter was so still suddenly, so cool when only a short time ago he had been burning with fever.

"No!" she sobbed. "You can't have him. He's mine!"

If only she dared leave Hunter long enough to light the lamp. Surely the apparition would vanish with the darkness. But something warned her not to release her hold on him or all would be lost.

"Damn you!" she seethed. "Leave this place. Now! We want none of your dreadful gifts. We want to be left in peace."

The black cloud swirled and reformed, closer to the bed now, hovering, waiting to strike. Cluney covered Hunter's body with her own, screaming, "No! Get away from him!"

On and on she fought, until she was exhausted. Her voice grew hoarse, her body limp with fatigue. It was no use. She couldn't protect him forever.

After what seemed hours, Cluney sensed a sudden change. Or was she only imagining what she had fought for so long and hard.

"No," she breathed. "It's gone!"

Hunter stirred against her and murmured her name. She opened her eyes to find that they were alone again in the room. The awful odor of sulfur and decay had vanished. The night seemed calm and quiet.

Had the black shadow been only a nightmare? The moon was shining again, too, casting its faint light across the bed. She was bathed in sweat, shivering in the chill of the air. Hunter once more felt hot, but, for a change, she welcomed his fever. His burning flesh meant that he was still alive, that he hadn't been whisked away from her by their ominous night visitor.

Quickly, Cluney rose from the bed and lit the lamp. A new wave of relief came with the light. She went to the pitcher and poured cool water into the bowl. With great care and tenderness she sponged Hunter's burning body, all the while murmuring reassurances to him.

Once he seemed calm and comfortable, Cluney lay down beside him again. But she knew she wouldn't sleep. Her nerves were raw. She dared not even close her eyes for fear that the threatening cloud might return. She must keep up her guard. Sitting up in bed, she glanced about the room, checking again to make sure they were still alone. Her gaze lit on Hunter's journal.

"I'll read to you, darling," she whispered. "You'd like that, wouldn't you?"

Hunter never heard, never answered. But Cluney rose quickly to get the diary. She decided to begin at the beginning. The first entry was dated 13 May 1846, and was written in boyish script.

*   *   *

Mother and Father took me up to Lexington today to pay a call on Colonel and Mrs. Courtney. It was an especially fine day, with the air as hot as summer and the sun shining bright. I'd have rather gone to the creek with Jordan and the fellows for an afternoon of swimming and sporting. But Father seemed to think that I needed to be with the men today, and, besides, Mother insisted. She always gets her way. Neither Father nor I can abide her hysterics.

You can well imagine my surprise when we arrived at the fine Courtney mansion, only to be ushered off to the horse barn by a certain surly servant wench, who declared to all within the limits of her powerful voice, "This ain't no barbecue. It's a birthin'. So you gentlemen get yourselfs on down to the barn and out from underfoot so's Miz Jenny can have some peace and quiet for her laying-in."

Well, I can tell you, my face went scarlet. Neither Mother nor Father had mentioned to me that Mrs. Courtney was even expecting a baby, so certainly I had no suspicions that I might get caught up in any such sort of female event. How I longed to be with Jordy and the boys!

However, the day turned out pleasant enough for us men. We spent a fine few hours in and around the barn, pitching horseshoes, swapping tales, and admiring Colonel Courtney's new foal, a fine filly he calls Dancer.

By the heat of the afternoon, though, Colonel Courtney was showing the strain. Being the youngest in the group of eight—husband and brothers of Mrs. Jennifer Courtney—I kept quiet and listened to their conversation, learning much about this process of birthing babies. It seemed Miss Jenny had been seized with the pains of labor at sunset the day before. Having previously lost two babies in childbirth, Mrs. Courtney sorely feared her coming travail. Although a physician had been summoned at the very moment "her water broke" (a term used freely by her husband and the others, but never explained to me) she begged to have word sent to my mother, who has been her best friend since they were girls, so that she might have a sympathetic hand to hold during her "long hours of suffering." (These were her husband's exact words. Which brings to mind this question: If a husband knows that inflicting his wife with a child is surely going to make her suffer, and he loves his wife, then why does he do such a thing? It appears my tutoring on such matters is sorely lacking.)

Mrs. Courtney's suffering became much apparent to us all as the afternoon wore on. Her screams were ever so much like those I heard once from a slave being whipped by Father's overseer. I shuddered and trembled at each outburst since it brought with it the well-remembered sight of that poor black man tied to a post while his back was laid open. During this period of Mrs. Courtney's labor, the men took to passing around a jug of prime Kentucky bourbon. I took a sip when Colonel Courtney offered, but only after receiving a nod of approval from my father. And so, another first for this day—my first drink of a man's liquor. It burned, tasted of smoke, and made my head swim. But I do see how a man might acquire a liking for its fire, its taste, and especially its euphoric aftereffect.

By sunset, Colonel Courtney was, as the men say, "in his cups." He told bawdy stories for a time, then began singing at the top of his voice in order to drown out the cries of his suffering wife. By the time a servant came to announce that Mrs. Courtney had been delivered of a fine, healthy daughter, the colonel was snoring away. My own father roused him and gave him the good news only to be faced with the new father's wrath. "A *girl?*" Colonel Courtney roared, all red in the face. "Why a girl? The two she lost were sons. This must be some other man's bastard." Then he set to moaning and holding his head, finally lamenting loudly, "Girl young'uns and bull calves are the poor man's doom, and surely I am one of those doomed."

Within a short while, however, Colonel Courtney was quieted and soothed by the others. His face washed, his hair combed, he made his way rather unsteadily up to the big house to see his long-suffering wife and the female she had spawned with such success.

I myself was allowed into Mrs. Courtney's bedroom to pay my respects and view the tiny, red-faced creature named Larissa Flemingate Courtney. Rather a grand name, I feel, for such an unlovely scrap of flesh. But I did as my father instructed me and assured the screaming infant's mother that Larissa was beautiful beyond my powers of description. Poor, weary Mrs. Courtney smiled at me, patted my head, and promised me that someday I would marry the homely little creature. I shuddered at her words!

Late tonight, long after we returned to Bluefield and were sleeping, I was awakened by a shower of pebbles against my windowpane. I knew, of course, that it was Jordan, who had sneaked off earlier, wanting a full report of the day's proceedings. I opened my window and he climbed up the sycamore. After telling him all that had transpired, I put several questions to my brother. Concerning the reason why men make babies on their wives, even knowing that the birthing will bring suffering, Jordan claimed that women thrive on such pain. He told me further that a woman who cannot give her husband sons is worse than useless. He went on to explain that a horse who can't foal can be sold the same as a slave wench who drops no suckers. But a wife with no sons is worth less than nothing to her husband, and that's why so many men form relationships in the quarters.

I confessed that I doubted the truth of all this. He bloodied my nose for calling him a liar, then ran off to his room, leaving me standing with my nightshirt clinging to me and turning scarlet as my nose dripped upon it. So ended this fine day in May—the day of Larissa Courtney's birth.

Cluney stared down at the page. As many times as she had read Hunter's diary before, this was the first time she realized that she was reading of her own beginning.

"Larissa Flemingate Courtney," she repeated. "Can that really be who I am?"

She glanced down at Hunter, who had written as a boy that she was an "unlovely scrap of flesh." Although he had remained asleep while she read to him aloud, his grimace of pain had given way to a slight smile and he seemed less restless now.

Cluney leaned down and kissed his forehead, then smoothed the covers over his chest. Suddenly the full impact of their relationship struck her. As difficult as it was to believe, she knew that she must be his wife, Larissa. This was her real world now. Her existence as Clair de Lune Summerland had been only a fleeting dream.

With new purpose, she opened her husband's journal once more, determined to discover a new understanding of herself.

Since dawn was still hours away, she would continue reading. The sound of her own voice would keep her awake, and it seemed to soothe Hunter, as well. She skipped over the boy's entries to read of Hunter as a young man, first discovering his love for Larissa.

Very soon, she discovered that she wasn't simply reading about the lives of Hunter and Larissa. She felt herself transported back through time to experience it all once more. To remember the life she had once lived, then forgotten. To wonder at the woman she had been. And to hope that she had learned a few lessons through the years.

# Chapter Fifteen

On that day shortly before her marriage to Hunter, when Larissa went alone to visit Jordan, she risked everything. But she did it for Hunter. She had so dreaded the thought of the two brothers meeting at sword point in battle, that she had put her own reputation on the line to stop that from happening.

She had been so young then, so foolish!

Jordan had deceived her, of course, begging her to come to him alone so that they could talk about his final decision on joining the army. He had said that he trusted her and valued her opinions. But Jordan had lied.

On that fateful day, Jordan had mocked her—making sure that her arrival coincided with his dalliance with his slave lover. He had shamed her—using her body as his own private plaything. And, finally, Jordan had ruined her—telling Hunter that Larissa had come to Broad Acres, on the very eve of her marriage, because she simply could not stay away.

The confounding contradictions of Larissa's life were all so clear to Cluney now. Was there any wonder that Hunter had seemed strange on their wedding night? Was

267

there any wonder that Hunter had left for the war, convinced that his marriage was a mockery?

Cluney, hugging herself and rocking back forth on the bed, let the tears flow freely. She felt dirty and used, remembering that afternoon with Jordan.

"How could Larissa have been such a little fool?" Cluney moaned.

Then she confessed to herself that the modern-day Cluney would have done the same thing for the same reasons. Not much had changed through all the years.

Cluney finally managed to calm herself by thinking, not of the bad times in the distant past, but of how wonderful her future with Hunter would be. He trusted her again. He loved her. And she loved him!

She looked down at his handsome face. "And damned if I'm going to give up that love without a fight!"

Dawn was breaking, tinting the sky with threads of amber and amethyst. She put away the journal, and set about doing everything she could to make Hunter comfortable. She bathed his fevered body, changed his bandages, and talked to him all the while about what their life together would be like back at Bluefield once he recovered enough to travel. She talked of riding horses while morning dew still clung like shining crystals to the bluegrass. She spoke of gay house parties with guests coming from miles around to feast and dance and make merry. She whispered of children—strong sons, loving daughters. And she promised him love—all the love that was within her heart and soul to give, all that she had been saving up for him so long.

So involved in her work and her dreams was Cluney that she never heard the soft knock at the door. Mary

Renfro stuck her head in just in time to hear Cluney talking to her husband about taking him home.

"Larissa?" Mary said quietly.

Cluney turned with a jerk, startled.

"Leave the major and come out here for a minute. You and me, we need to talk."

Satisfied that Hunter was still sleeping (comatose actually, if she had allowed herself to accept the truth) Cluney followed Mary out into the main room.

"What is it, Mary? Is something wrong?"

The older woman looked stern, worried. "I reckon there is! You ain't really got yourself believing that the poor major in there is gonna be fit to travel anytime soon?"

"Well, it might be a while, but he's stronger now, Mary." Her eyes glittered with hope. She wanted so badly to believe her own words. "He's gaining strength every hour."

"I hate to be blunt with you, child, but in a pig's eye!" Mary pointed toward the bedroom door, her hand shaking. "That man in there has one foot in the grave already, and I reckon it won't be long now till he crosses over."

"No!" Cluney cried. "That's a lie!"

"The only lie is what you're telling your own self, child. You don't even have to look at him no more to know his last battle is almost done."

Cluney cocked her head, not sure what Mary was getting at.

"He ain't gonna get better, no matter what you do. Best brace yourself for the end, Larissa. It's hard, I know. But you ain't the first woman to lose her man to this war, and, pity to say, you won't be the last." Mary shook her head sadly and gripped Cluney's cold hand. "I'm sorry, but it don't do no good for you to spin pretty tales that'll come to naught."

"But Wooter's on his way," Cluney insisted, nearly hysterical. "He'll be here soon—any minute—with medicine to make Hunter well. It's powerful stuff, Mary. You wait. You'll see."

Mary was still shaking her head. "Tain't likely anything can help him now. It's almost over. Go sit with him. Hold his hand and say a prayer for him. I'll be here close. Call me when . . ."

Cluney was furious. She whirled from Mary and raced back into Hunter's room. How dare the woman be such a doomsayer? Cluney had it all worked out in her mind. Wooter would come. She'd give Hunter the drugs he needed. In a day or two, there would be a miraculous change for the better, then a full recovery. In a few weeks, he would be strong enough to go home to Bluefield, where the two of them would live happily ever after.

"End of story!" Cluney said. "But not until we've raised a passel of kids and turned happily old and white-headed and senile together."

Just then a fierce gust of wind blew through the room. Cluney, who was sprawled on the bed clinging to Hunter, hardly noticed when the door blew open.

"Oh, Lordie!" came Wooter's voice. "Are we too late? I seen bad omens in the night. He ain't passed over, has he?"

"Wooter!" Cluney uttered a cry of soul-deep relief, her heart pounding with pure joy.

She turned toward him. The old mountaineer looked like he'd been to hell and back. His face was scratched all over. Twigs and leaves snarled his long beard. His clothes were torn and hung on him like rags on a scarecrow. But he was the most welcome sight Cluney could have imagined.

"You brought the medicine?"

"Yes, we brought it." B.J. Jackson stepped from behind Wooter and held out a paper sack.

Cluney uttered another cry. She wanted to run to her friend, but the sight of B.J. left her too stunned to move.

"B.J., can it really be you? What are you doing here? How did you get here?"

"There'll be time for a question-and-answer period later," B.J. replied, pushing the sack of pills into Cluney's trembling hand. "Right now, I think you'd better see to your patient, if you want this stuff to do any good."

For the next few minutes, all attention focused on Hunter Breckinridge. He was beyond swallowing the capsules, so Cluney opened each one and mixed the powdery contents with water. Then—patiently, laboriously—she dripped the antibiotics into Hunter's dry mouth. He never knew what was going on around him or that they were racing time to try to save his life. He knew nothing. At the moment, Hunter existed in his own world—a place of dark, swirling clouds, beyond pain or love.

"There, darling. You'll be better in no time," Cluney whispered.

Wooter and B.J. exchanged silent glances, but it seemed that Cluney had forgotten that they were even in the room. Sitting next to Hunter, holding his hand, she stared attentively at his still face, hoping to see the first sign of some change for the better.

"I'll leave you two now," Wooter whispered to B.J. "She'll be wantin' to talk to you in private in a bit."

B.J. nodded and closed the door after the old man left. She took a seat and sat quietly, watching Cluney watch

Hunter. Her friend's pain was a tangible force in the room. B.J. had stayed with Cluney through those awful days and nights after Jeff Layton's death. But somehow this was even more heart-wrenching. She recalled Cluney telling her about how she felt each time Jeff went away— that the last few moments were the most painful, even though they were still together. And so it was now. Hunter Breckinridge was obviously breathing his last, measured breaths. Yet Cluney clung to him, refusing to accept the inevitable.

The scene before her was so terribly sad that B.J. had to get her mind on something else. She didn't like thinking about her trip back into the past any more than she enjoyed dwelling on the scene before her. But it was difficult not to think about all that she and Wooter had been through. They had been whisked from the bright light of the moonbow over Cumberland Falls into some stormy netherworld, filled with moaning winds, flashing lightning, and formless, menacing foes. B.J. would believe forever that during their flight through time, she had come face-to-face with death in its most ghastly and horrible form. Now, here she was with her feet firmly planted on earth once more and that same ominous visage was still glaring nearby. Glaring, not at her, but at the handsome Civil War officer who had won her best friend's heart.

"It's not fair," B.J. muttered, unaware that she had spoken aloud.

"What?" Cluney turned at the sound of her friend's voice. She had forgotten that she and Hunter were no longer alone. "Oh, B.J.! I can't tell you how glad I am that you're here. Thank you for coming."

B.J. offered her a quick, unenthusiastic smile. "Yeah, I

know, girlfriend. Thanks accepted, but not necessary. So now what?"

Cluney frowned. "What do you mean?"

B.J. glanced toward Hunter. "Come on, girl, you know what I'm talking about. Are you staying here or going back where you belong?" She glanced about the room, which made her little apartment seem like a suite at the Plaza. "I mean, this is an okay place to visit, but I wouldn't want to stay here. I figured when I headed back, you'd come along to keep me company. I'm not nervous flying normally, but this trip was like from outer space. I could use your hand to hold. I'd say the sooner you and I get out of here, the better."

Cluney looked at B.J. as if she'd lost her mind. "Leave? Why, B.J., I can't believe what I'm hearing. You expect me to desert Hunter? He's my husband!"

B.J. let the last statement pass without comment. She was sorely tempted to point out the obvious to Cluney—that if he was indeed her husband—she was soon going to be a widow. Instead, she bit her lower lip and tried to think of some way to reason with Larissa Breckinridge. It was obvious that Cluney Summerland had been submerged in the other woman's personality, at least for the present.

"Has the medicine helped?" B.J. asked.

"Oh, yes!" Cluney forced a bright smile as she smoothed his covers and brushed a lock of damp hair off Hunter's hot forehead. "I expect he'll wake up any moment now. If the weather stays nice, he may even feel up to going outside to sit in the sunshine by then."

"Looks like rain or maybe even snow," B.J. muttered under her breath. This situation was obviously hopeless.

Hunter wasn't better and wouldn't be, but Cluney refused to accept the truth.

Suddenly, B.J. had a brainstorm. Yes, it might work! She allowed herself a small smile.

"Too bad there are no modern hospitals around here," she said as if thinking aloud. "I'll bet a crack nineteen-nineties internist could fix him up in no time."

Cluney whirled toward B.J. "What did you say?"

She shrugged. "I was just wishing he could see a real doctor in a real hospital. But I guess he's too sick to travel."

"Travel?" Cluney's eyes were glittering with hope suddenly. "You mean take Hunter over the moonbow?"

"Well, Wooter did say that we could go back tonight, if I want to. And I'm pretty sure I do." B.J. cupped her right ear and turned toward the window. "You hear that? Gunfire! There's a battle going on not far from here. Mrs. Renfro said we might have to evacuate if they move this way. I'm not keen on getting caught between the lines of blue and gray, and I don't think there are too many librarians' jobs around here for recently freed slaves." She nodded vigorously. "I'm going back tonight, Cluney, and I'd like for you to go with me. Hunter, too, if he can travel."

Cluney was across the room in an instant, hugging her friend with all her might.

"Oh, B.J., you're a wonder! Why didn't I think of this? Of course, we'll take Hunter back and get him right to a hospital. We can get the college ambulance to drive him to the medical center in Knoxville."

Just then, Hunter moaned—the first sound he'd made in hours. Both women turned to stare at him. His eyes were open, but glazed-looking. He moved his dry lips, but no words came.

Cluney went to him. She gripped his hand and kissed it.

"It's going to be all right, darling. We're taking you where you can get help. Hang on, please!"

A single syllable passed his lips. Had Cluney not been close, she couldn't have heard him say, "No." As it was, she pretended not to hear.


Hunter Breckinridge was more aware suddenly than he had been in some time. He knew, for instance, that Larissa and one of the servants were in his room. The young maid must be a recently purchased slave since he had never seen her before. But, no, that couldn't be. His slaves were all free. And even now he was dying from wounds he'd received while fighting to put an end to all slavery for all time.

His mind cleared a bit more, and he knew who she was—who she had to be. Private Lincoln's woman. Of course! Just as Hunter himself had found Larissa, Free had now found his Belle.

"Happy day," he murmured, but neither of the women heard him. They were talking about going somewhere, taking him with them.

"No," he moaned.

When Larissa leaned over him, he tried to form words to tell her that he couldn't go. He was too tired and the pain was too intense. He wanted to tell her to go without him. He knew he wouldn't be here much longer anyway. Exhausted with the effort of trying to speak, he let his eyes close again.

He needed to think pleasant thoughts so that he could forget his pain. Larissa! He would think of her. He would think about holding her in his arms, making love to her. She was sitting beside him even now. With great effort, he lifted his hand to her breast. Her nipple hardened under his fingers. He felt her cool hand cover his.

"Oh, my darling," she murmured, "I want you, too."

What happened next could only be a dream, but, oh, how it eased his pain!

B.J.'s eyes went wide as she watched Hunter reach up and caress Cluney's breast.

"Hey, I'm outta here. You guys need some privacy."

Before Cluney could answer, she found herself alone with Hunter. He might be weak, but he was awake and very much aware.

"I gave you medicine," she whispered. "It's helping, isn't it, darling?"

A weak smile played at the corners of Hunter's mouth. He dared not try to speak. He needed to concentrate all his effort on caressing Larissa's breast. He tugged gently at her gown, begging silently for her to remove it.

"We can't," she whispered. "As much as I want you, we just can't, my love."

When he continued the insistent gesture, Cluney rose and pulled the gown off over her head. Then she crawled into bed next to him. It felt so good just to lie close to him. She let her hands trail over his shoulder and chest. He sighed with pleasure. Encouraged, Cluney allowed her hand bolder moves. By turns, she stroked him with her fingertips and let her nails drag lightly over his flesh. And all the while, she talked softly.

"Everything is going to be all right, darling. I'm going to take you away from here. I know a place where you can get help. In a few days, you'll be yourself again. Then we'll go back to Bluefield. We'll start over again. While we've been together here, we've wiped the slate clean. All the old, bad things are gone from our lives. The war will soon be over, too. Then we'll have nothing to stand in the way of our happiness."

He caught her hand in his, the pressure of his fingers surprisingly strong. Cluney searched his eyes. What she saw there tugged at her heart. Such a depth of love, but an equal amount of sadness.

"Please don't look at me that way, darling," she begged. "You're wrong. Our life together isn't over. It's only beginning." She rested her head on his shoulder and sighed. "How can I make you believe me?"

Hunter wanted to believe. He wanted with all his heart to believe. But something told him Larissa's promises would never come to pass. Fate would intervene as it had in the past. But none of that mattered any longer. Larissa was right; they had thrust the bad times away. He knew now that she loved him. That knowledge would last him through his lifetime and beyond. She was his; the stars had proclaimed it so before the beginning of time.

Smiling, still feeling Larissa's soft hands on his flesh, Hunter drifted off to sleep.


"Belle!"

B.J. whirled around when someone called her by her given name. Nobody except her family even knew that her parents had christened her "Belle Joy Jackson" after a great-great-great-grandmother, who had come to

America over a century ago against her will on a reeking slave ship. B.J. had shed the name the minute she left home. She used B.J. as her legal name now.

"Who are you?" she demanded of the big, dark and handsome stranger grinning down at her.

"Aw, Belle, it's me. You ain't forgot your man, Jimbo?"

Belle stared into his wide, black eyes and recognized some spark there. Did she know this guy? She couldn't be sure. But she got some distinct feelings of warmth and safety from just being near him. She felt as long as she was in his presence that she would be protected from every bad thing in the world.

"Jimbo?" she ventured, thinking it an odd name at best.

"But I changed that once freedom come. They calls me Free now, 'cause my new name's George Washington Abraham Lincoln *Free*man." He put the emphasis on the first half of his new last name. "Won't that be fine to hand down to our children?"

B.J. stared, aghast, at the beaming stranger. "I think Wooter's been feeding you moonshine, mister. I've got no children. I'm not even married."

"Are too!" he countered. "Just 'cause all we done was jump the broomstick don't mean it ain't the real thing."

B.J. narrowed her eyes at him. She remembered her parents telling tales from their grandparents about slaves jumping the broomstick when their masters refused to allow them legal marriage ceremonies. This man wasn't part of her time. He belonged here, in the days of slaves and plantations and the Civil War.

Suddenly, he held out a worn snapshot. "Miz Larissa give me this likeness of you." He held it up beside B.J.'s face, then nodded. "That's you all right, Belle."

278

She took the tattered photo from his hand. "Of course that's me—B.J. Jackson."

"My Belle," he repeated stubbornly. "I'd know you anywheres."

"I'm sorry," she said. "I don't remember you. When and where do you think you knew me?"

He gave her a heartbreaking smile. "I don't just think, honey, I know it for sure and certain. Before you got sold off to that place in Kentucky, we grew up slaves together in Tennessee. When we was young'uns, we played around the dooryard of the cabins together. Then you was sent up to the big house and me to the fields. We axed the master could we marry. He said slaves don't marry no more than mules do. So by the light of the moon, and with all the people gathered round, you and me, we jumped the broomstick holding hands. We're married, Belle, whether you remember or not. You're my wife!"

B.J. had a creepy feeling along her spine suddenly. His words brought visions to her mind. She saw herself in a patched, white gown, cast off by the master's young wife. She felt the dirt warm on her bare feet and the light from bonfires searing her cheeks. And next to her, holding her hand, she felt the man she loved more than life itself.

Struggling to get the question out, she asked, "If we were married, what happened? Why have you had to search for me?"

Free's face went hard and his eyes flared with anger. "The young mistress, she say the massa foolin' 'round with you. She say she won't have you in her house or on her place. She make the massa sell you off to a man in Kentucky. He took you off to a place called Brodaker."

B.J. gasped softly. "Broad Acres!" Suddenly, she remembered the name of the run-down plantation long ago in Kentucky. She remembered, too, an unhappy young slave girl who was called Arabella.

"I tried runnin' twice," Free continued, "but they sicked the dogs on me, then whupped me good once they had me back. I was near 'bout well enough to run again when we was freed. Then I headed straight for Kentucky to find my Belle." He flashed a blinding grin. "And here you be!"

When Free mentioned the master in Tennessee and his attentions toward a young slave woman, the hair rose on her arms. Thinking of being sold off to Kentucky made her feel dizzy and ill. There had been a "massa" there, too, young and virile and cruelly demanding.

"Massa Jordan," she murmured, not even aware she had spoken aloud.

"Belle? What you say?" Free leaned down closer.

She shook her head, trying to clear it. "I need to sit down."

Concerned, Free took her hand and led her into the living room, to a chair. "What's done happened to you, Belle? What did they do to you to make you forget me?"

She stared into Free's eyes, her own shimmering with tears. She knew suddenly what had happened. Somehow, during that terrible, awesome flight over the moonbow, she had come back in time to take her own ancestor's place. She *was* Belle Joy now—former bedwarmer to two cruel masters. Wife of this slave, self-named *Free*man.

"I haven't forgotten you," she said softly. "I've been searching for you, too. I just didn't realize it."

Just then, Cluney came into the living room. The scene she witnessed there came as a shock. Her friend, B.J., sat in a chair, tears streaming down her face. Free was bending over her, his huge frame dwarfing the woman he embraced so lovingly. He, too, had damp trails down his dark cheeks.

Hearing someone enter the room, Free turned. His face split into an enormous grin. "It's my Belle, Miz Larissa. She come back to me."

Cluney could only stare in amazement.

"He's right," B.J. said. "I can't explain any of this, but I know I belong to Free." Then she added with wonder in her voice, "I love him, Cluney."

Cluney embraced each of them and offered her congratulations. The turn of events stunned her, and later she would demand to know all the particulars of this bizarre reunion. But right now she had more pressing matters on her mind.

"Have you seen Wooter?" she asked the blissful pair. "I have to talk to him right away."

"He went out yonder by the falls," Free answered.

B.J. studied her friend's face. "You're planning to go back, aren't you?"

Cluney nodded. "Yes. And I'm taking Hunter." She glanced at Free and then back at B.J. "I was hoping you'd go with me, but . . ."

"Of course I'll go," B.J. answered. She squeezed Free's big hand and smiled up at him. "We'll both go, won't we, Free?"

Free had no idea what the two women were talking about, but he'd go to the ends of the earth with his Belle. He nodded.

"Good!" Cluney breathed a sigh of relief. "Now all I have to do is talk Wooter into showing us the way."

"Are you sure Hunter's strong enough to make that trip?"

"He must be, B.J.! There's no other way to save him."

Cluney hurried out in search of Wooter. There wasn't much time and everything had to be ready. She only wished she felt more confident that this plan would work.

As she headed toward the falls, she glanced up at heaven and prayed fervently, "Please, God, save the man I love most in the world! Don't let him die!"

# Chapter Sixteen

A dark cloud passed over the sun as Cluney approached Wooter. She hugged herself and shivered. How would she ever talk the cantankerous old mountain man into going along with her wild, desperate scheme?

Before she could speak, Wooter turned. His bearded face was screwed into a frown and he squinted one eye at her piercingly.

"No need you explaining what's a-gnawin' at you, little girl. I figured you'd hit on a plan to take him to the other side sooner or later."

Cluney was so relieved, she felt faint. "If you knew that was what I was supposed to do, why didn't you tell me?"

"I didn't say you was *supposed* to do it. If you want my opinion, I think it's a damn-fool idea. Crossing the moonbow ain't no Sunday picnic, you know. It could kill him 'fore he ever gets to the other side."

Cluney shivered and clutched her arms more tightly. "Don't say that. Don't even think it! Taking him over is the only way I can save him."

Wooter turned, avoiding eye contact. He remained silent for so long that Cluney thought he had forgotten she was there until he spoke to her. "Whoever said you was sent here to save him?"

She caught her breath in surprise. Of course she was meant to save him!

"Why else would I be here? You told me yourself, Wooter, that only people who were needed could come over the moonbow."

Wooter kicked a rock with the toe of his boot. It flew over into the gorge and landed with a dull thud.

After he had waited to hear it land, he said, "Maybe you was needed to ease his dying. Did you ever think of that?"

"No!" Cluney stamped her foot. "That's not why I came here and that's not what I intend to do. I'm taking him back to a hospital."

Again, Cluney was forced to wait for what seemed an eternity before Wooter told her what was on his mind.

"What makes you think he'd be happy in that other time? What could he do? What kind of life would he have?"

"We'll be together," Cluney replied. "That's all that matters."

"To you, maybe. But it's different for a man. He needs his own place in life."

Cluney shook her head, blinking back tears. "We'll worry about that later. Right now, all that matters is getting help for him. And the only way I know is to take him forward in time to a hospital. After he's well, if he's not happy, he can come back. I'll come with him."

Wooter stared at her for a long, silent time. He was obviously trying to make up his mind. Cluney held her breath, waiting to hear what he would say.

"Well then," he began, "you dose him up good with

that medicine you're so keen on. If you got anything for pain, give him plenty of that. He'll need it. Then you dress him up real warm. Me and Free will get him out here to the edge of the falls come time to go. And I reckon we better figure on bringing that dog of his along, too. He'll be needing something of his old life with him for comfort."

"Is that all?" Cluney asked. She'd been hoping Wooter would explain elaborate preparations that would take all day—keep her mind off what they were about to attempt.

"No, that ain't all," Wooter stated in a flat tone. "If I was you, I'd take pains to explain to Miz Renfro how to give him that medicine in case this don't work." He stared at her hard, his gaze unwavering. "There ain't no guarantees, you know."

Cluney refused to let Wooter's cynicism dampen her hopes. She turned from the man and headed back to the house, back to Hunter. It was time for more lifesaving drugs.

But before she gave Hunter his next dose, she called Mary Renfro into the room and explained everything to the woman as Wooter had suggested, just to be on the safe side.

"I'm gonna miss you, Larissa," Mary told her after they'd finished with Hunter. "Having you here has been like having my own daughter, Lorettie, back again. But don't you worry, I'll take good care of the major once you're gone, and I'm sure you'll come back to him just as soon as you can. He needs you, you know. You're better than any tonic for that man. I honestly thought he'd be gone long before now. You've wrought a miracle, child."

In a sudden burst of affection and gratitude, Cluney

hugged the thin woman. "I'm taking Hunter with me, Mary. We won't be back."

"Not ever?" the woman cried.

Cluney shook her head. "If all goes well, we'll have a new life together, Hunter and I. I want to thank you for all you've done for him. You saved his life, Mary. I owe you so much and there's no way I can ever repay you."

"You don't owe me nothing," Mary said firmly. "You owe yourself and that fine man of yours a long and happy life. See that you both get it."

"I mean to do my level best, Mary. I promise you that!"

The moon rose huge and blood-red that night. The air was cold, with a threat of rain or even snow. Cluney and B.J. shivered, coatless, in the cutting wind. But soon, they knew, they'd be back in the warm Kentucky springtime.

The two women followed along as Wooter and Free wheeled Hunter's chair to the edge of the falls. He was bundled tightly in every available blanket, with the old hound, Trooper, lying in his lap. Hunter looked so shrunken and still that Cluney's heart gave a lurch of fear. She touched his face to make sure he was still warm—still alive.

"He's all right," Wooter assured her. "It's all them pain potions you gave him a while back. Mark my word, it'll go easier on him this way. He won't know nothing till it's all over."

Cluney knew Wooter was right. She only hoped she hadn't given him too much.

"Now," Wooter said, "let's all stand close together and right still. The time's nigh. Hold onto the one next to you and don't let go, no matter what."

Cluney and Free were on either side of Hunter's chair, holding onto its straight back. Wooter clutched Cluney's other hand, while Free kept a strong arm around his Belle. When Free leaned down to give B.J. a good-luck kiss, Cluney did the same for Hunter.

They were ready. All they needed now was the moonbow. The moments creeped by, silent and unbearable. When would it happen? When could they be off on their perilous journey through time?

Suddenly, the mist at the skirt of the falls shimmered with a faint glow. Then the light grew brighter and brighter, until Cluney had to close her eyes against the glare. She heard the familiar roar, and felt the earth shift beneath her feet. An odd dizziness overcame her. She thought she spoke Hunter's name, but she couldn't be sure.

The last thing she heard before the roar became deafening was Hunter's distant voice. "I love you, Larissa. I always have and I always will."

His words were punctuated by the baleful howl of old Trooper.

Then it seemed they were flying, with time racing past them like pages in a picture book. In those very first moments, Cluney was conscious only of the scenes flashing before her eyes. Then suddenly, she realized with horror that she was gripping, not Hunter's wheeled chair, but Free's rough sleeve.

Hunter was gone!

"No-o-o-o!" Her anguished scream echoed down through the gorge and out over the mountains. It wailed through time, spanning years, decades, centuries. It was the sound of all the pain and heartbreak and suffering in

287

the whole universe. It was a small, forlorn cry, lost in the blackness of eternity.

Before Cluney opened her eyes, she knew that the ground where she lay was damp and cold. As cold as her heart.

"Hunter?" she cried, scrambling to her knees.

She scanned the area quickly, hoping against all hope. The others lay sprawled around her, still stunned from their flight through time. B.J. remained very still, while Free's eyes were open already. He gazed about, obviously dazed and in wonder. Wooter climbed to his feet, his old bones creaking with the effort. His gaze swept the area, then he limped over to Cluney to help her up.

"I'm sorry, little girl. I was afraid this would happen."

Cluney was wild. "We have to go back for him, Wooter. Right now! We can't leave him. What will happen to him? We have to get him to a hospital."

Wooter shook his head sadly. "You know we can't do that. Not in broad daylight. Even come dark, it won't be no use. There's no way back till next full moon. I ain't even sure you could go back then. You see, little girl, he don't need you no longer."

"Hunter *does* need me!" she cried desperately.

"Not no more, little girl. You done all you could."

B.J., aroused by Cluney's cries, came to her friend and embraced her. "Don't Cluney! You did the best you could. Mary will take good care of him."

Just then, a tall, uniformed ranger strode over to them. "What are you people doing out here this time of the morning? Did you sleep by the falls? That's not allowed, you know."

B.J., fully aware now, recognized Ranger Sonny Taylor immediately. She felt a surge of relief to see a familiar face from a familiar time. "Hey, Sonny. How's it going?"

He gave her a closer look, then frowned. "Do I know you, ma'am?"

"I hope to tell you! I've bugged you enough about my missing friend." She turned and pointed at Cluney. "Well, she didn't fall in the gorge. Here she is! I found her just like I told you I would. Sheriff Elrod can call off his search for good now."

The big ranger looked more and more perplexed by every word B.J. spoke. Lifting his hat to scratch his head, he said, "Ma'am, I'm sorry, but I just can't recall ever meeting you or your friends. And I don't know anything about a search for anyone falling into the gorge. I think you all better come along with me and explain what you're doing in the park before opening hours."

"But, Sonny . . . ?"

He turned back and gave B.J. a hard look. "Come on, now. You all cooperate and I'll let you off easy. It's a mite cold to be standing out here. I'd rather hear what you have to say back in my nice, warm office."

Cluney realized he was right; she was shivering from the cold. Puzzled, she glanced up at the trees. The season had been well into spring when she'd left. By now, the branches should be thick and lush with the green of summer. Instead, they looked stark and leafless. How long had she been gone? It seemed only days—weeks at the most. Could it in reality have been months?

She turned to B.J. and whispered, "When you left here with Wooter night before last, what was the date?"

"June the sixteenth." Realizing why Cluney had asked, B.J. glanced about. "Hey, something's not right here."

"That's just what I was thinking," Cluney answered. "Summer should be coming on, but it looks more like late winter or very early spring."

Sure enough, when they crowded into the tiny ranger's office, the calendar on his desk read "27 February."

"That's why Sonny doesn't recognize me," B.J. whispered to Cluney. "We didn't meet until the night you disappeared, the eighteenth of May."

Suddenly, Cluney was shaking all over. She gripped B.J.'s arm for support. It couldn't be, but it must be!

"What's the matter, Cluney? You're as pale as a ghost." B.J. pulled the ranger's chair away from his desk. "Here, sit down before you fall down. What is it? What's the matter with you?"

"The date," Cluney managed after several wordless tries. "It's February the twenty-seventh, B.J."

"Yeah? So we missed our mark on the way back. We get to live a couple of months over again. After all we've been through, that hardly seems worth mentioning."

Tears were now streaming down Cluney's face and she was trembling as if she were having a seizure. Finally, she got out what she was trying to say. "Jeff! It's only February, Jeff's still alive!"

"My God! You're right, Cluney. His plane didn't go down until the first of March."

Free was so amazed by everything around him—the electric heater, the radio playing country music, the ranger's ballpoint pen—that he failed to notice anything else. But Wooter had been listening in on the whispered conversation between the two women. His frown deepened with every word he heard.

"Hey, hold on a minute," he interrupted. "Just 'cause we missed on our landing don't mean you two can go

290

changing anything that's already happened the first time around."

"Why not?" B.J. demanded, obviously ready to fight. "Cluney's fiancé was dead when she left. Now he's alive again, which means . . ."

"Which means," Wooter cut her off, "that she knows it's going to happen, so she can be a lot nicer to him before what fate has willed happens to him all over again."

Cluney moaned and covered her face with her hands to keep from sobbing aloud. She had just lost Hunter for the second time. How could she possibly endure the agony of losing Jeff again? And she couldn't even be with him. His ship was already in the Mediterranean by now. He'd left the States three weeks ago.

Before further discussion could take place, the ranger entered his office and shut the door.

"I'm surprised at the lot of you," he said, glancing from one to another. "You all aren't kids out on a lark. You ought to know the laws around here. Now what were you doing at the falls all night?"

"Come for the moonbow," Wooter piped up. "There ain't no crime in that."

Sonny nodded. "You're right there, mister, but we frown on people staying by the falls all night. It's too dangerous."

"We wasn't at the falls all night, but go the hell ahead and frown on us, if you like. Then let us go. We ain't done no mischief and we want to get home."

"Well, now, you just hold on a minute." Sonny obviously didn't care for Wooter's surly tone. "I've got my orders not to let things like this pass. You see, we've been having a lot of vandalism around here lately. Somebody even stole an old tombstone from the Civil War burying ground."

The ranger's mention of Hunter's grave marker drew B.J.'s immediate attention. "You mean that stone is gone?"

"Last time I looked." Sonny narrowed his eyes at her. "You know something about that, ma'am?"

B.J. started to remind the ranger that he'd told her all about it, that he'd even shown her the spot where Hunter Breckinridge had been buried. Then she realized that he wouldn't remember because at this point in time none of that had happened yet.

"I've heard about it," she answered simply. "Could we go have a look at the burying ground?"

"Right now?" he said. "What in the world for?"

"Just humor me, Sonny. Please?" She smiled at him and he almost smiled back.

"Well, I guess it couldn't hurt."

"Great! Free and I will go with you. Wooter can stay here with Cluney. She's not feeling too well."

B.J.'s mind was whirling. If Hunter's stone—indeed, his entire grave—was still missing from the burying ground, that would mean that he must have survived after they left him behind. Maybe Cluney couldn't do anything about changing Jeff Layton's fate, but it would certainly make her feel better, after all she'd been through, to know that she'd saved Hunter Breckinridge.

Not even sure why he was going along with such nonsense, Sonny Taylor escorted B.J. and Free through the woods to the old burying ground. Along the way, he explained again about the Renfros and the cabin that used to be in the clearing—about all the things they knew so well from firsthand experience. Finally, they stood in the midst of the tangled underbrush and age-stained tombstones.

Suddenly, Free realized exactly where he was. A tremor went through his big frame and he clung to his Belle. He remembered digging some of these very graves and helping to lay the soldiers' bodies in them. But the grave he'd started working on for Major Breckinridge was gone. There was not even space for one where it had been.

"It's the confoundingest thing," Sonny said, shaking his head. "See? It was right there, but it's vanished now, like the others just closed in around it and squeezed it out."

"He's telling God's own truth," Free whispered to B.J. "I commenced digging the major's grave when Miz Mary told me to. It was right between those two—Captain Van Dyke and Private McClenny." He pointed to the location. "Ain't no grave there now."

"All right!" B.J. cried with glee. Then, leaving the two men staring after her, she turned and fled back toward the ranger's office.

"What got into her, you reckon?" Sonny asked of Free.

The big man only shook his head in answer, but he was grinning ear to ear. "The major made it," he muttered to himself. "He don't need no grave."

Back at the ranger station, B.J. flew through the door, startling Cluney and Wooter. "Hunter's okay!" she cried.

Wooter frowned at her. He'd spent the past few minutes with the little Summerland girl trying to make her understand that what was meant to be couldn't be changed, no matter what day and age it was. He'd told her that the fate of both Hunter Breckinridge and Jeff Layton was decided long before they were born, and no mortal human could do nothing about it. Like it or not!

He'd tried to be gentle with her, but there were times when a man just had to be firm. Now, here was this wild, crazy woman, tearing in, screaming about how the major was just fine and dandy.

"Bull hockey!" Wooter growled.

"Listen to me," B.J. insisted, glaring at the old man. "If Hunter had died at the Renfros', he'd be buried in that graveyard, wouldn't he? Well, he's not!"

"How can you know that?" Wooter argued. "The ranger just said his marker got stole."

"His whole grave's gone—like it was never there." She turned to Cluney for support. "Free told me Mary Renfro told him to start digging Hunter's grave. Is that so?"

Cluney, fighting for control, nodded her head. She could still hear the awful sound of Free's shovel scraping at the hard earth.

"I begged Mary to make him stop digging," Cluney said quietly. "It was too horrible to hear the sound . . . to have Hunter hear his own grave being prepared."

B.J. turned a triumphant face to Wooter. "Well, that proves it once and for all! Free showed me the spot where he dug. There's *no grave there!*"

Wooter went to scratching his beard. His face was screwed up with puzzlement. Neither he nor Cluney said anything. They just stared at B.J.

"Don't you see what this means? Hunter didn't die trying to cross the moonbow. And Mary must have nursed him back to health. Otherwise, he'd be out there with the others."

Cluney still wasn't convinced. "What about the diary? It ended the night I went back in time. If he'd lived, why weren't there entries after that?"

B.J. couldn't answer that one. But she had to make

Cluney believe as she did. Surely, there must be a way, if only she could think how.

Just then, Free and Sonny came back in. The ranger's eyes immediately lit on the woman with silver-blond hair. She was real pretty, but her face looked tired and strained. And she was so pale.

"Are you all right, ma'am?" he asked Cluney.

She nodded. "I think so. I'm just so very tired."

"Well . . ." Sonny glanced from one to another of them. "I reckon I can let you go. I can't see as you've done any real mischief. Besides, I got another problem to take care of this morning first thing. We may really have someone missing in the area now. That yellow car's been out in the parking lot all night. I've got to run a check on it and find out who owns it. Then I reckon I'll have to get it towed down the mountain and impounded till we find the owner."

"Oh, no, you don't!" B.J. cried. "That's my car, my way home."

Sonny looked relieved, then frowned. "Can you prove it's yours, ma'am?"

Moments later, B.J. had produced both her driver's license and her registration. Satisfied, Ranger Taylor let them go, but not before one final stern warning about sleeping out by the falls.


Cluney was so tired by the time B.J. and Free dropped her off that she didn't even invite them in. All she wanted was a hot bath, a cup of real coffee, and then her own bed.

"If I'm lucky, maybe I can sleep right through the next month," she said as she peeled off her grubby clothes. "Then I won't have to deal with what's ahead."

She walked over to Jeff's picture and picked it up. He smiled at her from inside the frame. How well she remembered that cocky, confident grin—like he owned the world and knew all its secrets. His eyes seemed so alive and loving as she gazed into them.

"You *are* alive!" she said, trying to make herself grasp the fact.

Suddenly, Hunter Breckinridge and Larissa's love for him seemed like some distant, bittersweet story she had read long ago. There was still pain when she thought of them, but the tragic pair no longer seemed to have any intimate connection with Clair de Lune Summerland. Instead, Jeff Layton was once more her whole life, her lover, her soul mate. In some way, he seemed almost an extension of Hunter. Her love for the two of them intertwined in the deepest part of her heart.

"Oh, Jeff." She set the picture back on her bedside table and sighed. "If only I knew how to reach you. Maybe I *could* make a difference."

On impulse, she looked up the area code for Jeff's home base, then picked up the phone and dialed Virginia information. After a seemingly interminable wait, the operator answered.

"What city, please?"

"Virginia Beach," Cluney said.

A few clicks and buzzes, then a voice asked, "What party, please?"

The operator wanted a name, of course, but Cluney had none to give her. Instead, she answered, "I need the Naval Air Station Oceana."

"What party, please?"

"I don't know. Just tell me how to reach the base operator."

A moment more and Cluney had the number she'd requested. This might work. It just might! She dialed and held her breath, waiting for someone to answer. Surely, the squadron's home base communicated regularly with the ship. And certain emergencies were bound to arise while the men were deployed—births, deaths, illnesses back home. If she could only get them to transmit a message to Jeff for her . . .

"NAS Oceana," came the woman's businesslike voice at the other end of the line. "What extension, please?"

The question threw Cluney for a moment. "I'm not sure. I need to reach someone who is deployed to the Mediterranean. His ship is at sea now. Is there a number I can call to send a message?"

"Is this an emergency, ma'am?"

"I think it is. I mean, yes, of course it is!"

"A death in the family?"

"No."

"A life-threatening illness?"

"No, not exactly."

"Well, then, ma'am, I'm sorry. The Navy has strict rules regarding emergencies. Nothing else qualifies, I'm sorry."

Cluney wanted to reach through the phone and strangle the bland-voiced operator. But she managed to hold her temper.

"This *is* a life-threatening situation. The threat is to an officer on that ship. I have to get in touch with him immediately."

"I'm not sure I understand, ma'am."

"Look! We're wasting precious time. I *must* reach him! Right away!"

"The fastest way to send an emergency message is

through the Red Cross, ma'am. I can give you that number, if you like."

"Oh, yes! Thank you!" Cluney all but kissed the phone.

She hung up and dialed the new number she had written down. This time a man answered with the usual offer to help.

"I hope you can help me. The Navy operator suggested I call you. I need to get a message to someone on a ship in the Mediterranean. It's an emergency," she added.

"Are you a family member?"

Cluney almost admitted to being only Jeff's fiancée, but caught herself in time. If anyone other than family members could send messages, the man wouldn't have asked, she reasoned.

Crossing her fingers behind her back, Cluney said, "Yes, I'm his mother." She'd never met Mrs. Layton, who lived in California. But she was certain the woman would want to help save her only son's life.

"I need the name of the officer, his unit, and the name and relationship of the deceased, ma'am."

"I didn't say anyone had died."

"Oh! Sorry, ma'am. I simply assumed." He paused a moment, collecting his composure after making such a blunder. "Then the name of the family member who is ill and the relationship."

"No one's ill either."

"Ah!" He seemed to brighten. "Then you want to send word of a new baby. Congratulations, ma'am! You must be the grandmother."

"No," Cluney answered with a frustrated sigh.

"Well, I'm sorry, then, ma'am, but we can't help you. Any other messages will have to go by the normal route."

"What *is* the normal route?" Cluney demanded.

"Fax, regular mail, or by phone once the ship reaches port."

*Fax!* Why hadn't Cluney thought of that herself? She thanked the man, then quickly hung up. There was a fax machine at the college she could use. All she needed was the ship's number. She hurriedly dialed the Virginia base again.

She received an answer quickly. "I'm sorry, ma'am. We are not allowed to give out that information."

Discouraged beyond all hope, Cluney hung up the receiver. For a long time, she just sat there staring at the phone. She'd never liked telephones much. Right now, she hated the useless instrument.

She would try again later. Maybe she'd even phone Jeff's mother. If Mrs. Layton called, surely the Navy would be more helpful.

She picked up her towel and headed for the bathroom, weary, discouraged, and frustrated to the marrow of her bones.

"Maybe a hot shower will soak the ache out of my heart."

Cluney had shampoo foaming all over her when she heard the phone ring.

"Oh, drat!"

Blindly, she reached out of the shower for a towel, but soap got in her eyes, stinging, and blinding her. Before she could get one foot out of the stall, the ringing stopped.

"It was probably B.J." She went back to her leisurely lathering.

But the more she thought about it, the more she knew it wasn't B.J. Her friend had her own important agenda for the day. She and Free had much to catch up on. And

Free had a lot of adjusting to do, fast. No, the caller had to be someone else. But who?

The answer came to her with such a rush of love and longing that she knew she had to be right.

"Jeff!" she cried. "Oh, my God, it must have been Jeff!"

He had promised he'd call the minute the ship reached its first port.

Cluney hurriedly rinsed her hair, then toweled herself partially dry. She could live with being damp as long as she was sitting by the phone, waiting for Jeff to call back. And he would call again—she just knew it!

And maybe, when she heard his voice, she would finally be able to believe that he was really alive—that he would, in spite of everything that had happened, be here to marry her on the last day of June.

# Chapter Seventeen

Cluney sat staring at the silent phone until her eyes grew heavy. Forty-five minutes crawled by and then an hour. Finally, she gave up her battle against fatigue and stretched out on the bed. Instantly, she fell asleep.

Once her eyes closed, a collage of assorted dreams filled her head. She was a tightrope walker, precariously balanced on a slender beam of silvery rainbow. At one end stood a tall, solemn-faced soldier, begging her to come to him. At the opposite side of the moonbow, a handsome, laughing aviator winked at her and beckoned. As she turned this way, then that, trying to make up her mind which call to answer, a pair of pesky raccoons climbed onto her thin blade of light and commenced chasing each other, threatening to throw her off, into the deep, black gorge far below.

Suddenly, the two masked creatures ran into Cluney. Her feet flew out from under her. Down and down and down she tumbled. People and things shot past her as she fell through the dark spiral of her dream. She saw her mother and father, the brother she had never known. Mary Renfro was there, along with Wooter, Miss Redbird, B.J., Free, and Jordan Breckinridge. Cluney paused in midair to wonder what ever happened to him.

"No matter," she said in her dream. "He's gone now, just like all the others. All but Jeff." Then she went right on falling, calling Jeff's name until the sound spiraled up behind her like the funnel cloud of a tornado, sending out echoes in all directions.

Cluney watched a smile light her own face. "He should certainly hear that," she said, watching the cartoonlike corkscrew of echoes that her dreaming mind fashioned.

She came out of the nightmare still calling his name. "Jeff . . . Jeff . . . where are you, Jeff?"

Nearly two hours had passed and again the phone was ringing. Cluney reached for the receiver and managed to drag the whole thing off the table. It clattered to the floor beside the bed with a complaint of rattles, rings, and dings.

"Hello?" she said breathlessly.

"Cluney?"

Her mouth moved, but as hard as she tried to force them, words refused to come. Was she still dreaming? Most likely. Otherwise, how could she be hearing his voice?

Her glance caught the calendar on the wall over her desk. "February 26," it read. She hadn't yet turned it to bring it up to date since she got home. Today was the twenty-seventh and she knew it. She also knew that this flashback in time was how she was able to hear Jeff Layton's voice at the other end of the phone after she had already endured the pain of his death.

"Darling, is that really you?" she finally managed.

"Oh, Cluney, it's so great to hear your voice! I called earlier, but there was no answer." His statement neither accused nor questioned. He was simply giving her information.

"I heard the phone, Jeff. I was in the shower with soap in my eyes, so I couldn't hurry to answer it. I was so mad—before I could get to the bedroom, it stopped ringing."

She heard Jeff's deep laugh at the other end. "Oh, Cluney, you're a riot! Why don't you get an answering machine, darling? Then when you get calls, but have soap in your eyes, the machine can take the message and you can call back later."

"No, Jeff! You know how I hate all those modern contraptions. I despise talking to answering machines, and I will not subject my friends to a machine version of myself. If I'm not at home to answer my phone in person, I don't want it answered—period."

Suddenly, Cluney realized that Jeff was calling from somewhere in the Med and that his call must be costing him an arm and a leg while she chatted away about trivial nothings. After his death, she had thought of so many things she'd wished she could tell him. Now here she sat, arguing about a stupid answering machine. The two of them had far more serious topics to discuss—like the fact that he was alive.

"Jeff," Cluney said, her tone urgent now, "I have to tell you something—something *really* important! Listen to me, and please don't argue. It's imperative that you *not* fly anymore and that you get off that ship as soon as possible. Your life is in danger!"

He chuckled at the other end of the line. She could tell he wasn't taking her seriously. "And just how am I supposed to do that, sweetheart?"

"I don't know. Maybe you could get your mother to

write your commanding officer a note, saying she wants you excused from flying for the rest of the cruise because it's too dangerous."

Now, he roared with laughter. "The Navy isn't run quite like a prep school, Cluney. I'm afraid an excuse from Mom wouldn't carry much weight. But maybe someone in Washington could write me a note."

"I don't care *who* writes it, Jeff, as long as you stay out of the air. Promise me you won't fly!"

"Hey, Cluney, if you'll stop talking for a minute so I can get a word in edgewise, I have a surprise for you."

"What?" she asked. "Tell me, Jeff."

"First, how about you telling me whether or not you still love me?"

"Of course I do! More than ever. I never knew how much!"

"That's more like it. Then we're still getting married?"

"I'm certainly planning on it. I've even been looking at wedding gowns."

She was telling the truth. She had been, before Jeff's fatal accident. She glanced down at her bare left hand. She'd taken off her engagement ring before she went across the moonbow. Now she reached into her jewelry box for the diamond solitaire and slipped it back on her finger. She held it to the light and smiled when it flashed a rainbow around the room.

"A wedding gown, eh?" Jeff continued. "I hope it's something real old-fashioned, honey. Something with lots of lace and seed pearls and little satin roses. Victorian! Yeah, that's what I like."

"Why, Jeff!" Cluney exclaimed. "I guess I don't know you as well as I thought. I figured you'd prefer something simple, modern, and classic."

"Nope! I'm an old-world guy, through and through, darling. Besides, I have a reason for wanting an old-fashioned bride."

"Tell me!" Cluney begged.

He chuckled mysteriously. "I can't right now. It's a surprise, sweetheart. You'll find out soon enough. Right now, we need to talk about a wedding date. Cluney, what are you doing on May eighteenth?"

Instantly, Cluney's mind grasped the ominous significance of that date, but she hesitated to say to Jeff, "That's the day I'm supposed to leave for California to share my grief over your death with your mother. But I won't make it. You see, I'll get detoured over the moonbow, back to the time of the Civil War and into the arms of another man."

No, she couldn't tell her fiancé that. Instead, she said simply, "I've no plans that I can think of."

"Great! Marry me, then."

"That soon? But your ship won't be back by then, will it?" Suddenly, she gave an excited cry. "Oh, Jeff! That's the surprise, isn't it? You and your squadron are flying home early."

"You might say that," Jeff answered cryptically. "You're sure you don't mind changing the date, sweetheart? I don't want to rush you into this."

Cluney was grinning from ear to ear as happy tears squeezed out at the corners of her eyes. How could Jeff possibly think that she would have the slightest objection?

"Of course, I don't mind, darling! The sooner the better! It won't take much planning. A small ceremony in the college chapel with a reception in the social hall afterward—that's what we'd talked about before you left."

"That's what *we* talked about. But I'm afraid you'll

have to forget those simple pleasures, darling." Jeff sounded hesitant, his tone guarded. "You see, Mom's flying in from the coast in a few days. Actually, she's the one with the surprise in store for both of us. And you can bet it has to do with our wedding."

"Your mom's coming? Here?" Cluney couldn't hide her stricken tone. She'd been nervous for months at the thought of meeting Jeff's socialite mother.

"I hope you don't mind her helping with things, Cluney," Jeff pleaded gently. "Mom can be a little pushy at times, but she means well. And I'd better warn you in advance, she's big on theme weddings."

"Oh, not one of those black-and-white ones, I hope. Black is for funerals and sorrow. I'm a traditionalist. I don't want anyone wearing black or feeling sad at my wedding."

Jeff laughed. He obviously knew more about the plans for their wedding than he was telling his bride-to-be. "I'm sure, you don't have to worry about that, sweetheart. But, if Mom had her way, we'd be married in the Winner's Circle at Churchill Downs—the perfect Kentucky-style ceremony. You see, she's big on tradition, too. But don't let her bully you. Our wedding should be the way *you* want it, and I'll tell her that myself, if I have to."

"Oh, Jeff!" Cluney said suddenly. "I've missed you so much. I can't begin to tell you. I'll be so happy, and so relieved once we're married, no matter how or where. This has been an awful month for me. I wish I could see you right now. If I could just hug you and kiss you!"

"That's what you'd do if I were there with you now, darling?"

Cluney chuckled sexily into the phone. "For starters.

I'm not sure I can go into all the details on the line, love. The phone company might discontinue my service."

"That good, huh?"

"Wel-l-l . . ." she teased. "Do you remember the night before you left on deployment?"

"Yes-s-s-s!" he answered in a husky, drawn-out sigh. "Do I *ever*!"

"Where are you, by the way?"

"Well, I'm not on the ship."

"I know that," Cluney answered. "You're ashore. But which port—Greece, Turkey, Italy, Crete?"

Instead of answering her, he said, "Uh-oh! I have to hang up now, sweetheart. But I'll call back in a little while."

Cluney grimaced. "Some of the guys came up, huh?" It seemed whenever Jeff's buddies put in an appearance, he had to dash.

"No, it's not the guys. Stay right where you are. I'll get back to you in a few minutes. Hey, girl? I love you."

His words sent thrills all through Cluney and brought tears once more to her eyes. Such a short time ago, she'd never thought to hear his voice again.

"I love you, too, Jeff. More than anything!"

The phone went dead. Cluney sat for a time, cradling the receiver against her breasts. *Married*! she thought. *To Jeff*!

"Mrs. Jeff Layton. Clair Summerland Layton. Cluney Layton." She tried out all forms of her name, then added in a whisper, "Larissa Courtney Breckinridge Layton."

She picked up Jeff's picture and stared at it. How very strange! Until this moment, she hadn't realized how much he resembled Hunter Breckinridge. The bone structure of the face was slightly different, but their eyes . . . She could remember how Hunter had looked at her in those last moments before she crossed the moonbow, when he was telling her goodbye. Although Jeff always seemed to be smiling, at times she'd seen that same sweet-sad look in his gaze.

"If I believed in reincarnation," she began. Then she shook her head. "No, it couldn't be? *Could it?*"

The phone rang again just then. She snatched the receiver from the cradle and said, "Jeff?"

She heard a woman laugh gaily on the other end of the line. "Close," the bright voice said. "At least you have a member of Jeff's family. Cluney, this is Andrea Layton, Jeff's mother. I've tried calling you for the past two weeks, but there's been no answer. Then I phoned your friend, Ms. Jackson, but she apparently took me for a crank caller and hung up on me. I always forget about the time difference between California and the East. I'm afraid I woke Ms. Jackson well after midnight."

"Mrs. Layton, it's so nice to hear from you." Cluney was sure she sounded as stunned and nervous as she felt. Jeff's mother was the last person in the world she'd expected to talk to today.

"Please, Cluney, call me Andrea. If we're going to share Jeff, we need to be friends. Don't you agree?"

Cluney smiled. "Yes, Andrea. I do, indeed! Jeff just called a few minutes ago. We've set our wedding date— May eighteenth."

"Wonderful! That will work out perfectly for me. I plan to fly to Lexington in a few days to start setting all the wedding wheels in motion. I hope you don't think I'm being too much the doting mother, Cluney, but it will be such a joy for me to do this for the two of you."

"Jeff mentioned that you were planning a surprise for

308

us. That's very thoughtful of you, Andrea. I can hardly wait to hear all about it."

"Well, I'm not going to tell you a thing right now, not until I see you and Jeff in person. Rest assured, though, I have everything under control, dear. I will need your guest list. As many as you like. Invite the whole college, if you wish."

Andrea's expansiveness brought a smile to Cluney's lips. She could think of a dozen names at the most.

"I'll get right to work on it," she told her future mother-in-law.

"Fine, Cluney! I'll let you know my arrival plans. I'm so looking forward to meeting you. Jeff has told me all about you, dear. Do give him my love when you see him. I suppose I'd better cut this short. Now that you and Jeff have set the date, I have several calls I must make immediately, concerning the wedding plans."

"I'll look forward to meeting you. Goodbye, Andrea, and thank you."

"I *love* doing this! You have nothing to thank me for, dear."

"Thank you for having such a wonderful son."

"Well, we certainly agree on that! And I'll soon have an equally wonderful daughter. See you soon, Cluney."

Cluney hung up the phone and sighed. Reality was finally setting in. Andrea's call had made Jeff's seem all the more real. Suddenly, Cluney felt breathless with excitement.

How could she ever have guessed last spring, when Lieutenant Jeff Layton came to the college to give a talk to the seniors about the Navy as a career, that they would fall in love almost on sight, that she would lose him forever, then have a miracle occur that would bring him back from the dead to make her his wife? It seemed too good to be true.

When that thought crossed her mind, some of Cluney's elation faded. She realized that she would not feel completely confident until Jeff was with her again and she could snuggle close in his arms and feel his heart beating next to hers. But he was still thousands of miles away. It dawned on her then that she didn't even know exactly where he was. And she had no idea when he'd be home. He'd never told her.

"Wherever he is, he's a long way from here," she said with a sigh. "And I won't see him for weeks yet." Then true panic gripped her. "What if he keeps flying? Why, history will simply repeat itself! There's still a strong chance that I'll never see Jeff again."

Cluney had worked herself into a true frenzy by the time she heard the knock at her door.

"Oh, God!" she cried. "Who could that be? I look a mess!"

She cinched her terry cloth robe tighter, ran her fingers through her tangled hair, then headed for the front door. If it was a door-to-door salesman, he was going to catch it from her. She was in no mood . . .

Cluney jerked the door open. Her eyes went wide. Her knees went weak. And a little strangled cry got caught in her throat. The next moment, she was in Jeff's arms, sobbing her heart out.

"When . . . ? How . . . ? Where . . . ?"

Jeff dragged his clinging lover into the house, kicked the door shut, and silenced her whimpers with a long, deep kiss.

Cluney felt as if she were flying over the moonbow once more. But this time she wasn't making the journey alone.

Jeff was with her! Jeff, with his strong arms holding her, his hard torso pressing into her softness, his mouth devouring her with a sweet, savage need.

"Jeff," she moaned between kisses. "Jeff, darling, you're here? But, how . . . ?"

Again, he cut off her questions. She gave up trying to ask. The only answers she needed came with the taste of his mouth on hers, the feel of his hands on her breasts, the hard, strong beat of his heart, and the hot rush of his blood.

Touching, kissing, fondling, they staggered around the tiny living room like two drunks. They were drunk—on their love and their need for each other. Suddenly, Jeff swept Cluney up into his arms. For a moment, he stared down into her lavender eyes as if he meant to devour her with his gaze.

"God, you feel good to hold!" he moaned.

Without asking permission—he needed none—he turned and headed for the bedroom. Cluney's bed was rumpled, but still made up. Jeff never bothered with turning down covers. In a single, swift motion, he tumbled with Cluney still in his arms onto the spread.

Her head was spinning, reeling. Jeff's hands seemed everywhere at once as he tugged at her robe. The tie-belt slipped loose, tangling in Jeff's watchband. He cursed softly and ripped it away. It slithered to the floor. A moment later, Cluney gasped as both his hands slipped inside the opening of her robe, parting it so that she lay naked before his dark, hot gaze. She stared boldly into his eyes, inviting him to have her, here and now.

"My God, look at you!" he moaned. "Look at all this— all mine!" His hands played over her like a miser caressing his gold.

311

Jeff was stradling Cluney, who lay on her back. He leaned forward, his gaze locked on her breasts, but the heels of his hands pressed lightly to her hips. His touch gave Cluney the wonderfully odd sensation of being his captive lover, unable to do anything unless he willed it so. When he leaned down and kissed her breasts, the sweet-hot sensation shot through her like sensual heat lightning. She arched her back and moaned.

The minutes ticked away, but time stood still for Cluney. Jeff was here, and she was his—*all* his, *now and forever.*

Somehow, she could never remember afterward, Jeff shed his khaki uniform. His tie, shirt, and shoes vanished first. Moments later, the rest of his clothes were gone. Now, they were a writhing tumble of hot human flesh— arms and legs and mouths and everything in between groping for a loving hold.

Jeff touched her all over, as if he needed to know that she was really there and really his. Cluney was even more anxious to assure herself that her lover was real and alive and hers.

Their kisses went from deep to light to playful, then back to seriously passionate. Cluney was surprised to hear her own voice in the room time and time again, begging him for more, then moaning or gasping when he complied. She was shameless and wanton; she was in love and in need.

That need was something Jeff understood. When neither of them could wait an instant longer, he entered her. The long slide was pure delight for both of them. Jeff's first thrust was aimed with accuracy. He went only part way, then withdrew. The second time, he went a bit deeper, then deeper still. Each time he pulled back,

Cluney would moan and beg, feeling as if she might die unless she had all of him. When that final, full penetration came, it might have been missile-guided. It touched the very spot, the spot that set off rockets of colored fire in Cluney's brain to shower down over her entire body. She felt as if the moonbow were shining inside her—hot and silver and vibrant.

"And you warned me not to fly," Jeff gasped, letting his body drop heavily to cover hers. "If that wasn't flying, sweetheart, I don't know what it is."

He rested there for a minute before he rolled his weight off her. Lying on his side, he stared at Cluney, grinning. Then he chuckled, and then he laughed out loud.

"Lord, darling, if we aren't going to have some marriage! We're going to have to take vitamin pills to keep up the pace."

Cluney traced one finger over his generous, smiling lips. "I think we'll manage," she answered.

She kept staring at him—the brown shock of hair falling over his brow, the amber lights dancing in his brandy-colored eyes, the set of his wide shoulders, the wonderful line where his golden tan stopped, leaving pale, inviting wonders to be explored.

Suddenly, Cluney propped up on one elbow and said, "You devil! What are you doing here? And where were you when you called me?"

He gave her a low chuckle. "I just hit town. I phoned you from the pizza place. I was going to tell you I was here, but then I decided to surprise you. As for what I'm doing here, if you don't know that yet, I guess I'll have to show you again."

But when he reached for her, Cluney put her palms on his chest to keep him away.

"Not until you've answered some questions, mister!"

"Fire away!"

He gripped her hand and began licking her salty fingers, distracting her. But Cluney was determined to find out why he was here and not somewhere off in the Mediterranean with his ship.

"Back to my original question—what are you doing here, Jeff? How did you get leave to come back to the States?"

"I'm not on leave. I'm out, a civilian. Or I will be as of March first."

Cluney stared at him, her eyes as wide as her smile. "You never told me . . ."

"I didn't want to get your hopes up before I'd decided. I knew you were hoping I wouldn't make the Navy my career. After my last night at home, I decided that it might be a fine life for a bachelor, but not for an old married man. It tore me up to leave you, darling. I couldn't go through that for years and years to come. So I resigned my commission. It took a while for all the papers to be processed. But as soon as my discharge came through, I hopped the first transport plane back to the States. Back to the woman I love!"

He leaned over and kissed Cluney slowly and thoroughly.

Moments later, she asked breathlessly, "So, you're home for good?"

"For good and always, sweetheart."

"Oh, Jeff!" Cluney flung herself on him, hugging with all her might. "What will you do? Where will we live? I can find a job wherever you want to go. California, maybe?"

He smiled and fended off another loving attack. "Slow

314

down, darling. Let's take one question at a time. How would you like to stay here in Kentucky—live in Lexington?"

"I love Lexington!" she cried. "It's beautiful! It's so . . . so horsey!"

"Ah-h-h!" Jeff said, grinning one of his mile-wide grins. "Funny you should mention that. What would you think of living on a horse farm?"

Visions from another time flitted through her mind—rides threw dew-damp fields in early morning, long evenings with fireflies dancing in the rose garden, a feeling of belonging, to the land and to each other.

"Oh, Jeff, what a wonderful idea! I'd love it."

He let out a whistle of relief and wiped imaginary perspiration from his forehead. "Boy, am I glad you feel that way! You see, Mom's bought us a house as a wedding gift. I nearly fainted dead away when she told me about it earlier today. I could just imagine you refusing to marry me, if that meant getting saddled with this huge, old mausoleum to live in and a farm to take care of. I haven't even seen the place. I'm not sure Mom has either. I think she heard about it from one of her breeder friends over lunch, then bought the place by phone."

Cluney gasped. "She'd do that?"

Jeff nodded. "Yep! That's my mom! She's an impulse buyer on a worldwide scale. She once bought a small island kingdom in the South Pacific. But the government made her give it back."

"You're kidding me!"

Jeff raised his palms before him. "Would I lie to the woman I'm about to marry and raise horses with?"

"And children!" Cluney reminded him.

He nodded. "Lots and lots!"

315

"Well, not *that* many." They kissed again, then Cluney said, "Tell me about the house, Jeff. I'm dying of curiosity."

"Well, from what Mom said, it was once one of Kentucky's showplaces. That's been a while back, though."

"How long ago?"

Jeff frowned, dreading Cluney's reaction to his answer. "Back before the Civil War."

"It's *that* old?"

"Yes, it is, darling, but well-built, so Mom says."

"Of course, she hasn't seen it."

"Not yet," Jeff admitted.

"How did she happen to buy such a place? I mean, it just seems a bit odd to me."

"Once you meet my mother, you'll understand. She's not only an impulse buyer and a racing buff, but she's a sucker for historical landmarks as well. It seems this place was about to be leveled to make way for progress, and she couldn't stand the thought of all that history being destroyed."

"I can certainly understand that. But still—a place like that must have cost her a fortune."

He chuckled. "Hey, money's no object! I'm her only son and heir, remember? And I guess the cincher came when she heard that the house still had all the original furnishings locked up inside and the other prospective buyer meant to auction all that stuff off. She couldn't stand thinking about the belongings of some Civil War hero being scattered to the four winds. She said she even had nightmares about it. She claimed the guy came to her in a dream and begged her to buy all his old stuff."

Cluney rubbed her arms. "You're giving me goose

bumps, Jeff. What's this place called? Maybe I've heard of it. I do teach Kentucky history, remember."

He tilted his head back and looked up at the ceiling as if he might find the answer there. "Aw, gee! What did she tell me? It had a color in the name. Graystone? White-hall? Bluebell?" His face lit up suddenly. "*Bluefield*! That's it!"

Cluney could only stare at him. Her heart was pounding frantically. She felt hot and cold at the same time. "Bluefield?" she whispered. "It can't be!"

"That's it, I'm sure, darling."

"But I thought it had been torn down to make way for a shopping mall."

"Mom outbid the corporation that was trying to buy it. So Lexington loses it's new shopping mall and we get an old house called Bluefield. Aren't we lucky!"

Tears sprang to Cluney's eyes. A million thoughts raced through her mind. She had been a bride at Blue-field once before. As Larissa Breckinridge, she had spent her honeymoon there. And she had tried desperately to bring Hunter back to his home, but she had failed. She thought of the man in Andrea Layton's dreams—the Civil War hero, who had begged her to save his home. It had to be Hunter!

"Bluefield," she repeated again.

Jeff was leaning close, staring at her oddly. "Do you know the place, darling?"

"Yes," she whispered, "but I haven't been there in a long, long time."

Jeff drew her into his arms and kissed her tenderly. "It will be our home soon, sweetheart. We'll live happily ever after there, and raise beautiful daughters and strong, handsome sons."

317

Cluney clung to Jeff, trembling in his arms as she heard him repeat the very promise that she had made to Hunter so long ago. One thought imprinted itself on her mind: Jeff had a second chance at life and she had a second chance at love.

*I must not fail my husband this time! I will not!*

# Chapter Eighteen

Three days later, Andrea Layton blew into Kentucky like a chic, diamond-studded whirlwind. Cluney had worried about transportation for the three of them. She certainly couldn't haul Andrea around in her old van, and Jeff's sportscar was a two-seater.

"Don't worry about it, sweetheart," Jeff had told her. "I'm sure Mom's made arrangements. She doesn't miss a trick."

Andrea had, indeed, arranged things, ordering a chauffeured stretch-limo before she left California to be waiting at the airport in Kentucky. The chestnut-haired beauty who was Jeff's mother—although she looked more like his sister, Cluney thought—traveled all the way across country wearing white. Cluney was amazed. The woman stepped off the plane after her long flight, looking as if she'd just leaped to life from the cover of a fashion magazine.

"My darlings!" Andrea called the moment she spotted them. "I've arrived!"

"So she has!" Jeff said, grinning down at Cluney.

"Brace yourself, sweetheart. You're about to meet the rest of the family."

Cluney didn't say anything. She just clung to Jeff's arm and tried not to look as intimidated as she felt. Andrea certainly looked nothing like any mother-in-law Cluney had ever seen before. She looked more like a centerfold. At least Cluney had had the presence of mind to wear an attractive lavender summer suit instead of her usual jeans and T-shirt. That gave her some needed confidence.

Jeff swept his gorgeous mother into a bear hug. They were both talking at once, so Cluney couldn't understand what either of them was saying. She stood back, forgotten for the moment and completely bewildered. But her time came soon enough.

The moment Jeff released Andrea, they both turned to Cluney, both smiling that blinding Layton grin.

"Mom, this is my beautiful, blushing bride."

Cluney's cheeks warmed even more when she realized that Jeff was speaking the truth about her hot-pink cheeks.

Andrea hugged her future daughter-in-law soundly, enveloping Cluney, not only in her arms, but in a cloud of expensive perfume. "Joy," if Cluney's nose did not deceive her.

"My dear, the pictures Jeff sent didn't do you justice." Andrea stepped back and beamed at her son. "She's a beauty, Jeff!"

Jeff slipped his arm around Cluney's waist and gave her a hug. "Don't think I don't know it, Mom! And she can cook, too."

"Well, that will hardly be necessary. You see I intend to hire a full staff for Bluefield. Cook, housekeeper, butler, gardener, stable hands, trainer, and, of course, in time a nanny for my grandchildren."

Jeff and Cluney shared a secret glance, rolling their eyes at each other.

"Mrs. Layton?" The husky, uniformed chauffeur interrupted their family reunion. "I am Pierce. Your car is ready whenever you wish."

"Shall we, my dears?" Andrea invited, motioning toward the long, white limousine. "I don't know about you, but I'm *dying* to see Bluefield."

The mere mention of the name sent a shiver through Cluney. She wanted to see the place again, too, but still the thought frightened her.

"By all means!" Jeff answered. "We're eager to see our wedding gift, aren't we, Cluney?"

"Oh, yes!" she said, forcing enthusiasm. "I can hardly wait. This is really so generous of you, Andrea."

"My pleasure, dear, believe me."

Cluney had been worried about carrying on initial conversation with Andrea Layton. After all, the two women were worlds apart. Jeff's mother would hardly care to hear about life in a coal miner's shack, or the antics of Wooter's raccoons, or old Redbird being born with a caul. But Cluney needn't have been concerned about making conversation. With Mrs. Layton holding forth, no one else could get a word in edgewise. All Cluney had to do on the way to Bluefield was sit back, smile, and nod at the appropriate moments.

Before they arrived, Cluney realized that she adored Jeff's mother. Andrea was pushy all right, but in the nicest sort of way. Mother and son were actually very much alike. It was impossible to love one without feeling genuine affection for the other.

*It's going to be a lovely life,* Cluney pondered silently. *Yes, a lovely life, indeed!*

* * *

Cluney's breath caught at her first glimpse of Bluefield. She felt as if she had once more crossed over the moonbow into another time. The house stood—large, imposing, and handsome—just as she remembered it. Granted, it needed a good deal of work. A paint job was overdue, and some of the windows were broken. The garden was overgrown with weeds and brambles. But she could easily picture it the way it had been and would be again. Even the rose garden remained where Hunter's mother had raised her prized blooms. Cluney half expected to see Hunter himself come striding out through the wide front door.

"Well, darling? What do you think?"

Jeff's voice brought Cluney out of her reverie. "Wonderful," she murmured. "It's a real home!"

"I just knew you'd both love it!" Andrea enthused. Then she launched into plans to get the place into shape in time for the wedding. "You'll want to be married here, of course. Won't you, my dears? The broker told me there's a gorgeous staircase inside that will be perfect for a bride's entrance."

"The stairway . . ." Cluney murmured, remembering her other wedding, but her words went unnoticed as Andrea chattered on.

Pierce pulled the limo up into the circular drive. Andrea was so excited, she couldn't wait for him to open the door. She was out of the car in an instant and heading up the stairs to the veranda.

"Well, come on, you two!" she called back over her well-padded, white shoulder. "I can't wait to see what

322

Major Breckinridge has left for us. I adore antiques, don't you, Cluney?"

Cluney didn't answer. Andrea's mention of Hunter's name had set her heart racing. Had he really recovered and come back to Bluefield after she left him behind? Surely she'd know the answer to that question within minutes.

"Are you all right, sweetheart?" Jeff sounded concerned. "You look so pale suddenly."

She forced a smile. "I'll be fine, darling. It's just all this excitement. Let's go inside. I do want to see our new home."

By the time Cluney and Jeff reached the house, Andrea had made an astounding discovery.

"Come in here, both of you!" she called. "You simply aren't going to believe this. Why, it's uncanny!"

They followed her voice to the front parlor, a sunny room Larissa Breckinridge had always loved. Andrea was standing before the fireplace, staring up at a portrait on the wall.

"Look at this! Can you believe it? Why, this could be *you*, Cluney!"

Andrea reached for Cluney's hand and led her over to stand beneath Larissa's wedding portrait.

"My, God!" Jeff breathed. "You're right, Mom. I wonder who she was."

"There's a little brass plaque on the frame." Cluney went up on tiptoe, pretending that she had to read the name. "Larissa Courtney Breckinridge," she said.

"She must have been the major's wife," Andrea reasoned. She came closer then, and looked from the portrait to Cluney, then back at Larissa. "I simply can't believe this. Larissa Breckinridge could be your double, Cluney.

And this gives me the most wonderful idea. I'm going to have a wedding gown made for you exactly like hers. Won't that be charming? And so appropriate since you're to be married in her house."

Cluney glanced toward Jeff. *Yes, most appropriate,* she thought, *since I'll also be marrying her husband.*

Jeff, too, was staring up at Larissa. In the shadows of the parlor, he looked more like Hunter than Cluney had ever thought he could. Then she glanced up at Hunter's portrait.

"That must be Major Breckinridge," she said, pointing to the other gilt-framed picture.

Andrea exclaimed over the major's handsome, brooding face, but failed to comment, if she saw any resemblance to her son. Perhaps only Cluney could see the similarities because she knew in her heart that they were there.

For the next hour, Cluney and Jeff explored the house while Andrea, with Pierce in tow to take notes for her, listed repairs that needed to be made before the wedding.

The last room Cluney and Jeff entered was Hunter's bedroom—the room where he and Larissa had spent their honeymoon together. His things were still there—a clean uniform laid out as if he might come in at any moment to dress for some special occasion. His boots, dusty, but polished to a high gloss. His books, his papers, everything, Cluney noted, except his journal. Her heart fell. She had so hoped that she would find the old diary here and be able to read Hunter's entries after that night of the moonbow.

"You look tired, sweetheart," Jeff said suddenly. "Why don't we go back outside and wait for Mom. Surely, she won't be much longer."

Cluney nodded, almost afraid to trust her voice. "Yes, I could use some fresh air."

"You aren't unhappy with the place, are you, darling?"

She forced a smile, trying to hold back tears. "Oh, no, Jeff! We belong here—both of us."

Cluney slipped her arms around his neck and clung to Jeff for a moment. He lifted her chin with one finger. Staring down into her face, he said, "Tears? Why are you crying, Cluney?"

She bit her lips and shook her head. "It's nothing, darling. There's just such a feeling about this room. It's almost as if he's still here."

"You mean you think it's haunted?"

"Oh, no! It's not that kind of feeling, Jeff. It's a good, warm, welcoming sense I get. I love this room."

"Then, that settles it!" he said with finality. "We'll spend our wedding night here."

Cluney smiled and blinked back the last of her tears. "Yes, I'd like that, darling. Very much!"

Before they headed outside, Jeff took advantage of their privacy to give Cluney a long, searching kiss. If Andrea hadn't been downstairs, they might have begun their honeymoon at that very moment.

A short time later, they wandered—hand in hand—out to the rose garden. A few buds were sprouting, but the weeds seemed to have the upper hand.

"This will be beautiful once it's been cleaned up and the roses pruned," Jeff said.

"Yes, we'll be able to smell the flowers even in the house—in the library especially."

Jeff looked at her oddly. "Now, how would you know that, sweetheart?"

"Just guessing," Cluney lied.

Walking slightly ahead of Cluney, Jeff stumbled on something and cursed loudly. "Would you look at this? It's a grave right in the middle of the rose garden."

Cluney caught her breath. She felt a coldness flood through her. She stood back as Jeff stooped to get a closer look at the headstone.

He laughed. "Just a family pet. A cat or a dog probably. The stone says, 'Trooper' and there's a date." He rubbed at the stone to remove years of dirt and lichen. "1865."

Cluney dropped to her knees beside Jeff. She smiled as she rubbed her hand over the cool, old marble. "Good ol' Troop," she murmured, her heart brimming. This was her proof that Hunter had made it, that the uniform and other personal items in the house were really his, that he had lived long after she left him by way of the moonbow. He and Trooper had returned to Bluefield together.

Yes, Cluney thought, Hunter Breckinridge came home long years ago. And now, at last, his bride was about to return as well.

She glanced at Jeff, who was still kneeling beside her, pulling weeds from around Trooper's stone. How could he ever know how much it meant to her that he loved her, that he was going to marry her, and that they were coming home to bring her story and her life full circle?

*Someday*, she thought. *Someday, I'll tell you everything, my darling.*


The next weeks were the busiest of Cluney's life. She and Jeff worked tirelessly, side by side with Andrea, setting Bluefield to rights. Painters, cleaners, gardeners, upholsterers—the place was awash in laborers for every job that needed to be done. As the day of the wedding approached, Cluney could almost feel Hunter's shade, smiling down on them and nodding his approval. Bluefield now looked exactly the way it had when Larissa Breckinridge was a bride. Cluney remembered every detail and made sure that everything was just as it had been so long ago.

Early May found the engaged couple involved in a dizzying round of soirees. Parties for Derby and parties for the bride and groom overlapped, making every day more exciting than the one before it. The festivities culminated in a huge bash, hosted by Andrea Layton, the night before the wedding at the hotel in Lexington where they were staying. Everyone who was anyone was there. Hollywood friends of Andrea's who had flown in from the West Coast for the wedding rubbed elbows with Kentucky's horse fanciers as well as a dandied-up Wooter Crenshaw and old Miss Redbird in a bright sequin gown that she swore she meant to be buried in.

"Why this party's near-about as grand as my wake's gonna be," she told the hostess.

Mr. and Mrs. George Washington Abraham Lincoln Freeman were there, too. B.J. and Free had eloped quietly a few days after their return to the present via the moonbow.

"Our wedding wasn't anything like as grand as yours is going to be," B.J. told Cluney. "The justice of the peace was in his bathrobe, and his wife had curlers in her hair. But we're married, good and proper, just the same."

Free, darkly handsome in his tux and beaming with newfound confidence, smiled down at his wife. "We been married all the while," he told her, "ever since we jumped the broomstick, way back when."

B.J. looked solemn suddenly. She whispered for

Cluney's ears alone, "Free's right, you know. All that stuff really happened. For a while I thought I must have dreamed it. But I didn't. I remember so clearly now, Cluney. Everything!"

Cluney nodded. "I know what you mean," she said in a hushed voice. "I remember, too. It's a pretty odd feeling, knowing that I'm about to be a bride at Bluefield for the second time. But it's a good feeling, too. I won't make the mistakes I made the first time."

B.J. laughed gaily. "From the way you and Jeff look at each other, I'd say nobody's making any mistakes. This marriage was meant to be, girlfriend. Meant to be so much that you managed to call back time to get your one and only. Does Jeff know?"

"Not yet," Cluney whispered. "I'll tell him, of course. But I have to wait for just the right time. It won't be easy for him to understand. I'm not sure I understand it all myself."

Free interrupted their private conversation just then. "Can I tell Cluney our news, sugar?"

"Tell me what?" Cluney asked. She looked at B.J., who was grinning from ear to ear.

"That me and my Belle are expecting," he blurted out.

"Oh, B.J.!" Cluney hugged her friend. "That's wonderful news!"

Jeff sauntered up just in time to hear. "Is that legal, sweetheart? A pregnant bridesmaid?"

Both women laughed. "It is if she's my matron of honor, darling!"

The evening wore on, with more music, more champagne, more congratulations. By the time the last guest left, it was after midnight.

"Oh! I should have planned this better so that everyone

would leave earlier," Andrea fumed. "Get out of here, Jeff. Go to your own suite. You're not supposed to see your bride on her wedding day."

"It is, isn't it!" Cluney cried. "This is the eighteenth of May!"

"It certainly is," Andrea said. "And you need your beauty sleep." Turning an adoring look on her son, Andrea relented, saying, "You may see Cluney to her door, Jeff, but *no fooling around* and don't you dare go in with her!"

"Yes, Mother," he answered.

Good to his word, Jeff left his bride-to-be at her door, with only a soft, sweet kiss to savor until they were officially man and wife. But before he said good night, he pressed the moonstone necklace into her hand.

"I almost forgot this," he said. "B.J. gave it to me when she came in tonight. She said you'd lost it and a ranger up at the falls found it and asked her to return it to you. Here, let me put it on for you. I fixed the broken catch. I was sure you'd want to wear it with your wedding gown. After all, Larissa wore it, didn't she?"

Cluney searched Jeff's dark eyes. "How did you know that?"

He laughed nervously. "I'm not sure. I don't even know why I said it. She must have been wearing it when her portrait was made. Yes, I'm sure she was." Now, he was frowning at her, but at the same time some light of recognition seemed to be stealing into his eyes. "But how could she have worn *your* necklace?"

Cluney wanted desperately to say, "The same way that she married *my* husband." But it was late, and explanations would take too long. Another time.

"Maybe my necklace only looks like the one she was

329

wearing, darling." She went up on tiptoe to kiss him one last time. "Good night, my love. I'll see you at Bluefield."

"Home!" He smiled at her, and Cluney could have sworn he had tears in his eyes. "*Our* home, my love, *forevermore!*"

She slipped silently into her room and closed her door before she let her own happy tears flow.

Dawn came early, and with it came Andrea Layton.

"Rise and shine, my dear! Our chariot awaits without!"

The plan was for Andrea to speed the bride off to Bluefield by limo, where Cluney would dress in the reproduction of Larissa's wedding gown and prepare for her wedding. Jeff got to sleep in and get ready for the big event at a more leisurely pace.

The first hour after dawn was a blur to Cluney. She felt as if her head had barely touched the pillow before Andrea rousted her out. Dressed in jeans and a sweatshirt, sunglasses covering her unmade eyes, Cluney climbed into Pierce's chariot and accepted a Bloody Mary from her cheery, perky, fully made-up mother-in-law-to-be.

"Wasn't the party last night simply delicious, darling!" Andrea enthused. Then she proceeded to tell Cluney all the gossip she'd heard about everyone there from everyone else who was there.

"However," Andrea said, frowning, "I'm still stymied by that strange little mountain man, Wooter Something-or-other. Are his parents truly still alive? He seemed rather put out with me, I'm afraid, because I didn't invite them. But how was I to know? You should have put them on your list, dear."

Cluney choked on her Bloody Mary, picturing the pair

330

of raccoons racing about at last night's fancy do, trying to wash their caviar in the champagne fountain. When she could get her breath, she said with a straight face. "I really didn't want to invite them, Andrea. They don't behave well in public."

"Oh!" she said. "Oh, yes, I know how old people get—spilling drinks, dribbling food, telling the same stories over and over. You were probably right not to include them, Cluney."

Just then, Pierce rolled to a stop in the circular drive at the front door of Bluefield.

Andrea turned serious suddenly. A tear even slipped down her cheek, marring her perfect makeup. She pressed a hand to her breasts and took a deep breath.

"You'll have to excuse me, Cluney," she said with a sniff. "I'm afraid it's just hit me that my baby boy is about to be married. Such an occasion is a bit frightening for a mother."

Cluney smiled and touched Andrea's hand. "It's frightening for the bride, too. But I think we'll both survive it happily, Andrea."

Jeff was awake long before his mother whisked Cluney away. Actually, he'd hardly slept all night. After seeing Cluney to her room, he'd gone to bed, falling asleep immediately. But then the dream had begun. It was the oddest damn thing! Actually, it had been more like a visitation from the spirit world than any dream he'd ever had.

"Major Hunter Breckinridge," he said aloud to his image in the mirror as he shaved. "Was he here, or did I only imagine the whole thing?"

He wiped the last of the shaving cream from his smooth, square jaw and reached to pour himself another cup of coffee—his fourth since dawn. He couldn't seem to stop shaking.

"Wedding jitters!" he said with a laugh, but he knew he was lying to himself.

He was shaking still from the strange experience he'd had during the night. The dream had begun with him in the parlor at Bluefield, staring at the major's portrait. Suddenly, the picture changed and he was gazing at an image of himself. Next, it spoke to him.

"You've done well," the portrait said. "You're bringing Larissa home at last. I've needed her here. I can rest now."

Before Jeff could reply, the figure had stepped from his frame. He advanced on Jeff, staring him right in the eye.

"What the hell is this?" Jeff remembered saying. "Get back up there where you belong."

"I *am* where I belong," the spirit, ghost, or paint-and-canvas had told him. "I'm here at Bluefield, my home, and I am part of you and you are part of me."

Jeff had backed away from the apparition, not sure how to react. Should he be afraid? He didn't feel fear, only confusion.

"How can you be a part of me?" Jeff had demanded.

"She has made it so. We wanted a second chance. You have given it to us, and for that we both thank you."

"Who are you talking about? This is outrageous!"

"No, this is love," the specter answered. "And you know who I mean. She is our wife, the love of both our lives."

They had argued and discussed on and on. Much of

what had been said was lost to Jeff now. But his fatigue told him that the confrontation had been genuine.

Suddenly, he remembered the ghost's parting words and gesture. He had handed Jeff a book. It had seemed very real at the time. Jeff remembered flipping through the pages and seeing handwritten entries.

"My wedding gift to her," the major said. "Give it to her, but tell her you found it in the house. Don't mention that I was here; it would only upset her, and I won't come again. Be gentle with her. And no matter what she tells you, try to understand. She'll need your understanding and your love."

Jeff drained the last of the coffee from his cup, then slammed it down on the sink so hard that the thin china broke.

"That book!" he said. "If last night was real, it will still be here."

He hurried into the bedroom, searching as he went. The bureau, the bedside table, the closet, the floor.

"Nothing!" he said at last, feeling relieved. "I imagined the whole thing."

When he sat down on the bed, something crunched under the covers. He flipped back the spread. There it was—an old journal of some sort, its leather cover badly stained with water and blood.

"Damn!" he said, staring at the thing. "What the hell kind of wedding gift will that make for my bride? Cluney will think I've gone nuts. I'm not giving it to her and that's that!"

But before he left for Bluefield, Jeff found himself wrapping Hunter's diary in silver paper left from a gift they'd received the night before. It was as if some other force moved his hands. He could no more have left the diary in his hotel room than he could have stayed there himself and missed his own wedding.

Dressed in Hunter Breckinridge's Union army uniform, which had been altered to fit his slightly larger frame, and with the journal wrapped and under his arm, Jeff left the hotel, headed for Bluefield and his bride. Headed, although he never guessed it, to play out a hand fate had dealt long ago.

# Chapter Nineteen

Dressed in a perfect copy of Larissa's shimmering white gown and long mistlike veil, Cluney waited on the landing at the top of the stairs for her signal to start down. Nervously, she toyed with the moonstone at her throat. Her talisman warmed at her touch and seemed to send out tiny vibrations, giving her strength and courage.

She was feeling truly odd this morning, as if she weren't sure which time period she was in. One moment, she knew that she was Cluney Summerland and that Jeff Layton was downstairs waiting to make her his bride. Then in the next instant, she'd feel Larissa's presence and wonder if she might find Hunter there when she descended the long stairway.

"Are you okay, girl?" B.J. hovering at her side, adjusting her veil, sensed that the bride had a bad case of jitters.

Cluney looked at her matron of honor, absolutely glowing in her satin gown of forsythia-yellow. "You're going to make a great mother, B.J. But do you have to practice on me? I'm fine! And I'm Cluney!"

"Say what?" B.J. demanded. "I hope to say, you're Cluney! If not, then I'm at the wrong wedding, girl."

Cluney tried to laugh off her statement. "It's just that I feel strange. Everything is so familiar. Everything is just like it was before. I keep thinking that maybe I've slipped back in time and I'm actually Larissa again and Hunter's waiting for me downstairs and I'm going to blow the whole thing again."

B.J. knew Cluney's whole story and decided it might be a good idea at this moment to remind her of her origins. "You *are* Larissa, girl! Don't you remember? You were born Larissa. You only became Cluney after you crossed the moonbow the first time. So, it's not odd that you feel like Larissa. The odd thing would be if you didn't. But that doesn't make any difference now. You're about to marry Jeff Layton, the man you love. And you're both going to be happy."

"Thanks, B.J. I know all that, but it helps to hear someone else say it."

Just then the music began, the matron of honor's cue.

B.J. gave Cluney a quick hug, then said, "See you downstairs, Cluney. Good luck, girlfriend!"

Wooter suddenly appeared at Cluney's side, ready to escort her down. Cluney thought to herself that he cleaned up real nice. Andrea had seen to it that he was perfectly groomed and outfitted for the occasion. Jeff's mother had balked at first when Cluney said she wanted him to play the part of father of the bride, but Cluney had stood firm. After all, if it weren't for Wooter, no wedding would be taking place today.

"Smile, little girl," the old man ordered. "This day's been a long time comin', and it ain't no place for long faces."

Cluney beamed down at her escort as they began their long descent of the staircase. Below, as she had expected, the bride saw the glamorous array of guests Andrea had invited to witness the marriage ceremony. Oddly enough, it came as no surprise for her to see several movie stars, directors, and producers among the guests. The shock came when she spied the groom.

Andrea had decided to keep Jeff's costume a secret until the very moment that his bride entered the parlor. Her surprise nearly cost her a daughter-in-law. Spying the old Civil War uniform, in her present frame of mind, Cluney assumed Hunter Breckinridge was waiting for her at the altar. She all but fainted. Only Wooter's strong arm and steady, commanding voice kept her on her feet.

"Don't give out on me now, little girl. We got a ways to go yet," he urged in a husky whisper.

Somehow, Cluney made it into the parlor to stand beside her groom. At the moment Jeff took her hand, all else faded from her mind. His presence, his touch, and his love were the only things that mattered to her in the whole world.

She smiled up at him through a mist of happy tears. They spoke their vows in voices trembling with emotion. When he took her into his arms to kiss his wife for the very first time, Cluney thought she had never felt such love flow between two people.

Jeff clung to her afterward for a moment, whispering into her ear, "Darling, this all seems like a dream. I feel as if I've loved you since the beginning of time."

"And we'll keep on loving each other," she whispered in response, "until the end of time and beyond."

The magical spell was broken when Andrea rushed forward to hug them both. The poised beauty was sobbing with happiness—embracing them, kissing them, showering them with her generous affection.

The rest of that fine, golden spring day passed in a blur for Cluney. She seemed to be slipping back and forth between the present and the past. One minute, she would be talking to Andrea, then the next moment, Larissa would be talking to her mother-in-law, Mrs. Breckinridge. The guests' clothes would change before her eyes. The conversation among the guests would be of jockey Pat Day's first win in the Run For The Roses earlier in the month, then flow without pause to talk of the Civil War. Only Jeff remained the same. She knew at all times who he was and how very much she loved him.

Not long after sunset, the last of the guests departed. Andrea lingered only a short time, then left, after more hugs and kisses, to have Pierce drive her back to her hotel.

Cluney and Jeff stood on the veranda, waving goodbye as the limo roared down the drive. When it disappeared beyond the trees, Jeff turned to his wife and slipped his arms around her.

"At last!" he said with a sigh. "I have you all to myself, sweetheart."

Cluney snuggled against him, smiling. "It was a wonderful wedding, thanks to Andrea's planning."

"Hey, Mom's not the only Layton who knows how to plan things. Wait till you see what her son's planned for your wedding night."

"Tell me," Cluney begged.

Jeff swept her up in his arms. "I'd rather show you, sweetheart."

He carried her all the way to Hunter's room—their room now. Waiting there, he had champagne on ice, cold lobster, and a wedding gift wrapped in silver paper.

*"Another* present, darling?"

Jeff shrugged. "Just a little something I thought you might find interesting. You can open it later. Come here, wife!"

Gift along with food and drink were soon forgotten. Jeff set Cluney on her feet, then pulled her immediately into his arms. His kiss was deep and sweet and thorough. Cluney came out of it trembling and wishing she were wearing far fewer clothes.

"Excuse me, darling," she whispered. "I think I'll change now."

She slipped into the newly added bathroom, then reappeared moments later in a gown and negligee of sheer, snowy lace. Jeff gave a low whistle when she posed sexily against the door frame for him.

"You look good enough to eat, sweetheart."

She gave him a heavy-lidded look. "You're not so bad yourself. Red silk pajamas, eh? Three guesses who picked those out for you."

"If you don't like them, I'll take them off."

"Why don't you do that?" Cluney invited.

Jeff made a silly, sexy show of stripping for his bride. Once he'd slowly unbuttoned the top, done a few bumps and grinds, then tossed the hot-red silk at her, Cluney slunk toward him, a mischievous grin on her face. She paused at the vanity to take something from her purse. A moment later, she stood before him, gazing sensually up into his eyes. She ran her hands over his bare chest, nipped at his shoulder, then tucked a dollar bill into the waist of his pajama bottoms.

"There's more where that came from, if you take it *all* off, big boy!"

Instead of dropping his bottoms, Jeff gripped the lace at

Cluney's shoulders and slid her negligee off. Next, he slipped one nightgown strap down. And then the other. When she, too, was bare to the waist, he drew her close, letting their hearts beat together. Her nipples puckered against the heat of his bare chest.

Cluney's head fell back. "Ah, that feels good," she moaned.

Moments later, their nightclothes lay tangled on the floor as the old bed ropes sang a song of love.

Cluney forgot everything else. It was her wedding night. She was lying with her husband for the first time. She must not—now or ever—disappoint him. She had learned long ago, that she would find her pleasure through pleasing her man. She meant to do just that. She meant to go on pleasing him forever.

She kissed him and stroked him and licked him until he thrashed in the bed, moaning her name. As she sensed his desire building to the point of no return, hers flamed as well. When he covered her at last, their love was like nothing she had ever experienced in this lifetime or any other. It was as if the universe flowed into her and all through her. The ecstasy seemed to last on and on. They kissed and touched and clung to each other, sighing with happiness, crying for the sheer joy of that one perfect moment.

By the time it was over, a clock somewhere in the house was striking midnight. Cluney lay back on her pillow, her breasts heaving, her whole body limp with blissful exhaustion.

Jeff murmured several times, "Never anything so good! Never, never, never! I love you, Cluney, so much!" Then he slipped off to sleep.

Cluney lay very still, not wanting to disturb her husband. She thought she would drift off, too, but her mind was awake and alert. Suddenly, she remembered the gift, still wrapped in its silver paper. She slipped out of bed.

"I wonder what it could be?" she said quietly.

She ripped the paper, and a moment later stood speechless, staring down at Hunter's journal. She glanced toward the bed. "Oh, thank you, my darling."

Quickly, she pulled on her gown and negligee, then tiptoed to the adjoining sitting room. She switched on a light and settled in a comfortable chair.

Trembling all over, she turned the pages, hoping against hope that she would find the answer to the questions that had plagued her these past months. Quickly, she located the entry from the night she crossed the moonbow. On the next page, a new passage began.

"To my darling wife, Larissa. It is November now and you have been gone for nearly a month. The night you went away, I was sure I would die without you. I knew sorrow that is as deep as my love for you. I wanted to die. I begged to die. But Mary Renfro is a pillar of strength. She insisted I take the medicine you left for me. She bullied, cajoled, and threatened until I had no option but to fight back. And fight I did—I fought for life. You see, my darling, I've come to understand something. The fact that you are not with me does nothing to diminish our love for each other. We live on in each other's hearts as we always shall. A love as strong as ours can never die. And someday, perhaps I will find a way to return to you. Believe me, I will try.

"I am getting well, my darlng. And for the first time in months, I look forward to my life ahead. I mean to go back to Bluefield and set it in order. If you do manage somehow to return to me, I want you to find our home just as you left it. I will be waiting there with open arms, a brimming heart, and more love than has ever been lavished on any one woman. But then, there was never another woman like my Larissa."

Cluney had to stop reading. She couldn't see Hunter's words for the tears in her eyes. What a dear, dear man he had been! Still was! she reminded herself, glancing toward the bed at her husband's sleeping form.

When she had dried her eyes once more, she went on reading the precious journal, devouring every sweet word.

Hunter had made a full recovery and had returned to his cavalry unit for the duration of the war. During one battle, he had, as Larissa had feared he would, come face-to-face with his brother Jordan.

"He saved my life, Larissa, darling. True to the end," Hunter wrote. "Another Reb had me in the sights of his gun, ready to pull the trigger and end my mortal life. Jordy threw himself in the path of the bullet, stealing my death for his own. God bless him and rest his soul! I never lost faith in my brother. As he lay dying in my arms, he confessed to me the terrible thing he had done to both of us. He told me how he had tricked you, then lied to me in order to create dissension between us. He begged my forgiveness and received it before he drew his last breath. We shall meet again someday as friends in the heavenly hereafter."

Hunter had endured the rest of the war with no further injuries. He had returned to Bluefield with his old hound, Trooper, after Lee's surrender. He told of his struggle to put Bluefield back to rights.

On a single, tear-stained page, he wrote a poem of tribute and remembrance to his faithful dog, who succumbed to old age. He told of burying Troop in the rose garden and having a fine piece of marble carved to mark the spot.

Hunter had never married again—never given up hope that someday Larissa might return. For the next forty years, he marked her birthday and their wedding anniversary in his diary and wished her happiness "wherever you may be, my dear, darling wife."

The final entry was dated "November 27, 1905." He wrote in a feeble hand,

> "Winter is upon us again. The fields lie white with snow. And soon I will rest under that sheltering blanket. If there were time, my darling Larissa, I would write our story again, the way it should have been. I would begin, 'Once upon forever, there was a lonely warrior who found his lovely maiden. He took her away to his castle called Bluefield and they lived happily ever after.' But there is too little time left to record so much love—the love I have for you, my Larissa."

Wiping tears from her eyes, Cluney closed Hunter's diary slowly, savoring his final words.

When she returned to bed, she looked at her husband in a whole new light. She had loved him before, but now her love for Jeff Layton was total, all-consuming, everlasting. It was a love complete.

She slipped into bed beside him and let her arms steal around him. He smiled in his sleep.

"We're together again, darling," she whispered. "Once more under Bluefield's roof, Larissa and Hunter will have their chance at a happy ending. And you and I, Jeff, through our love, will see that they get it."

Jeff hadn't heard Cluney's exact words. He only knew that she was whispering to him and holding him tenderly. He'd been dreaming a wonderful dream.

"Once upon forever," he said softly, "there was a lonely warrior who found his lovely maiden. He took her away to his castle called Bluefield and they lived happily ever after."

He pulled her close and buried his face in her fragrant, moon-silver hair. "Do you know why, sweetheart?"

"Why, my darling?" she whispered back, feeling her heart flutter with love, hope, and desire.

"Because he loved her not just for now, but forever."

"And she loved him," Cluney replied. "She loved him across time and space and even across the moonbow."

The moon showered its light through their window, shining its silvery gleam over the entwined bodies of the master and mistress of Bluefield.

They were together again . . . at last . . . for all time!

# *Author's Note*

When I first visited Cumberland Falls with my husband and son in October of 1987, I knew that the magnificent setting would be perfect for a novel. The thunder of the falls, the riot of gold and scarlet autumn leaves, and the peace and silence of the forest seemed an ideal backdrop for romance. Then, too, I guessed the place was haunted.

When I returned to the falls in 1992, my story was already taking shape and a life of its own. I needed only to fit my characters into their proper setting. Old maps and photos were available at the Bob Blair Museum at the Dupont Lodge. With the help of staff members at the lodge and Ms. Kim Burchett of the Cumberland Falls State Park staff, I dug out some intriguing historical facts about the area. There had been stories of a silver mine under the falls. Reverend and Mrs. Renfro did run a recuperative facility for wounded soldiers at the edge of the falls during the Civil War. And they were forced to leave the area suddenly in 1875, under mysterious circumstances.

The moonbow fascinated me most of all. It spans Cumberland Falls in the Daniel Boone Forest near Corbin,

Kentucky, and is one of two such phenomena in the world. The only other lunar rainbow can be seen at Victoria Falls on the Zambezi River at the Zambia—Zimbabwe border.

On clear nights when the moon is full, or nearly so, the moonlight turns the mist around the falls into a luminous arc—sometimes silvery-white, on other nights faintly shimmering with all colors of the rainbow. Known as the Niagara of the South, Cumberland Falls is 60 feet high, 120 feet wide, and sends ten thousand gallons of water per second crashing down on the boulders in the gorge. A magnificent sight, day or night!

Cumberland Falls is a favorite haunt of students from nearby Cumberland College, in Williamsburg, Kentucky. They're always eager to talk about the many legends that surround the falls and its moonbow. Long ago, the Shawnee Indians worshiped the falls, believing that the moonbow had mystical powers. Visitors have long reported seeing the "Bride of the Falls," a lovely, weeping woman, gowned all in white. Others have seen faces in the moonbow or heard ghostly wailing on full-moon nights.

So the next time you find yourself in the mountains of Eastern Kentucky, don't miss your chance to see the moonbow, and perhaps a whole lot more!

Becky Lee Weyrich
Unicorn Dune
St. Simons Island, Georgia
July 11, 1993

# About the Author

ONCE UPON FOREVER is Becky Lee Weyrich's eighteenth novel. She is also the author of four novellas. Since she began publishing fiction in 1978, she has written for various publishers in a variety of genres, including historical romance, fantasy, saga, Gothic, horror/mystery, contemporary, and time travel.

Her first novel, *Through Caverns Infinite,* is now a collector's item among New Age aficionados. In 1991, Weyrich won *Romantic Times* magazine's Lifetime Achievement Award for New Age Fiction, and in 1992 she was awarded the Certificate of Excellence in Career Achievement in Historical Fantasy and the Reviewers' Choice Certificate of Excellence for *Sweet Forever* (Pinnacle Books, May '92). Her novels, *Gypsy Moon* and *Forever, For Love,* have received the Reviewers' Choice Award. Weyrich's books have been translated into ten foreign languages and recorded as books for the blind.

Beginning as a nonfiction writer in 1960, Becky Lee Weyrich did freelance work for several newspapers and magazines. She also wrote and illustrated two chapbooks of poetry before turning full time to fiction.

A member of Romance Writers of America and a board member of Southeastern Writers' Association, Weyrich is the originator of the Becky Lee Weyrich Fiction Award, presented annually at the Southeastern Writers' Workshop on St. Simons Island, Georgia.

After roaming the world as a Navy wife, the Georgia-born author now resides in a vintage beach cottage on St. Simons Island with her husband, six cats, a beagle named Barnacle, a pet 'possum, and assorted sea creatures. They have a daughter, a son, and four grandchildren. Weyrich's hobbies include golf, beachcombing, cruises to exotic shores, and collecting Victorian antiques.

If you would like to receive Becky Lee Weyrich's newsletter, please send a self-addressed, stamped envelope to P.O. Box 24374, St. Simons Island, GA 31522.

**ANOTHER TIME... ANOTHER PLACE... ANOTHER LOVE—**
*Let Pinnacle Historical Romances take you there!*

LOVE'S STOLEN PROMISES                           (631, $5.99/$6.99)
by Sylvie F. Sommerfield

Mitchell Flannery and Whitney Clayborn are two star-crossed lovers, who defy social conventions. He's a dirt-poor farm boy, and she's a South Carolina society belle. On the eve of the Civil War, they come together joyously, and are quickly and cruelly wrenched apart. After making a suitable marriage, Whitney imagines that she will never feel the soaring heights of passion again. Then, Mitchell returns home seven years after marching away. . . .

VELVET IS THE NIGHT                              (598, $4.99/$5.99)
by Elizabeth Thornton

To save her family from the guillotine, Claire Devereux agrees to become the mistress of the evil, corrupt commissioner, Phillipe Duhet. She agrees to give her body to him, but she swears that her spirit will remain untouched. To her astonishment, Claire finds herself responding body and soul to Duhet's expert caresses. Little does Claire know but Duhet has been abducted and she has been falling under the spell of his American twin brother, Adam Dillon!

ALWAYS AND FOREVER                               (647, $4.99/$5.99)
by Gina Robins

Shipwrecked when she was a child, Candeliera Caron is unaware of her wealthy family in New Orleans. She is content with her life on the tropical island, surrounded by lush vegetation and natives who call her their princess. Suddenly, sea captain Nick Tiger sails into her life, and she blooms beneath his bold caresses. Adrift in a sea of rapture, this passionate couple longs to spend eternity under the blazing Caribbean sky.

PIRATE'S KISS                                    (612, $4.99/$5.99)
by Diana Haviland

When Sybilla Thornton arrives at her brother's Jamaican sugar plantation, she immediately falls under the spell of Gavin Broderick. Broderick is an American pirate who is determined to claim Sybilla as forcefully as the ships he has conquered. Sybilla finds herself floating upside down in a strange land of passion, lust, and power. She willingly drowns in the heat of this pirate's kiss.

SWEET FOREVER                                    (604, $4.99/$5.99)
by Becky Lee Weyrich

At fifteen, Julianna Doran plays with a Ouija board and catches the glimpse of a handsome sea captain Brom Vanderzee. This ghostly vision haunts her dreams for years. About to be wed, she returns to the Hudson River mansion where she first encountered this apparition. She experiences one night of actual ecstasy with her spectral swain. Afterwards, he vanishes. Julianna crosses the boundaries of her world to join him in a love that knows no end.

*Available wherever paperbacks are sold, or order direct from the Publisher. Send cover price plus 50¢ per copy for mailing and handling to Penguin USA, P.O. Box 999, c/o Dept. 17109, Bergenfield, NJ 07621. Residents of New York and Tennessee must include sales tax. DO NOT SEND CASH.*

# FEEL THE FIRE IN CAROL FINCH'S ROMANCES!

**BELOVED BETRAYAL** (2346, $3.95)

Sabrina Spencer donned a gray wig and veiled hat before blackmailing rugged Ridge Tanner into guiding her to Fort Canby. But the costume soon became her prison—the beauty had fallen head over heels in love!

**LOVE'S HIDDEN TREASURE** (2980, $4.50)

Shandra d'Evereux felt her heart throb beneath the stolen map she'd hidden in her bodice when Nolan Elliot swept her out onto the veranda. It was hard to concentrate on her mission with that wily rogue around!

**MONTANA MOONFIRE** (3263, $4.95)

Just as debutante Victoria Flemming-Cassidy was about to marry an oh-so-suitable mate, the towering preacher, Dru Sullivan flung her over his shoulder and headed West! Suddenly, Tori realized she had been given the best present for a bride: a night of passion with a real man!

**THUNDER'S TENDER TOUCH** (2809, $4.50)

Refined Piper Malone needed bounty-hunter, Vince Logan to recover her swindled inheritance. She thought she could coolly dismiss him after he did the job, but she never counted on the hot flood of desire she felt whenever he was near!